D0292354

the art and practice of explosion

Also by G. F. Michelsen

To Sleep with Ghosts

Hard Bottom

Blues für Nansen

THE ART
AND PRACTICE
OF EXPLOSION

a novel

by g. f. michelsen

University Press of New England
Hanover and London

University Press of New England, 37 Lafayette Street, Lebanon, NH 03766

© 2003 by G. F. Michelsen
All rights reserved
Printed in the United States of America

5 4 3 2 1

Library of Congress Cataloging-in-Publication Data
Michelsen, G. F.
  The art and practice of explosion/by G. F. Michelsen.
  p. cm.
  ISBN 1-58465-308-6 (cloth: alk. paper)
  1. Autobiographical memory—Fiction. I. Title.
  PS3563.1336A88 2003
  813'.54—dc21   2003000546

Excerpts from "Autumn," "Consciousness," "Medallions," and "Diamonds" are
from *Perched on Nothing's Branch* by Attila József. Translation copyright © 1999 by
Peter Hargiti. Used by permission of the publisher, White Pine Press, Buffalo, NY.

acknowledgments

My thanks go to Gabe Von Dettre, Fran di Lustro, Tom Cook, The Writers' Room, Joanie Warner, Pete Sessa, Jochen Buck and Fred Barthet for their help, succor and protection in the writing of this book.

to Olivier

Linear systems are meaningless in the sense that the question of semantics need not arise within their universe of discourse. The implementations, artificial or natural, of mechanisms by which a linear system could be inferred are themselves non-linear.

—James P. Crutchfield
Santa Fe Institute paper 91 09 035

Voilà ce que j'ai pensé; pour que l'évènement le plus banal devienne une aventure, il faut et il suffit qu'on se mette à le raconter. C'est ce qui dupe les gens; un homme, c'est toujours un conteur d'histoires, il vit entouré de ses histoires et des histoires d'autrui, il voit ce qui lui arrive à travers elles; et il cherche à vivre sa vie comme s'il la racontait.

—Jean-Paul Sartre
La Nausée
(Samedi, Midi)

the art and practice of explosion

one

(. . .)

No birds sang, and this formed a void at the heart of the country.

Around the lack of song lay, in order of diminishing distance: a ridge covered with vines; a brown, willow-worshipped river; a village of stone farmhouses.

Closer by, a small and not very ambitious stream ran alongside a field of corn, a small road intersected one even smaller, a windbreak of tall chestnuts paralleled the lesser road.

Two railroad tracks on a bed of gravel slashed the country. In the center of the curve they made, a train consisting of one locomotive, one baggage car and seven passenger carriages stood immobile on the northern track.

The last two carriages were crooked. Although they had not left the track bed both were angled against the trend of steel, and the next but last was canted on broken bogeys.

There was not much left of that car. Almost a third of its metal skin was missing. Much of the rest was bent and folded outward, as if a terrible force dormant in the carriage's structure had chosen this quiet place to punch itself in all directions to freedom.

Flaps of aluminum rising from the roof looked like wings broken in a struggle for flight. Wreckage strewn around the train and for two hundred meters to the west lay in broken sequence. A portion of crumpled panel hung in an elm, moving in rhythm to the wind; in a patch of pink-and-white flowers a steel frame bent into a shallow "U" lay next to a red-colored volume of poetry that had suffered no damage at all.

Where the road came closest to the track bed rescue vehicles had congregated. They flashed fairground lights and gave off treble static to encourage the men who walked among the wreckage or stooped over light-blue blankets spread on the ground beside. Occasionally a truck would leave or arrive but there was no urgency or haste to the movements. It seemed almost as if, in this place from which birdsong had vanished, time also had been suspended while men tried to rearrange the broken bits of space against which they measured their slender histories.

two

The small events of man, de Fontgibu once said, can be understood as chance tending toward larceny. However to Frank Duggan, turning in the crystal of the lost moment from a chair he had been sitting in, what happened next had a more immediate cause.

The sum of factors that came together to create the event included the low friction coefficient of the varnish used to paint Frank's chair. Another cause was the high noise-to-signal ratio in Frank's brain that prevented him from seeing that his grip on furniture as well as on events less material that day was loose or gone altogether.

The chair stood at Angelina's, at 226 Rue de Rivoli in Paris. The time was 3:16 in the afternoon of July 13th. The sky was overcast and the temperature seventeen degrees Celsius. Women clad in the fur of arctic animals met daughters to plan their weddings to men with whom they had this conceit in common: that time was an event around which others could be organized and marshaled.

The tearoom was warm and glowed with a light the color

of calla lilies. In wall frescoes, cicadas buzzed under Aleppo pines in the morning sun in Mediterranean villages of ninety years ago. Frank had finished his African cocoa and paid the bill. He was pulling the chair sideways, out of the path of waitresses, when his thumb slipped on the slick lacquer of the crest rail. The chair tipped, and fell on the back of a Lhasa apso wearing a lamé waistcoat. The dog screamed. From this point onward the Newtonian laws, while they remained in place, governing the trajectories and up-front forces, took second rank to more obscure principles whose sense was hidden in the rush and statistics of accident.

Frank, shocked from his thoughts, bent to pick the chair off the dog at the same instant as the dog's owner leaned over to rescue her pet. Their heads met with a musical knock. Frank recoiled, backward. His buttocks bounced off the occipital bone of an elderly Neo-Gaulliste seated at the next table. The Neo-Gaulliste, who had been about to swallow a mouthful of cream and chestnut meringue, knocked his false teeth into the fork. The dentures came loose, obstructing his airway. He began to choke, and set his cup of hot chocolate half on, half off the table. It tilted toward his daughter's lap and a dress for which she had just shelled out 1800 euros in the Place Vendome. The daughter's fiancé, whose money it had been, shot his hand downward toward the cup, catching one knuckle on a spoon whose tail extended from his own saucer.

The lip of the dish acted as a fulcrum, the force of the man's gesture provided propulsion. The spoon, which was of plated steel and heavy, was launched upward. It spun, relaxed as a satellite in space, snagging the various caustics of light reflecting off the angles of mirrors at Angelina's, shining them out again as if in celebration of the implement's brief but mathematically elegant escape from gravity. Its flash caught the eye, five tables across the room's diminishing noise, of Eva Koszegfalvi where she sat stirring, with an identical spoon, the remains of her own hot chocolate.

Eva, glancing upward, took in the spoon, saw a cloud of chestnut shrapnel suspended for an instant in midair. Above that, a face and a correlation of patterns: black hair tightly curled; plates of lip, jaw and chin pressured into synthesis as if by some powerful industrial process; eyes that slanted down so that often he looked as if he were winking when he wasn't; despite that, a watchful quality, as much in the set of shoulders as in his face.

The spoon reached its apogee, and started downward again.

The owner of the dog, observing Frank's shoes, made a remark in French about his inaptitude for life in a society founded on deep respect for the subjunctive.

And epinephrine, at the arse end of a process she understood well, was pumped from the medulla of the adrenal glands to jack up Eva's metabolism in response.

Frank! She thought. And then, Yes, Frank Duggan.

"Il faut savoir ce qu'on veut, dans la vie," the woman announced, checking her head and then her dog for apnea over and above the usual.

The adhesive used in the glue securing the neo-Gaulliste's dentures was a vinyl acetate compound containing twenty-seven ester molecules. This was exactly the same number as in the vinyl acetate used in the varnish covering the chairs at Angelina's.

The French own one dog for every three families.

"Je m'excuse," Frank said, in an accent that gutted every open vowel in the phrase.

There was a taste and smell attached to strong memories, Eva thought, and it could blend well or poorly with the flavor of thoughts passing through your mind when the memory occurred. In this case they added up, not similar but harmonizing, like different instruments playing melodies in a fashion that made more acute the great sense of things-coming-apart associated with all of them.

Disjunction, of course, a sense of overriding strangeness,

from twelve years before, when Eva saw Frank Duggan's face for the first time; but strangeness, more strongly and proximately, from this very morning, when she went to the clinic on Rue de l'Essai, and entered the domain of Doctor Makabeus.

three

Her apartment looks out on what was once a garden. A young woman from the Bouktoub Wilaya used to tend the plants, with a care she might otherwise have devoted to infants, singing songs in Kabyle until she was deported under new legislation passed by the neo-Gaullist parliament. Eva, partly from a sense of political guilt, tried to take over the care of the flowers, but she is not good with plants and now most of the garden is dry and dying.

Eva has been awake since 4:20 this morning. The few blooms surviving her black thumb produce a strong sweetness and, in turn, cloying sensations of both nostalgia and indifference. The duality as well as the strength of smell plus memory astonish her.

She starts to brew coffee, then remembers she is to take no food or liquid other than water for twelve hours beforehand. She showers. The avocado soap is full of the lanolin and juices of this spring and others. She thinks, a film, any film, requires a screen to project on and what would it be like if one day the screen were gone? Banality, she realizes, is the anesthetic of choice; pressing down fear with memory, hurting herself on the scrub brush.

In the crack of window she sees the berries of a surviving pyracantha, scarlet drops espaliered against the courtyard's stucco, dying, a tiny vegetable Guernica. Automatically she looks down. The water runs down her pubis, twists ropes of hair and polishes in a thin coat the ivory cellulite of her inner thighs.

The water today is clear.

It is blood, though, that is the common denominator here. Blood at the wrong time, subtle betrayal of moons, first announced the possibilities in a slim thread of color among the alkaline Île de France water coursing across the enamel below her.

Tendrils of iron oxide among the chalk, a very light pink, really.

The first time she ever saw anyone hurt it was Tamas; *had* to be Tamas, who in his Alfold arrogance must prove no horse too raw or strong for him. When she thinks of Tamas she thinks of tanbark, the simmered musk of animals. He rides the new Kazakh stallion in performance before it has been lunged or circled the required time. The horse, instead of being spooked by the crowd and music and lights, ingests from the noise an energy so high that it requires passing on in the form horses know, an explosive buck, again at an odd time, off-stride. The orchestra hesitates in the middle of the *Zigeunerbaron* overture, the horse's mane sprays like a cresting wave at the broken rhythm. It surprises the rider, so that he slips off, landing deftly but still irretrievably in the path of the half-Lippizaners behind, there is no margin for escape. The hooves rip a patch of flesh from his scalp and break his left forearm so hard that the jagged endosteum cuts through muscle and skin and splashes his blood against the pale tanbark—bringing to Eva's mind, then, every time, the dreams from which her father was always too late to save her; the Rusalkas with red hands, the wolves with incarnadine maws. Fear of menstruation, of sexuality, the analyst called it, as if looking it all up in his encyclopedia of post-Freudian clichés, but what difference can it make to know the reasons for a flood if the river is already in your fucking cellar?

She towels herself off. The appointment, the second appointment now, is marked in blue on the calendar. The familiarity of her flat seems like an agonized plea, her external life praying to her internal. Photos of Erzsébet Bridge, of Serge frowning through the smoke of his Silk Cuts, totems of normalcy stacked on her escritoire. She drives alone to the clinic. She wears a green silk dress with long sleeves and matching scarf, and many thin silver bracelets on both wrists.

The Clinique Nicolas Bourbaki is built of dark granite from Brittany according to a design that emphasizes scarcity, the retreat from curves and arcs. Eva, who likes to draw conclusions from architecture, supposes this is fair enough for an institution dedicated to technological dominance over the uncontrolled and organic. Yet there are so few windows, and that carries its own message. The building is like a black needle thrust into the vein of a street already narrow and medieval as Gregorian chant. From the roof of a seminary three buildings down, limestone gargoyles vomit dust at the cobbles.

The assistant who summons her is new. He is tall and lean and wears a black suit. The halls are so white they might as well, in their absence of color, be black. She will not see Doctor Makabeus until after the tests. She feels in her a slight, desperate thrill of resistance, of refusal to give in to the cheap drama of the whole affair. She strips and, before putting on the johnny, mimes forgetfulness, removing a dress that is no longer there. It is a reflex that goes deep, to the centers where fear, and how to live with it, are structured.

Nobody laughs, or smiles even. They cannot know she once did this for a living. Her bracelets are placed in a plastic box and tagged.

As the assistant takes blood, a drop breaks loose from the syringe and hangs on the inner lip of the test tube, englobing, in its capillary completeness, in the tension between gravity and the float of electrons, between the holism of plasma, hormones, salts, nutrients and dissolved gases, and the partiality that causes her presence here in the first place, all of the strain building within her. The redness, filling the glass, paints history into the tube: Rusalkas, Tamas, her enameled tub; Guernica, and the Xelixec River that ran with the blood of Indians.

A crucifix hangs above the sharps disposal. The flesh of the Christ figure is whiter than the wall. The blood of his stigmata has faded utterly. Eva thinks, without logic, that its color has been absorbed by the incompleteness in all the tubes of diseased blood taken beneath.

They lead her to the same x-ray room she was in nine days before. The scanners are painted in colors clinically proven to suggest natural life, the order of forests and meadows. She knows the equipment well; not an atom from copse or sward taints its kilometers of circuitry. The hole in its mass, where her body is inserted and moved at precisely calibrated angles, contains in the darkness pinpricks of orange light, as if a constellation had been captured and imprisoned in the CT scan.

She sits and looks at magazines. Most of them, for some reason, are in Swedish. Fifty minutes later she is admitted to Makabeus's study. It is bare as a Trappist's cell. One wall is built of the same ebony granite. The desk is of polished black marble with a flexible reading lamp scavenged from some fallen spaceship. No books or journals are visible, as if the medical territory he travels lies beyond published charts. Makabeus himself is taller and thinner than his assistant. His suit is of dark blue with the tiny drop of the Legion of Honor at the buttonhole. On his face every facet of skull stands out, skin stretched like a drum head over the supraorbital margin, the maxilla, the zygomatic bone, so tight she can mark each vein as on an anatomical dummy. He has a camel's chin and finely carved lips and hides his eyes behind tinted glasses. Makabeus does not chat; he returns to a black leather chair and reads the printouts. But it has all been growing, accumulating in her to a point where her mind, because it is female, because it is Hungarian, because, Kossuth forgive her, it has even become somewhat French; because, most of all, her years in neuropsychology have taught her the value of assymetry, of the jolt given to causality; at any rate she no longer can accept the blanket unilinearity of this, mainframe, centrifuge, the four meters of printout, and it expresses itself in the only way it knows, a conceptual buck, a stupid joke, behind the wide-eyed grimace of the circus clown, used for scrim and contrast; "*Vous devez acheter vos gueules d'enterrement au prix de gros ici.*"

For thirty long seconds Makabeus says nothing. Then his voice comes, silky and cold as a casket opening. "*Mécanisme d'auto-défense, vous compensez, Docteur Koszegfalvi,*" to which of course there is no real answer except "*J't'enmerde,*" or the ubiquitous "Fuck you," which she does not, in the end, quite dare to utter.

four

Eva, sitting with a hand frozen in the second of an arc of stirring, felt one zone of her brain, pushing past the Clinique Bourbaki and its implications, move her to rise, call out, gain friction on Frank and what he represented, a piece of time resuscitatable to a partial extent in the shape of what they remembered together and apart.

The other section of her curled tighter than a cut caterpillar around its damage.

Finally she got to her feet. "Frank." And louder, "Frank!" The hard Anglo-Saxon rasped her Gallicized palate. Finding only that, once again, the respect she held for the possible beauties of chance was greater than her talent for damage control.

He turned then, rubbing a finger where the dog had snapped, though its teeth had not come close. His eyes narrowed to slits.

"Eva? Eva! My God."

Could it be, she thought, I startled him?

Frank picked up a canvas bag that read "UTA" in white letters on blue. He backed out of the area in which the young woman sponged obsessively at a brown stain on her silk dress.

"*Excusez moi, encore.*"

The woman ignored him.

Eva's table had only one chair. They moved to a corner, below a mirror and a fresco where the sun rose on a quiet, tree-loved creek in the elbow of warm ridges.

"My god." Frank swung his bag over the table, narrowly avoiding saltshakers. Tourists cringed. "Eva. The usual. I won't go on. What is it, eleven—twelve years now? But to have you see—that?" He smiled, jabbing a thumb toward the miniature dog.

The table they sat at had been used, sixty-two years earlier, by Helmut Knochen, the leader of Himmler's Paris *Sonderkommando*. Here he conferred with a former deputy head of the Paris office of German Railways, which was a front used to collect the names of Jews and democrats. Two other men attended: Deloncle, a leader of the Fascist "Mouvement Social Révolutionnaire," and an anonymous subaltern in the Vichy *milice*. Knochen visited Angelina's often for it stood near his old headquarters at the Hôtel du Louvre. That afternoon in 1941 the four men discussed specifically and in general the implications of the Gestapo Section IV-B (4)'s demand that France deport from its territory upwards of 100,000 Jews.

"It reminded me," Eva said.

"No shit."

He sat back, still feeling the sough from the chemicals of humiliation. For the first time he could relax enough to take in the depth of shadow around the neck tendons, the angle of her head, the slope of pupils and eyelids. She looks scared, he thought, and this surprised him. He said, gently, "I guess it's a shock."

"Well. Not since Xelajú. Of course."

"Waiting for the train."

"The rebels."

"The hotel."

It was the fear, she thought. Not strangeness at all, or at least not entirely, but in good measure a component of fear that provided the link between seeing Frank then and seeing his face now. Both times she had been afraid, without guilt or embarrassment; scared the way a child is scared. When it comes down to it, she thought, it's always wolves with yellow eyes under the bed. What comes later, the adult part, is how you explain it to people, the excuses you make. In the end the extra years meant nothing.

"It seems so—" he rubbed his moustache. A lot of the hairs were silver now but the gesture was something she remembered unaltered. "I mean, like a cartoon. A stupid soap-opera melodrama, eh? With the colors kind of wrong."

"They had drama," she said, taking a pen out of her bag. "The rebels, anyway."

"No, they all did. Even the Gardia Nacional. Remember the uniforms, like Hollywood Nazis? An', an' those fucking volcanoes, the ten volcanoes, smoking over our heads like, you know, like the gangway to hell—did you—" he waved away a waitress— "do you ever hear from Rohan?"

"Rohan," she said, ordering a pastry she did not want because otherwise they would have to leave and she was too tired suddenly, too tired to cope with getting up, the compression of rituals, goodbye, hello, the forms of it exhausted her in advance. "But he is in Paris now and—"

"Here?"

"Yes. And, oh, I haven't, no."

"But—"

"But I saw him, you see. Listed. I get their magazine, the UNESCO magazine, the *Courrier* or whatever. It said, he was appointed something, something temporary, oh with the archeology of ships—"

"Huh."

She remembered that "huh" of his. He used it as a badge of interest. The interest was not always real but the "huh" was catching. She had used it herself, in English, for months after meeting him.

"We can call him there," she went on. "At UNESCO."

"You mean, like, a reunion." Frank smiled, but the way his cheeks sank in as he did so qualified the gesture. "Survivors of the *emergencia*, the three of us."

"And Leila."

"And Leila." He looked at her without blinking. "But you can get in touch with Rohan."

"Why not?"

"Why not, indeed."

"No, but. I mean this." She was leaning forward from the waist, drawing birds on scrap paper as she always did when anxious. Tall, gawky birds with necks made of a single penstroke, angular wings, and headfeathers that stuck out in all directions. "I have a mobile phone, we'll go outside. I'll pay my bill—"

Proserpine Strauss, a writer of small literary novels that veered toward the sadomasochistic, walked into the rear of the tea-room and spotted Eva. Strauss was to be nominated for the Prix Montcorbier and she glowered ferociously at Eva; this was her way of being noticed. Eva paid no attention.

"It's okay," Frank was saying. "There's no rush."

"Yes. But Tuesday is a holiday here and people do *le pont*, the bridge? You know, days off, they take—"

"A long weekend?"

"Exactly." She unfolded a twenty-euro note and wedged it under her cup. She had finished her pastry to the last crumb. She did not remember eating it.

"It would be nice to catch up with you," Frank added, "I'd have time for that."

"Yes." She screwed the paper coaster into a ball. "I'll just call, quickly. It will be interesting, don't you think?"

They stood outside, in the arcade of a hotel that had served as the Wehrmacht's western headquarters during World War Two. Eva's shoulder hunched around the thin black instrument as her call went through.

"It's him." She half-turned toward Frank, scrabbling in her bag for the pen.

Frank turned away. Germans fingered postcards beside the Meurice. A woman with dark hair and plump hands, her mouth masked by a thrown shawl, leaned on a nearby wall, consulting a guidebook. Eva's voice rose and fell in modulations meant to convey surprise and delight past the distortion of electronics. She tapped his arm.

"Listen. Oh, Frank. Ludovic—Rohan—he's going to the country for the weekend. To Alsace. He wants us to come. You and me. To Alsace," she repeated. "It's so pretty this time of year.

"For the weekend," she added, looking hard at Frank's features, "day after tomorrow. Are you going to be here? Are you busy? No. There are mountains," she added more quietly.

Why am I pushing so hard, she asked herself, suspecting the answer; because it's a box, an isolated compartment in which she could move and react without taking bearings back to Doctor Makabeus and what his presence in her mind must signify. Even if the box would come apart on Wednesday morning. Even if it proved to hold, as boxes from the past often did, as she suspected this one might, as many rotted bones and green organs as the computer printouts, by implication, contained at the Clinique Bourbaki.

Frank looked up at the Meurice. He could feel the inertia in him, as from a Valium taken earlier, and wondered at its source. She looked scared, yes, and tired too; she must be close to forty, and the cells of her skin and the ligaments in her neck were starting to let her down when it came to furnishing the brutal tribute a phallocratic society sought from a woman's looks. Still she looked good to him, with that vastly long and subtle mouth that seemed made to play *agon* and comedy without ever stooping to melodrama, even of the kind they had shared once; and that architecture of breadth in bone and cheek; and eyes so brown and fathomless you wondered what kind of creatures had been trapped in their La Brea ooze, reptiles of horned elbow and webbed wings, birds of plumage and hue long lost to the world, whose only trace was the shades they left in her brain and which came out, unconsciously, in unguarded moments, through her fingers and pen.

Frank had no particular desire to go to Alsace. But Eva was sketching birds once more, in felt-tip on the borders of her address book. Finally he said, "Tell him maybe."

"He has to make plans—"

"I just can't decide now. I have to call the airline, my department—"

The traffic turned and roared as it funneled into the Place de la Concorde. It jammed, backed up, flowed again in whorls and patterns that recurred at intervals you could measure, if not explain. Bastille Day banners stirred in the slipstream, diesel exhaust ebbed into the Dufy sky. In the fountain of the Tuilerie gardens, children sailed model boats with straight stems and patched sails. Goldfish big as pike turned in the graying water.

five

Schedules rearranged, Frank stood two days later in the great hall of the Gare de l'Est, hunched a little, his normal posture, one thick hip shot protectively over the UTA bag, his nylon travel jacket flapping in the commuter breeze. Above him the iron arches of the station soared to meet with frosted glass where pigeons feared to shit, while, lower down, a stone staircase rose like a hymn to the lost and found and other railway offices over the forecourt.

Frank touched with one finger the marble tablet dedicated to the railwaymen of what was then the Chemins de Fer de l'Est, the eastern region railroad. *"Aux Cheminots de la Région Est,"* it read, *"Morts Pour la France."* Inside the nearby "Crypte du Souvenir" were carved thousands of names of men killed in the 1914–1918 war. It seemed to Frank a continuation of the conflict's iron logic that it did not spare even the conductors, the switchmen, the crossing guards. These names once had belonged to the slightly rotund fellows in cloth caps who functioned as initiators into the rites of steam, linear travel, foot-pounds of pressure; of speed and gears and the other back-casting arcana of manhood; shamans of the flattened franc piece, role models for generations of three-year-old boys, all smelted in the hot breath of conflict.

In the archway leading to the hall of tickets, a glass-encased 75-millimeter cannon from the battle of the Marne stood as if in testimony to Frank's loose thoughts.

His great-uncle had volunteered, Frank remembered. He had joined a New England infantry regiment late in the war and died in battle to the east somewhere. Perhaps he too had taken the train from this station to meet the German fire.

Frank fingered the magnet in his pocket. He felt a sudden desire for booze, so urgent it was almost sexual, an erection of the liver. The smell of beer was strong here. He looked around, trying to place the source of the smell—

(Honey-rotten, spreading over the worn spruce in puddles)—

An Algerian boy wrung out a mop at the entrance to a brasserie, twenty feet away, dunking it in a galvanized bucket, twisting the fibers in a ball against the metal, the gray water pissing freely—

—flowing in a run of sour Narry that led away from Frank, a bubble river you had only to follow, Speke-like, upstream, to find the source of his Nilotic confusion.

It was too early for a beer today; just as it had been too early in the halls of twisted parsing, at PISR, in Somerville, ten days ago.

six

Every time, he is late.

Frank, stashing the can of beer in one coat pocket, pedaling his twelve-speed up the wheelie ramp of PISR, notices that this switchboard girl, hair stuffed in a rasta snood, currently reading Kolmogorov, is not wearing her headset.

She never does, he remembers.

"Professor Duggan," she begins, "you're late, an'—"

"Don't you ever answer?" He points to the console. "The phone." His annoyance is not directed at her.

"I have this theory?" She pops gum. She is one of those students who pronounce their "o"s Cockney style and end each sentence with a question-mark. "The same people call in, like, patterns, ew-kay? So I'm doing a graph, and it works out, they call in cycles of around fourteen-point-seven minutes, ew-kay?"

"Terrific."

"Yeah?" She puts down her book. "Well, Dean Kopper—" she adds this in spite— "he's auditing your seminar today?"

"Better and better."

"That bad, huh." She doesn't bear a grudge.

"It's kinda like getting a visit in the shower," he tells her in a stage whisper, "from Tony Perkins."

She pops her gum at him. She's not sure who Tony Perkins is. In the classroom Kopper sits in the corner, bald, handsome, a whale among whiting. He looks at his watch and makes a single tiny mark in his notebook.

PISR—the Phillips Institute for Social Research—is attached to Kenmore University. The endowment of this megalith of academic mediocrity has substantially declined in recent years, and the board of governors is threatening to shut down some of the less influential faculties, with PISR high on the list of targets. It must be said that Dean Kopper for all his faults has fought back. After complex negotiations he has obtained funding from Integrated Information Incorporated, "Triple-I" for short, for certain "pragmatically oriented" fields of research. Pragmatic, in the new lexicon, means what can eventually be spun off for profit. Frank's field, the politics of aid and development, does not qualify. Now he listens as a precocious kid from Metro Park tries out on the seminar what he hopes will form the basis for his Ph.D. and subsequent employment in a better-funded college or think tank. The kid wears a dolphin-shaped lip stud and a ski jacket; they all wear coats because PISR, for budgetary reasons, only heats its buildings in the afternoons. Frank takes off his coat and hangs it on his chair. He has never had a problem with the cold. "The relationship between the cycles of aid and the harmonics of army year-classes in the Nigerian officer corps," Ascanio ("Skip") Sobrero intones, consulting his notes. "The paper will be based on—" he chalks out a differential equation, gripping the tip of his tongue between his teeth. Frank peers at the numbers, feigning puzzlement, scratching his bald spot. Someone in the back row burps.

"What ranks are you considering?" Frank asks the kid.

"Captain only. The equation—"

"Have you included"—Frank feels the magnet in his pocket, twists its clean rectangle between thumb and fingers—"Galt's work on rank reduction as a function of time, that is, how coups which followed closely on each other, five or three years, less even, they tended to be carried out by lower and lower ranks. Colonel to major, major to captain, to lieutenant etcetera?"

Sobrero continues writing symbols on the board. His breath makes lacy puffs against the green. "These are the deep harmonics I believe I've found, I was examining the records of the Nigerian Military College, they are expressed by this polynomial, and—" he turns, eyes fired, looking only at Kopper now—"I believe they will have a statistically non-insignificant correlation with the military assistance harmonics of five major Western donors, which is in turn expressed by—"

"Wait." Frank knows he shouldn't do this. He is conscious Kopper is waiting for him to do something stupid like this. Finally that realization changes to a fatalism that allows him to commit actions he understands to be irrevocable. He strides to one end of the blackboard. "Wait a second, Skip."

Outside, the cold bricks of Sumner Redstone Hall meet the clapboard chestnuts, the pricking drizzle of Somerville. PISR is invariably pronounced "Piss-ah," which, in Boston dialect and an inverse relation to the root connotations of urine, means something terrific, amazing; the opposite, in fact, of the fad scholarship and tech-oriented papers PISR has resorted to for survival under Kopper. "Skip, baby. Who did you *talk* to in the officer corps? Skip."

As he'd asked Jodee earlier this morning to whom, exactly, she had talked among Jack's teachers.

He shouldn't have bought that beer, let alone popped its top. He can smell it now, faint and musty; an odor too weak, he is sure, for Kopper to catch. Sobrero is another matter.

"I didn't want to deal with the army. You know how they are, even after Abacha—"

"You didn't want to deal?"

Frank strides back, around his chair. He feels blood speed up, hot as lava under his eyes. "You won't talk to the Nigerians and yet you want to do a thesis on this, this *relationship*—"

Sobrero is young enough to blush easily but he looks at Kopper, and what harmonics exist between these two who should not even know each other?

Yet in fact the link is clear. Frank is only coincidentally Sobrero's supervisor, because of the aid angle, and Africa. The real thrust of his research is in Cheung's field, which involves cyclical organizational reaction to labor-market fluctuations and is therefore a Triple-I-approved endeavor.

"This relationship, as far as you know, how much of coincidence—"

No coincidence, earlier—that Jack, his own eight-year-old, sullen, back-talking Jack, should be found at the wheel of a Hyundai six boys were pushing into a barricade that had blocked fucking Laurel Street for god's sake. Half of those kids wearing the doglike virtual-reality game masks, four hundred bucks apiece of distortion of whatever was going on in their fields of vision and sound to fit into the parameters of some punk-chivalry program synchronized between them and the Uragiri software in Jack's laptop, and where in hell did Jack get four hundred bucks to begin with? "An electronic rumble," the police sergeant called it, using a term that managed to be both an oxymoron and out of date. "We never seen that before."

—"The real harmonics, huh, the truly significant relationship here being;" Frank strides behind the desk, swinging his arms now; "being between Triple-I, our corporate sponsors, hallowed be their name, who want more research in this Ruelleian theory, waves, rhythms, harmonics in chaotic market systems, to hook up with each other, no, no what they want is not research but *results—*"

Kopper makes two, three marks in his notebook now. He does not look up. Frank, aware of the doom in him, the Wagnerian roller he might as well surf because diving under will not work anyway, continues, spates—

"Results, Skip?" He raises his arms, lets them fall Guignol-fashion. "That you will damn well supply them with, oh, so they can have some precious illusion of deep structure in social movements, put it all in those parallel networks to hook up with their arbitrage software, more neat equations, with post-Kondratieff cycles, 'n Lorenz curves, 'n—"

Swinging by the chair on which his overcoat is hung Frank's knee bangs into the arm and his coat slips half off the back, changing the slope of pocket so that the can of Narry cants upside down from the opening and hangs there for a full second, gurgling, then falls to the floor with a thud. The can finds on the warped boards a slope that will allow continued pursuit of the earth's massy core: it rolls under a desk into the aisle, then rumbles on, straight toward the chair where Kopper is waiting, notebook poised—cheap Pawtucket-brewed beer smelling like stale bread, penicillin, semen—flowering in the taste buds, exploding in the related synapses of the eight people in this classroom as it gushes foamy down the planking and forms a puddle near the dean's deck shoes. And everyone, Frank included, looks on in silence and the kind of empathetic awe that is the factor onlookers at all catastrophes do share, as Kopper makes one final mark, stands up, smiles vaguely at no one, and walks out the door, shutting it quietly as in a chapel behind him.

seven

Airwhistle echoes rose, fell, chased each other around the Gare de l'Est and died among the geometric girders.

The twelve-sided clocks hanging over the Hall of Lost Footsteps read 12:16. Frank leaned on the zinc counter of the Saturne snack bar, near the board announcing "Départs Grandes Lignes." Loudspeakers, the roar of electric train engines, the flapping of the Solari board punctuated the space around him. He ate a sausage fornicated with hot mustard into a slice of baguette. He was opening a book, finishing a *demi* of Kronenbourg when he saw a tall man dressed in well cut corduroys, a tweed jacket, and desert boots come to a halt below the sign and look distractedly around him. In his head Frank clicked off conflicting characteristics. The man had less hair than Frank remembered. He was ten or fifteen pounds heavier. Despite the extra weight everything about him was still long and narrow; his nose and chin were essays on the vertical, and the clothes hung off him as they might from a hook. He had the same beard, so thin-cropped you could not tell if it was deliberate or just a bad shave. A chcroot fumed in cupped palm, a coal of green simmered in his look as the man turned.

"Rohan?" Frank dropped change on the zinc.

"Frank—ah, Frank."

They shook hands.

Rohan thought, Frank Duggan does not seem twelve years older, though the lines of his face have grown harsher, more pronounced; the shelf of his nose, the bulkhead under his moustache. He wears the same off-fashion clothes. Frank has fans of gray at his temples, but then Rohan's beard has brindled as well. The truth is, Rohan decided, we are all aging at similar rates and, like boats in the same current, we cannot tell how fast we go by looking only at each other.

"So." Rohan carried a leather doctor's satchel, cracked and shiny with age, and a canvas musette; now he unloaded these at his feet. "You decided to come, after all."

Rohan always spoke very slowly, Frank remembered, as if he had to measure each syllable and phrase before it could be allowed to see daylight.

Frank's mouth twisted.

"I had some spare time, I teach at a small faculty, they are flexible—"

"You are lucky."

They looked to the side of each other as men and dogs often do. On quai 14 a ringing grew. In the overexposure of daylight at the station's end a metal snake made its way toward the foot of the quai, building in control and size as it came. *"Arrivée en provenance de Nancy, TGV numéro 1618, le 'Lorraine,' quai quatorze."* It looked more and more like a snake the closer it got, so that when the train came to a halt its tapered orange snout and inset headlamp eyes and the sinuous unity of its body gave it the same air of confidence in speed and strike as might be possessed by a huge viper.

Men in business clothes, desperate to be first off the platform, hurried from ports in the train's side.

"Waiting in a station, yes? Again."

"For a different woman, this time."

They said nothing more for a moment.

"Is that the one we're taking?" Frank asked finally.

Rohan glanced at the TGV, then turned his gaze downward.

"No," he said. "I am afraid we are on a slow train. It will take us six hours to reach Colmar, and we have to change in Bar-le-Duc. If we took the TGV it would be only three hours to Strasbourg."

Frank chewed at nothing.

"You see—" Rohan looked up suddenly. "I like it better." His cheroot was in his mouth, smoking into one eye. The eye did not water. His mouth stretched in a smile so wide it contorted his face to a point close to ugliness. "I did it on purpose."

"Did what."

"The slow train—"

"For what?"

"To go slowly."

"Huh," Frank said, raising his eyebrows. He remembered the Frenchman's habit of zipping off on some argument or other but did not recall his doing that so soon after a conversation started. Perhaps the years, instead of softening Rohan, had eroded the loose stuff, the way the sea wore at a cliff, washing away topsoil, exposing the rock beneath.

Rohan dropped the cheroot. His accent in English was weaker than Frank remembered. "Unfortunately this is the last time I can take this slow train. You see next month it too will be replaced by a TGV, like that one. But you take that TGV, you will see nothing. The train goes so fast everything outside the windows is like this—" his hands made a horizontal slice—"a blur only, just streaks of colors. By the time you see something that interests you it has gone. Poof.

"And the people. They are these types, Sciences-Po, Polytechnique, the technocrats. They design the TGV, they finance it, they ride it; they have seats like an airplane. You *must* look at the seatback before you, you look *away* from the window—away from the person next to you. Do you understand?"

Rohan's eyes slid from the orange snake back to Frank, who shrugged.

"You wanna see things. It's only—"

"No. It's more than that. It's—it's—Eva."

Frank followed his gaze. "Eva."

"Eva."

Frank felt a buzz of irritation. He'd never been able to talk easily to Rohan.

Rohan's hands stopped moving. To Eva he seemed frozen in mid-gesture on the black concrete. Rohan, for his part, felt disoriented by her physical presence. He noticed the contrast of cut-rate jeans and a silk blouse and an expensive leather coat but it was her mouth that silenced him, the strength of its memory and the power of its rose curve over him, which in turn caused him to wonder at the strength of whatever, in the twelve years since he'd seen her last, in the many miles they'd all put in since the Hotel Continental, whatever had prevented him from keeping track of her.

"Eva," Rohan said again. He stood straight and brought her hand to his lips in a courtly gesture that was half a joke and mostly what his father taught him. Then he put his arms around her shoulders. The scent of her neck flooded his nostrils—

—the scent comes among the hot bodies, through the odors of death and rotten water—

But she was late. The association dimmed for Rohan as he checked his watch. A squad of CRS riot police marched by. The cops wore navy blue jumpsuits tucked into combat boots and led two Alsatian dogs by the leash. Someone yelled across the forecourt. Frank turned. In the corner of one eye he saw the Arab boy who had been washing the floor of the brasserie drop his mop and sprint around the World War One exhibit for the métro entrance. One of the cops let go his leash and the police dog set off across the concrete, moving in lovely predatory lopes through the vacationers, jumping at the kid's waist, bringing him down. The incident was veiled by the sound of whistles and the backs of the curious.

"Another illegal." Rohan looked at his watch. "We're going to have to run." But he looked up again, almost reluctantly, to where the police dogs barked in hollow tones.

"I'm sorry I'm late." Eva had seen nothing.

They turned, following Rohan. Their train, as befitted its obsolescent status, stood at the most inaccessible quai. The coaches were of the old olive green variety with the longitudinal corridors and separate passenger compartments of the pre-'90s SNCF. The engine had the rectangular shape and flat prow of the BB 9004 series. The drilling of the quai bell, signaling the train would leave in less than one minute, seemed to grow louder. A conductor waved impatiently in their direction and looked up and down the platform. Frank took Eva's arm and pulled her up the steps of the last car. The conductor blew his whistle. Rohan climbed up beside them. Worn couplings gave, then jerked taut; Eva and Frank fell slightly together, and Frank's arm slipped to her waist, in the ease of the body, in the stopped time of man's arm and woman's thigh, as if the things, the separating things that happened in more than a decade, had not come and gone in between.

eight

Round her waist.

She is lost and getting nervous the first time Frank Duggan slips his arm like that.

The area of Xelajú Eva has wandered into is a warren of crumbling adobe and open sewers. The streets are jammed with Maxeño Indians with their sharp machetes and wide-brimmed straw hats and faces that six hundred years of Spanish rule have taught to show nothing whatsoever. She has seen a man's body lying in one of the sewers and the only difference there is, the smell of shit is stronger.

Going with the thrust of the crowd she finds a market dominated at one end by a white church with two bell towers half crumbled from the recurrent earth tremors. Indian priests squat at the base of the stone steps, burning incense wrapped in corn husks into sharp clouds. Something about the church reminds her of Krisztina Templom, in Buda, where her mother sometimes wound up when she was lost. She joins the lines of Indian women entering the church.

Inside is fire and fog; columns of tapers create a ziggurat of orange light, at the foot of which the Indians place offerings of maize and foxglove petals. The haze creates shadows that graduate around each other in a progression of darkness to the invisible roof. The miasma of incense, pollen and damp seizes up in her lungs. She turns for the exit. A hand touches her elbow. She spins, panicky, to find a European in a cheap nylon suit at her side.

"You know what they're offering for?" he asks her.

"It's Uazeb," she answers, when she gets her breath back. She repeats what Julián told her. "It's the end of the Mayan, er, the calendar year. The feast starts today. It lasts nine days. The last five days are considered the most dangerous in the whole year."

"Do you think they are?"

"What?"

"Dangerous."

She looks more closely at his face.

"I was lost," she tells him.

"You're at the Continental," he says, "I saw you at breakfast." Though his clothes are stateless and his shoes are *chulo* sandals his accent is purely American. He walks her outside. The crowd around the shamans has grown so thick they have to lean against each other to stand upright. His arm slips to her waist. Somehow she knows this is in protection not affront. He has thick forearms, like a wrestler. He leads her to Avenida Bolivar and they find a taxi back to the hotel.

He does not ask for her name or room number. She does not see him the rest of that day. Julián is nowhere to be found. She spends the afternoon at the Neuropsychiatry Convention at the Maya Excelsior. It exhausts her, as usual. When she returns to the Continental she orders dinner in her room.

But the food never comes. When the gunfire starts she thinks it is fireworks. At first the rebels announce their takeover politely; they call up the guests, as if the revolution were a new form of room service, and request that everyone assemble in the lounge. The elevators inexplicably are manned by young Indians wearing jeans, bandannas and automatic rifles. She is standing in the corner of the lounge, timing her pulse, looking for Julián, when Frank appears beside her.

"Just another fucking convention," he tells her.

"It's not funny," she says.

Some of the rebels wear hobnail army boots that scar up the parquet. The hotel's manager, a Swiss-German, stalks into his office, sobbing audibly. A rebel leader climbs to the band podium. He tells them they have nothing to be afraid of. The Armed Front for the Liberation of Los Altos is making certain rational demands of the government, and once those demands are met they shall all go free. A tall unshaven man in elegant French clothes breathes out his nose sharply, in irritation; looking straight at Eva, he makes a face. She thinks, that man wants to sleep with me, then curses herself for her irrelevance. Down the lobby Indians with guns try out the plush couches. She makes a comment to Frank but he is staring at a dark-haired mestiza who leans on the podium piano, somewhat in the manner of Lauren Bacall singing for Harry Truman. He does not answer. This time she and Frank do exchange room numbers; it seems a basic precaution, a geographic alliance; the mestiza says they can all go back to their rooms for the night, as long as they do not lock the doors. Already Eva appears to know, in a manner more physical then mental, that her contact with Julián is dissolving.

Anyway he told her from the first that he could be nothing to her—that he was already taken, a thousand times over, by whom or what he would not say. She had accepted that. Stupidly, she had hoped nonetheless.

Back in her room she immediately gets into bed. At first she keeps the curtains drawn, but after a while she gets up and opens them. The city seems peaceful; only the perimeter lights of the hotel, the knots of rebels setting up heavy machine-guns, the strobes from the Gardia Nacional jeeps on the other side of the compound wall speak of activity beyond the normal. A quarter moon washes in tinny light the barrios of Santa Maria. She always feels less afraid in bed. When the first tracer bullets arc past her window she has no idea what they are but the explosions this time are too different for mistake. She is out of the room before she knows what she is doing, for the violence of what she learns later are rocket-propelled grenades has shorted all basic hesitation in her brain. She finds Frank's room and walks in without knocking. He is lying under the bed. His head sticks out, protected by a pillow. He looks at her silhouette, then sighs.

"Eva."

"You were expecting someone else?"

She crouches beside him. Then she slips under the bed with him.

"I hate this," he says, and puts his arm around her waist almost automatically. "I hate it I hate it I *hate* it." Real anger rises in his voice, as if there were a manager, in life as in a hotel, to whom he could complain about such problems.

"Tell me a joke," she suggests, desperately.

The detonations succeed one another, drum-rolling the windows. Yellow blooms of high explosive throw brief hard shadows on the wall. She wonders where Julián is and tries not to think about what would happen if one of those shells or rockets found its way into this room. The lack of hesitation in her brain is linked somehow to an unacceptable need for cheap humor, and this in turn is linked to a very sexual burn. She files this information for future reference even as she feels herself loosening. Her waist is very warm. The wetness makes her underwear heavy. She puts a hand on his neck. He rubs the small of her back. The firing hesitates, starts again, tapers off. A siren sounds, and is shut down. His hands are meaty and strong where Julián's were supple as a lake reed; almost weak. They shuck each other's clothes off like Frenchmen opening oysters.

He is slow and gives her opportunities to go her own way—democratic, she thinks; Californian. She cannot as usual remember the pleasure, only that it is sharp and brings comfort to the contrast of silence. For some reason the forgetting bothers her this time. Her memory is eidetic, near perfect, except for this void. In the suspended moments after sex she traces in her own brain the rush and backwash of signals among the basal ganglia.

They lie on the bed. He switches on the television. A black-clad Zorro brings justice to Indians in back-lot Mexico. The Indians, dubbed in Spanish, are played by white people with makeup. On a second plane, outside and below, the rebels rev engines as they move Mercedes to block the gate of the hotel compound. Across the valley, highlighted by the moon, the dark cone of Santiaguito writes a thin cursive smoke into the purple sky.

"Nothing in the universe has an essential order to itself," Frank says, quoting a monk she has never heard of.

Later she decides that, if she'd known it would last nine days, she would have found some way to get out, but at the time the warmth of Frank's arm around her is enough to restore hesitation.

nine

Consider the size of this train station, and imagine the confidence of its builders.

The cornerstone of the original Gare de l'Est is laid by King Louis-Philippe in 1843. It stands at the end of a wide boulevard that Haussmann, the royal planner, has built through slums in order to both diminish their area and provide the cavalry with easy access to heads they might want someday to crack.

Even the initial station is vast. Covering an area of 160 meters by 30 it takes until 1877 to finish and when done looks like a monstrous Greco-Roman temple dedicated to the gods of steam. Its stone apex supports a female statue of "Strasbourg" holding a clock so huge you can tell the time halfway down the Boulevard de Sépastopol. Forty-eight years later this first temple will be joined to two others of equal size, linked by an enormous roof built of wrought-iron and glass in the shape of an inverted hull.

During the 1870 war the Gare de l'Est is the focal point of a railroad débacle. Trains being marshaled for the east are blocked, shunted aside, misdirected in their attempt to feed the war with fresh fuel and cannons and men. The French high command consistently demands trains of the wrong length for the units involved. The Germans, who have studied the only book on the subject, *De l'Emploi des Chemins de Fer en Temps de Guerre* (published in Paris in 1869), run their trains like scientific instruments, even to the inclusion of special expresses carrying Christmas gifts for the troops. "By what association of ideas can the same people regulate the normal use of the cutting torch, fuel and *Liebesgaden* [gift] trains?" Baron Ernouf fumes at the time. Nevertheless the French eastern railroad manages to haul 220,000 men, 32,000 horses, 3,000 pieces of artillery and 1,000 tons of munitions before the ceasefire.

In 1914 the traffic directors headquartered on the Rue d'Alsace, only 70 meters from the meeting place of Frank, Rohan, and Eva, are better prepared. At 3:30 P.M. on the 31st of July they put into operation the so-called Plan XVII. Plan XVII was conceived by the army general staff. It calls for initial movement to the border, via an integrated system of marshaling and dispatch, of frontier troops, followed by the first call-up of reservists and finally the cavalry divisions.

Despite problems caused by enemy action as well as the scale of the logistics involved, Plan XVII's system works smoothly enough to ferry five army corps as well as five infantry and three cavalry divisions from Lorraine to the Marne, in 740 trains between August 26 and September 3.

ten

Hurry and crowds were not in evidence nor were they expected on the slow local that left the Gare de l'Est at 12:32 bound for Meaux, Château-Thierry, Dormans, Epernay and Bar-le-Duc, with connections in Bar-le-Duc for Strasbourg and Colmar. Rohan found an empty compartment in the second car from the end. They placed bags on the racks and left coats on the spare seats to deter strangers. They sat, tugged clothing from their joints, watched the granite cuttings and electrical equipment of the station yards go by, getting used to the increasing roll and screech of wheels. Eva unfolded a copy of *Le Monde*, then put it aside without reading. "German Irredentists Plan Campaign of Terror," the headline read. "Bombings in Lorraine, East Prussia, Tyrol Form Pattern."

The conductor started collecting tickets before they were past the first *poste de triage* at the end of the Paris yards. He wore the standard blue uniform and low-peaked cap. Rohan, seeing him framed unexpectedly in the door's square glass, thought for a second that the police had followed them on board the train; the CRS and the gray-tan Alsatian dogs with their almost weightless way of moving.

He had felt compelled to look back at the dogs where they pinned the little Algerian to the cement. It was not because of the event's meaning, though he despised the xenophobia behind it, and the weakness festering, soft as abscess, behind that. Rather, it was because of those eyes; their almond shape, their lemon color—

"Billets, s'il vous plaît, messieurs-dames."

—the quadrant in every hound's heart, excepting only the most abject of lapdogs, that remained essentially wolf.

eleven

It is early autumn. He is eight, maybe even nine. Rohan's parents take Nathalie and him out of school in the middle of the trimester and they all travel by train to Bayonne, and by bus to St. Jean Pied de Port. In the morning of the next day they are driven up a mountain valley above the line of snow, as far as the car will go.

No explanation, of course. Their father never conveys any beyond the minimum: we are going on a trip. Pack your warm things. Henri Rohan has on the dark woollen over-coat he always wears. He carries, as he always does, the black briefcase which in all his life Rohan has never seen un-locked. Their mother never says much of anything when Henri is around although on this trip Rohan has noticed a curious light, like the static you get from rubbing a cat, play-ing in her gaze and around her when she moves. It cannot however be cat static because Marielle Rohan is seldom rubbed.

In the clearing where they stop a sleigh is waiting. It is a crude wooden affair drawn by two shaggy *Pokkatat* horses but it is the first sleigh he and Nathalie have ever been aboard. The driver is tiny and hunched. He wears a raw sheepskin coat and a beret that leaves all his face in shadow except for a long nose and eyes that are slightly slanted and of an odd color. Nathalie is so happy she is silent. Rohan is allowed to sit up front, with the driver, but his excitement is altered by the nervousness the small man induces in him.

The sleigh slides without sound up the valley. Snow falls gently and the air seems to grow darker, though it is barely noon. They skirt a forest. Behind black granite walls the beeches rise interminably to become one with the white. The horses' hooves make a muffled drum noise and the heart-shaped bells on their harness shake out sounds like bronze raindrops. Rohan watches, fascinated, as snow builds up on the thick insulating hair on the animals' rump. The coachman asks, "Do you know why that wall is there?"

Rohan does not reply.

"It's because of the wolves," the coachman says. "Every winter, the wolves come down. They eat the sheep and the little children. That is why they built the wall."

He can see them, long dark shapes coming together in the lack of pattern between snowflakes, disappearing when the wind blows the snow into some kind of order. They lope in long, easy strides through the drifts. The path starts to wind. The sleigh leaves forest and wall behind. The sides of the mountain, blow-dried with drifts, grow steeper, closer.

"Listen, children," his mother calls suddenly. The gold star of David around her neck winks dully as she moves. "Do you remember the story of Roland, I told you when you were younger . . . He was coming back, with Charlemagne, it was in the pass above this, this valley, and then the Moors attacked. Charlemagne wanted to go back but Roland's uncle, he said, 'No.' The uncle was jealous, you see."

"Roland blew his horn," Nathalie volunteers.

"He didn't play Mingus," puts in Henri Rohan, whose humor is scarce and, usually, fathomless.

"It was not the Moors," the driver mutters.

It was wolves, Rohan thinks. And then he wonders how this man, with his yellow eyes and long nose with thick gray hairs sticking out of the nostrils, would know that particular fact. A cold spot deep in his chest grows bigger and colder.

"They took the tourist road to Compostella," the coachman whispers, "but we knew the paths above them."

Nathalie watches the ravens that cruise silently among the falling flakes.

Finally the driver stops his sleigh in front of what once was an *olha*, or summer farm. They have long left contrast behind and the tiny house appears like a cave in the snowy mountainside. The door is opened by a man with the breadth and beard of a mountain troll. "*Alla Jainko*'," the troll says, "You got my letter."

The house consists of one large room. It is smoky and lit by kerosene lamps. Books, their spines blackened by the fire, line a long wall. Even in the miserable light they can see the troll is filthy. Their mother, who seldom hugs and touches, who cleans her floors the way other mothers scour dishes, puts her hand on his arm. In the light of the hearth he tends the troll's face seems made of the same angles and faults as the mountains around them. Only when he looks at their mother does the mouth subvert his Mesozoic solidity.

Light is slowly sucked from the air outside. Their parents drink from unmarked and dusty bottles. The troll starts to talk in a low voice that allows no full stops. He speaks of mountain people; they are fierce, he says, and know the high passes. Their way of government is based on free farms and the protecting circle of granite peaks, and accepts no chiefs or peons.

Mostly he talks of a people who speak a language so twisted it has thirty-six different variations for each noun, and every verb changes according to whether it relates to reality, or just possibility. And in Rohan's mind this language sounds as the modulation of a howl, and what he sees is a race of wolves that course across the snowy passes hunting exhausted children. Their number is legion and their speed is greater than the wind.

34

Nathalie grows bored and starts to whine. Their father fidgets and peers out the tiny umber windows but for the first time Rohan can remember he does not deliberately extend his discomfort to others around him. Finally he walks over to the hearth where Rohan and his sister are sitting.

"Listen," he tells Nathalie. "Your mother owes this man a debt."

Rohan and Nathalie both look at the troll. They cannot believe that Marielle Rohan, whose skin is white and smells like lilies, could have anything to do with such a creature, let alone owe him something.

"He is very old, and sick," their father continues. "But during the war, when she was a little girl, he helped her escape from the Germans. He hid her in a place like this. For two months he hid her. Then he carried her over the high passes, into Spain."

"I'm hungry," Nathalie says.

"He's a very educated man," their father mutters, as if trying to convince himself, "but the Spaniards will not let him back into Spain."

"He's a wolf!" Rohan whispers. "That's what the coachman said."

"Don't be an imbecile," Henri Rohan replies. "The last wolf in the Pyrénées was shot in 1933."

The hut's roof is hung with herbs that smell of hollowness and almonds. The troll's intestines are twisted and blocked. Their mother gives him medicines she has brought; these the troll stashes carelessly under his bench. Behind Rohan the fire gives tongue, in a language as diverse as Basque, to the concept that histories conceal within them, like meats in a shell, other histories, which carry in turn the shells of further secrets. The driver, who has been drinking silently in one corner, gets to his feet.

"*Allez*," he says, "before it grows too dark."

The troll tries to touch Nathalie, and she starts to cry. He watches them leave from the doorway of his hut. "We will survive," he says, "we will come from the shadows," but the words sound more like a prayer for something he no longer believes will happen. On the way down Rohan refuses to sit with the coachman. Nathalie tries to crawl under the furs with their mother but she is whiter and more silent than usual and after a while Nathalie moves next to Rohan. "Sit still!" their father yells at her; he holds his briefcase on his knees like a table before him. He brushes away the snow accumulating on its black leather.

Nathalie snuggles defiantly under the rug that covers her brother. Eventually she falls asleep. Rohan stays awake, carefully watching the driver, but the little man never turns around. The snow, still falling, covers his beret and sheepskin coat until finally he is as white as the horses that trot, in endless, silent cadence, before him.

twelve

"Service de restauration ambulant aprés Dormans—Messieursdames, merci."

The focus of Rohan's gaze pulled back somewhat as the conductor left. The milky square of window became sharp again. So did the faces of the other two passengers in the compartment. Both were gazing at him in mild expectation.

"I'm sorry? I was, ah—thinking—"

"I was just saying." Eva's voice held an energy almost too bright. "It's like seeing phantoms. You know."

"Twelve years dead," Rohan agreed. "Almost." He did not look at either of them. Though he had not seen many changes the first time he did so, the little clocks that indexed his thoughts kept insisting time *had* passed and that the analogy of ghosts, with its own peculiar resonance for him, was on target.

The train, rolling over junctions, made a rhythm like this; *Clunk (click-click)—clunk (clack-clack)—clunk (click-click clack-clack);* which Frank in his middle consciousness realized was the same as the opening bar from *Lucy in the Sky with Diamonds,* three-quarter time from a song that had been high on the WPRO charts when he was a kid.

"It's eerie, almost," Frank muttered, rubbing his moustache. "The fluke of it—"

"Well." Rohan lifted his eyebrows. "But once before," he pointed out, "it happened. I mean, we were all together."

"That's the coincidence," Frank answered. "That's what I was saying."

"By definition," Eva put in, and raised her left arm to shake down the ten or fifteen bracelets around that wrist.

Rohan looked downward. "In my work," he said, "or what used to be my work, well, you learn that they are so common. Coincidences. Someone should write a paper: 'Coincidence as an Engine of History'; like that." Frank stared at him with an odd expression, as if he'd just smelled sewer gas. "Well." Rohan shrugged. "Maybe I will write it myself."

In the Maya-Ki'iché culture of Xelajú the Indians consider white people to be ghosts who have been put in charge of the living world as part of some joke of the gods that is considered by the shamans to be inexplicable, and in poor taste. This is a fact whites are mostly unaware of.

"If it happens often," Frank observed, "it's not coincidence."

"But that's what I'm saying," Rohan replied. "If you look at coincidence." He brought his eyes up suddenly toward Frank's. "You find it is a creation of the mundane. This nail, that is missing from the horseshoe of the king, 'for want of a nail,' you know the one? Or a message is misplaced, very simple. The 'flu, or someone wants someone else's girl . . . a battle is lost, the culture is destroyed.

"Look," he added, and the fingers of his left hand moved higher to touch an object hidden behind the fabric of his shirt, "look what brought us together. I was going to see, check out this wreck on the Pacific coast. I mean, my flight—I spend one night at the Continental—well, something stupid, there was rain in Miami."

"I had a business meeting," Frank said. "Normal, right?"

"You were buying guns," Eva spoke up suddenly. "I remember."

Frank looked at her with a certain absence of expression.

"The fat man told me," she added. "Calderón. I remember what he said."

"You're serious?" Rohan leaned forward. "I thought, those days, you worked for an aid group, something—"

(The rebels, Frank thought, in their cut-rate jeans, their guayaberas and bandannas, their World War Two-era Sturmgewehr submachine guns he had come to Xelajú to buy. When he saw the MP-40s in their hands he knew it was useless. The Gardia had a stash of well-tallowed Sturmgewehrs that Nagyratoth had sold them, hidden in an armory in Oriente. He realized then the rebels must have taken the garrison, or bribed the officers in charge. He didn't mind their having done so, in the abstract—it just screwed up his business.)

"I *was* working for an aid group," Frank said slowly. Between phrases, his jaw chewed at gum that wasn't there. "We were helping some insurgents in Uganda. It so happened that, what they needed to survive, it wasn't medicine, or water or CARE packages or bread; they needed *guns* to survive."

"It is always the reason, don't you think?" Rohan objected, and his face was pulled tighter in cords of curiosity. "I mean, those guns, they go around, around, like bad money—"

"I was always careful," Frank replied.

"Do you think your guns," Rohan asked him, "do you really think they helped anybody, in the long run?"

"We all met in the ballroom," Eva put in, looking at each of them in turn, very seriously.

"It was true," Frank told him. Abruptly his chewing ceased.

Silence for a space of time, broken by the sound of wheels, the variations in tilt of older rolling-stock.

"An odd thing," Rohan said, changing the subject to draw most of the perceived aggression from what he'd said. It was a longish trip and there would be plenty of time for wrangling, if such was inevitable. "I thought I saw, well—"

"It was no amateur thing," Frank interrupted, "it was *professional*. I was in the business of helping people in practical ways."

"Maybe I knew it," Rohan waved his hand, "but I forgot. What I remember is, you told me you worked for a relief agency."

"It was in the ballroom," Eva repeated.

"I saw you first in the bar," Rohan told her, "the day before the rebels came. You were with Julián."

Outside, the climate of the North Atlantic swirled its soup of mist, wind and drizzle over the indifferent suburbs. Inside the compartment the three shared to varying degrees memories containing small common denominators: sense perceptions that were either strong enough initially, or amplified to such an extent by the force of coeval events, to have been imprinted in mutually recognizable fashion on each of their minds:

• • •

The smell of mold, and Swiss floor wax. The smell of copal resin, too, for amid the mirrors and polished stainless-steel columns of the Continental's bar, not far from the door, stand two Maya-Ki'iché stelae carved in limestone. One represents a fanged, long-nosed god with a head-dress. The second consists of a squatting figure, painted black and white. This one has skeletal features and a ring of bells around his neck. It is to this sour deity that the rebels mostly come, burning small cakes of incense that they must have carried along with their spare clips of 7.62-mm ammunition. After the Gardia assault, and the death of the two Brazilians, the rebels herd everyone down to the ground floor, essentially the ballroom and bar. In the middle of the ballroom they rig up an explosive device made of eighteen L-1A1 anti-personnel grenades taped inside a wine crate with a wire looped through all the firing pins. They assign one of their number to sit next to it. He will yank the wire if things go badly.

At some time during the first night the electricity is shut off from outside. The hotel staff, or what is left of them, light dinner candles, myriads of tapers that are reflected in the shiny paneling and fake Indian motifs lining the ballroom's walls. Many of the guests sleep on couches and armchairs and the rest stretch out on the carpeting, with the exception of a Dutch musician, who lies on a buffet table, head pillowed protectively on her guitar case. It is hot during the day but at night the temperature drops and condensation courses down the walls in thin waterfalls. The armored cars ringing the compound carry loudspeakers that play Souza tunes transmitted from the air force station. From his cage in the bar a tame macaw curses in Spanish. An English businessman tries to use the phone and is told that only one set in the bar now functions and in any case that is off limits. The Englishman works himself into a great fury and is knocked silly with a rifle butt for his pains.

• • •

"Sweating," Eva said, and felt her skin grow warm in memory. "Sweating, all the time."

"Our clothes, they were always soaked," Rohan agreed.

"Like the métro at rush hour," Frank put in.

Outside, a commuter train passed, moving quickly in the opposite direction. The blast from its passage shook the windows and made their ears hum.

"I wonder what happened to Julián," Eva said softly.

"You know what happened," Frank told her. "You saw, he was arrested, after the rebels left. The Gardia knew exactly who he was, he—"

"I knew that." Eva took one bracelet and tried to fit it through another. "What I mean is, who told the Gardia? No one knew who he was, not even the guerillas, no one knew he was the, Julián was in command of the rebels."

"Ah." Rohan touched his chin with one finger, "Exactly. What they call, the sixty-four-dollar question."

"Twenty-four hours a day," Frank looked outside, "that phone was guarded. There was no way."

"Except during the radio broadcast," Eva corrected him, "the rebel radio."

Eva let her breath out slowly.

"If it comes to that," Rohan added, "how did *we* know who he was? Julián."

Frank looked at Eva. "You told me. You told me he worked for the rebels."

"Eva." Rohan looked at his hands. "You told me also. I remember now." He grunted, and looked up. "So the question is now, how did *you* know?"

She dragged down one corner of her mouth with a finger, as if to forcibly prevent herself from laughing.

"In bed," she said finally.

"Men tell me things," she added, "in bed."

In December of 1523 one of Cortez's captains, Pedro de Alvarado, was dispatched at the head of 900 men with the stated reason of taking control of the Central American highlands for the glory of the king of Spain and, of course, the Catholic god. What Alvarado truly coveted, however, was the golden wealth of the legendary "Seven Cities of Cibola." They followed the coastal plain to the Rio Suchete, then began climbing, occasionally skirmishing with Ki'iché raiding parties on the way but meeting little serious opposition until, threading a path between two of the ten volcanoes surrounding, they came into the plain of Xelajú.

thirteen

And surely, Frank thinks, he has told the truth. He *does* work for an aid agency, before, after—during, as he told Rohan.

And as principal humanitarian assistance officer to Bahr el Gazal and Darfur for the Boston-based International Relief Organization he puts in weeks, months, in a small dusty town called Birea, in the autonomous prefecture of the same name, in the Central African Republic, just fifty-four kilometers by truck across the growing desert from the people he is supposed to be helping.

Birea is a collection of mudbrick warehouses and administration buildings, and, around these, a cluster of beehive huts surrounded in turn by the cities of flapping cloth in which live traditional nomads as well as 6,300 refugees from a war in south Sudan. This war, because it has until now gone unreported by Western media, can fairly be said not to exist.

Around Birea stretches either desert, or land that in twenty years time will be desert; ochre without end, cut by dry rivers, nailed by thornbush, swept in its rare marshes by silver grass; hammered by sun and drought to a hardness close to metal; buffed, not so gently, by the Khamsin wind.

It is the country where man first left the dying trees and learned to walk on his hind legs, to see over the thornbush, the silver grass, thus freeing his hands for weapons.

To the Europeans, lost or driven, who end up in this town, Birea is the Hôtel du Terminus, a former *Tirailleurs Sénégalais* post in the main square. Here, in the courtyard of the Terminus, is where Frank meets Chapman and Jouget.

They are sprawled under the parched fig tree that dominates this tiny yard of beaten earth. It is late afternoon and shadow changes the dirt to the color of gun-metal. On a stone bench to one side sit three cameramen from a Western news organization at last attracted by the very absence of publicity this no-war across the border enjoys. Chapman is broad, fifty-ish, right-wing. He holds himself as if he still had access to the Greenjackets mess; his pale eyes bulge over drink-eroded features like two cool blue moons rising over Arizona.

Hakim Jouget is the son of a British artilleryman and a Gazali woman. He has the fine features and long build of his mother's race. His smile is full of even, healthy teeth. He bears the rank of colonel in the Gazali "army" but now wears the robes of a Sudanese Muslim. Later he will call himself simply "Colonel Hakim." They drink warm beer imported from Kampala.

Europeans, even half-Europeans, form circles in these places. Frank complains: both his diesels have broken down; the sand seeps through the gaskets. The commander here wants a bribe to guard the trucks against pilfering. Frank has no money, because the relief group stopped sending funds after they had not received a report from him in four months. Frank has been mailing a report every ten days. The airstrip is out of commission in any case.

"We'll give you a job," Chapman offers, as the owner lights kerosene lamps and hangs them in the tree.

Frank says nothing. He does not know exactly what Chapman and Jouget are up to but they are not UN or NGO or church and therefore can only be smuggling; ivory or diamonds, guns or gold.

"Look," Jouget says in delight, "he has scruples."

43

"Africa's not a healthy place for those, my son," Chapman tells him, opening another beer. "Scruples are for places with a surplus of water."

"And public loos," the African adds, chuckling. He has taken courses at Sandhurst, whose buildings, during his tenure, contained many lavatories separated by rank but not sex.

Across the courtyard, the three film men check their equipment. They are small intense Venetians. They seem to live only within the context of their electronics. The two cameramen constantly peer through their viewfinders, framing everything, anything, as if the world had no solidity unless it could be taped and edited.

"*Due punt' otto,*" one of them says. "*Luce. Più presto.*"

"We need a driver, lad," Chapman says. "We'll pay you a hundred pounds for three days work. Sterling. Cash."

"What are you running?" Frank asks him.

Jouget leans forward like a tennis player at net.

"What are *you* running?"

"Ground corn," Frank tells him without hesitation. "Powdered milk. Antibiotics." With his beer he swallows pills reputed to prevent malaria, Dengue fever, amoebic dysentery. Jouget waves a handful of long, graceful, pink-tinted fingers.

"Do you know who you are helping?" he says. "You are helping the Sudanese army. They find out where you send your trucks. Then they come into the villages and shoot everyone. They take your food and sell it, in the north."

The Italians move around the courtyard, testing their equipment. Chapman automatically turns his back.

"*Più forte. Vai, vai. Ecco.*"

Frank has heard the rumors but he ends the conversation. Two days later half his cargo is stolen in Birea, probably by the local commander. A week after, he learns that the village in which he left supplies last month was indeed sacked by the Sudanese Army.

He works for Chapman for four months. The work is easy and occasional, with just enough risk to keep an edge on. He pilots a Mercedes truck loaded with ordnance, at night, under a sky so heavy with stars it seems likely to bust open at any moment, spilling the tiny bright lights like a basketful of conflict diamonds across the Sahel. He drives through checkpoints where Jouget has bribed everyone in sight. Eighteen miles beyond the Sudanese border he leaves the rutted track, steering for the dark shape of the mountains where the rebels camp. Sometimes the métis rides with him part of the way. His accent, a compound of African glottal stops and Sandhurst drawl, seems to color in what he says. He allows Frank's political affirmations, forced in the soil of American labor organizing, to bend with Jouget's own. They talk up a system based on principles that function only on a small scale, if at all. It includes produce markets and cheap trucks, tribal councils and Rhode Island town meetings. All of this is crossed with the precepts of an irrigated garden agriculture that Jouget, who once visited Stourhead, seems curiously enamored of.

"Water is the secret of politics here," Jouget says wistfully. "There is so much water in Wiltshire . . ."

Jouget often stops to cut the strange flowers of the thornbush.

After two months have passed Jouget makes him a proposition: he will give Frank the name of a "munitions merchant" in Larnaca if Frank will arrange to ship arms to Jouget for a third of the commission Chapman charges.

Frank does not hesitate.

For six years he sends German mortars, American rifles, Chinese hand grenades, Russian RPGs to Jouget's camps in the Djebel Marra. He makes enough contacts to score other deals: a cargo of AK-47s for the Guatemalan *Frente*, 900 third-hand Katyusha rockets for the Kurdistan People's Party (flown as "drilling pipe" via Cyprus); 250 mortars with 10,000 rounds for the Papuans, landed by a Filipino coaster west of Kokonau. He learns the tricks of the trade: how to shuttle arms around Europe, backed with legal end-use certificates, till they wind up in places like Minsk or Piraeus whence they can be shipped virtually anywhere. He learns what cargo planes, like the Lockheed Connies, carry doors that open inward for parachute drops; how to buy passport holders that look like diplomatic papers, for added comfort in passing Customs; how to hide your nationality in drip-dry Italian suits and shoes purchased in the country you work in; how to carry on your keychain a magnet that will tell you the percentage of iron used in a "bronze" shell casing. He talks Arms-speak, saying systems instead of weapons, transfers instead of import, conflict instead of war. Though he never falls in love with the merchandise as some do, he ends up admiring the gear that works well with low maintenance: the FALs, G3s, Kalashnikovs. He distrusts the Ingram, knock-off Uzis, Chinese weapons.

Above all, over the course of many trips, mostly between the Near East, Africa and Europe but occasionally further afield, he collects names. A credit manager in Berne, a customs chief in Lagos, a dealer in antique guns in Birmingham. He meets an ex-Ojukwu pilot in Cairo, a former Polish cavalry officer in Port o' Spain, a Franciscan friar in Peshawar who offers him a book by John Duns Scotus along with confirmation of a deal in the mountains. He does not get rich; he will not emulate Basil Zaharoff, who sold Maxim-Nordenfeldt machine guns at big markups to both the Italians and the Austro-Hungarians during the First World War. He sends exactly fifteen percent of his earnings to the Boston relief organization. He is careful, to the extent possible, to trade on account for people who are being, by and large, slaughtered by their central governments. He averages two successful contracts per year, and makes few serious miscalculations.

He is not naive. He knows the arms will end up killing people. But he believes, on balance, that it is a case of self-defense;

that the world works, on some level, like the south end of Central Falls, Rhode Island; that his guns, as Jouget once said, have done more to help the dispossessed than the relief agency's corn and powdered milk.

And one day, almost seven years after first meeting Chapman and Jouget, Frank hears a BBC account of a key defeat sustained by the Sudanese regular army at the hands of dissident forces in southwest Sudan. A rebel spokesman named Major Chapman states that a new provisional government has been set up, led by Colonel Hakim.

The next week Frank flies to Birea. He cadges a ride with the three Venetian filmmakers who, like him, have come back for the kill. Frank is tired but hopeful, looking forward to seeing Jouget. They drive for thirty hours. Then the driver turns off the track, aiming for a broad column of smoke. He slows as they approach the remains of a Darfur village. The Venetians become part of their vidcams and Nagras once again. The huts are all burning. Men, women, children and cattle lie spavined on the stone-hard ground. They have been shot with rifles and maimed with knives. Their blood turns the ochre ground purple. Already the heat has caused the bodies to rot. Their stomachs are huge with corruption, and the buzzing of flies is so loud it competes with the diesel's rattle.

An old man crawls from the ruin of a *boma*, a cattle enclosure. The driver asks him when the Sudanese came. The old man stares at him. The cameras whirr.

"It was not the army," he says finally. His eyes are glazed with cataracts and thick with flies. "I cannot see, but I can hear. It was the Gazalis."

The old man is quite naked. Working entirely by feel he has been lining up in rows the corpses of his children or grandchildren. He refuses to leave. "There is too much meat here," he keeps repeating. "It will all go to waste."

Next to one of the rondavels lies the cut flower of a thornbush.

"Guardi," the Italians say. They hook into each other's powerpacks, focusing on the roseate bud. *"Da mi piú forte."*

Frank realizes that, all this time, he must have been vaguely in love with Jouget.

Frank works as a munitions merchant for another eight months. It is during that time that he goes to Xelajú. When a job opens up coordinating a famine-relief project in Tigre for the IRO he applies. Partly because of his experience, mostly because of his donations, he is accepted.

He reads many of the works of John Duns Scotus.

The image of the lined-up children, and the humming of flies, does not dim with time, and he has trouble thereafter eating steak, which he used to enjoy.

fourteen

Men you did not know had found you a place.

A cozy flat with lace curtains. It belonged to a woman. You pulled on a pair of surgeon's gloves and bolted the door carefully behind you.

You found a desk in one of the children's rooms. It was a simple matter to clear the video toys and schoolbooks, wipe off the surface with a sponge, and bring over a good lamp. You placed on the desk the parcel wrapped in paper from a Paris department store.

There was Ivory Coast coffee in the kitchen and a small espresso maker. You brewed a pot because you liked coffee, but you would only drink half because you didn't want your hands to tremble. That would not be smart.

Inside the parcel was a box, and inside that a cellophane bag half full of white powder, and a plastic bladder tight with pink paste. Securely wrapped in cottonwool and taped to the box beside them lay a two-inch copper tube with a pair of wires extending from one end.

You took the three objects and placed them separately on the desk; three objects that on their own could do little. The process involved here was one of combining. You added and blended, step by step, until you created exactly the conclusion you had planned for.

The bag was full of pure ammonium. The bladder contained nitrate paste. On their own, or even side by side, they were inert, you could let off a hydrogen bomb beside them and they would simply melt without adding any more destructive power to the conflagration than could be expected from gravel. These two products were manufactured by ChemImpex of Prague, a division of the Banque Atlantique group with headquarters in St. Peter Port, Guernesey. In this case they were purchased from ChemImpex by Hun Hau Holdings of Caracas, Venezuela. From Caracas they were shipped to Industries Mitnal (International) SA of Georgetown, Bahamas, and re-exported to Industries Mitnal SA in Villeneuve, in the north of France. On the first two legs of the trip they were undervalued as imports and overvalued as exports, earning their companies, which were all controled by Banque Atlantique in the first place, substantial savings in tariffs and tax credits.

To combine the first two ingredients you simply squeezed the paste into the bag of ammonium and kneaded the two together until the substance within turned a uniform rose color. It was easy to shape the bag into a triangular form. At the apex of the triangle you cut a hole in the plastic and inserted the bronze tube, with the wires protruding.

The paste now consisted of 1.7 kilograms of ammonium nitrate. No longer was it inert; it could be set off by a small explosion, like an M-80 firecracker. In fact, it had the explosive power of ten sticks of dynamite, enough to open a rock face, or break an armored car in two.

Truly, you thought, this was a case where the whole had become greater than the sum of its parts.

The bronze tube was a blasting cap containing a solution of lead azide stabilized by three percent dextrin. It was manufactured in Indonesia before 1998, which meant that the serial number printed on the side did not correspond to anything. The triangular shape of the explosive, and the position of the detonator at its apex, would ensure that most of the force of detonation would be directed toward the base. If you wanted to destroy something, you made sure you pointed the base of the triangle at it.

You finished a cup of coffee and waited to pour yourself another. You had an hour to finish. Plenty of time.

You did not want your fingers to tremble.

fifteen

A half dozen men from a highway construction gang leaned over the side of a cut in the suburb of Villemomble, watching the train rush by.

Inside the train the passengers sat in silence for awhile. Frank stared out the window, not seeing the men. Rohan stood, opened the sliding door and entered the corridor. He lowered the window and took out a flat pack of cigarrillos. The wind of the train's passage, cavitating in the sudden gap in the carriage's surface, pushed back his hair. The smoke of the cheroot was sharp and thin and easily made its way through the poorly sealed door and into Eva's nostrils.

Eva understood exactly how smell worked. She was aware of the great elegance of the human capacity to smell and taste, which was more or less the same thing. She knew that while men could detect musk at levels of only one part per

10,000, an ovulating woman could smell it at the level of one part per *quadrillion*. She did not know if she was ovulating or not. She was aware of how the cilia of the olfactory molecule worked like a neuron's synapses, swapping ions of potassium in one case, calcium in the other, to alter the resting potential of the nerve. She knew that nerve chemicals flowing down a pathway in the brain caused more chemicals to be stocked up, which in circular fashion made that pathway more apt to be traveled in the future; and that this process, arbitrarily drawing order from random information, constituted the basic brick of which sense, memory, and intelligence were built.

Eva knew that smell worked differently from the other senses in that no buffer zone existed between the olfactory membrane and the lobe of the brain that received its messages. Also, the olfactory nerve sent its messages straight to areas of the brain associated with emotion; and for all these reasons the impact of smell on memory had to be more powerful than that of any other stimulus.

But comprehension was a mere twist on the swift fractal surface of the message she was decoding. That primary neural association with tobacco summoned inside her umber shades, an odor of cabbage, of dirty laundry. It built with efficiency the *taste* of twinned boredom and contentment that was the legacy of her and Anna growing up in the apartment in Szentkarolyi Ut.

sixteen

The neighbor, Andrassy Maria, whenever she smells the cigar smoke, reports their father to a man she knows on the local Party committee. The man, who also smokes cigars when he can get them, takes no account of this grave proof of bourgeois decadence. But there is always the possibility that things will change, that one day it might affect them.

Things already have changed. After '56 their father, who supported Nagy in a mild sort of way, was stripped of his position at the University of Pesht and assigned to menial jobs in an aspirin factory. Now, almost fifteen years later, he spends long hours staring at the newspaper without reading it. His hair is white, though he is only forty-one years old.

Their mother says she cannot stand any more such disruptions. She was always quick to emotion but as the years go by the lag grows lesser, the volume louder, whether in dispute, mirth or tears. There are times when she acts like she used to; when she sits on their beds defending them against the onset of night, for darkness is something both girls are afraid of; telling them stories of how this house used to be, the levées and cotillions, the horses and carriages coming to the door, the dukes and princesses dressed in gold-shot clothing who disembarked from them. The stories always are related to her grandfather, who attended many parties until he was seconded to a West Prussian Grenadier regiment and killed in the Great War. She plays comic-opera waltzes on the Victrola and her eyes seem to sparkle with the light of a hundred candles. But these episodes grow less frequent.

When their father takes out his cigars she seems to whirl like a dancer in the music of her anger. In summer she closes all the windows and crams wet sheets against the sill of the door.

It seems like every month but it really only happens two or three times a year that she does not whirl out of her rage as quickly as she spun into it. She is a small woman with rich brown eyes and black curls and cheeks that one day will sag but that in her late thirties are still round and cheerful. When the spin does not trigger its own recovery, though, the life seeps from her face and even her curls droop as if the very elasticity in them had been removed through some delicate process of chemical subtraction. She cries and slams the doors on the two girls. From behind the cracked panels they can hear words she must know they will catch: despair and separation. Suicide. Divorce.

Anna is older. She is just as frightened by all this as Eva but since she has been given a role to play she lives up to it gamely. They cut paper figures with blunt scissors, waiting for their mother to leave.

She always leaves. The door bangs, the neighbors' windows creak, a rattle of shoes sounds from the courtyard. She comes back when they are at school or asleep. Their father ignores the newspaper. The next morning she is more affectionate than usual.

One morning in autumn, when Eva is ten, the storm starts early. For two hours they can hear her shouting at or around their father. "I will leave you," she says, "I cannot abide how none of this ever changes." This is news to Eva, who always thought her mother preferred things the same.

The door slams before Eva and Anna have left for school. By now Anna is thirteen and has discovered boys, who tell her secrets that seem to insulate her, to some extent, from what her mother does. But Eva has found her sensitivity to all this increasing. On impulse, and for the first time in her life, she follows her mother out.

Teresa Koszegfalvi wears cheap heeled pumps and a worn, fur-lined overcoat that is her second-most-precious possession. It billows, unfastened, in the chilly wind. Eva has grown up on accounts of the autumn of '56. It was a mild season, and the Russian mortars shook gilded leaves from the trees; but this November, like all the others she has ever known, is misty, bleak and cold. She supposes, in some unlit corner of her mind, that the Russians took away the golden fall weather along with Imre Nagy and a lot of other good Magyars.

Attila József writes,

Drooling between the bricks.

Mother and daughter like ducks down Museum Korut, Kossuth Ut. She crosses the Erzsébet Bridge and pauses so that Eva, her heart suddenly pounding, almost runs to stop her, but it is only to watch the black-headed gulls gliding almost stationary in the wind. With the fog coming off the Danube in a flat streak the birds look like notes on a rolling score of gray music. They cross into Buda. After a while Teresa slows down. She turns right into Kagylo Utca, a street of steps and old-fashioned lampposts that rises steeply to a church. The two climb slowly, in unconscious unison.

A children's park lies at the church's base. Teresa sits under the statue of a bear with his paws in a honeypot. A few paces away, a bronze fox walks hand in hand with a goose of the same metal. She stares at the houses below, then, after five minutes, continues walking.

They cross the hill, northward, and descend. Teresa is almost strolling now. Eva has to hide more than once to avoid being spotted. By the foundry museum her mother abruptly enters an apartment building. Eva hangs around the door, uncertain, but in the fear and arrogance of being ten decides she must try to affect what she can. She goes in.

Only one door seems to offer welcome in the courtyard. Above it a sign reads "Grunros Anton: Mechanical Workshop." The courtyard is tall, sooty, green with moss. Wrought-iron balconies tense and twist in the sky above her. She goes down the stairs under the sign.

Inside is very dark and hot and smells of coal and cigarette smoke. A bell jangles as Eva shuts the door. Something moves on her right-hand side. Atop a rickety sideboard a clockwork man, no doubt activated by the door's opening, reads from a scroll, then bows jerkily. He is five inches tall, made of wood and tin and dressed in antique clothing that would probably be garish if she could see it better.

Her eyes grow used to the light. Behind a six-foot passenger ship, all lit up, she spots her mother bending over some kind of exhibit. In one corner, beside a coal stove with many blackened pipes leading from its back, a man dressed in work clothes and a leather apron turns to examine her. He has pale, pudgy features. A cigarette wedges his mouth open. He wears a skullcap and is the age of most of her teachers. He turns back without a word to his bench, which is buried in drifts of what appear to be clock escapements.

A model of a locomotive's cab is hung against one wall, with a man, also five inches in height, frozen in the act of shoveling coal.

> *Weariness squats on a boxcar*

(Attila József again),

> *watching the steam engine*
> *as it winds home on the tracks*

She takes a step inside. To her left black-robed metal figures stoop in attitudes of judgment. A strong bearded man, stripped to the waist, stands chained against a stone wall. She recognizes the man and the scene. Dosza Gyorgy, hero of Hungarian school histories, was a farmer who raised an army of 100,000 peasants. Instead of fighting the Turks as he was supposed to, he turned on the Magyar nobles, with bad results. She touches a figure in the montage. He is dressed in a leather apron, like the man in the corner. A whirring starts. The figure, in jerky, partial movements, raises a whip over its head.

She gasps, without knowing she does so. Her mother is beside her. Eva starts to stammer, expecting anger, lectures, but Teresa takes her hand and walks her over to a high box in the back of the shop.

"Look," she says. "Look at this, Eva."

Teresa winds a crank in the box's side, then folds open the front panel. A wooden bird stands perched on a branch inside, but it is like no bird Eva has ever seen, it has an expression, a sarcastic smile, of the kind she would get slapped for in school. Emerald eyes gleam, and feathers in fifteen different hues sprout everywhere. As the mechanism unwinds a fan starts in the box's side, and the bird begins to move. It lifts its wings, then, responding to guidewires invisible in the dark of the box, rises from the branch. The wild feathers fold in a streamlined pattern, the beak veers into the draft and suddenly the whole thing is planing in the fan's wind exactly as the gulls did over Erzsébet Bridge in the breeze off the Danube.

"You followed me."

Eva nods dumbly, watching the bird.

"You'll have to make up a day in school. Look at this one, sweetheart." Teresa's eyes now are calm as well water. She brushes her hair back and touches a button. Light falls on a miniature pit. A bear moves and turns, swiping with one paw at three dogs who jump and snap around him. Eva can see the rods and gears on this mechanism but still she turns away. There is blood on the bear's shoulder. A dog lies still to the side.

"They used to do that as a sport," Teresa says. "The men would pay to look. But here, we don't have to. Pay, I mean. Or look." She turns off the switch and gives her daughter a smile that is quite clear of obstacles.

Eva looks at the ship. Officers stand watch on the bridge and passengers stroll on the boat deck. A man, hypnotized by the wake below, leans deeply over the stern-rail. The French tricolor flaps above him. Her mother shows her a dozen other mechanisms. Many of them carry tags saying they are destined to go to such and such a museum. Eva remembers a carousel with horses that trot in circles under their own power, and a steam-powered forge where a smith pounds iron in a live fire. As the steam hisses, the springs turn, the tiny electric motors hum, her mother seems to lose her proximity to whatever cliff she walks in normal life.

In 1944 the SS regional command, angered by the Budapest government's lack of cooperation in this matter, rounded up and deported the Jews of the rural districts of Hungary. The Hungarian leader, Admiral Horthy, eventually put a stop to the deportations, thus sparing many of the Jews of Budapest a similar fate. Still, 400,000 Hungarian men, women and children disappeared forever to the west that year.

The commander of the SS in Hungary at the time was SS Hauptsturmführer Theo Dannecker.

Before they leave, her mother buys the carousel. She gives the man a tiny ruby ring she fishes from her coat pocket. "Wrap it, please," she says, "I'll pick it up later." As they go out the door the man takes Eva's hand and shows her the ring in his own.

"We do this every time," he whispers. His voice is scratchy, like an overused record. "Next month, she will take it back." His breath is mighty with tobacco.

Later that day they eat ice cream for lunch at a café by Krisztina Templom. Later still, many years later in fact, Eva and Anna are summoned home to find their mother strapped to rough hospital sheets with a tumor eating the occipital region of her brain.

It happens so quickly there is not much time for grief. But in one of the lucid moments Teresa Koszegfalvi opens her eyes and they are as calm as they were when she was looking at the mechanical people in Anton's basement and Eva has a certainty, as irrational as it is strong, that despite or because of the intrusion in her brain Teresa once more stands in the ghetto workshop, watching five-inch men whir and bow in a world she will always be able to control.

seventeen

Toward the end of spring 1918 the exhausted armies of the Allied powers face the worn-out armies of the German states across a desert of broken trenches, rusty barbed wire, and undiscovered bodies. The desert, which is called "no-man's-land," has been shelled, gased, machine-gunned, fought over hand to hand, and traded countless times over the preceding three years and eight months. Like other deserts it has its own metabolism, its isostasis. Millions of men and tens of millions of tons of munitions and supplies have been sacrificed in order to maintain a precise balance between the two armies and thus preserve in time and space the integrity of this place where nothing whatsoever can grow. The German trains running from the Rhineland—the French trains running from Paris on the same line Frank, Eva and Rohan one day will travel—keep the process alive.

But generals are the natural enemies of isostasis they cannot end at will. In April of 1918 Feld-Marshal Luddendorf, the German commander, decides to launch yet another offensive. The idea behind this one is to attack directly toward Paris across Champagne, causing the French to draw their reserve troops away from the Flanders front; at which point Luddendorf, abandoning the feint, will strike a decisive blow against the British troops remaining in Flanders. The night of May 26 is very quiet, according to a Hungarian artillery officer seconded to Von Boehm's Seventh Army. The nightingales are singing and the croaking of thousands of frogs disguises the trundle of advancing cannon. At 1 A.M. on May 27, 1500 German artillery pieces begin lobbing gas shells into the Allied positions across no-man's-land, which in this case lies on a ridge the homesick Germans call Winterberg, because the exposed limestone to them looks like the snow of the Bavarian Alps. At dawn the fifteen divisions under the command of Kronprinz Wilhelm invade the desert. Wading through flooded shell craters, clambering over acres of barbed wire, their feet mashing three years' worth of unclaimed corpses, they bust through the seven French, American and British divisions on the other side of no-man's-land and advance twenty kilometers into Champagne. They cross the Aisne river, then the Vesle. They reach the Marne on May 30 and re-take Château Thierry on the thirty-first. Luddendorf and Wilhelm, delighted by the unexpected success of their offensive, decide to press on toward Paris, but their impetus is checked by the French Second Division on the Marne's other side.

Still, 50,000 allied troops have been captured; 12,000 allied troops, compared to only 10,000 German, have been killed. In the beginning of summer, the mood on the German side is good.

eighteen

Easing the window further down, taking air from the slipstream, the smell of anthracite from the rail bed and the cigar smoke pricking at his nostrils, Rohan saw the train as a continuum that led from this point and instant all the way down the seamless steel rail to Colmar and the platform in which all color values would be preempted by the brightly dyed garments favored by Dominique and her daughter waiting for him, Dominique standing quiet, but Chloé always moving, restless with hormones.

He wondered what they would think of his guests. Probably Chloé would appreciate Eva's looks and silk blouses and hold judgment on the rest.

Dominique might wonder what lay behind Frank's watchfulness, his explosive laugh. She would use them all as grist for analysis, to determine what he wanted, what they wanted. She would smile and she would analyze, her capacity for one augmenting, not detracting from, her capacity for the other.

She did it from the first, he knew now; from the very first.

●

nineteen

Rohan, the first time he meets Dominique, is convinced that he has seen her face before. The structure of it comes back to him with strength and frequency, a phrase from a melody he cannot quite place.

Of course he does not tell her that, then or for a long time after, because it seems so coercive, even if true, which he has doubts about anyway. But there is power in that connection, some pop justification of events to come.

All right, then, Scene One: the Sirius Underwater Cinematography Center in Summit, California. This is originally a site of some political and economic drama, when Pacific Light and Electric obtains Federal approval to build a 1.2-million-kilowatt nuclear power station on a flat sandstone shelf full of piñon and truck repair services between Summit and Hesperia in the San Bernardino Mountains. They get as far as casting in heavily armored concrete a gigantic round containment vessel before a team of geologists hired by what PL&E calls "a bunch of tree-huggers" points out in court that this shelf lies over a previously ignored tributary of the San Andreas fault. PL&E, aware that the legal fees will cancel out any profits it could garner from the project, shuts it down.

The containment vessel lies there for years after the court case, a great cement fossil left behind by forgotten seas, until the technical director of Sirius Pictures, scouting for underwater production facilities for their new historical subocean epic *Fathom 500*, happens to fly over it on his way to New York and realizes what is sitting below him: seven cubic acres of watertight container going cheap within a hundred miles of Culver City. The studio has three underwater films booked. It not only rents and adapts the disused structure but, in an excess of enthusiasm, decides to invest in historical accuracy by hiring an expert in both underwater archeology and underwater films.

Enter Rohan, to borrow a term from the jargon that defines them all. The day is hot but dry and clear, a welcome change from the miasma of L.A. He has worked out most of the technical problems on *Fathom*. It is on the historical stuff that Kevin McCann, the producer, is refusing to give. "Every authentic touch," he likes to shout, holding all his fingers up, "ten thousand bucks!" However Rohan already has learned how far he can and cannot go, which is what passes for serenity in Hollywood.

The second unit is starting to shoot scene 45 in which the diver who, in scenes 24 and 30, evinced his belief that "something is wrong" with this wreck, seeks to repair their single phone link to the surface. Behind him the companionway to the galleon's great cabin slowly opens. The skeleton of Ponce de Leon's navigator leans out of the blackness. A fifteenth-century Spanish cutlass severs the wire and the diver's neck for good measure. Rohan takes the elevator to the operations deck. Aimé Barthélémy, in full wetsuit, is shouting in mangled English at a group of Teamsters. Edie Parnell—*the* Edie Parnell—stands to one side. In the next scene she is to struggle briefly in the water before her double takes over.

"*Bande de cons*," Barthélémy yells. He looks like a miniature containment vessel himself, he is round and tough as cement. Barthélémy spent eighteen years as a French Navy commando. On patrol outside Djibouti he singlehandedly gunned down five men in French uniforms waving from a streetcorner, on the theory that only FRUD would be present in this area. He was right. He sports a bristly crew cut, a brushy moustache, he bristles generally. He is the best diver Rohan has ever worked with. "You not touch that gears!" His "r"s are heavily rolled, like those of a stage Frenchman. He points at the winches that control the underwater lights and film platforms.

"How we gonna move the lights then?" one of the teamsters says.

"You," another teamster tells him, "you can't tell us what to do, anyways."

Barthélémy turns. His face is red as sunset. He sees Rohan and shrugs apologetically. Then he reaches over, switches off the winch control board, and pockets the key.

"Hey!" The first teamster takes off his hard hat and pumps his chest at Barthélémy. "Fuckin' frog."

In an interplay of knee and elbow that looks simple Barthélémy pulls the teamster off the platform and drops him, yelling, into the water seven feet below.

"You're outta your mind," Edie Parnell says, in some awe. "They're *Teamsters*."

"You want to swim, too?" Barthélémy moves toward her in a stance Rohan knows is a joke but that looks all too real from Ms. Parnell's point of view.

The Teamsters walk out. Parnell calls her agent. Barthélémy disappears. Gottlieb, the second-unit director, ignores Rohan and walks in circles, shouting into a cellphone. A limo shows up at noon and someone pages Gottlieb for a conference. Rohan suits up and works on one of the underwater camera railways. He likes L.A. well enough but he would rather get a grant for another archeological site. Unfortunately the money has dried up since the affair in Edremit Korfezi.

Rohan comes out mid-afternoon. He cleans his gear, changes and wanders over to the trailer he and Barthélémy share. From inside he hears shouts from his assistant and, incongruously, music. He opens the door and sees a woman sprawled across the couch. He can tell her mouth has just been stretched in laughter. The shock comes, conducted by the high current of dark straight hair lying like a broken powerline across her cheek. The curves of her nose, eyes, and mouth all seem to duplicate each other—and are duplicated, in turn and in miniature, in the features of a four-year-old girl dancing clumsily in the middle of the lounge area to Georges Brassens singing *Supplique pour être enterré sur la plage de Sète*.

> *When my soul will have taken off for the horizon . . .*
> *I ask that my body be brought from afar*
> *on the* Paris-Méditerranée *sleeping car,*
> *terminus; Sète station.*

She is from Guebwiller, in Alsace. They are drinking diabolos. She is one of McCann's assistants. The girl is her daughter. The woman, whose name is Dominique, was dispatched here on short notice to fire Barthélémy, with minimal severance, in French if necessary. She brought the child because no day care was available.

"If he goes, I go," Rohan tells her.

"That can be arranged," she replies.

"But *mec*, now she tells me, maybe she can save us both." Barthélémy burps loudly, causing the girl, who has eaten too many sweets, to feign hysterics.

"Only if you are willing to kiss their asses," Dominique says in English. "I mean, the Teamsters. And McCann."

She talks like a Parisian, Rohan thinks. There is nothing sunny or unilinear about her whatsoever.

She lives in Topanga Canyon, near the French Montessori school, in a cabin with a studio where she makes unsaleable sculptures. He has rented a place in Venice, a broken stucco bungalow off Speedway with a garden so overgrown you cannot see its structure from the alley. She is that rarity: a Frenchwoman with an innate sense of self-reference; she can laugh at herself without looking in the mirror.

The first time they sleep together—the fog creeping like dun commandos through the garden, the Pacific clawing at the beach—she tells him she plans to leave. "If I had balls," she tells him, "the Industry would cut them off. You think I cared whether I fired you or not?"

He does not believe her. He would never let them move in with him if he did. Dominique only quits Topanga because Venice is closer to the airport as well as to the Eurotrash cafés of Santa Monica and Venice Beach. In a way he still does not believe her, about the Industry, about her leaving even, two years later, when he is driving her to LAX for the last time.

He has worked out several issues by then. First, the strong infatuation they shared at first has worn off, as both expected. Second, in both their cases it has been replaced by a feeling of *foyer*—there is no equivalent in English, hearth, perhaps, with flavors of "home" and "family" included— that has to do mostly with Chloé and to a lesser extent with the way the three of them live together, a way that is smooth and seems to build slowly on its own building.

He has stopped asking her why she is going because she always says the same thing. "You will leave too, eventually." When he presses her she quotes Brassens; "Glory to he who / having no sacred ideal / limits himself to leaving / his neighbor alone."

And third: he realizes he saw her originally, in Venice, at the Rose Café, outside.

She was, as far as he can recall, with a group of people that included Brooke Adams and Edie Parnell. It was sunny and she sat in the periwinkle shade of the hedge. And, although his memory is not clear on this, and because he has never grilled her on this point; because, finally, it is without importance; he has the distinct impression she was holding the hand of a producer of gaudy horror epics named Kevin McCann.

twenty

Outside, the farther outposts of Chelles and Vaires had given way to relative countryside. Corn and beet fields stretched away on both flanks. Incongruous in that gentle landscape, a California-style oilwell donkey-nodded docile in the midst of wheatstalks. The tracks moved in close to a wide green-brown river and cleaved to its placid curves the way lovers nestled—then, without warning, jumped the water on an iron bridge.

Rohan threw his cheroot out the corridor window and stepped back into their compartment, sliding the door shut behind him. It was immediately quieter.

There had been silence in the compartment for most of the time Rohan was smoking. Eva leaned over abruptly as he sat down. She opened a straw bag and pulled out small packages, of differing shapes but all neatly tucked and wrapped in waxed paper, and tied with string.

"I brought pastries," she explained, "it's good to let them breathe. You know, the tastes, oh they get all mixed up, otherwise."

She laid them on the seat beside her. Rohan watched her hands move in and out of a wedge of cream-colored light that shifted and pulled left as the tracks turned against the sun. Her fingers were not long; her hand itself was thin and square. Not an artist's hand, he thought, or even a surgeon's, but one you could visualize tying those parcels with economy of movement, or cleaning a baby's bottom, or leafing through old letters in a sere, quiet room.

Frank, looking at the parcels, was visited by what he thought of as a "travel-ghost": a quick blurring where boundaries of time zone and country shifted suddenly, canceling the common denominator of his presence, highlighting the difference at the core.

He remembered vaguely that the Chinese had devised a

philosophy out of wrapping packages. You lined up the corners of the paper with the points of the compass and placed the object at its exact center and at the cusp of the world thus created.

He could smell something sweet: pastry he thought, burnt sugar; and the smell was familiar in a light, unvectored way. The volume of noise from the carriage grew. Frank's eyes narrowed as he looked outside. The train was crossing a bridge over the Marne River. A péniche with a compact sedan on its after-hatch moved stately toward Germany. He saw water pinned black and green in the shade of a concrete sluice. The sight was more powerful in its associations than the smell had been. Casting back in his mind, he became aware that this was because it was nearer in time, something to do with Boston and the harbor all black, the wind lifting off the water, fanning his hair as he moved . . .

twenty-one

. . . Fast through the black draft of his own bike speeding. It is a good road for a twelve-speed late at night. The pavement has been resurfaced to the consistency of rayon all the way to Fresh Ponds Reservoir, where he turns back on the downslope. Slicker than a guilty feeling he rides past the road to Cambridgeport and the house he left from, pushing hard on the level stretch by Inman Square, hitting thirty, well twenty-five anyway on the hill past the "T" switching yards onto the Salt-and-Pepper bridge and then over the Charles.

At that speed with his head going down on the gearshift the lights blur in peripheral vision and he can almost see himself moving through the green or orange traffic lights and red brake lights, parting the blinking signals like some new force in the electromagnetic universe, something that can skank space and flout the very stars in their perigee.

It is early in his nightly ride and he has not got to the level where there is nothing but himself and the bike so he cannot avoid the first association, the shape of his new hands in the September phosphorescence; they looked like the paws of a galactic monster swirling 10,000 suns at a stroke, moons and comets streaming from the night between his splayed fingers, as he and Jodee swam naked in the lagoon at Tisbury only a month after they met, the slim V of her body outlined against the greenish advertising of diatoms.

He pushes so hard at the pedals he can feel their serrations through his sneakers. He listens to the pressured clicks of the dérailleur, the breathing of his tires, the sudden, disinvolved, treble chunk of chain as he switches gears on Charles Street, a snap and catch as the sprockets engage and hold. The wind in his ears echoes the sough of his own breath. Sweat funnels down his back, though it is autumn and not warm. He veers left, up Beacon Hill, changing the gear ratio up, and up again. Around Louisburg Square. Graceful streetlamps polish the brick night of the rich. He has worked hard enough by now for the chemicals to have altered. He is no brain surgeon yet he knows this much: the endorphins bring a high, a respite from relevance, gears of the mind clutched out. At the end of the hill he swings dangerously wide and the lights of Mass. General rise overhead when he turns east, just as he thought he'd missed them.

The trouble with endorphins is they narrow and flatten the flow of consciousness to the point where it can be filled by something as essentially shallow as a bike ride or a jog. This is good because it restricts access to other stuff less rich in the ores of Zen but the trouble is, once the other stuff does manage to get in, it takes over every band and channel and this is what happens to Frank now, push hard as he might down Tremont, then Summer, seeing not the road but the other hospital rising at all points in his inner vision.

Inside, it is not so pretty. Rhode Island Hospital lacks the endowment of MGH. High on the eighth floor, at some kind of chill epicenter of state-funded med-tech and smells of ether and spilled bile—someplace where the septic dreams of mind and body quite deliberately are never afforded privacy from the lights and beeps always watching, watching—the vinyl-siding expert lies hooked up to a machine that washes poisons from his bloodstream like some robot prospector sluicing sludge out of a hematological Klondike. The doctor is Indonesian. He chuckles when Frank tries his few words of Bahasa. He is encouraging. Diabetes at this stage is treatable. He sees no reason why the patient cannot lead a normal life, even with the heart the way it is; et cetera. Both know how formulaic the words are, and each knows the other knows. The vinyl-siding expert lies in a stainless steel bed so hostile it looks like it could fold around him like a giant clam and digest him. And after all the deceit, the bright anger; the petty forgiveness that only reinforced what there was to pass over; Frank looks at the salesman and for the first time in his life sees more light going into his father's eyes than comes out.

He feels cheated, like a fighter who triumphs by default.

He has never seen his father helpless.

"How 'bout them Paw' Sox, huh?" the vinyl-siding expert offers hoarsely.

Frank ignores this question which is not a question.

"How's the food?"

The expert puts a finger in his mouth to simulate a gag. The finger trembles.

"Are you in pain?" Frank continues. "I can make sure you get medication."

"Tell your mother," the expert croaks. "Don't let them fuck her with the Medicaid." The wife of the expert is shopping. Illness causes her to buy shoes.

Frank thinks, He will never get out of this place. He experiences a rushing sensation, as of wind howling down a stone tunnel.

He turns the bike left at Roxbury, onto Morrissey Boulevard, into McConnell Park. He is seeing bright lights on EKGs and the shadow within cells. He does not catch the odd flash from reflecting discs on the mountain-bikes blocking the parkway from one side to the other until he is almost on top of them.

They surround him at once. All are women, mostly dressed in black spandex with black and yellow bike helmets. Some of the women are large. Many carry motorcycle chains wrapped around gauntleted forearms. All pack cell-phones in belted holsters. "The Honey-bees." Frank, startled, says it out loud. They are a lesbian bicycle gang that controls wedges of Roxbury at night. "Sting like a bee," one of the women agrees. "Get his bread," another orders.

Hands pat him down, neither gently or pruriently. "No money, just house-keys, ID card. Prick." In the hospital he felt like he was standing outside himself and he feels the same way now. He has read, somewhere, that sixty-five percent of murders committed by women are carried out in the three days before menstruation; only three percent are committed in the week after. Women living together will tend to run on the same cycle. He sees no humor in the pun. He wonders what part of their rhythm is applicable here.

Frank knows of a PISR study that parses the menstrual system into rhythms that, attractively, match the triggers of chaos: events like water boiling, or the abrupt migration of Arctic rodents.

"He works at Piss-ah." One of the women is checking his ID.

"Cut his balls off."

"He's a perfessor, he don't have any."

They let him go, after ripping off his bike pump. Rolling down Fox Point to the harbor he starts to laugh. It is the

70

usual reaction to fear. He wheels cautiously onto a town pier, watching for cracks between the planks. He can hear the water, smell its bad breath. The docks are old teeth in a mouth of dead marsh, heavy metals and sewer. Yet in the middle of the filth he can taste something that remains clean: the good salt; the change, perhaps, that works in and out with moon tides.

She would have listened to this once. Even his inability to describe exactly what he'd felt would have meant something to Jodee. She would have tried to decode it. That time they'd gone swimming had been during a weekend of academic softball league, John A. Walker Jr. College versus Kenmore, but they had sat alone most of the time, talking. They could not get enough words from the other, as if each were a dry field and talk the water that would make it green.

Yet the water table had fallen fairly quickly, or maybe it was the bad salts that had risen with irrigation, small but cumulative dissatisfactions, crystalline tempos out of synch. He believes now that in fact it was a building up of gutless events, the ones each saw in the other of course not as damaging as those exposed in oneself. He recalls her inability to love a given logic enough to labor at it. And yet she needs very much the false buttresses of academia. When she was a girl in the Canuck part of Fall River she read the *New Yorker* cover to cover every week in the library, desperate to understand the jokes.

The laptop that never leaves her side. She has a way of assuming for you the cultural pretensions she aspires to. "I was talking to Seamus Heaney the other day—do you know Seamus?" "I was having lunch with Paul de Fontgibu and his wife, you must know Paul . . ." Yet somewhere fairly deep she realizes he does not know, nor care to meet, Seamus or Paul.

He walks the bike back onto solid ground. He pushes off, lifts his leg high over the seat. It is a move first learned at age five that has never quite lost the aura of freedom and acceleration it first imparted. He remembers the vinyl-siding expert insisting he needed training wheels for months when he did not, then stabilizing the bike for him long after Frank had mastered balance. He starts pedaling, gently at first, then, as the pavement improves, faster.

Sometimes, when he is biking hard, he imagines what would happen if he fitted wings to his bike. They would be fantastically light, built of balsa, Kevlar and wire. They would extend twenty feet on either side. He would deploy the wings by pulling down a lever, much as he switches into highest gear now, with Dorchester coming up on him like runway lights. He would lift gently on the mephitic air of the harbor and, tilting upward, see only stars before him.

He knows Jodee wants him to leave.

He would not glide for long but flight, after all, is defined by the ground to which you eventually return.

twenty-two

High in the air over the ten mountains of Xelajú a propellor-driven scout plane from the Fuerza Aerea glides in circles over the Continental Hotel.

Inside, flying beetles have incubated in the day's great heat. They are large, clumsy, Paleozoic-looking. They buzz and bumble in silly counterpoint to the aircraft's whine. The tame macaw caged in the bar has expired for no reason. No one bothers to take him out of his cage. The colors of his feathers contrast sadly with the disordered heap in which they lie against his water dish.

It is the third day of the siege. The Gardia by now has fig-ured out how to shut off the water. A smell of mold, mingled with the pointed odor of human shit from backed-up toilets, has come to dominate the bar and the ballroom where the hostages are confined. The people too are beginning to smell, although since they are all growing dirty together this is not as apparent to the individual as it otherwise might be. There is food, and enough water from the cistern to go around, but the whipsaw effect of day's heat and chill of night combined with the general discomfort are beginning to take their toll. Shouting matches erupt, even fisticuffs. An elegant woman whose husband owns one of the country's largest *fincas* has taken to standing and bawling "*Cojones!*" without provocation. People avoid each other's eyes. The young Indians have removed their combat boots. They watch impassively, MP-40s set across their knees. Heat and fear and boredom are old hat to them.

The medial pulse rate of the Highland Maya is fifty, compared with seventy to eighty for the average Caucasian.

No one gets enough sleep.

Frank and Eva have laid claim to a corner of the ballroom formed by a green couch and a couple of coffee tables under a loud tapestry depicting Maya-Ki'ichés chucking spears at Spaniards. The first night Eva walks around restlessly, waiting for Julián. He never shows up. Frank spends time watching the man Eva thinks wants to sleep with her. His name is Ludovic Rohan.

Rohan is friendly with the rebel woman who moves like Lauren Bacall. This woman's name is Leila but she will not tell Rohan her last name; revolutionaries have no families, she says, although it is clear, from her ease and her good English, that someone put serious money into bringing her up. She is very dark of skin and has hazel eyes, high cheekbones, and hair that snaps black as a Nihilist's banner.

Frank invites Rohan over to their couch. By the second night Frank has thrice talked to the rebel woman, and Rohan has become a permanent resident of the corner.

Eva is glad of Rohan's company. She likes to have men around at any time, it makes her feel more closely engaged with life. Even the full realization that Eva was only cover for Julián has not sapped that illusion for her. Rohan does not try to talk when she takes refuge in reading. She scans the manuscripts Serge gave her for the trip, as well as her medical notes.

One paper in particular, *The Role of R-Frequency Waves in Catalyzing and Blocking Activity in the Temporal P-7 Zone*, delivered early in the Xelajú conference, has set a thought to germinating inside her. She finds herself growing furious at her position, not because she is being held captive but because fear seems to have the effect of stalling her fledgling ideas before they can achieve takeoff. She already has come to believe, through her own research and that of others, that memory is constructed of fluid neural networks constantly rearranging themselves to fit in what she once termed, in a fairly notable paper in *Journal de Neuro-psychiatrie*, a "synaptic story." The hippocampus/hypothalamus dyad, she now theorizes, functions as a kind of cerebral navigator with a role in locating and arranging sequences for different parts of the brain associated with memory. It's an astonishingly flexible system, functioning both down the railroad lines of dendritic spines, and cross-country, over the chaos of short-circuits and phosphor connections; constantly weaving new links between mnemonic nodes even as it rubs out the old, the insufficiently stimulated. What if—the conclusion is within her grasp, she can feel it. Yet every time she reaches for it something intrudes, a dispute, someone crying, the shouted *Cojones!*, a thought: they will start shooting hostages, it's inevitable; and the image, shivering, evades her grasp once more.

In the bar the Swiss manager has raised prices by two hundred percent. "It's the law of supply and demand," he explains stiffly, "see how price functions as a rationing agent." The fat man, Calderón, leans over the bar and grabs him by the lapels, but the Swiss squirms away and out of the room. Calderón turns to an American sitting beside him. They are the only people in the bar excepting a barefoot rebel who squats in an armchair ten feet away guarding the telephone. As if it formed part of the same conversation Calderón goes on, "You know, this is quite intolerable. The Gardia demands the rebels to turn over their *jefe*. He calls himself 'Capitan Vent'uno,' after the date of the first rebellion. But no one knows who this man is." Calderón slumps over the bar again and pretends to sob. He wears a pin from the "Club Fútball Hernan Cortes" on his lapel. Under cover of the histrionics he slips two bottles of Alvarado beer and a quart of *Balche* liqueur from the shelf underneath. The rebel, picking dead skin off his big toe, notices nothing.

That night Leila disappears into the stinking moist darkness. Waking at 3:20 A.M. Frank discovers Rohan has gone as well. The next day the Swiss decides they will cook and eat all the food spoiling in the dead freezers. In the evening the candles are lit once more. They sit in a row, rebels and hostages alike eating boiled veal and salmon with their fingers. The food is flavored with *hierba buena*, an herb that grows wild, an import from the Mediterranean, in the surrounding mountains. One of the guests picks at a classical guitar. Frank asks Rohan where he went the night before. Rohan says, "If I ever get out of here I am going to buy a caique. I will also buy an air compressor and scuba gear. I will order lots of draughtsman's pens, and India ink, and paper made of linen rag. Then I will anchor the caique near a wreck I found once near Antikythera. I will live on figs and *retsina* wine and I will work the wreck. It will take me the rest of my life. I will do it slowly and right. I will never publish the results. What about you?"

"I bet," Eva comments, "you will never do it."

At length Frank answers Rohan's question, but he looks at Eva as he does so. "I'd buy a large old house in a bad section of an old city," he says. "It would have a huge kitchen with a big old coal stove. An', an' I'd let people stay, anybody who needed a place, cats, kids, see? Old people, anybody. Only five at a time, though. But, I mean, they could stay with me.

So what happened," he turns back to Rohan, "what happened to you last night?"

Rohan says nothing. He is looking at the tapestry that dominates their corner of the ballroom. The shadows of candles smear and tremble, making the figures in the weave start with ephemeral life. The scene in the tapestry tells this story:

When Alvarado reached the plains of Xelajú he found several thousand Maya-Ki'iché waiting for him under the shadow of the volcanoes by the Xelixec River. Alvarado was no coward; also he knew that his guns, crossbows, and horses gave him a real advantage over the Indians, who had never encountered such weapons before. He attacked head on. The Indians fought gamely. Tecún Umán, the king of the Maya-Ki'ichés, wore golden anklets and silver bracelets and an emerald necklace; he ran into the fight with his *nahual*, or familiar, flapping above him. His familiar was the quetzal, a bird with long, brilliantly colored tail-feathers. But Alvarado rode into Tecún Umán's path and cut him down with one stroke of his sword. As Tecún died—so the Indians tell the story—the quetzal faltered and fell dead to the ground beside him.

A lizard, crouched at the top of the tapestry, snaps at a flying beetle, then pauses with the insect's abdomen and feelers still sticking out of its mouth.

The rebel lieutenant, whose name is Suchil, brings food to the Indian guarding the grenade bomb in the middle of the ballroom. None of the guests ever look at the guard, with the exception of Frank. Frank knows these L1A1 grenades; they are filled with twelve ounces of Baratol, a compound that at such concentration is equivalent to forty pounds of TNT.

"All I'm asking—" Calderón, whispering, leans in Leila's direction— "do you really think your *Indios*, whose chief qualities are stubbornness and a taste for alcohol, could do any better than the Fourteen Families, whose chief occupations are canasta and incest?"

"He's crazy," Eva mutters nervously. "She's one of *them*."

"He's drunk," Frank says.

"*Balche*," Rohan agrees, "a whole bottle at least."

Eva tenses. She has spotted Julián at the back of the room. She fancies she can see his eyes gleam as he restlessly surveys the crowd. For some reason she thinks of what he told her, three nights that seem like three months ago: that he grew up watching *The Untouchables*, dubbed in Spanish, in local open-air cinemas; and that not far from Xelajú, in a ravine under the eastern slope of Santiaguito, runs a waterfall so thick and clean that if you stand behind it, under the dawn, the lens of its falling will turn you and everything else the color of purest gold.

When the last dishes have been cleared the elegant woman, who, though she does not realize it, is a third cousin of Julián's, stands up and raises her skirt gaily.

"*Cojones!*" she yells.

Eva cannot chase from her mind the image of a golden Elliot Ness standing under ribbons of water like sheet-rolled fire.

twenty-three

A medium-sized *fête foraine* which included a small circus in the midst of its sideshows and rides had set up for the national holiday in a field outside Mareuil. The field was lush and shaded by linden trees and next year would be covered by rows of middle-income housing blocks financed by state and private monies. In the meantime the circus was in the process of dismantling and a couple of the carnies paused as they worked to glance at the train trundling east.

Eva had been staring out the window, not seeing anything

but an occulting wash of reflections and shapes outside. Her mind, taken by events that had occurred twelve years earlier, stood without reserve in Xelajú.

But something in the view now framed in the square of SNCF Securit got through.

One scene faltered, shifted, and allowed another space. Perhaps it was the pennants, flapping impertinently against the dull sky and Bovary roofs of the small town. Or the overall pattern: the merry-go-round with its gaily painted horses, the serried lights, the stage-set arches that, incorporated into the tent, inevitably built a code of celebration on whatever ground they were erected on.

Whatever the catalyst, she felt her pulse speed up as it always had at this particular code, no matter the slurry of years between. A classic, if small, *chapiteau* tent, four masts erected in the middle with the ritual stable square of roulottes and cages set out at the main entrance. She saw a splash of brown nearest the tent, where the wild animals would be kept. It was arranged in this way for a reason, so the fiercer beasts would lead the parade and the gentler bring up the rear, reducing the risk of stampede.

And the strength of what she felt at this point was so great that the images of Xelajú stretched, folded and collapsed without fuss—and were replaced almost immediately by smells she was much too far away from the *fête foraine* to have gotten from that source, a strong compound of manure, of tanbark, of sweat from acrobats and musk from elephants—and from her own top hat, the raw stink of industrial alcohol.

Eva twisted in her seat, trying to keep in sight the colors and guy ropes of the closing circus.

• • •

For Eva becomes interested in the circus only a few months after she follows her mother to Grunros's workshop, that is, at the same age and in the same way it happens to most children, with two vital differences. In the first place, she is a shade more enamored of the horses and of their portable drama of tricks and gallops than most kids; in the second, unlike most children, she can take action to feed her interest. Budapest has one of the few circus-training schools in the world, an academy modeled on the Moscow school and situated on Bornemicza Ut, in Pesht. Her father mentions the school, not seriously, and for months Eva militates to sign up for the entrance exam. Teresa Koszegfalvi is vaguely against the idea for she was brought up in an environment that equates circus with gypsies, and gypsies with all things soiled and dishonest. Her father backs Eva, a little less vaguely. Among the few citizens offered a chance to leave Hungary on a routine basis by the regime of Janos Kadar are graduates of the circus school. She takes the test and to everyone's surprise, for the competition is stiff, gets in.

And leaves fourteen months later. The standards are equally high inside and Eva, though physically agile, does not have quite what it takes to be a top gymnast, juggler and acrobat, as the school requires of all its pupils. She tries out for the equine act but is turned down early. The only field where she consistently does well is the tumbling and vaudeville. It is almost a relief to abandon the rigors of the circus schedule to go back to her normal school—though she cannot keep the blood from rushing harder through the valves of her heart every time she comes across a circus poster with all its gaudy ability to make you forget for an hour or two the dreary colors of 1970s Hungary; "Wild Lions from Africa! Death-Defying Aerialists! 20 Arab Stallions performing the World-Famous Viennese Courbet!"

Partly by way of compensation Eva becomes interested in boys. She does not stand out academically, except in mathematics, but with a little help from an ex-colleague of her father's she is accepted into the university at Szeged. Eva lives in a hostel. She starts an affair with a young man who like herself is from the Kalvin Square area of Pesht. They talk late, subscribing to the habitual clichés, drinking *palinka* or *dupla* coffee from espresso machines where the barman puts a coin on top of the pressured grounds to strengthen the brew. After three months she discovers she is bored. She is specializing in math and the courses are too easy for her. Most of her fellow students have been selected for their total inability to think up trouble. The boy from Pesht is going to be a systems engineer and his idea of peril is to drink three glasses of Chain Bridge brandy the night before an exam. They take long walks by the river or among the dark fields of paprika plants outside Szeged and soon the inoffensive Alfold hillocks begin to feel to her like the walls of Karzon Prison.

The only consolation from those days is her discovery of Attila József. She has always shirked Hungarian literature and especially those writers praised as "socialist" so that, opening *Medvetanc* out of pure ennui in a bookshop on Arpad Street, she is stunned by the force, the steel-bright humanity of his poems.

> *Yes; Let us never forget that we row*
> *With fists instead of*
> *Oars, and everything has to be stroked lovingly*
> *The wolves as well as the frogs*

One night in April, after another ragged fight with Stefan, she is kicking fallen horse chestnuts through the cobbled streets of Szeged when she spots a large negro pasting up a poster. "Cirque von Andau," it announces, "Wild Lions from Africa! The Incredible Cossack Horses of Petofi Tamas!" She attends almost every performance, spending all her coffee money. When the circus moves on to Morahalom she hops a train and watches them set up. By then she has talked to the entrée clown, a drunk named Fredi, who in turn has informed Madame von Andau that Eva once attended the famous circus school of Pesht. Madame spots her hanging around the stable square. The Cirque von Andau has no alumnus of such a prestigious institution. She sends Fredi to tell Eva there is an opening for a groom and assistant clown. Eva nonetheless catches the train back to Szeged.

Two days later, when the show leaves Morahalom, Eva is riding one of the trucks.

The Cirque von Andau is a small and frankly not very talented show of the sort that once was a familiar sight on the medium and small roads of Europe. It travels in the summer, leaving big towns to the prestigious outfits like the Knies, Meranos and Knocks. Its biggest attraction is Petofi Tamas's equine act. Tamas, though somewhat lacking in the finer points of *Haute École*, is an agile rider and acrobat; more importantly, he knows how to make horses do what he wants. He has reintroduced a couple of the older stunts: the "St. Petersburg Post," in which eight horses dressed in the colors of neighboring countries gallop clockwise and single file underneath a man with one boot on each of two horses moving abreast, at a gallop, *counterclockwise* around the ring; and the double-backward somersault from one horse to another, famously executed by Chotachen Courtauld in 1930 at the Cirque Merano; this Tamas will attempt only for the bigger audiences.

The von Andau follows a route seldom interrupted by war or political troubles that takes it from the east of Hungary through central Austria, northern Tirol, Bavaria, Alsace, central France and finally, in the early fall, to the shores of the Mediterranean in Languedoc-Roussillon. At first Eva shares a trailer with a female midget and a woman named Haleytey who works as a human cannonball. Haleytey, who bills herself as a Sioux Indian, never stops talking about Petofi Tamas, in low Russian, even in her sleep. The trailer, or "roulotte," is organized more neatly than a ship. Eva soon realizes that the organization inside reflects the tightness of the small independent nation-state that is the Cirque von Andau.

She carefully notes the routine; it is, after all, what she once trained for. It is complex enough to require real survey and vigilance. It works like this. Different trucks of the convoy race each other to the next town, vying for the best camping sites, the most level ground closest the water source. Some of the sites are meadows beside clean brooks, or parks in the shadow of a church the grace of whose spires almost seem capable of creating a presence of God out of the Leninist void. Other sites are mundane and ugly. In any case when Mme. von Andau arrives she marks the tent's eventual center using a spike with a red ribbon attached, hammered in by the large negro, Haddad. Then with a cord she measures out the emplacement of the four masts, tagged this time by green ribbons. The tent men go to work hauling up the masts and canvas with trucks, guying the lot with cable. The stable square is set up. Haddad and Haleytey walk into town to paste up posters and the rest get to work rehearsing. The constant practice is something Eva remembers with no great fondness from Bornemicza Ut.

The first performance comes well before dusk in these latitudes of northern summer. The "band," two trumpets, a drum and an accordeon, marches down the central street, trailing Loki, the younger of the two elephants. The older elephant, Darshan, who lived through the bombing of Hamburg, is left out, for she is apt to stampede at loud noises. Bobo, a tame European brown bear, scratching at fleas, shambles along at the tail of the parade followed by his trainer Hansi who, since he shares everything with Bobo, including parasites, scratches also. Madame counts tickets and looks at the change; if there are a lot of copper coins and small denominations it is a poor town and they will not stay long. The performance is the usual. But in the middle of the second act a drum roll sounds. The Rhinelander tent men drop dry ice in the smoke machine and an argent mist fills the ring. The spots dim. And suddenly from the darkness, cantering in unison, come ten white horses with a man standing astride the first two. The horses are so white they seem to spill their own light into the fog. The man, in Cossack dress, holds his head high and looks like the Lord of Storms.

Eva spends a first week with the circus. Every new town she vows will be her last. Now, however, it is the striking of tents that appeals to her. She is growing addicted to the feel of leaving. When Mme. von Andau says she can get her a visa for Austria Eva signs a paper apprenticing herself to Fredi for the season.

Part of the motivation of course is Tamas. He is difficult and condescending but there is a softer side to him that comes out with animals and women. Despite Haleytey's best efforts, he is single, which, in a world whose tight cohesion would be destroyed by the trauma of marital cheating, is of consequence. Above all he is quick and unpredictable as arson. They make love in a horse stall one night, the half-Lippizaners farting and stamping around them. The next morning she feels no debt to gravity. The riding master, Radetski, a former Polish cavalry officer, from that moment on does not look at or otherwise acknowledge her.

In a town in Styria, at 3:40 in the morning, a thunderstorm comes up from the south. A big wind blows. The entire circus turns out to haul at the guys and fight the flogging canvas to prevent the big tent from collapsing. Once the tent is steadied Eva and Tamas struggle to calm the horses. Hailstones big as plums fall on all sides and a bolt of lightning strikes a tree nearby. The sound is awesome, but not as terrifying as the high, uninterrupted trumpeting that rises from the elephant's enclosure. In the mind of Darshan the elephant she is two years old once more and Hamburg is folding into vast sheets of fire, sound and death-smelling metal that have already stilled her mother. She crashes through one side of the horse enclosure, guy wires and canvas trailing like crushed sloops in her wake, knocking aside stalls, horses, tack chests, and disappears into the nearby woods. Eva finds herself lying, one leg trapped under a stunned half-Lippizaner, with this thought looping in her forebrain: "Things happen *without us*." She is unhurt. They find Darshan two hours later, calmly ripping off a haystack.

They cut across northern Slovenia and into the Carinthian Alps. Eva sees no correlation between the thinness of the children and the force of their reaction to the circus. Sometimes when the moon is up, moving higher into the mountains to the next town, the clouds lie below them in the valleys so it seems the mountains are islands and the rest of Europe a sea of indigo and silver. Sitting beside Tamas Eva feels a power in her, as if she could take off like one of their horses with strides the breadth of a mountain chain and cross Europe, the oceans, the world entire in the space of a midsummer night.

twenty-four

Veering easily around a bend of track, the train passed through the hamlet of Villenoy, and then slowed. Fields gave way to small garden plots, cement water towers, low-income housing blocks. The air brakes hissed. Now as they drew near the center of a bigger town the houses grew older, progressing backward down the architectural time-line; Empire, Ancien Régime, Renaissance. Where the train drew into the station platform a Gothic cathedral threw its loom over monastery buildings converted during the revolution into a lycée.

A sign announced "MEAUX" in broad blue letters.

It was in Meaux, on April 6, 1229, that King Louis VI forced Raymond VII, Count of Toulouse, to sign a treaty forever renouncing the independence of the southern regions of France.

●●●

More recently, Meaux is the first step in the series of ceremonies that mark the opening of the original Paris-Epernay segment of the new Strasbourg line. On the second of September 1849 Prince Louis-Napoleon, recently elected president of a republic risen like a dazed bird from the ashes of 1848, takes a special train from the gleaming new Gare de l'Est eastward. He is accompanied by the board of directors of the Compagnie de l'Est, including the Comte de Ségur, the Prince de Soubise, and Baron James de Rothschild. In Meaux they are received by an honor guard of soldiers and firemen. The bishop walks solemnly from the ancient cathedral and blesses the tracks, the train, the president and his moneymen. From Meaux the sweating Number 73 steam engine drags them all to Soissons and finally Epernay, collecting more blessings from additional bishops at every stop. In Epernay Louis-Napoleon and the director of the Württemburg railway, who is angling to have his line hooked up to the new network, each give a speech.

"If Emperor Napoleon had known the steam engine," his nephew intones, "never would we have seen foreign troops invading the capital of France. Let us therefore honor the railroad for these reasons; in peace it promotes prosperity and commerce, and in war it promotes the independence of our homeland."

The director of the Württemburg railroad strikes a more pacific note. "When the Germans come back to Strasbourg," he says, "it will not be to the sound of guns but to the noise of locomotives, those powerful engines of progress and peace."

"We shall consult our common interests," the Comte de Ségur says to a German engineer, "we will forget geographical divisions, we shall believe in European nationhood!"

The line to Strasbourg is completed in 1852. The German army invades Alsace eighteen years later.

twenty-five

It took the Bar le Duc local only a minute to embark and discharge passengers at Meaux. It departed on schedule, accelerated slightly through the outskirts, straightened as it passed through Poincy. The engineer ratcheted up power. The connecting meter of rail welds adopted the rhythm of a minuet. Rohan eased back in his seat and enjoyed the rock and hustle of a train moving fast into strange country. He breathed in happily the scent of these old carriages, a smell that he believed included not only the cloth of the seats, the corridor polish, the grease of the couplings but also the smoke and chatter of every man woman and child it had ever carried; just as the rail bed below secreted at some gravel stratum a bit of the waste of each human who had ever pissed, shat or puked down the open W.C. hatch in the 150 years this line had been in operation.

Under half-lowered eyelids he took in the beaten cream paneling of the bulkhead, the black-and-white photos of Amiens Cathedral, of pines surrounding some cicada-ridden harbor near Menton; watched Frank shift in his seat, Eva push her dark hair against odd breezes. And the combination of inputs, as it always did, triggered in him a change that was like colors shifting, shades of mote and city lye turning to sun-green and yellow, a sense of ease that morphed into a tinge of finality if held too long; as usual it worked into a touch so powerful he did not have to analyze or think of it directly to know in the pith out of which all pith grew where it came from.

Like an old farmer with land so often ploughed that whether he thinks of it or no it lies always mapped within him, first landscape in the geography of his mind.

North, in apposition to the old beliefs, is Hades while south is where the goodness of ease creeps in. This train, the *Hérault*, is like an old friend, the same train that always takes them south, he and Nathalie with no escort but the ache in him and the pressure of excitement also in their chests blooming with every kilometer that separates them from the iron garden doors of Passy. He cannot escape Passy entirely on the last trip for the guilt remains inside like a cold stone; and does their grandfather know? And will his welcome turn as a result? But then the train rocks round a curve in the river and they experience the sex of color and smell in this country where the sun cooks perfume in every wild ditch.

On the Micheline from Béziers—so tradition dictates— he and Nathalie hold hands. They have done this since they were seven.

Their grandfather does not smile much but he touches them as always so he cannot know as yet. Pé shouts instead of talking. He has a sharp nose and a pointed goatee and smells of dry wood. He is thin and cured with the salt he mines. As always it seems odd to address him as "tu" when they use "vous" with their parents. The hills of Languedoc are red, the wind sometimes comes yellow with sand blown across the sea from the Sahara.

The first night Rohan wakes up whimpering without pride, the ache cold inside him and Nathalie shaking his shoulders. They sit side by side, feeling their ribs pump in and out together. This, too, they have done for years.

Pé knows, after all. The next morning he sits Rohan down on the stone *couradou* in the shade of the big Aleppo pine. Pé drinks watered rosé and black coffee and gums shrunken olives gathered from trees behind the kitchen. The "housekeeper" this year is new and fatter than usual but he calls her Madeleine like all the rest. "Evil is stronger than good in this world," Pé announces, "as if you hadn't noticed, but it won't help for you to just accept that, eh *pignouf?*" Rohan will work out his punishment helping to fix sluices; Pé runs one of the last salting marshes on the coast.

Rohan is sixteen and work is not something he is overly fond of. His skin burns, then blisters from the salt. Pé's half-witted crewman, Pascal, giggles ceaselessly, drools, and works twice as hard as Rohan. However Pé lets Rohan run the flat-bottomed skiff and the sea skills, painfully learned over an accretion of summers, fill him with hard pride. On his days off he can take the skiff west to a *calanque*, or inlet, and dive for dappled fish under the cliffs, his new knife gripped dramatically between his teeth. Or with Nath riding Pascal's old white horse he climbs the mountain behind the villa into a ravine under a ruined tower. Pascal is their ally and will not tell Pé of such sorties. The ravine is so isolated you cannot see from there the tall concrete hotels being built near the *marais salant.*

Even out of sight of the sea he is aware it is near, and the feeling is like the knowledge of an escape tunnel.

Without him around most of the time Nathalie grows bitchy. One day she "borrows" a bike and free-wheels dangerously down to Montagnac. There she lopes the streets, aware of the boys wolfing, their noses lifting as she walks past, making sure they realize how thoroughly she ignores them. Word gets around. Madeleine tells Pé. From then on Nathalie works the salting marsh with her brother. Striped with sun and white with salt, whistling between her teeth.

When the *Marin* blows, flooding the saltworks, they read in the cool limestone rooms of the villa. The library belonged to Pé's father-in-law, who knew Aubanel and Tavant. Rohan is too lazy to read the volumes on Languedoc dialect, but he acquires a taste for a series of novels based on the short independence of southern France. Curled in the tile dust around stories of the heretic nobles who united the

Midi and its dialects and also its turn of thought for one sharp moment before the convulsing forces of pope and king brought their towers low. Sappy stuff of blood and deceit. "The 'Bons Hommes' practiced ancient and secret rites that enabled one to navigate around the demons they knew were in control . . . they advocated a pure, chaste love and killed themselves in droves rather than abjure that faith." Because the hormones are making stew in his veins he accepts also the texts Nathalie likes, the silly passions of the troubadours, listening to his sister recite them in her catching voice, sniffing out the raunch and chuckle of sex beneath their verses of *amor de lonh*.

> *Ye know aught of love*
> *If ye expect no grace*
> *For if ye have consented*
> *To grief without solace*
> *In a trice will she cure*
> *Ye, and wipe away*
> *The pain she hath caused ye*
> *For many a day,*

Nathalie recites; she has learned many of the *lais* by heart, aware in some gut fashion that the steps and rhythms of the couplets, with their hidden patterns and repeats, are tailored to fit the shapes of memory the way clothes are cut to the body.

The most a human memory can absorb in the short term is five to seven "bits" of information per second. It is likely a coincidence that many of these *lais* are written with five to seven words a line in stanzas of five or seven lines.

Neither the work nor the days off make Rohan's ache go away.

During one of these nights of wind, lightning painting stark crabs on the walls, five days before their parents are due to arrive, he wakes up mewing once more in the dark. Nath is there, a little cross but cool, faithful. They lie as they always have lain. Only a difference creeps in. He never resolves the ontology of what happens; is it the muscular decompression that comes with sun and rough work? The bounced light of the sea with its ability to destroy the shadows cast in pain? Or is it simply a function of the contrast between the shut misery of Passy and the physical happiness they know here in Montagnac—the impulse to make comfort total by destroying all *memory* of what came before? He is not even sure who initiates the soft chain. Perhaps it starts as a slight rise in the body heat of one, which causes in their symbiosis a rise in the heat of the other. The growing heat loosens muscles, allowing more heat to escape.

It is he who kisses her. They kiss on the mouth anyway but this lasts a fraction longer than it should.

Her hair is black and her eyes very big, and dark as the soil under a rock. Each touch of flesh leverages sensitivity. She touches him and immediately he explodes over her.

She dries him and herself with a shirt. The action is sisterly but a new role is included in the circle of her wiping. The next day, though, she avoids him. For the first time he has no idea what she thinks. She talks too much with Pé yet when he corners her she will not talk. This goes on until their parents arrive and in the silence they bring it is she, now, who cries out in the night.

Henri Rohan has forgiven nothing, forgotten nothing. He sits out on the *couradou* drinking mint tea with his jacket on and his briefcase rests beside him. Marielle stares at the distant line of sea. On his next free day Rohan skips breakfast and walks alone to the ravine. Her cutoff has been so strong that he does not expect her at all, but in some way neither understands that is *why* she comes at noon, riding Blondel.

He watches her walk up to the shade of the hut. He thinks, She moves differently, she uses her hips more. In the hot shadow she looks at the ruined tower on the hills and speaks words made lighter by the *lais* she has read. "I love you, Ludo," she says, "I can't help it." Later, when he thinks to check, he understands that for a while the ache had diminished in both of them.

The hut is full of rolled barbed-wire and broken scythes. Their bodies race in RPMs scored in increments of softness. She guides him with words and fingers; it seems to him quite normal that the woman should know the secrets. She milks him the first time, then draws him inside. It takes no time at all, it takes a lifetime and she pushes him out so he can fertilize her small breasts and stomach with his warm and salted water.

The legend goes: the tower above this valley belonged to an old nobleman who married Sérémonde, a fifteen-year-old girl with eyes like a cat's. A young troubadour named Guillem de Cabestaing stopped at the tower and he and the girl fell in love. Sérémonde's jealous husband ordered Guillem ambushed and killed and served his wife the troubadour's heart, *pané*, for supper. "Do you like it?" he asked wittily. "I love it," Sérémonde replied. "I love it so much I will never touch another dish unless it is as good as this." And she starved herself to death.

They have the time of a heartbeat to get used to this. He has cut his elbow on a scythe but does not know it yet. She looks out the narrow window and sees crows swooping among the sere rocks. "I feel like I am flying, too," she whispers. It is a banal statement but she is barely fifteen and unaware.

In the backdraught pebbles crack. The door squeaks. The good sun falls on the mocha blood, the sky reflecting blue on her thigh. Pascal's jaw hangs, and a string of saliva dangles into their silent space. Then, before going down to tell Pé, he grins. In that grin resides the lies they will utter, and the slamming of doors, and the heart of Guillem de Cabestaing. For once Henri Rohan chooses to believe their lies; this constitutes a lesson in itself. Pé, confronted by the fury of his son, goes silent. Marielle continues to watch the horizon and says even less than before and that, of course, is worse. Nathalie, loud in her misery, argues for herself and her brother, the lies she speaks for him burning in the air like a witch.

> *And so I would sooner*
> *Die of a pure love*
> *Than to joy in a heart*
> *From which love hath gone*
> *Thus love conquered me*
> *From the first moment on,*

the troubadour Bernard de Ventadour sings.

There is no warmth or blue of sea in the schools of the Jesuits where Rohan is sent for the next eighteen months, on cold trains running into the rains of the north.

twenty-seven

"Guebwiller," Eva asked, "is that far from Colmar?"

Frank looked up, then across at Rohan.

"Ludovic?" Eva said. She smiled slightly, in reflex, because Rohan's lips were also turned in a slight smile, nothing much really.

Rohan pulled his eyes down from the luggage rack where his gaze unaccountably had come to rest.

"To Guebwiller," he said, "it is maybe fifteen kilometers. Her chalet, it's up in the mountains from there, it's quite isolated."

"She has a daughter—you said?"

"Chloé." Rohan nodded. The blister-water feeling that for some reason had welled in him over the last few minutes seemed to emanate from his stomach and in an occult way had spread to his scalp and toes. Though it antedated the question it seemed to resonate with the anticipated warmth of seeing her.

"What does she do," Frank asked, "way the fuck up there in the mountains?"

"She goes to school—what do you think?"

"No. Your friend—"

"Dominique," Eva finished for him.

"She makes pottery, *terre-cuite*." Rohan caught Frank's hardly disguised amusement. "And yes, I know what you're thinking, but it's not that kind, she's not like that, they're sculptures actually, she's quite good." They certainly were not pots, they would not even hold flowers, or water; they looked like shapes of music and tendrils of fog blended out of the loins of ghostly women. They were formed from a clay she imported from Germany, a mineral so white and thin you felt that it could not come from the fire unscathed; sensed that the sculptures would break where she lay them to cool under the brooding weight of clouds coming together over the old, cold volcanoes of the Vosges.

"We know so little about each other," Eva breathed. "It's incredible, how people can lose one another. Just lose them, as if they were, oh, socks, or something."

They drew into silence.

"Got to celebrate this," Frank said suddenly, "I mean it, it's not every day, we should have brought champagne."

"I brought wine," Eva said brightly. "It's a good one, if you like sweet wine. Tokaj."

"From home?" Frank was fumbling with the zipper of his UTA bag.

"From a place I used to go," she agreed, "near a big lake, in the hills in the center of Hungary."

Rohan got to his feet and pulled his doctor's satchel down from the rack. "I have wine as well," he put in. "I mean, it is not a great wine, but." He found the plastic bag full of ice, and the bottle inside. "I often buy it, because—"

Frank caught a whiff of spiced sausage coming from Rohan's leather bag.

"Chilled," Frank whistled. "There's fancy for you."

"*La Tour Guillem*." Eva squinted at the label. "*Listel des sables. Montagnac rosé.*"

"It's from the cooperative, where my grandfather's grapes went."

"Oh, that's good," Eva said, pulling her lip down on one side, "we each brought wine from our countries. Frank, did you—"

Frank got the zip to draw. He rolled pill bottles to one side and pulled out a litre of rouge from under his Fruit of the Loom. The smell of sausage still was powerful in his nostrils.

"No," he said, "I know what you're gonna ask, I mean there's New England wines I know, there's even a winery in Newport but not where I come from. I mean, what do you want, *Château* fuckin' *Central Falls*? Portygee-American table wine? A nice *Mouton-Pawtucket '86*?" He paused. A label that did not exist popped into his head bearing the skyline of Central Falls etched in black and white, the cold smokestacks and rotten gables, the electrical factories and granite mills.

"No," he said, "I brought, let's see, I forget—" he twisted the bottle around, his eyes loose in their focus.

"*Lynch-Graves*," Eva read, "at least you found one that was Irish." Nobody laughed. "So, which shall we open first?"

—*and among the fixed-up Victorians that one crazy saw-toothed intrusion of chimneys and pennants and skewed stairs*—

"We should open the Listel," Rohan suggested softly. "The rosé, well, since it's cold." He spread his hands.

"What do you think, Frank?" Eva repeated.

"Frank?"

"Oh, sure, whatever," Frank said.

twenty-eight

The phone call from Central Falls comes in the middle of a shouting match. Manny Carvalho of the Pawtucket Action Movement (PAM) and Esther Moon of the Mothers Against Toxic Emissions (MATE) are accusing each other of trying to co-opt next week's protest at the gates of the Vulcan Electronics plant. The protest is mostly symbolic. Vulcan closed the plant three years ago. All that's left is an office that deals with pensions, maintenance, and legal fees.

"I got a ten-year-old kid who can't go to the bathroom alone you don' have—"

"Yeah but that don't mean you haven't got your own ax to grind in—"

At first Frank does not recognize the voice. By choice and habit the Hallorans don't use telephones. "Lou?" he yells in disbelief, plugging his free ear with one finger.

When Frank does get the message he cuts the meeting and turns the conference over to the RI-PIRG rep, and never mind the fact that in the last eighteen months of organizing southern Rhode Island communities to sue large industrial polluters he has had to fight Rhode Island Public Interest Research Group for territory along with everyone else. Outside, the 650 Yamaha Special grins chrome in the light rain. He guns it like fired mercury up route 114, the piss-off puking up in his throat despite the salving speed.

Carbo's house stands shot-roofed beside freshly bulldozed lots. Frank rumbles the bike up the ramp and inside the second porch the way he always does. A new sign is nailed to the big oak outside; "CARBO CROSVIK the Fixit Man all repairs appliance and marine engines" it reads and, underneath, "House of Thousand Rooms / Guided Tours $2." He finds Lou Halloran on the third level of kitchen, dangling his legs over a balcony of perverted lizards and deranged frogs deeply carved into the pine.

"Hayyadoon."

"Beer?" Lou tosses him a can.

Frank pops the Narry. "Where is he?"

"East rooms."

Frank sips the cheap brew. The east rooms are the more cheerful ones, in terms of interior decoration. Carbo seldom goes up there unless he is feeling low.

"So what's going on, exactly."

Lou shinnies down to level one. He reaches around a stack of *Yankee Traders* and fishes out a paper full of legal script. Frank reads down the document. "A condemnation order. That's bullshit, the house is sound. The work he put in—"

"Yah, he never got zoning permits."

"That's not the problem, is it? I mean, I saw the building sites, down the street."

Lou is shrugging on his EMT jacket. For some reason, despite or because of their personality disorders, the Hallorans all ended up doing med work, even the twins; even Sue, who got her MD though that won't help her up in Cranston now.

"Yeah," Lou grunts. "Moncenigo wants it. He's got some deal going with an outfit called London Erie. They're gonna put up a discount jeans mall. This," he waves, indicating the whacked-out carpentry, "is the ornamental landscaping."

Lou is gone. Frank listens to the house shift and creak like a ship-of-the-line trying to tack clear of shoals. Then he climbs the hidden staircase, through a door crafted to look like a china hutch, down a hallway painted with crude Polynesian motifs, up a couple more ladders and trapdoors to the east building.

Tiny rooms of different shapes open on either side. One holds painted mustangs cropping cornflowers. Another is constructed entirely of driftwood boards, many still covered with barnacles; it smells of seaweed. The floors are warped, the windows round. Frank stops outside a room he built himself. It looks like the cockpit of some mythical flying machine. The controls all come from his grandfather's junkyard; hubcaps, bits of dishwasher. The windshield is from a crashed Beechcraft. He finds Carbo in a plain room at the end, daubing seahorses on a chartreuse ocean. Outside a Norwegian flag slaps its flagpole. Even Carbo cannot tell it is upside down.

Without seeing Frank, Carbo stands up. It takes him a long time. Where it has not been stained orange from tobacco his beard has gone off-white. He spots Frank and nods.

"Ah, Frankie—you came."

They shake hands.

"How's college?"

Technically, Frank is finishing an M.S. in social work at URI. The Community Anti-Pollution Association will be his thesis. Frank does not answer. Carbo eventually shrugs.

"They got me, Frankie."

"But you'll fight it?" Frank asks.

"Too tired."

"I'll fight with you. That's why I came."

Carbo's eyes are the color of the mains water downstream from Vulcan's Pawtucket plant after a big rain. Even his red woolen cap seems to droop despondently. Carbo looks away; the wrinkles deepen.

"You fightin' the mayor, Frankie. Him and Moncenigo, they buddies, ya?"

Carbo holds the big hammer and looks for somewhere to use it.

Frank has experience in this kind of fighting. When he worked at CAC they sent him to apprentice with Barry Greaver, who organized Harlan County against the Coal Operators' Association. He takes a leave of absence from the Pawtucket coalition; he even puts off an interview in Boston for a job with International Relief in central Africa on which he had pinned a lot of hope. He moves into the flying-machine room at Carbo's. He spends days at Providence

City Library and the Secretary of State's records office on Westminster Street and goes quietly square-eyed from the thousands of ghost-lit microfilms. He finds that London-Erie Holdings (Rhode Island), the property company handling the mall transactions, is a big, if legal, contributor to the mayor's reelection campaign. Also, the person listed as secretary of the property company has the same address as the brother of City Councilman Moncenigo. A records search at City Hall proves she is in fact married to him. Moncenigo sits on the planning board that approved both the mall variance and the condemnation action and never recused himself from voting on either motion.

Frank gets wound up in the fight. Carbo still works on the east rooms but you can tell he gets a surge of energy when he comes down and finds Frank roostering with anger or exultation. "We got 'em now, Carbo!" Frank crows, shaking a fist high, "by the *balls*!" "Ya, great, Frankie," Carbo says, and talks about Barcelona that he saw as a bosun on a tramp steamer, just before the Falange took it in '37. And he starts to play the accordeon again, tunes like *The Red Flag* and *Nu Takk for Alt Siden*. At the end it seems that Frank's coming has made Carbo more nostalgic than anything.

Frank establishes meaningful communication with an assemblyman who is not bent. He hand delivers material to the state ethics commission. Then he contacts a reporter he knows at the *Journal Bulletin*. The newspaper and Channel Nine snap at the story like sharks at offal. Frank has less success at the neighborhood level because the area has changed in the last few years. Young lawyers and venture capitalists bought houses locally looking for fast profit and they want the mall to go up and raise real estate values so badly they are wetting Y-fronts just thinking about it. Carbo's more immediate neighbors—with the exception of the Hallorans, who live three houses away—have always bitched about the junk, the unmowed lawn, the unauthorized additions. What they do not know is that when the complaints got too thick

Carbo stopped building additions on top of the house. Instead he concentrated on tunneling, down and outward from the cellar.

Frank plows through the red tape, the threatening phone calls, the garbage dumped on the first porch. The matter is brought up on an emergency basis before the city council, which considers the issue in closed session and, on a Friday evening well after the *Journal* has gone to bed, lets the mall variance stand.

Frank learns later that London-Erie told the mayor, a convicted kidnapper with the morals of an irradiated tick, that if they could not have the entire property they would move the project and the 245 jobs it carries to Taunton. Under pressure from the mayor the council caved in. The ethics inquiry is allowed to continue for a week until the media lose interest.

In a separate decision, the condemnation order also is upheld.

The night of that decision Frank goes to the Hallorans' kitchen. Mrs. Halloran is cooking pies and New Bedford boiled dinner. The aroma of burnt sugar and linguiça—a sausage made of garlic, smoked pork, and red dye—fogs the room. Frank likes linguiça but its smell tonight disgusts him.

Lou, too lazy to get up, is pissing in an empty gallon jug of Chablis. Carbo sits on the couch, sipping peppermint schnapps from a pint bottle.

"S'okay, Frankie. I tole you." Carbo is slumped against Lou's obese hound. His big hands, holding the schnapps, are like stunned animals.

Frank, though he loves Carbo with something close to a child's singleness of emotion, feels his disgust build. He goes out on the porch. He looks down the street at the patchwork of portholes, towers, and ladders; at the five hundred angles and contortions of Carbo's roof against the Fanta-colored sky. Sue Halloran comes out and touches his ass but Frank is thinking of all the carefully carved troll heads and lion paws, the scenes of Port Said and New York and other places the old man had been or imagined, painted with no great skill but with huge love and attention on three-ply or pine that with the touch of Carbo's knife or brush have taken on a nobility not normally assumed by trash wood.

It's no use, he thinks, no use at all. Everything and everyone he cares for will end up as fodder for outfits like London-Erie, and Vulcan, and people like Moncenigo. Even the bluefish in Pawtucket harbor are contaminated with their undirected poisons.

Esther Moon's son was crippled because she liked to eat fish when she was pregnant. The anger, rising hot as super-heated steam, meets a pool of desolation like radioactive sludge and before he knows it he is making sounds like a dying seagull as the newly smashed hopes struggle to escape his ribcage.

"*Fuck,*" Sue says in some wonder, and hands him the Gallo bottle, from which Frank, because he's been away, because he is upset, takes a deep, unthinking swig.

"Gaaahhr!" he croaks, spitting out a mouthful of Lou Halloran's piss.

"You're the cunt!" Sue shouts, as Hallorans will after a nasty and successful prank.

twenty-nine

Here was the tricky part.

You took the coffee cup back into the kitchen. You used the bathroom. You wondered idly who owned this place, what she thought about when she awoke at four in the morning, what they called "the hour of the wolf." Did she see her life as an empty succession of wasted minutes, or did the kids burn up her faculties for worry? She bought cheap tampons from Monoprix . . .

It was a way of clearing your mind.

Then you returned to the desk. You eased the putty-like pyramid of ammonium nitrate to one side, making sure the copper wires of the detonator were firmly bent in opposite directions. You took the clock, the wires, the epoxy glue, the battery and wire cutters from your kit bag and placed them in the cleared space before you.

The clock was an old-fashioned travel alarm with a square glass-covered face and metal levers in the back for adjustments. It was not easy to find such clocks these days, they were mostly digital and plastic, and plastic timepieces were useless for this work. You had found this clock in a pawnshop. You'd removed the minute hand and predrilled a hole in the glass. Now you picked up a length of red wire and pushed it through the hole in the glass until it was far enough in to impede the hour hand's passage, but a strong millimeter shy of the clock face. You glued it in place with a drop of epoxy. You wound up the mechanism, listened to the tick to check it worked, then set it back again; hours, and two centimeters, before the spot where the wire poking through the glass marked a particular point in time and space. You picked up a black wire, wound it tightly around the alarm spur, and secured that with epoxy. As you waited for the glue to set you opened the suitcase and strapped the pyramid of explosive to the suitcase's base with gaffer's tape. Ten centimeters away from that you taped down the battery, the six–volt Mazda kind with the copper ears for terminals. You taped the clock ten centimeters from the battery, on its side, so front and back were both accessible. You took a deep breath and flexed your fingers.

Then, without benefit of much oxygen, you made all the connections: red wire to battery's positive terminal. Black wire from battery's negative ear to "minus" pole on detonator.

A telephone rang inside, a car honked without, it did not concern you. You checked once more to make sure the wire had not shifted through the clock face and that it was well away from the hour hand. You felt a drop of sweat surf your chops and wiped it carefully out of the path of the electrics.

Finally you fastened the red wire that led from the alarm spur to the positive pole of the mercury detonator. The circuit was now complete, except for one gap between the minute hand and the wire protruding into its path. You coiled all the slack wire and taped it to one side. You sat back in your chair and held up your fingers. They shook, but only very, very slightly.

It was ready.

You wanted coffee more than sex.

thirty

Eva put her glass down, carefully wedging it against the wrapped packages lying in the next seat. She had assumed they would drink from the bottle but Rohan pulled out three glass goblets for godssake, insisting fine wine tasted better from good receptacles, and she liked him for that; it was something Serge would have done. She pulled string from the parcel labeled *E. Vaillant artisan boulanger* and revealed coffee éclairs. One unlabeled parcel held cold chicken in *forrás*-paprika *gelée*, as well as leek tarts. The other contained sticky pastries from the "Arabe" on the corner. She got to her feet. Whether it was because her bladder was getting weaker with age or for some more doom-laden reason, now just a few gulps of wine induced in her the need to pee.

She said, "I need to pee." Rohan stood up politely. Frank,

his face stiff as a wet rag in the freezer, nodded. The train bounced her in ribald fashion down the corridor.

The WC, like all such, smelled of shit and wind and camphor blocks. When she pulled down her jeans and panties and sat the wind rushed up the poorly sealed trap and fanned the crack of her ass with slipstream and it was not unpleasant. Her nipples were hard but it was not because of the air, which was warm. Cool air hardened them, as did sexual arousal or nervousness. Or nervousness and arousal together, as had happened at Sainte Anne . . .

She felt the flush spreading from the bottom up. She could do nothing to stop it, though no one was there to see in any case. She was not ashamed of the memory but it was only six weeks or so ago and Holy Mary she was brought up Catholic, the closet Communist kind which was the worst. And he was, or had been, a *monk*—

Bazhd!

thirty-one

Chartreuse is not something she normally drinks but she is feeling premenstrual and the liqueur helps quell that tension. Her vision holds burred edges from fatigue for the lab is taking fifteen hours out of every day and on top of that Serge's publishing house is in litigation over the Ermisen sequel so she must make time for that as well.

The office party, held by the anti-neo-post-Lacanian cabal, is a bore. Only anti-neo-post-Lacanians would feel the need to require costumes outside the holiday season. She has few friends here, and attends purely for political reasons. Eva's colleagues at Sainte Anne tolerate her project because her CNRS research money rubs off on them;

previous grants, and those who earned them, signify worthiness for other monies. She wears a cheap paper mask with the features of the current French president bought cheap from a toy store. Her stomach clutches a little as she sees her assistant Bernard Vauclair standing, like a line at a convention of circles, at the door. For costume he has but a rubber pig's snout strapped to his face. He is short and thin with an army haircut, heavy cheekbones, the pale eyes of an inquisitor. The typecasting makes sense; he took his *maîtrise* from a Franciscan seminary.

He spots her and plots a course in her direction. She thinks, How did he find me; for she has been trying to avoid him. Nervously and in obvious association she thinks of SEM—sees it in her mind, the Sequential Stimulation Encephalograph (Mitnal).

"Doctor Koszegfalvi's phrenology machine," they call it. Like a child it is unlovely in ways only a parent could appreciate. In fact the hardware, bolted to metal frames, festooned with varicolored wires, arranged over a dentist's chair, does appear somewhat Victorian.

The SEM consists of four twenty-seven-centimeter double metal quadrants, each with one vertical and one horizontal track that line up around the subject's head. Four Mitral Mikrotech electronic pens, laser adjusted, that fire a light voltage along a very precise vector, speed up and down the curved vertical quadrant on ball bearings and a moving belt. The vertical quadrant itself runs in the same way along a curved horizontal track.

But all of that, though it cost a lot of time and money, is mechanics. The art is in the software behind, which they call the Navigator: the jewel in the matrix. This program, hooked up to the sensors of an EEG, picks up the subject's wave activity. With the help of an atomic clock it triangulates exactly where in space and time that activity is occurring in the patient's brain and feeds the coordinates to the four quadrant systems. Within 1/140th of a second the pens line up and, like little cannons sighting down an enemy position, fire brief, simultaneous impulses at the area in question—which of course reacts since it is now absorbing three times more amps than any other part of the brain. The EEG picks up the heightened activity, leaving the Navigator a choice: either plough back energy into the same activated area, or divert stimulus to other zones.

She finishes her Chartreuse. Bernard stands in front of her, Orangina in hand.

"How did you know it was me?"

He does not answer.

"I was coming," she adds defensively.

"It was this afternoon. We agreed."

She looks away. "This is silly, Bernard."

"You're scared."

Her eyes snap back to his.

"What are you talking about?"

"I'm talking about 45 and 81."

Both 45 and 81 are experimental subjects who complained of depression after their SEM sessions. Neither came back for the follow-up exam.

"I'm not scared," she says, taking off the mask so she can see better, "but I told you; we have to go slowly."

"It lacks courage," Bernard Vauclair says, "to test it mostly on others."

In the end, she thinks, it always comes down to pride. Pride in your ideas, your ethics, in who you hope you are, finally the details do not matter.

The lab lies behind an office that shelters the mainframes, fourteen Uragiri 3800s in parallel that add up to half a teraflop of capacity. Desks, bookshelves and piles of journals surround the terminals. They wash their hands automatically and sit down at the keyboards.

"Feedback or proto-Penfield?"

A hesitation. "Penfield."

She originally conceived of the SEM as a device for

studying and even initiating memory in accordance with her theory, that memory is a narrative process involving many fluid "neural structures" in scattered areas of the brain. And the device has suggested graphically how the hippocampus/hypothalamus dyad works; how it "navigates" the areas where data are stored, drawing coordinates, making a priority list based on the strength of different inputs, remembering in what sequence to retrieve them, transmitting its theta waves accordingly. Memory, Eva is now convinced, must be identical to the way humans tell a tale, in that it records different bits of observation — subject, object, action; mood, smell, relation to other observations — in a fashion that strongly favors narrative coherence over accuracy.

What the SEM does is, it overstimulates an area of the subject's brain that they know has been linked to a particular memory or type of memory; when that memory triggers another strong memory the SEM both records the output and gooses that area of brain. In early experiments, the point was to track how different areas were connected, and how the hippocampus regulated their sequence, and how the memory was linked to new nodes or unhooked from old ones — how it changed over time.

In later case studies, they started changing the memory story, to see how the brain coped with and tracked such alteration.

Although it is too early to make judgments she believes the "cascade" of memory stories emanating from the subjects so far will support her thesis.

Working at the SEM terminal brings back in a circular way the early excitement.

"We'll go straight to Gemini," she says.

He looks at her with the light flat in his eyes. Fingers spidered over the aphid keyboard. He has forgotten to take the rubber pig's nose off his face, he is the type who seldom notices himself. Either he is absolutely egotistical, she thinks, or egoless, and wonders if that could be the same thing.

"We should warm up on our own," Bernard says.

"But we know how that works."

"It's too soon."

"*Now* who's scared?"

"Gemini," Bernard agrees. His voice is battened down tight.

Gemini is a subprogram on the Navigator network that links the two SEM units they have online. The idea is, using two subjects instead of one, to coordinate the firing menus of the different units while the subjects try to think back to a common "memory." The hope is that the two brains, like fishwives reminiscing, will reinforce and expand each other's recall of the event.

The more she works on SEM the more she thinks of "memory" as something in quotation marks.

"I had alcohol," she says.

"This is hardly a controled experiment, Eva."

"What do you want to target?"

"The party. Keep it simple."

They program the two units and then the Gemini, setting trigger time at five minutes. They enter the workshop: small, windowless neon, stuffy with equipment, warm with LCDs and baked circuitry. He fastens the EEG cap to her forehead and she does the same for him, deliberately leaving the pig's nose in place because Christ knows they can use a little humor around here. He still has not noticed.

They strap themselves in and wait.

She watches the clock, wondering what will show up on the tapes, the graphs.

They already have found anomalies. Three weeks ago Bernard, purely for the hell of it, programmed the computer to graph the entire 63 hours of SEM recordings. He found two patterns where none should have existed at all. One consisted of a recurrent 19.69 minute cycle for short-to-midterm mnemonic events. Another, choppier cycle—it averaged out at 14.32—surfaced specifically when the subject was asked as a control to make up a "memory" from scratch.

This last frequency interests Eva the most. It involves more separate neural structures than any other cycle; its microstructure oscillates between rhythmic pulses and a febrile, random activity.

It reminds her, somehow, of Charlie Mingus. She wonders if the true role of a healthy navigator might not be akin to what a jazz improviser does—inventing new structures, linking them to old riffs, making a structure of novel patterns that in itself will become a base upon which to build further improv—the key here being a balance, between the act of creation and the exploitation of what has already been made up.

"Thirty seconds," Bernard says.

She snorts like a pig. He still doesn't get it.

Some but not all subjects experiencing the short frequency have reported extremely high levels of affective input at the relevant time. Subjects 45 and 81 belonged to that group—

She cuts outside thoughts. Her limited experience as a SEM test subject has hinted at a suspect ability on her part to shut down certain memory centers completely. She has a theory that this may be the flip side of an eidetic memory, but now is not the time to theorize. She closes her eyes and tries to think of the party. The taste of chartreuse. Bernard. Her nipples are hard. Bernard is right; she *is* nervous. The servomotors start to buzz. The quadrants zip and fire so fast they sound like one continuous tearing. And now, coming into her shut vision like slide shows run by spastics she sees pictures. As usual they are fuzzy, bubble images, filmscreens melted in a slow fire, without definition or margin; star-filter on. Tiny Professeur Jules-Falret dressed as Genghis Khan, eating *petits fours*. A burp smelling of chartreuse;

the tweed transactionalist, body odor, his cheekbones. Bernard. SEM, a pink-white flower, a Frankenstein strapped in, a rhythm she cannot place. She feels a tingling sensation, as if her feet had been sliced off in a way that feels nice. And her hands, Bernard's hands, herself—*herself standing there looking at him*—and when did she ever look so thin? Her nipples erect in fear, the shadows charred under her own cheekbones. The colors grow hot, the floating feeling has claimed her stomach now.

And then of a sudden this is all speeding up and the speed doubles on its own doubling, the temperature has spread to her womb, opening, the fear and tingling, the fear and *tingling*; she wants to open her eyes but cannot, opening her chest, her throat in waves conducted by this blasted rhythm, this waltz—*dum* da, da—*dum* da, da. Bernard's porcine nose, obscene, his eyes wide and startled like a boy caught wanking. Then the heat and rhythm and eyes merge implode, odd but they shine like those of Julián in the dark of the hotel with the glow of Gardia searchlights electroplating the outside. And the pleasure hits her undisguised, white horses running their way, free of gravity and him with the horses running under, three, six, nine waves of horses, tidal waves of horses backed up in colors and her eyes fly open.

And she loves, loves. And she loves like honeysuckle the embrace of a fence.

The colors are leaf, Balaton; the flaking gold and copper of the Alfold stretching to a horizon beaten purple with coming rain.

The Navigator program automatically shuts off when the looping tightens down, exceeds a certain threshold.

She has stretched out her left arm. The warm Barthelin seep spreads down her inner thighs to the dentist's vinyl. A smell of stale beer.

Her index finger touches his, at the farthest point of reach.

And she loves.

thirty-two

Out of a sense of urgency, because the crowds in Munich are snarling for a decisive victory, Crown Prince Rupprecht of Bavaria asks for permission to carry out Luddendorf's original plan in Flanders; and, as a direct result of getting bogged down at the Marne yet again, Luddendorf is willing to oblige. However the preparations take time and in the interval Luddendorf decides further to exploit the bulge created by the May 27th offensive. He plans a second assault to be led by the Prussian Kronprinz, Wilhelm. The action is scheduled initially for July 13th or 14th against the low-water mark of allied positions in Champagne. Luddendorf, who is highly religious, believes the prayerbook texts for these dates to be propitious.

The French in the meantime have learned of the planned offensive. A patrol behind German lines, led by Sergeant Joseph Darnand of the 161ème Régiment de Fantassins, takes prisoners who inform Deuxième Bureau interrogators that the attack has been delayed. It is now set for July 15th at 00:20 hours. Petain decides to leave only token troops in the front lines so the enemy will exhaust his *élan* and artillery on near-empty trenches.

Foch, in overall command, assigns Mangin to lead the Tenth Army, independently of the German assault, in a flanking attack from the forest of Villers-Coteret on the western side of Luddendorf's bulge.

Twenty minutes before the German barrage is to start, Allied artillery sends up a counterbarrage along the Champagne front that takes the German rear positions by surprise. Just east of Château-Thierry, near Courpoil, an Austro-Hungarian artillery unit supporting the Fifth König Frederic I Grenadiers is badly mauled when one of its ammunition dumps blows up. A young Hungarian lieutenant commanding a battery of 15-cm Krupp howitzers is knocked unconscious by the explosion and falls into a cross-trench.

He wakes up breathing French mustard gas. He lies against the bodies of two other artillerymen, coughing desperately, waiting for his own side to fire.

At 00:20 exactly, upward of 2,000 German artillery pieces puke flame in unison. "It was," Kronprinz Wilhelm will gloat later, "a scene from the Inferno, an apocalyptic symphony of destruction."

Excited by news that five million bottles of champagne are stored on the other side of the line, and finding virtually no resistance in the first French trenches, the German troops advance all day along the entire front, but as soon as they reach deeper positions they find themselves heavily engaged. The König Frederic I Grenadiers and the German 36th Division cross the Marne on pontoons and lose so many men in the process that the river downstream darkens from their bleeding. A private in the U.S. 38th Division dug in behind rows of corn flanking the embankment of the Paris-Epernay railroad line aims his M-1 at a grenadier but his arm trembles so hard that he misses his target. Pétain, upset by the scale of the German onslaught, requests two reserve divisions from Foch. In addition he asks Foch to call off Mangin's attack in case Pétain should require the Tenth Army to defend the road to Paris.

Luddendorf, too, is worried, for although things seem to be going all right the psalms for July 15 speak of death and ruin.

The Hungarian lieutenant drowns in the fluid of his own damaged lungs amid the flicker and tremble of friendly guns.

Sergeant Darnand is decorated for his daring raid; he survives the ensuing battle and the rest of the war. Twenty-four years later, as assistant chief of the Vichy police under René Bousquet, he helps direct the roundup of Jews in occupied France and their ultimate transfer to the German SS.

thirty-three

Using his fisherman's knife to open wider the package Eva
already had spread out in an inviting position, Rohan eyed
the pistachio sweetmeat sitting on waxed paper. The pastry
was not French, he thought. It looked Turkish and probably
was Lebanese, or Algerian. He took a sip of rosé while he
sized up the cake. It had a hard-looking crust and was covered with what appeared to be honey glazing.

Eva, coming back from the W.C., thrust the sliding door
sideways with the weight of her thigh. Frank noticed that
her face was the color of the rosé he was drinking and without giving it much energy put her flush down to wind in the
passageway. "Go ahead, Ludovic," she told Rohan. "I brought
them for all of us."

Rohan grunted and picked up a pastry between thumb
and forefinger. The shadow of concrete fell on them as the
train passed under the A-4 highway leading from Paris to
Reims. The crust was indeed hard. The filling was soft and
sugary; it seemed to take over his tongue, his whole mouth,
like a horde of taste infantry charging previously softened
up terrain. But more astonishing than the fact of this blitz-
krieg sweetness was the way the flavor of pistachio paste,
honey, and mint could seize him almost without transition,
thought, or great perception; wrestle his conscious thoughts
and thrust them, a function of the specificity of taste and the
power of the time, by the scruff of dendrites through a door
opened in his mind by the simple fact of *kataif*.

thirty-four

Reading and eating to excess the crew lives under the blue canvas awning of Suleiman's rusting but much-loved coaster *Karayel*. The small ship's after-hatch serves as table for Rohan's team. At most times one can find thick brown tea and baskets of *kataif* and apricots and goat cheese on its worn tarp, deep in the rolling shade along with chunks of scuba gear, bottles of suntan oil, trash paperbacks. A half-mile to the north the orange cliffs leading to Cape Bababoro rise into the complete lack-of-distortion of the eastern Aegean; in the southern distance loom the arid slopes of Lesbos, so clear you can almost make out the Samothracian shrine atop Cape Mithimna. The sea is very calm and, through the shards of sun glare, seems to have absorbed quite ridiculous quantities of Prussian-blue pigment.

Rohan stands in the saloon watching TV monitors and computer screens. They are using a tracking device in which a diver holding an ultrasound "pen" simply points it at an object he wishes to catalogue. The soundwaves are picked up by three transponders positioned around the wreck and the computer automatically draws lines of position to the object being surveyed. "Wine goblet, tag 1213," the diver says. His voice is hysterical with helium. "That clump of gravy-boat lamps, ahh—1214." Carl types in the data next to the reference numbers. A quiet day on a deep site. Generators thrum, Turkish descants wail from the crew's quarters, silt gushes from an airlift tended by grad students on the foredeck. Rohan has tacked up an x-ray of a star-measuring device he helped excavate when he was a graduate student under Sanders. It has sophisticated gears and differential pawls that lock in lunar cycles with solar and the whole with the circling planets and stars behind. It was probably assembled in Rhodes around 80 B.C. based on the calculations of an astronomer named Geminos for use by navigators in finding celestial bodies. Among the zodiacal symbols inscribed on the device is a lozenge containing a star, a bird, and a beery-looking fish or dolphin that is puzzling the hell out of Sanders. Rohan is staring at the x-ray, thinking that the Chinese used musical theory to calculate the sun's orbit and wondering, vaguely: If you could convert this device into music, what would come out—Bach? Coltrane? noise?—when a crackling erupts as if the intercom to below has itself taken a shocked electric breath. "*C'est—putain, c'est un bras!*" "It's an arm"—

People arrive out of nowhere to cluster in the saloon. Two hundred and twenty-five meters below, in the deep-sea laboratory the *Marine Nationale* has loaned them for this excavation, Barthélémy, who came with the lab, zooms in on the closed-circuit monitor and snarls "Whore of narcosis!" But they know it can't be, not with the oxygen–helium mix the divers are breathing.

"Hold it," Rohan tells the divers.

"Let them do it," Marie suggests, "they found it."

Rohan looks at her. It's an old issue. She has a wide face gone over to freckles, made lively by oversized eyes the color of jungle moss. She was once his graduate assistant and for ten months now has shared his bunk. In the screen Barthélémy announces, "Time's up, anyway." There is no arguing with the clock on such a dive.

Below, the two divers swim carefully through the nacred darkness to the white lights of Deeplab.

That night the team vibrates with tension. The ship below them is one of the oldest wrecks anyone has worked on, a (probably) Cycladic merchantman from (most likely) 1800 B.C. It is also one of the deepest, and best preserved. When they spotted it on sidescan sonar they watched as on heat-sensitive paper an outline of ship and broken mast drew itself clear as a bas-relief carved on Minoan stone. The photon magnetometer indicates bronze ingots in the hold. They have all seen the hull itself emerge as the airlift sucks silt off bulwarks and deck timbers. They all feel they own it. "Why don't you let Per continue," Carl says, "he's good, you know it." Suleiman adds, "You don't *scangiavarda* in mid-watch." "Scangiavarda" is Roumja, the ancient sailor's tongue of the Levant. It is a compound of Venetian words and terms from the Greek that are much older than the Venetian.

Rohan is the project director. He first heard of the wreck from a Turkish fishing skipper shooting deep trawls on thinning fish off Bababoro; he wangled the equipment via the base commander at Toulon, who was Rohan's CO during his year of national service. "I'm going down," he insists. He has an agreement with Sanders not to push this dig too fast or hard, nor to publish in haste at the end. But it is his responsibility to make sure nothing fucks up below. He fights off a feeling that by defaulting to the command role he is giving in to the part in him that most resembles his father. The diving schedule is changed accordingly.

The weather forecast is poor, and they may have to bring the Deeplab up anyway.

Sure enough, by four next morning the wind has veered southerly, a bad sign. *Karayel* rolls sloppy to a bitch-minded swell. Suleiman frowns. Neurotically he rechecks Decca fixes. Rohan, Carl and Marie suit up. They pass Per, Jean-Marc and Barthélémy, all reading sodden paperbacks, still decompressing at 100 meters.

The Mediterranean is clear but at 20 meters you lose all green tones and at 30 all yellows. After 70 meters everything is gray. The Deeplab and the wreck show up as two planets of light. They drop off Carl, who will monitor the cameras from the submerged lab. They change airpacks and move toward the second shadow under the artificial illumination.

One of the reasons the Med is so clear is that it is quite poor in oxygen and therefore in life. Below 75 fathoms no shipworms live. In the Bababoro Sink, under a protective carpet of silt from the Landimiri River, the merchantman has lain like a larva, undisturbed, unrotted; almost as if time were something that happened only in light.

The airlift, two long strings of pipe suspended from the ship and flotation balloons, hangs near the site. Using up too much of their breathing mixture he and Marie drag the airlift's snout to the deck. Rohan asks for power and compressed air rushes from the thin pipe up the nose of the thick one, creating a suction effect. In the bigger spotlights set around the wreck they can make out the stem of bow, the curve of ship's waist, the raised platform of her stern. They swim slo-mo over the structure. The deck beams are clean, up to a wall of black mud rising a third of the way into a small cabin. Next to the drinking goblet a dogleg of what looks like more dirt sticks out from the wall. Taut wires, coded rulers number the darkness into grids. Marie holds her lamp high and aims the sonic locator like a gun.

Close up, Rohan can see what appears to be frozen leather stretched over a clutch of joints and tendons. He looks at Marie but cannot make out her eyes through the lights reflected in her dive-mask. He checks the time. His breath rasps in and out. He can hear Marie's breathing through the radio. He holds the airlift closer and silt magically begins to pull away from the lack-of-color.

Rohan works to the right, arbitrarily. They reach a round knob overlaid with something dark. "*Merde,*" Rohan squeaks into the mike, "it's cloth!" He can feel his heart slam, like a kettledrum in a Tchaikovsky climax. He forces himself to breathe more slowly. He pulls the airlift back a bit to weaken its force, and aims it to the left.

By the wrist joint they find another drinking goblet. And then, slowly, a hand emerges. The ligaments are clearly strained under the calcified skin. The fist is fastened around a splay of sticks with tiny black shells at the end. It is small, neatly shaped. A circular object, two centimeters in diameter, lies on the silt beside. "*Anneau.*" Marie's voice is choked as she points toward the object. "Ring—it looks like." She reaches out, picks it up with difficulty through neoprene, and holds the ring up to the white lamp beam. Rohan sees a thin band inscribed with a lozenge of symbols. A star, a bird, a boozy-looking dolphin.

Silt is sucked from the starkly outlined extremity like emulsion turning in a bath of developer. There is nothing more personal than a hand, Rohan reflects. Nathalie's hands are as delicate and determined as she is. Marie's are more powerful, less defined. This one before them is competent, clenched—terrified. Rohan's gut seems to quiver and open.

The "sticks" are fingers trapped inside the palm. A *second* wrist extends at an angle from the first, into the silt. He takes the underwater minicam from his belt and films what they have found; and then, without looking, he reaches out to touch Marie, finding her knuckles through the thick glove. She has dropped the sonic gun.

"Today," Heinrich Schliemann wrote after watching the features of a soldier he had just dug up turn to dust beneath a funerary mask at Troy, "I gazed upon the face of Agamemnon." Schliemann was wrong; Agamemnon lay at a different level. But this sailor has been pickled like a herring in his own sea.

Carl's voice crackles in the earphones. "Three minutes." Rohan barely hears him. He has never felt star-touched or mystical but the emotion that soaks him now is like that. He knows this man; somehow, across 3800 years he can feel his fear and loneliness like an oil-lamp burning in the pelagic dark. He is a merchant, skipper and probably part-owner of this argosy trading in wine, oxhide bronze and blue glass between Crete and Asia Minor. But the south wind has come up and I have drunk too much. The sea is high, the rocks are near. I have forgotten some navigational check-point and now I am going to die, stupidly, because of it. He squeezes Marie's hand and she squeezes back. He has never been sadder or more completely happy; never felt more alive, in every nucleus of his body.

The Sirocco snaps out of the south like an adder striking. Barthélémy has to winch up the Deeplab on an emergency basis; this, too, will be used against Rohan later. He, Marie and Carl spend ten hours in the decompression chamber on board *Karayel*. The thrill of their find crackles like St. Elmo's Fire around them.

That thrill still moves and charges the air around Rohan eight months after they wind up the season when he is awarded the Throckmorton Medal and addresses the ritual luncheon in London. As he talks about the site he can feel, immediate as taste, the warm air and the *kataif*s on his tongue and the sea bleeding sapphire around the rusty coaster. Rohan, anxious that press coverage not warp what he has found, has hurried to publish his early results, and in particular his theory concerning the symbols on the ring. Because of that Sanders already has sent a critical letter to *Journal of Marine Archeology* but Rohan does not comprehend the impact of this as yet. Down in the pit of the audience he can see Victor Klaudius shaking his jowls and flatulating dourly over a copy of Sander's letter clasped in one sloth-sleek paw but Rohan does not let this bother him either. Now—tonight—he, not Sanders or Klaudius, is more famous, more successful. Already offers have come in from publishers and universities.

Yet, in all of it, what makes him feel best is not the award, the stipend, the applause. What touches him most is the sight of an old man sitting beside Marie at the front table with a locked briefcase on the floor beside him.

The old man is smiling in reserved fashion and nodding at a tablemate. Rohan cannot hear what his father says but he seems to be acknowledging approval, as if he'd had something to do with this; as if he had not fought with every talon and bribe he possessed to keep his son from history and the sea from the moment Rohan quit the Jesuit school without leave at seventeen and a half years of age.

thirty-five

A long slope hauled itself out of afternoon shadows to their right. A medieval steeple stood, harsh in its associations, on the ridge that ran roughly east and west on their left. A river, the same river they had followed from Paris, ran brown and lazy as a vacationing schoolboy through fields of stubbled wheat. A few kilometers north of them, the village of Pisse-loup marked the western frontier of Champagne; north of that, the trees of the ancient forest of Villers-Coteret still darkly grew over the land.

Among ancestors of those same moss-eaten chestnuts, King Louis XI issued in 1230 what became known as the edict of Villers-Coteret forbidding the use of Langue d'Oc or Provençal or any of the other southern dialects in the *Midi* of France.

Frank chewed gently on the remains of his *kataif*. It tasted strange to him, although the combination of nuts and orange was not unpleasant. Eva peeled more paper from the package, offering him another, but he held up his hands in refusal, pointing at his belly to indicate he'd had enough. Rohan also was munching absently, one hand rasping his crew-cut chin as he stared at the photo of a coastal village framed on the compartment bulkhead. Eva folded shut the package.

"You're married, Frank?" she asked casually. "I'm sorry—" she caught herself—"I just noticed the wedding ring. I didn't mean to ask, oh, personal things." For Frank was looking at her without response or expression. She rattled her bracelets nervously. In fact she had noticed the ring ear-lier but, preoccupied with something or other, forgot to ask him at the time.

Finally Frank nodded. "It's okay," he told her, in answer to the confusion rather than the question. "I mean," he went on, "we've separated. We're s'posed to get a divorce in February."

"You have children?" Rohan asked.

Frank nodded again. "One. A boy."

"I never know what to reply," Eva said, "to that statement."

"What? 'A boy?'"

"No, of course not. I mean, that people are 'separated.'"

"Huh," Frank commented, chewing at the crumbs of *kataif* though there were none left in his mouth, "I mean what can you say to someone who no longer *knows* what to think, which is the way people who are separated think, usually, you follow what I'm saying?"

Eva shrugged.

"You weren't married when we met."

"No."

"And you?" Frank asked her.

"Me? Married?"

"It's like these reunions they love, in America." Rohan looked down suddenly. "High school, college. These people, they have not met for ten, or twenty or even thirty years, and suddenly there they all are—back in the same gym where they have played tag and volleyball when they were kids—all eating pretzels or crackers with scallion dip. 'You look just the same,' they always say. As if life could reverse itself. As if what happens in twenty years does not change you—"

Eva asked him, "Do you think it does?"

"I don't know," Rohan said, looking up at her, "not for certain."

"You didn't answer the question," Frank told her. She was wearing a wedding band on her right hand, European-style.

"I was married," Eva said.

"You got divorced."

"He died," she told them, making sure her tone did not carry too much burden, though the thought of dissolution was strong in her these days.

"I never know what to say," Frank replied, after a pause, rubbing his moustache.

Eva's lips twitched.

"It was six years ago," she said, "and you learn, even the death of someone you love, or who loves you, it can be, oh, maybe not good, but it can help you in some ways."

"It is information," Rohan said, "even death. I am not sure," he went on, "if I believe now all information is good. I used to, though."

"Do you think love is information?" Eva asked.

"Yes," Rohan replied, "I think so; but that is definitely an example of information which does not always help."

Frank looked at Eva. She was pulling her mouth down to one side again. The gesture made her seem curiously young, a schoolgirl. He took a bottle of stomach pills from his bag. "What about you," he asked Rohan, without enormous interest, "you married?" But he watched mostly Eva.

"No," Rohan replied. "I never really believed in it.

"If something exists," he continued softly, "then why build a wall around it? If it does not exist then building a wall will not make it exist. No?"

Yet he had been thinking about marriage of late.

"You talk about love," Frank said, "like in a Sandra Dee movie, like it's a unitary thing for you, everybody knows exactly what it is."

Rohan shrugged uncomfortably. "Well, there is something there," he said, "we use that name, to describe it. Perhaps Eva can tell us," he continued, "it is more her department."

"I think," Eva said slowly, "we spend the first part of our emotional lives, oh, we are hoping love exists. The second part, we find out it does exist, in some form, as Ludovic says; and the third part, we spend wishing it did not exist."

"And the fourth part?" Rohan asked, not seriously.

"I spend that," Eva said lightly, "trying to find where it lives."

"So you can track it down and kill it," Frank suggested,

remembering a T-shirt that had been popular around PISR once. Eva's eyes glinted as she smiled once more. She had a quick vision of triggering a flame-hot sexual affair with Bernard and the idea made her smile deepen further. Bernard believed that what people called "love" was simply an explosive restructuring of short-term mnemonic routings based on navigational coordinates furnished by a deep-cycle stimulation structure—a new story, with plotlines written in bicarbonate sensors and cyclic AMP, violently forged out of the old.

He would cringe with embarrassment if he could read her thoughts right now.

In another part of the forest of Villers-Coteret once stood the stone fort of a nobleman. In the dungeon of that fort was a locked room where the nobleman killed and ate the women who loved him, or who, at any rate, had married him. To the south of the forest, north of the railway line, the ridges grew even more pronounced and collected shadows like nasty secrets in their lightly flowered valleys.

Frank saw the ridges from his window seat, but the rest of his mind had pulled back into itself. He knew that one phrase in what had been said over the last few minutes had touched him, reversed a factor in one of his internal algorithms, and he found himself going back over their words, feeling their texture the way a man will prod the different muscles of his lower back, looking for the tendon or vertebra that has pinched a nerve.

He was embarrassed by how the term "love" generally was used to veil fears and desires, but embarrassment would not explain the altered valence in his thoughts.

Of course the way he felt about Jack was based on fear of his own death as well as on the hackneyed and related desire to pass along his own genetic coding. It was not necessarily relevant that a kind of warmth grew in him every time the subject came up. It had always been there, unaccountable, solid, from the moment they had dragged him kicking and screaming into the scrubbed air.

The image that came to Frank now was not the kind of daydream that wrestled you through every detail, yet it was strong enough for him to be quite conscious of its arrival and power . . .

Dragged Jack willy-nilly and arse-first into the cold of a day exactly eight years, eight months and ten days before this one.

thirty-six

"Gee honey, you jiving me?"

A pneumatic black woman playing a surgeon on a rerun sitcom challenges her attractive kids and her handsome husband (a kind, intelligent African-American playwright) over who is to borrow the spare DVD player in their 3.2 million dollar New York City townhouse. This apparently is funny because the laugh track roars and Jodee laughs and her water breaks.

Just like that.

"Oh, *Jee*-zus," she says, staring at the soaked orchid-pattern couch beneath her.

"*You* just wanna listen to Boyz II Men all night," one of the handsome TV kids complains.

"Oh fuck," Frank whispers, thinking in one sector of his brain that maybe this is not happening and there will be a commercial soon.

Still, he has been to all the Lamaze classes and prenatal clinics and co-birthing seminars and he knows what to do. He telephones the hospital and tells the maternity ward they are coming in. He packs a bag full of nightgowns, tennis balls for back massage, a lithograph of Kate Chopin she wants to use as a focus point during labor. He remembers the pocket camcorder. Around him the house, full of furry toilet-seat covers, awning-stripe wallpaper and needle-point carpeting, slumbers placid and in terrible contrast to what could happen to his wife in the next two or twelve hours but he does not want to think about that. The contractions start way faster and stronger than they are supposed to and soon Jodee is groaning and going pale as if she has been kicked in the stomach every seven or eight minutes. He gets her and all the equipment into their new, unpaid-for, family-size van and takes off as fast as he dares toward Brigham and Women's, swerving around the nascent potholes.

"You okay?" he asks at every light.

"I'm—fine," she whispers, and covers his thick hand on the gearshift with her thin one.

"We'll be there soon."

"Don't forget to film it," she tells him. "Promise me, Frank? I want to see it. I want to see her come out."

"I won't forget," he says, though deep inside him he thinks this craze for watching birth scenes is silly and even somewhat sacrilegious. Some things should be unique, non-replaceable, not susceptible to rewind. Otherwise your mind will get mixed up between what is important and what is merely well-edited.

Jodee is certain their baby is a girl. She has swung the wedding ring on a thread over her stomach twenty times and mostly it has spun counterclockwise.

Inside Brigham's the staff treat this with amazing calm. They make her sign forms at the Ob-Gyn triage-and-accounting center while she sits around in a wheelchair. Frank explodes at the nurses, who act like they have seen it all, including his outburst, a thousand times before. They get to the birthing room as it turns out with a good five hours to spare.

This is the hip place to have your kid. The idea is to mimic a room in a community where women gave birth at home surrounded by butterchurns, country midwives, and maiden aunts. However the latest in computer monitoring and space technology stands ready next door should the need arise. The walls, like home, are covered with awning-stripe wallpaper and the bed is made to resemble a metal four-poster and Frank actually is supposed to do what he has trained for, which is hang out with his wife and help her through the contractions by breathing slowly in through the nose and out through the mouth and counting off the elapsed seconds and mopping her brow and so forth.

So he sits by her head and counts and breathes and mops and does not look while the nurse comes by with the enema and wipes and leaves with the tray and the obstetrician checks between her legs and sterile cloths and basins are placed to hand.

They hook her up to a monitor and above their heads the baby's heartbeat pumps out tiny regular sawteeth on the emerald screen and Jodee's contractions appear underneath like a crazy mountain range of pain organized from a background of zero and infinite information.

"It's going all right, isn't it?"

"It's gonna be great."

She smiles and turns white. Globules of sweat pop on her face and he mops diligently. After an hour of this Jodee asks him to leave before he wears out her forehead. The midwife smiles in the way women have when they are doing women things and men are around to fuck things up with the best of intentions. "It looks dramatic, honey," she tells him, "but it's gonna be another two–three hours at least, why not go outside, take a break, get something to eat."

"Don't forget the camera," Jodee whispers.

"I love you," he tells her. It is something they say all the time on sitcoms but he feels in him the sunken burn that proves to him he means it with no acting.

He buys acidic coffee at the canteen downstairs. Because of the women-authority in the midwife's voice he buys a hamburger he doesn't want and that turns out to be a disgusting greasy lukewarm gray thing of which he can barely manage to choke down half. He refills the coffee illegally and walks out the Emergency entrance to Longwood Avenue all hard and slick with November rain. His watch reads 21:41. Trying to keep the night safe for white Irish people the city washes the sky with orange. Frank's heart still pounds with a complex panic and he feels a space grow inside him, dug out by the fear he feels for Jodee and for the lump of trainee life inside her uterus and it makes no sense to him that this space should fill slowly with other worries, as if the squalid accretions of fear brought in only their like, the doubts and turgid discomforts sludged up over the last few months.

He walks harder, wishing he could jump on his twelve-speed and go for a ride, to fight off the goblins in his head.

It's not serious anyway, it's just that of late he is sick of the organized search-for-happiness he and Jodee apparently are engaged in. The Lamaze classes are fine and necessary, he does not mind the breastfeeding seminars or the co-parenting group, though he is sick of the edge of man-hatred he feels from the instructors there. Nor does he like the way they use words like "care" and "parent" in danger-ously inaccurate ways, subverting the sturdiness of nouns and the monopoly on action that verbs once possessed.

She was right to take him to AA meetings and Al-Anon for his brother and codependency for both of them and he is glad they drink less and "talk about" their deep-rooted problems with regularity and feeling but finally he is sick of the people who go to these groups; everybody's facile and frantic search for someone else, parents or society or the planets, anything, anyone other than themselves to blame the trouble on.

Like those two PISR fellows in AA trying to detect some deep harmonic relating their abuse of California Zinfandel to the sociopsychology of Roadrunner cartoons.

They should all reside in Bahr el Gazal for a month, he reflects. That would demonstrate to them that the only thing wrong with their lives is they have too much time and money to do anything but worry about what's wrong with their lives.

The gripe comes, bites, is gone in a flash. Jodee is upstairs, groaning in agony, and he is down here behaving exactly like the people he complains about—he chucks the coffee in the gutter and hurries back up and she is pathetically glad to see him.

In his absence the fetal monitor has been hooked via a suction device directly to the baby's scalp. The medic says there has been some fetal distress but everything is fine now. Frank nods while trying to control his own breathing. He doesn't believe a word of it. He is sweating worse than she is. He wipes her face again and in contrast with earlier she looks unbelievably fresh and young to him, exactly like when he met her at CUNY, after the trip to Nooristan, after he quit the munitions business. She was finishing her teaching diploma and he was giving a guest lecture in his new capacity as relief coordinator for Tigre for the Boston relief group. Everything about her, from her walk to her way of considering novel ideas with head cocked to one side, made *him* feel fresh as unprocessed film—almost innocent again. He was the one who wanted to get married, though it meant in the end that he had to give up the relief job because there was too little money in it to float both of them. When the research post at PISR came up he grabbed at it like the apple of all salvation and from the blossom of their infatuation he looked at it as a kid might; *this* was growing up. This was understanding there were limits to what you could achieve, and those limits were identically equal to the opportunities you grasped. All a lie probably but he wanted and still wants Jodee so much that his need seems the greater truth.

And then she screams, and screams again. The midwife props her in a half-squat by the head of the spavined bed and the real business starts. The baby's head is turned the wrong

way. Jodee is crying and trying to dislocate his fingers and repeating "Oh God" in a thick voice. Frank whispers anything
he can think of and mops like crazy. "It's a shoulder-hook,"
the midwife calls out, and the medic appears from nowhere
and a nurse grabs Frank and hauls him out of harm's way.
They wave big gleaming steel tools around. Frank trembles
as he watches the crowd move around his wife. He hears her
scream "Camera!" like some demented Hollywood diva and
he picks up the minicam and walks around the bed on knees
that barely clutch in. He sees a gap between the nurses, they
are bent like a single organism with eight tentacles all
pointed at his wife's vulva and pulling at a ridiculously miniature curled red paw protruding from her.

The baby does not want to come and for the rest of his
life Jack will have the same bad attitude about doing what
he's supposed to do on time. Later Frank, reasoning with
the quest for limits when Jack is two; or trying to convince
his boy to do housework or homework or anything rather
than sit and Nintendo and mope and watch TV and suc-
cumb to the Grendel impulse to let life happen to him instead of the other way around; watching the kid's face so
wretched in his lack of information, his lack of memory—
Frank will remember that tiny hand being hauled and
yanked by masked, capped and latex-gloved monsters. He
will recall how all this was sprung on Jack already undergo-
ing the trauma of a critter snug and warm and everything
taken-care-of in an accurate miniature of the salty sea in
which mammals first were spawned suddenly being forced
to use his lungs to pump in freezing air and move against
cold and stainless steel and choke on his own saliva and accept in those fragile retinae the blue neon light, now and
forever *on his own* . . .

Though Frank knows it's partial, whenever he remembers the details of Jack's birth he wonders less at the boy's re-
luctance to travel the indicated path.

"Here it comes," the medic says.

He sees blood gush and stain their gloves a deep and lovely rose. Frank lifts the camera but he is shaking so hard he is unable to aim or trigger it.

I have *seen* blood, Frank thinks. I have witnessed the death of men. A whole village slaughtered in Sudan. I saw the two Brazilians lying like thrown out mops where they'd been shot in the lobby of the hotel with dark pools thickening around their chests and legs. I am experienced, goddammit!

Yes! Only the difference is, This is Jodee, who to him is everything those dead children lined up must have been to the people who cared for them; this is Jodee who to him and his body is the small calm harbor where softness lives and where all the softness in him will continue while around them howl seas of metal and destruction and the depredation of those who understand and control metal.

One of the monitors beeps in warning.

"Forceps!" the obstetrician grunts. "Don't worry about that just pull."

The difference is his body's refusal to accept that hardness can touch her, that she is bleeding, that she and the frail sac still within her could die. And the tension between that refusal and what he is seeing in front of him subtracts balance and direction from the circle of his normal function. He feels dizzy and sweaty at the same time. Before he can think of what this implies his stomach heaves and he is puking coffee, half-digested ratburger, and the barbecue-flavored nachos they were eating while watching TV all over the camcorder and the sterile birthing room, and he is thrown out to cling, smelly, sweating, his shirt congealing in vomit, at the glass square set in the birthing room door as in the light of false neon day the midwife holds up a scarlet bundle still thickly wired to its previous place of residence, and he can tell by the smiles and the baby's enraged face that everybody is going to be okay.

•

thirty-seven

Every hour of being a hostage, in a place where learning curves are the first victims of the flattening effect of force, comes to seem like every other hour that passes.

In the crenelated view offered by the blocked gates they watch tanks brought from the disputed areas of Oriente blatting chundering up the hill, to squat like metal idols and surround the hotel compound with the potential of fire and metal's combining. For the rebels all hope of escape now is gone. They conceivably could have attempted a concerted breakout past the armored cars before, but the tanks now make this flat-out impossible.

The sun climbs like a zombie aerialist on the tightrope of its meridian. The tank crews leave their hatches open and prop up green awnings. On the fourth day, ignoring a chorus of pleas from the manager, the rebels shot out half of the big plate-glass windows in the ballroom so that now during hours of daylight a scalding catspaw strolls among captors and hostages.

Through one of these broken windows, above the distant lingam of the Torre del Reformador, one can see the pass between Santiaguito and Monte de los Spiritos that leads over ravines and mountains to Gumarcaj. It was in the fortified city of Gumarcaj that the Maya-Ki'iché survivors regrouped after the rout of Xelajú and the death of Tecún-Umán. There they decided that if they could not vanquish the invaders by force they would do so by deceit. So they invited Alvarado and his men to a peace parley in their capital. The plan was to start negotiations then discreetly pull out, destroying the sole bridge over the ravines outside, leaving the Spaniards to starve to death in the redoubt. But Alvarado's eyes narrowed as he looked at the high defiles going in. He knew ambush country when he saw it and he turned his troops around and got out of the area before the trap could be sprung.

Officially neither side will talk to the other but the rebels now are indirectly negotiating with the government via the guarantees and good offices of the Mexican chargé d'affaires. A gray-haired man in a double-breasted suit and professorial glasses, he shuttles mouse-foot back and forth through the compound gate. He spends hours locked in the bar with Leila and Lieutenant Suchil. Julián is nowhere to be seen.

Leila comes by their corner on the evening of the fourth night. She looks very thin. Her hair straggles, her olive-green shirt is black with sweat, and she bends in odd ways from fatigue.

"They are talking," she tells them quietly, when no one else is near. "They do not want the bloodshed, it is bad for tourists." She licks her lips, which bear a thin ivory rime left by thirst and stress. "But there is a problem. They will let us go, they will let everyone go. Only this, they want—they must arrest him."

"Commandante Vent'uno?" Eva asks.

"Yes." Leila struggles with her hair, using wrists that impart little tension. "The Gardia insists on this. They know— they think—he is here."

"How would they know?" Rohan objects quietly. "No one knows who he is. You could give them anyone, if you didn't care what happened to this person."

"We would not care," Leila replies, looking away, "but they would find out, don't worry."

Eva looks calmly at Leila. She notes the greasiness of the thick hair, and how the crow's feet seem graven so much deeper. She can feel a memory node shutting down inside her brain; she is content to let it suffocate.

"And if you don't," Frank asks, "what then?"

"Then, after tomorrow, it will be too late." Leila waves a hand. "They will take the hotel by assault. They will use the tanks." She speaks low and without inflection. "I *hate* tanks," she adds, in exactly the same tone she might use to say she prefers chocolate.

Leila rises to leave, then turns again. She drops on one knee. It is almost an attitude of prayer. Few candles are left and her face is like gold left in tombs against the dark.

"Somehow, you know." She does not look at any of them but especially she does not look at Eva. "You have found out who he is. The Commandante."

They none of them shift position but acceptance is implicit in their stillness.

"Please," she whispers. "For God's sake—for your sake, also—do not tell anybody." They can see her eyes move in the few splinters of candlelight. She grips Rohan's knee and repeats, "Do not tell anybody."

She vanishes behind a candle. An hour or so later, when he believes Eva to be asleep, Rohan disappears also.

Many Maya-Ki'iché legends center around an enchantress by name of Xtabay. At the full moon she sits naked under a ceiba tree and combs obsessively her long thick black hair and any man who passes nearby after midnight falls under her spell. These stories seldom end happily.

• • •

If three days before the stink and heat were bad—seemed, in fact, impossible to add to—they have tripled and tripled again by the seventh day of captivity.

The Swiss manager has grown more not less overbearing, and he doles out supplies with a grudging hand, invoking his authority as a captain in the army of his homeland. They are limited now to a quarter-liter of water every twelve hours. The food ration consists of half a tin of assorted gourmet fare: hearts of palm, cling peaches, quail breasts with pine nuts in minted aspic. In the crucible of discomfort and boredom, of thirst and fear, the hostages have begun further to break down into their component elements. Now when fights start they turn into full-scale brawls. The last one pitted two Americans against the remaining Brazilians and the Englishman. It soon involved ten people including a South African woman. One of the rebels fired a burst from his SturmGewehr into the ceiling to break it up. Stucco fell and people sobbed, covered with a fresh plaster snow.

A Canadian tourism executive has begun singing top-forty hits and will not stop even when one of the Brazilians threatens to punch him in the face. In the corner someone has been defecating behind a couch at night, although this, in an already stinking environment, makes no great difference. The older odors of floor wax and copal incense are memories only. Rumors incubate around the clumps of armchairs, and multiply with the soft determination of slime-mold. "They" are drugging the water with painkillers. "They" will call the Gardia's bluff and shoot half the hostages before the deadline.

The process by which individual spores combine into the single animal of a slime-mold can be described by the same equation that details how water boils, or how rumors gain a measure of currency within a crowd.

Now the deadline is tomorrow, and at last time starts to move a little faster again. Over tins of brutally tapped Kalamata olives people watch each other like survivors on a lifeboat wondering who will be picked next to feed the group.

By the evening of the eighth day the hostages are too strained to talk in whole voices. Thunderstorms passed two nights ago, and between what came in through the smashed windows and what always condenses from the broken ceiling, the floor of the ballroom is half covered with shallow pools of asbestos-laden water. Whole sections of the ballroom are practically off-limits and people congregate on the islands and communicate, when they do, as through a swamp. Frogs have entered the premises like Japanese tourists invading a theme park; when the sun goes down they start to croak and burp and soon the chief noise is the dripping of the thousand rivers of condensation and the frogs and the Canadian tourism man singing *Honey* and *MacArthur Park* to the occasional shriek of "Shut the fuck up!" and *"Cale a boca!"* and *"Cojones!"*

Eva falls prey to a keen despair. She spends a full ten hours convinced she must inevitably die and writes long letters grayed with tears on the back of Serge's manuscripts. Finally, bored by the self-pity, she goes back to reading the manuscript's front, hunched over the poor literature, pulling her mouth down with one fingertip. Frank strokes his moustache in his sleep. Awake, he invents games and jokes and is the first to tire of his own inventions. Rohan shows up and leaves and shows up again. He has bought cigarettes from the Indians and he smokes as they do now, with the fire glowing inside his cupped palm. He mutters words addressed to no one, comic in their bitterness, then catches himself with a grunted *"Merde!"*

The guerrillas have retreated to the bar and the podium and the ballroom's entrances. They are as silent as ever but they look at each other more. The man in charge of the booby trap sits motionless beside the trigger-wire.

"Isn't that dangerous?" Eva asks Frank at one point, nervously eyeing the box of grenades. "What if he slips or something?"

"They know what they're doing," Frank tells her. "Those grenades are designed so the pin won't come out easy. That kid is aware, I've been watching him.

"There's an art and practice to it," Frank finishes. "To explosion, like anything else."

Later that evening, with less than fifteen hours to go before the next day's deadline, the small Dutch woman stands up brave as Joan of Arc and sloshes around the hostage archipelago carrying her guitar case like a cross under one arm.

"I am going to play a recital," she tells them in good English, "if you would like to visit . . ." She gestures to the main island, a place of couches and coffee tables where by some accident of carpet or leveling little water has collected.

"Damn good idea." Frank attempts, without success, an Oxbridge accent. "Good show, what? What?"

"Be quiet," Rohan says. He wades across the ballroom to the island and squats against a couch. They slosh after him. It is almost eight o' clock. Others have clustered on the island, bringing candles or lamps improvised out of saucers and cooking oil with wicks of cloth. The Dutch woman sits on the edge of an armchair and tunes her guitar endlessly. The damp has played havoc with the strings. The Canadian sings *The Ballad of the Green Beret* but they are used to him now, he is part of the background, like the dripping, like the frogs.

The first notes of *À Tant de Bonnes Chansons* come from somewhere in the dark curved silhouette of the Dutchwoman. In all the half-tones of their reduced lives here the notes acquire a wholeness greater than that of music in other places. People strain to listen and the Canadian senses their tension and falls silent for once. The Dutchwoman plays short pieces; *Amis, Qui est le Plus Vaillant*, Gibbons's *Do Not Repine Fair Sun*, Purcell's *Fantasia;* retuning between each. Most sense a pattern in them like a ballet of invisible motes of light weaving choreographed to a modified three-four time in the blackness of the ballroom. Rohan grunts out loud, *"Allez,* it's not so beautiful as all that." Eva touches his shoulder with her fingers and he turns away.

The concentration is such that few notice when the transistor radio on the piano is switched on and the crow voice of the rebel announcer squawks from the podium. He does this at the same time every evening. The barefoot guard leaves the bar to listen for guerrilla news: the "Revolution Show." But his eyes are on the guitar player.

Frank thinks briefly of a turn in the Blackstone River where an egret used to stand in the swart and poisoned water like a poem speared in a soap factory.

The Dutchwoman is technically excellent and she has good dynamics as well. When the next to last movement ends a collective sigh rises from the smelly, exhausted audience. The first few notes of what is to be the last piece rise like doves. Eva looks around for Julián, who disappeared again this morning and has not surfaced since.

thirty-eight

The fact is, three types of memory may fool the person remembering into a belief that he or she is actually reliving a given event.

Of the three, the most successful is the trick memory, where a combination of inattention and some unexpected catalyst switches tracks in the mind so that for a fraction of a minute, with no effort or pain, over ninety percent of the consciousness lives in the circumstances of another time and place.

The least effective is probably the night dream. In the bizarre release of memory's sludge lies always fifteen or twenty percent of awareness, like the reticular system of a cat, that knows it is being played upon by sleep.

In the middle lies the induced recall, caused by an accumulation of props, relaxed concentration and stacked ancillary memories; these, given a critical mass of volume and frequency, can trigger a far more intense level of flow that will divorce the subject, mostly, from the present. And that change in levels happened now to Eva. In the enduring space-out of what had occurred inside her body, the resonance of what they had talked about and specifically the circumstances of her marriage worked for her as magnetite to a compass needle, pointing the way to a whole of detail and sensation that began not with the wedding, or even with meeting Serge, but three years before that, in a skanky, cluttered apartment in the Impasse Lathuile.

thirty-nine

Occupying an area squeezed between the old soap factory and the Boulevard de Clichy, the apartment, the whole building, are geographically doomed; all will be razed by a company named B.A. Constructions (S.A.) to make way for Lego apartment blocks from which B.A.C., with the unofficial aid of various allies in the current government, can pry more money.

They lie, perhaps fittingly, under the Butte Montmartre, whose original village was leveled in 1873 by the Catholic church and the usual associated financial interests to make way for the monstrous whited tumor of the Sacré Coeur. The stated aim of this operation was to wreak revenge on the people of Paris for a rebellion called the "Commune" that started in 1871 on this same butte.

The operation was successful.

At the time Eva goes to Stefan-and-Marya's party she is in her second year of med school at Cochin. She is ending things with Tamas, a little callously but it has to be callous, he has grown gloomy and unpredictable and at the same time he will not leave her alone. Now she runs with a hyperactive crowd of East European exiles, self-styled poets, professional students. At the party—the floor awash in spilled Nicolas wine and *palinka*, the air a fug of proto-anarchist gossip, paprika chicken and brown tobacco—she spots someone who does not fit. He is slim and good-looking, somewhat older than the average here, with a World War Two aviator's moustache and a straight nose and jaw and dark eyes that are calmly observant like a cop's. But he is no *poulet* because something about him reeks of caution, and a degree of risk. He makes his way to her side and invites her to come to a window. She chatters on about her studies; she is having trouble with the anatomy, after two years the sight of blood still makes her feel ill. She is fascinated by the neurology courses, which is why she signed up at Cochin in the first place. The handsome man smiles a little at her squeamishness. He talks quietly yet she can tell people listen nearby. He asks her if she believes anyone can locate the part of the human brain where the hunting and killing instinct is situated. She says, of course, the primitive instincts of aggression and territory reside in the lizard brain, the cerebellum. He shakes his head. *"Ça n'a rien à foutre avec le primitif,"* he tells her, glancing down again at the street, which looks like a set from *Bohème*, four-hundred-year-old *hôtels de passe* and Arab squats stacked anyhow around lampposts and crooked cobblestones. "It has fuck-all to do with the primitive . . ." Later, when Stefan tells her the man was Jacques Ermisen, a robber of armored cars, a killer of cops and the most notorious outlaw in France, she realizes the setting was perfect for him because despite its name the Impasse Lathuile contains at least seven different ways of exiting the neighborhood.

She works hard that year and the next and survives all dissections. Already she has come under the wing of Professeur Behren, the dean of neuropsychology. She has little time for men. She sees Tamas at intervals that grow ever longer because although he tries to be civil with her he always ends up criticizing or flying off in one of the uncontrollable rages that started, she now understands, after he got knocked on the head doing a *saut perilleux* at the Cirque von Andau. "I can't help it if you love me," she tells him, "always someone loves more, and someone loves less, and it's not new and it's not my fault." He refuses to let her run tests on him. This is ironic since it was his injury that to a significant extent catalyzed her interest in the brain.

One day in early autumn she gets a message that Tamas is in St. Vincent de Paul being treated for an overdose of barbiturates. She rushes to the hospital but he has checked himself out without permission. At his lodgings the concierge says he has gone back to Hungary without paying back rent. Eva tries to phone his mother, without success. By a trick of fate she meets d'Abruzzi the following weekend.

> The sun's flaming train
> Rushes past melancholy crossings. Go
> Your footprints no longer hurt. Silence.
> Only a splash
> I give back my fat fish to the river.
> Just go
> I give back my frail bird to the field

so Attila József writes.

As parties go this one could not be more different from the one in Clichy. Through Behren she has been invited to a soirée held by a rich neuropsychology groupie in Passy. The house is full of recognizable art and tropical birds whose plumage flames in silver cages. The men are graduates of ÉNA and Sciences Po and occupy high positions in large multinationals and the ministry for urban planning. The women wear dresses from boutiques on Place Vendôme and talk mournfully of Angkor Wat. Everywhere she recognizes a typically Parisian dyad: intellectual speed, and a closed-mindedness of epic proportions.

She finds, here as in Clichy, one who is different. d'Abruzzi is tall and stooped and resembles Yves Montand in midcareer. He has eyes that are yellowish, like a friendly adder's. He makes money as an impresario and spends it publishing small books, mostly radical erotics or stinging indictments of the business-as-usual, stuff no one else will touch. His elegance of language and, frankly, the exoticism of his obvious wealth charm her off a perch she had no idea she clung to. When an old man with dentures who is the deputy minister of housing starts to deliver a facile and amusing speech, d'Abruzzi woos her from the party to a grimy bar on the Rue St. Jacques where African intellectuals play chess and listen to ancient music. Leonard Cohen, the Doors. He is comfortable, as she is, in the dead zone between incompatible worlds. His apartment is vast and cluttered with old things, most of them more curious than beautiful. His collection of jazz is superb. She is not in love, the endorphins have not showed up for muster, but what is present (she believes) is depth. With Tamas the endorphins were around in great crowds, and little else, and it finished quickly. With Serge she finds ease, and room to work; a frequency of longer wavelength. She moves out of her sister's. They are married seven weeks after that.

They spend their honeymoon riding horses along dark mirrored rivers and rice paddies in the Veneto. Afterward she continues riding, hacking out in the Bois twice a week. This is her single extravagance, her one concession to Serge's wealth.

She obtains her MD, then the neurology certification. She lives in Serge's apartment almost as a guest; the only change she makes is to remove a life-sized oil of a brown bear, the sight of which always makes her gloomy. One day she finds Marya waiting for her outside Sainte Anne. Marya takes her to a Vietnamese cafe on the Rue Tolbiac. A man is waiting inside, drinking *cây bạc hà* tea by an ancestors' shrine near the rear exit. She recognizes Ermisen, although he now wears glasses and a sculpted beard. He places a manuscript on the table before her. "I would like your husband to publish this," he says. The title reads, *Death Is My Business*.

When she shows the manuscript to Serge he looks at her curiously. "How do you feel about publishing a killer?" he asks.

"I see him as mostly political," she replies, "he does not kill innocents."

"How do you define innocence?"

"I know what you're getting at, Serge," she tells him, "but he has his own context and he is true to it." Serge lets the Silk Cut smoke drift like fog between them. He insists that if he buys it she will have to edit the book.

She meets Ermisen again and again, always in almost farcical secrecy. Their fifth meeting takes place in a small room on Rue Thiers, named for the nineteenth-century politician who enlisted the help of German invaders to crush the 1871 Commune. With little editing and no words he takes her in his arms and she does not resist. Their lovemaking is sharp and quick like a wound and doubly exciting to her because of the danger in the man and the danger of Serge observing this with his snake eyes in her own but basically it is all too dangerous, she is far too busy to spend the energy required to protect herself. She stops it cold. Ermisen looks at her with suspicion bright as a scalpel in his own gaze when she tells him.

As it is, between the book and her research she is working sixteen hours per day and going thin and bruised-looking. On Marya's advice she signs up for a yoga course. The space this discipline pulls out in her strained body becomes the only room she has to relax in.

The Ermisen book, when it is published the following June, is a stunning success. It sells over 200,000 copies and, despite or because of the extra publicity of government lawsuits, overnight pushes Editions d'Abruzzi into the big leagues. Serge nominates her to the editorial board. She is selected to sit on the jury for the Montcorbier literary prize, an honor that, despite the extra work involved, she dares not refuse. She is at one of the Montcorbier luncheons, spooning sherbet, the big editors belching and squabbling over whose turn it is to get this year's accolade, when she learns of Ermisen's death. The man from Editions du Seuil announces, "They followed Ermisen's girlfriend. The *Brigades Spéciales* surrounded the house. There was no warning or attempt at arrest; they gunned him down like a dog." The publishers eye her warily.

Because of this the sales of *Death Is My Business* climb once more into the charts. With the proceeds she can finance the translation of the poems of Attila József, which, in the end, is the one book she truly wishes to see come out. Serge can publish the investigation of the de Broglie scandal that links a government minister with the shady deals of Banque Atlantique through its wholly owned subsidiary, B.A. Constructions (S.A.)

Then, two months after Ermisen's death, Serge goes to meet someone in an underground carpark off the Champs Elysées. He does not tell her who it is, as he once might have; in any case their lives have been growing steadily more separate. An attendant finds him on the concrete floor in a lake of motor oil and his own blood. They figure out later that someone wired the door of his Jaguar to half a kilo of plastic explosive.

The culprit is never traced.

She grieves for Serge, though not to excess. Now that she owns the publishing house she has to squeeze yet more time for work out of a schedule that was already crammed to the limit. The government has used death duties to come down hard on Editions d'Abruzzi and the József project is once more put off. She cuts her hair very short, then, changing her mind, lets it grow long. She cuts down on yoga. She realizes slowly that something has occurred quite deep inside her; something internal has been damaged, a gland that made laughing easier than not, something that believed firmly in her own coherence.

She is not sure if the damage occurred after or before

Serge's death but the realization, at any rate, is new. "Things happen without us," she finds herself thinking, and this too seems a new truth to her.

She stops riding altogether. She finds she cannot look at horses because the grace of even the clumsy ones causes her throat to clench. When she visits Hungary she makes calls and attends the performances of the circus, any circus, trying to find Tamas.

She is unsuccessful.

forty

Crossing the river Marne once more the train slowed slightly, as if intimidated by the scarp that grew in its path. Without warning it was engulfed by a tunnel. The compartment lights failed to come on, the passenger cars went dark and the noise of the rails curved around the walls to come back in those windows left open.

In this tunnel through the ridge of La Brussette, over a half-century before, a *rame* of Compagnie de l'Est passenger wagons carrying exactly one thousand men, women and children slows in the same manner, then comes to a clanking stop. Ahead of it a freight train hauling gray PanzerKampf-Wagen III(F) tanks to the east has taken refuge from a wedge of RAF Lancasters bombing the freightyards ahead at Château Thierry.

If you could reverse time's arrow; if an observer could combine the eye of a crow with the recall of a witness he or she could trace that train backward from the La Brussette tunnel, on exactly the same track bed as the Bar-le-Duc local, through Poincy, Meaux and Chelles till it splits off the main line at the *triage* at Noisy-le-Sec. Still in reverse, rolling more slowly now through the outskirts of Paris, it ends up back at its origins in the station of Le Bourget.

There, in an hour and a half from nightfall on August 9 to 11:25 P.M., ten platform buses of the STCRP company, under the guard of French police and militia, ferry passengers from the transit camp sited next door in the town of Drancy.

The Drancy camp was under construction as a housing project for poorer Parisians when its buildings were drafted to house those deemed "undesirable" by the German occupation forces. In particular, a horseshoe-shaped section of four-story buildings has now been designated as quarters for Jews. Within days of their arrival the tiered flats are filthy. The drains are blocked and the whole estate smells of human waste. Of the thousand taken from Drancy that August, a good half have spent over three weeks in the Jewish block. The other half have been transferred, also in STCRP buses, from temporary quarters in the old Vélodrome d'Hiver, since razed to make way for middle-income apartments, located at 1 Rue Naloton in the 15th Arrondissement.

Were he or she to track yet further back the witness would find that every one of the thousand was picked up in the same wave of arrests, carried out in the early dawn of two successive days in July by nine hundred special teams from the Paris police. This roundup—originally aimed only at adults—is called for by Theo Dannecker. The German plan initially is opposed by the Vichy chief of police, René Bousquet, during two meetings taking place on June 15 and July 2nd, 1942. Subsequently, however, Bousquet agrees to the use of French police for the arrests; indeed Laval, the Vichy premier, on his own initiative suggests including children "in order not to break up the families."

It should be emphasized that at this point it is not clear if the Jewish detainees will suffer a fate much worse than that of tens of thousands of non-Jewish Frenchmen already deported to work in Nazi factories.

Paperwork for the *rafle* is signed by Bousquet and drafted by a *Milice* lieutenant known only by the initials "JLM."

A year after this deportation Bousquet joins the resistance. After the war his crimes under Vichy are forgiven as a result. He becomes a director of the Banque de l'Indochine until further revelations concerning his wartime activities force his resignation in 1978.

JLM's identity has never been revealed. For the last six years he has held ministerial rank in a right-of-center French political party currently in coalition with the government.

The horseshoe block of Drancy, known as the "Nouvelle Ville de la Muette," now houses several hundred families, mostly from north and western Africa, in a squalor that most nonetheless find preferable to their homelands.

forty-one

Acceleration seemed an unattainable goal in the echo of noise the train generated for itself as, obeying the bright diktat of an orange "block-code" ahead, the train braked further in the tunnel of La Brussette. No outside light penetrated at all. No other trains were near.

The block-code—a system of signal lights triggered by a locomotive's passage—was a safety feature making it theoretically impossible for two trains to occupy the same section of track. It was adopted, for the first time in France, on this section of the Paris–Strasbourg line in 1867.

In the third compartment of the second to last car the three passengers found their visual sphere confined to afterimage. It felt to all three of them as if the solid presences they had been reacting to were gone and that for now at least they were reduced to dealing with people who existed *only in their own memory;* that "Frank," "Eva," and "Rohan" were entities you could solely define, who only existed by observations that had gone before; the way a ship's captain, in midocean in heavy weather in the days before satellite navigation, could plot his position only from the last sextant fix, hours or even days ago.

For Eva the darkness remained an enemy, and she crossed her arms against its pressure.

To Rohan, who had spent so many hours underwater, the dark was not a frightening thing, but his experience had never cut the isolating effect of it. Even diving with a "buddy" in the penumbra of ten fathoms he felt alone. There was a reason why the touched signal was so essential to diving, and it was not just because on most dives you did not carry radio. Darkness isolated you from the outside and in so doing made you more vulnerable to inner thoughts and tides, and especially to those dreams or messages linked to darkness.

Especially, though not uniquely, her—

—she who is darkness in an already somber room.

• • •

They keep the lights low in the Continental's bar, partly for the usual reasons, that is, to conceal the throat wrinkles of women and allow men, in the dearth of detail, to get away with a matador's strut; but also because the inward turning that darkness brings stirs the viscous creatures inside, causing one to drink more heavily in self-defense.

She sits at the bar in a narrow striped skirt, a ruffled blouse and a gaucho jacket, curved at the waist over her Lillet. Her hair and eyes all possess the kind of black that speaks more of what it hides than what it may reveal. She smokes nervously, cheap *chulo* cigarettes—bad cover, as it turns out.

146

Rohan, washed up like driftwood by the currents of airline schedules, compensates for jet lag with whisky and Alvarado beer. He sits two stools away and worries aimlessly over the delay. The wreck he is involved in is important for him. His book on what he calls the "navigational heresy" is, once again, on hold. For three years, because of all the controversy, he has been offered no good digs and this one, worked by someone else, gives him a chance to branch out from pure archeology. He will handle the technical details for filming the salvage of a sixteenth-century plate ship sunk off the eastern coast of Nicaragua with a cargo of Inca silver. Galleons are not lovely to him but in the patterns their bones make with the sea lies a certain harmony. In fact the only thing wrong with this wreck is that it will keep him far from Nathalie at what seems to be a pivotal stage in his sister's life.

The balance in the woman's features and in the double-V of her mouth soaks in with the burn of liquor. Inside his brain the slipped harmony of ships thrown on a lee shore washes into the loose grace of a woman fetched up in a hotel bar. Her skin is the color of Burmese teak. She has a way of looking around, looking for someone, like a pilot in poor weather hoping for runway lights, that confers on her persona urgency and vector. She is more gamine than beauty, but so much energy is conveyed in the dip of her nose and the crow's-feet at her eyes and how her hands are never still for a second that she comes across far more strongly than would someone merely beautiful.

He says nothing because some of the parts of him that respond to women are still occupied with a girl in Cros-de-Cagnes, a twenty-two-year-old with a buzzsaw wit that he particularly misses. Mostly he says nothing because this is Latin America and you don't accost a woman without confronting her brothers and to some extent her bishop as well.

It turns out this one is different, for *she* picks *him* up.

The details are unimportant. She calls herself a student in

history and the coincidence makes them both feel lucky. She went to Paris Cinq for a year and drank in a yellow-fronted café he knows, by Mabillon, where the *Porteños* play small guitars and smaller harps. As they walk out of the bar together Eva comes in with Calderón, but Rohan does not know them yet and anyway he is watching Leila as they pass.

They amble around the hill outside the compound, watching the lights of Xelajú below shimmer in the suspended humidity, the silver worm of the Xelixec River trying without success to hide its track from the moon. Without meeting his eyes she asks if she can spend the night in his room.

He does wonder at this; he is old enough to be aware of the dry rot in his male image and he knows just enough about her to see she is driven by a kind of religion that has little to do with the cross hung from her slender neck. However at this point AIDS is rare south of Juarez and he does not hesitate more than is called for by the sham of sensitivity.

When they get to his room she hangs her bag on the coathook and it gapes open and he catches sight of the blued metal of a .44 Molina. He says nothing. Outside the compound, in the shantytowns, *chulos* eviscerate each other with machetes for the price of a pack of Marlboros. A gun in Xelajú is more useful than aspirin.

Because of Leila he further puts his job at risk by postponing his departure for twenty-four hours. The following evening, of course, much becomes clear. She who has disappeared all day, to his mounting frustration, shows up at his elbow in the bar and whispers, "Something is going to happen soon, Ludovic. I know. Just keep down, keep quiet, OK?" A snapped smile, a fold in her crow's-feet, a whip of her loosely bound hair. She vanishes to one side of the twin limestone stelae with their faces of smirking gods.

And like magic the hotel is full of men with much bigger guns than hers. Rohan, following her advice, sits in the bar, downing Alvarados, watching rock-faced Indios direct soft tourists. He understands now that she needed him for his room and the cover he provided, but the realization does not disturb him overmuch. The religion she follows is clear enough now, and it would forever separate them, not because of the direction it takes but because the need exists within her at all. When she climbs to the podium and leans on the piano he thinks of her sweeping her hair across his stomach and chest, back and forth, like an artist using a sable brush on the canvas of his skin; that was not for the revolution, he thinks. It is like stealing something she does not care about, something that he will save and treasure despite her. Anyway, in one of those telescopings of events that seem odd only from the point of view of normal time, he spots Eva a minute or so later.

His first reaction to Eva takes the form of a key turning in a door he had thought was solid wall. Rohan understands later that it is the power of what Leila did to him that allows him to react so reflexively to this new woman; or, as Eva might have explained to him, such a surge of data would have excited a channel of calcium-ion/phosphor links broad enough to red-flag the hippocampus, making it more likely the navigator would direct similar traffic down the same route. And in truth his interest in Eva is short-lived. Still, in the instant, the tensions in her face, the shadows in her cheeks, the darkness of eyes and hair that are like Leila and yet not—because these colors reveal more than they hide— trigger a response in him that is as basic and fine as the resistance that both bonds and separates dendrites.

Eva however stands very close to a stocky man with a broad moustache, dressed in stateless clothes and *campesino* sandals, whom Rohan will later learn is Frank Duggan. As Rohan observes her he becomes convinced that her emotions are not directed at the stocky man. She looks around, alert as a springbok, in much the same way Leila did. What is even more interesting, Frank also pays no attention to his companion; instead he seems to be interested in *Leila*.

To Rohan it seems at this moment that the circles of fantasy of these three people must be turning in on each other, like the shapes in a kaleidoscope, arc touching radius, cord matching arc.

The American wangles an introduction to Leila from Rohan, as if this were some kind of high-pressure convention that he could network like a salesman. Rohan nevertheless obliges. Leila looks at him like he has gone mad and says little to the American. Rohan, in turn, uses the backwash from that favor to meet the girl Frank Duggan was with.

Later, when he and Frank and Eva share a corner of the besieged ballroom, Rohan notices Eva and Leila together eyeing a tall, thin Castilian type with horn-rim glasses and sloth fingers and the expression of a man living nightmares or dyspepsia daily.

Julián.

Both women look at Julián with a shared intensity, of the kind that distinguishes lovers, and assassins.

Rohan refuses to acknowledge the implications of this.

However, Eva continues to tender him only the forthright smile of alliance, with none of the hoarded energies and slower movements of seduction, and Rohan resigns himself to what this finally has become: a Molière farce played in a different country with guns in lieu of calling cards and couches standing in for bedrooms and the threat of death standing over everything like a grim theatrical device, the way discovery and dishonor worked for Poquelin.

The background grows more jagged, of course; such concerns dim for all of them as discomfort occupies their bodies and their minds are stretched back and forth between physical fear and mind-freezing boredom. The taste of those days is familiar to Rohan because of a dig he worked on in Africa that was to some extent hampered by guerrilla actions. He remembers the uncertainty, the fear-hollowed gut, the feeling of being both irrelevant and a table stake in someone else's card game. As the physical parameters draw tighter, as the electricity is shut off and water is rationed, he begins to sense himself shrinking inward. It feels like everything, not just the lack of light, is a form of dark, forcing him to look inside his own body for the solutions that come out after sunset.

Leila senses this also. The third night she pads over to their corner and talks softly to him for an hour. When she walks off she beckons him and he follows her through the pools of candlelight. She enters the bar and slides behind one of the limestone idols, where a closet is concealed.

The heat inside is twice what it was in the ballroom. She is breathing hard and her voice catches in her throat. She lights one of those homemade lamps the rebels are using; they are sauce boats from the kitchen, full of cooking oil with strips of cotton dishrag serving as a wick. The sight of her loon's neck and dark hair falling over the thick gold glow of the lamp triggers a wave of passion in him. It is not a passion for Leila, or for her body even; it is a feeling for the lamps themselves, which he has seen in virtually the same form, sauce boat, wick and oil, in a Sumerian midden and the Cycladic wreck and a shrine in Samothrace and a shepherd's hut in Sicily. It is a fondness for the way women have always bent like this, with the nape hairs exposed as they brought light to cave or palace; it is for all the men, women and children who have watched their light make sense of the night surrounding. She pulls his clothes off as if hidden underneath were the solution to all the chest-scraping terror of what she is trying to do. In this they are halfway between dance and fight and the sweat is so great that they might as well be swimming. She bites his shoulder till it bruises, thrusting against the stacked brooms and mops until they tumble in a great clatter of household zinc, and cans of vicious chemicals splurt on the formica floor.

They lie amid the mops and cleansers. They grow high on spilled ammonium. Her eye-wrinkles bunch as she looks at him. She strokes him down like a racehorse, using the edges of her palms like the rubber currycombs stablehands employ. Her hands are clumsy and plump and she is embarrassed by them; *chuletas* she calls them, that first night. She says, "You know I am using you—to."

"*Como*," he asks.

"To equalize," she says, in the breath-short way she has, "the differences in me. Between what I need, and—and what must be."

He is only half listening. In the slack-tide of his own coming he thinks of his sister, who went into the law because of her love of argument and married a solicitor who is drowning her in the vast ocean of his inabilities.

Leila is gone the next night but at four in the morning the night after that Rohan feels her hand on his shoulder and follows her to the broom closet again. This time she brings no lamp. They are in too much demand elsewhere. They find their way only by touch. The great heat and darkness inside of her seems to fold back and forth with the vast heat and darkness without. They smell and gasp. The floor is slippery with their juices. In the shapes his mind must make to counteract the awful lack of form in this closet, as the nerve pleasure surges up his body and back into her like a tidal bore, he distinguishes, briefly, Nathalie's way of looking—and behind that, as always, the calm of her; the deep calm of her, when she was happy.

Leila lights a cigarette. The smoke smells like burning *garigue*.

But he did not give Leila even the grace of thought in coming and for an instant he feels like a compound of every cad and liar in every age of mind. And then she whispers, "*Donde por l'amor de Dios puede ser?*" and he knows he is not alone in this abandonment.

"Julián?" he asks, unnecessarily.

"*Si*," she tells him. Sex temporarily steals English from her. "*Fué mi marido*."

I wish I could love her, Rohan thinks. The force in her is too precious to waste like this. He wonders what could be so strong that Julián would abandon this woman for it. The revolution is an old, spasmed thing, like a broken lizard; surely he is not fooled.

Even though they can see nothing Rohan senses Leila looking at him with no feeling other than loss. The likelihood of more loss to come is a solid shape in the darkness between them.

forty-two

Running northeast under the ridge again, the train emerged only briefly from the tunnel darkness. The tracks followed the valley for a few kilometers after La Brussette. A short stretch of country grew ever more hilly, and vines were revealed to the left as they caught the southern sun. A pumping station, a church steeple. Then they plunged at higher speed into another tunnel, this one transecting the great hill of Chezy.

Those susceptible to darkness like Rohan barely had time to loosen the hooks of whatever darkness brought to mind before the same barbed association snagged them once more. Rohan settled a little in his seat, crossing his legs and hiding his crotch with prayerful hands. The exhale and inhale of pressure as the train pistoned air in the tunnels had set drafts ambling through the compartment. The disturbed air carried forth some of the smells that had been lying doggo in packaging.

Frank, pulling his collar tighter in reflex against the draft, recognized the same wraith of sausage that had touched his nostrils before. A number of memories had flowed through his brain since then; perhaps their passage had washed from his circuitry whatever stopped him making the connection earlier.

At any rate, this time he realized with no delay that the sausage he was smelling reminded him of linguiça; and this in turn activated in Frank's mind the sickeningly complex chain reaction of synapses linked with that particular smell.

forty-three

Rehoboth Street is all Irish and every kitchen is like that of his parents—which means "foreign foods," that is, anything more "weird" than beef, potatoes and peas, never gets an inch past their lintel except under the disguise of the *Gourmet* magazines his mother sneaks in from the library discard bin. "Portygee" food like linguiça is considered especially low status, so their kitchen never smells of wine or strong sausage or garlic, or anything much other than potato water and the kind of unhappiness that seldom gets rich enough to be interesting, but just incubates, like a weak virus, breaking out in patches of anger, the occasional slap; its vector boredom, its symptoms chronic.

Frank's father Eddie has started a business from scratch in Central Falls. He puts up vinyl siding on the wooden houses of those too sick, old or broke to deal with traditional clapboard or shingles. And he does well for a while. The vinyl is easy to work with; a little careful measurement, two days of pneumatic hammers and it's up—"final," as he likes to tell his customers. Final vinyl. There are thousands of Coolidge-era frame dwellings in the lower-middle-class suburbs around Providence. In the prosperity of the sixties Eddie Duggan covers square-miles worth of Rhode Island with his indestructible, impermeable, low-maintenance plastic product. He believes he is the top expert in Rhode Island in this field of home improvement. The cash from vinyl siding enables Clara Duggan to join a country club outside Providence that lets in Irish Catholics. She wears golf clothes. She possesses all the symbols needed to upgrade her social "standing" and this makes her smile secretly to herself.

In some ways the Duggans are the first victims of their own success. By the mid-seventies Eddie has run out of houses to vinylize in northeast Providence. Competition has shut off markets further afield. With interest rates going up like SAMs during and after the Asian war, loans taken out in times of plenty turn into paper shackles. Eddie has to sell the workshop. Clara hangs on to the country club for dear life but the members look at her crosswise. The strength with which Irene Duggan denies the reality of these changes is the only element of heroic proportions in that household.

The worst of it is, nobody is fooled. The Brown University types, the RISD artistes, the old-line WASPs whose elm-shaded Victorians encroach on the Falls from North Providence and Fairlawn, still term them "Townies" and "white trash." Jack, Frank's brother, goes to work on a tugboat at seventeen, mostly to flee the shame of her pretence. Frank, at fourteen, cannot do the same. Instead he joins the Aces.

The Aces run the Central Falls waterfront, or the part of it, anyway, between Third Street and Hobart, if you can call it a waterfront since the "water" consists entirely of the delta of a thin river lined with decaying mills and so polluted by PCBs and polymer by-products from what industry is left that on warm days it bubbles like the first scene from *MacBeth*—if you can call it "run" given competition from the black gangs of Mill River and the Italian gangs from Federal Hill and the interventions of cherry-topped cruisers and the difficulties anyhow of enforcing a protection racket in illegal fireworks, dirty comics, and the nickel-bag trade in Connecticut Valley dope.

Recruitment to the Aces is easy. You have to be Irish or non-Italian Catholic anyway and swallow a raw egg and say "motherfucker" a lot. You should participate in the fights with the 31st Street Wolverines and the Guinea Posse but that involves chains and iron bars and even shivs. Frank hangs around a couple of the fights but something in him is not ready to cross that line. He sees an Ace slashed with a broken bottle; the blood dripping on the black road looks to him both beautiful in its color and repulsive in its volume. Perhaps the first step toward desperado status is recognizing that he is only a bag of liquids like the rest.

The night of that fight he sits by the electric plant and watches an egret stand in a pool of opal water. The egret is streaked with tar and too ill to move. Frank feels, for the bird, for himself, both pity and contempt.

The Aces are OK. They don't call him sissy because he doesn't fight; he is too young for the knives, they say. A stability exists in their codes and passwords that he does not enjoy at home or school.

He meets a couple of girls, twins, who are his age and in his grade and who hang around with the Aces the way he does. Their names are Amy and Sue Halloran. They are skinny tomboys with orange hair and a uniform of grimy T-shirts, jeans and sneakers that they never take off, even in sleep. They have short, retroussé noses—the kind that Frank, even at thirteen, knows he likes. Amy and Sue attend the gangfights and holler like cheerleaders and run like greyhounds. Frank and the twins go to the abandoned freightyards with the Hallorans' obese dog, whose name is "Dog," to sit and smoke cigarettes and sometimes dope; or drink Narragansett ale, the cheapest available, hidden by ragweed and cattails and a hundred defunct dishwashers.

The twins are already planning a life of outlaw action. They shoplift everything, from pork roasts to radios. Dog steals fruit from Italian vendors. But the greatest coup of all is the Great Entenmann's Heist, planned by the twins and carried out with all the icy competence (it seems to Frank) of the Doc Baldwin character in *The Getaway*. They study the driver's routine, how he leaves the engine idling when he sleazes a cup of joe behind the Stop & Shop. They practice driving a similar truck owned by a contractor Eddie works with.

One morning Amy and Frank creep up in the truck's lee while the driver is scoring coffee, and drive off. They meet Sue near the tracks, shove two-thirds of the cargo overboard, then drive a mile into Rehoboth and ditch the vehicle. The Danish pecan rings, the raspberry twirl coffee cakes, the coconut custard pies, the fudge marshmallow angel-food cakes, the boxes of "rich frosted" doughnuts and chocolate chip cookies are humped to their hideout in the ragweed. After that day and for the rest of his life Frank will never again be able to eat raspberry twirl.

Two months after he meets them the twins lead him to their house, a shabby place apparently held upright by its sixties-era vinyl siding, the brash growth of vines and ivy, and a tight ring of junked cars around the walls. Both porch-light and TV are perpetually lit. Their father is long gone and their mother, the twins say, is "weird." They live with an uncle they call "Chink" who was shell-shocked in Korea. The rest of the household is made up of Dog, and three brothers: Lou, Sam, and a boy known for some reason only as Bendix. The one thing that really interests the brothers is topping each other at a scatological sport they call "gross-out." Their language in its descriptive power is beyond Frank's ken. In the first week he sees Lou shit into a canteen on the living room floor and Bendix trick Sam into drinking piss from a jug of Gallo as Lou screams happily, "Yer the cunt! Yer the cunt!" Bendix collects large water snakes that often take refuge in the toilet, to the astonishment of the casual crapper.

Mrs. Halloran, on meeting Frank, accuses him of sleeping with Amy. She is certain half of Rhode Island is fucking the twins. On two separate occasions she chases Frank around the house with a can of E-Z Off. Bendix advises him not to take it personally; any male visitor is apt to incur this treatment. Oven-cleaning spray is Mrs. Halloran's first line of defense, and her last.

Her accusation is not, at that point, justified.

Mrs. Halloran is Portuguese and likes to make big stews full of mussels and spicy sausage and wine. Everyone drinks Narragansett and swears and argues like they are just about to pull flick-knives. Frank acquires a taste for linguiça. After a while he spends more of his waking time at their house than at home or school.

One day the twins suggest they "say hi" to Carbo next door. That is the first time he visits the House of a Thousand Rooms. Amy and Sue make fun of the old man and Frank goes along with that a little but really he is attracted to the Moses beard, the jay-blue eyes and the red woollen cap Carbo wears at all hours. Carbo is building a new room in the north tower. He offers Frank a pneumatic hammer and this presents a problem since Frank and the twins are by unspoken principle opposed to work; but Frank later makes the argument that since the House of a Thousand Rooms is by its nature and the by-laws of Central Falls illegal it should be exempt from their gangbangers' boycott.

The thing is, Carbo *shows* Frank how to use the hammer, and the power jig, tablesaw, and mitre box, and this is more than Eddie Duggan ever did. He lets Frank make a wall of any colors or shapes he wants. And, in his own queer way, he is interesting. He tells stories—not well, they are often rambling, disconnected, out of sequence, but he relates them with a spit-spraying, arm-waving gusto, a commitment and an attention to odd detail that prove, to Frank anyway, that he has really done the things he says he did. Carbo claims he helped erect the George Washington Bridge in New York City. He was torpedoed by a U-boat on a grain ship near the Arctic Circle, he helped dig the Fleet Line underground in

London, he mashed grapes with his bare feet near Bordeaux and manned pickets in the rubberworkers' strike in Akron. He knows the history of the places he went and when he forgets he goes down to what he calls the "book room" and looks up details. Years later Frank will start to spot holes in the continuity of some of these tales but the important thing remains that whether Carbo was there or not he *checked the facts.*

Forever after Frank will have a real respect for the ore you can mine from a reference book.

Frank spends more time at Carbo's now than at the Hallorans', and one day Carbo, in his lilting accent, tells him "I am getting in trouble because of you."

"How come?" Frank asks.

"You don't learn nothin'. Your school finds out—" Carbo draws a finger across his throat. "I can't make you go to school more," he continues, "but you sure as hell gotta study, you vant to stay here."

This is not funny. Frank hesitates, then, queazy at the thought of having to sit in class instead, agrees to try it. Carbo gets hold of the course list and chooses what he knows: mainly, in school terms, social studies. Frank's gut sinks. They talk over this stuff while they work on Frank's airplane room, the first project Frank has been allowed to design himself. Frank is bored half the time but otherwise the way Carbo has of tying in this arid material to what he has seen, and discarding the rest, makes it come to life somewhat.

More important, perhaps, is the fact that Carbo is a committed Union man, and his vision of a country divided into bosses and workers, outdated though it might be, taps into an anger in Frank that had remained up to this point inchoate and sapping.

Thus does Frank, now fifteen, begin vaguely to discern a pattern in the world around him. Tutored by Carbo he suffers the illusion that he understands how power works; how, in Rhode Island specifically, Quaker tolerance gave way to the tyranny of Yankee millowners, who fought to keep out Catholic immigrants. And after Dorr's rebellion those same immigrants, people like Councilman Moncenigo and Mayor Cianci, gained control of the throttles of power and simply took over where the Yankees left off. Or that, at least, is how Frank understands things. Always the new poor getting fucked by the previous.

It is many years before Frank realizes that Carbo, the Union man, was using Frank as unpaid labor as he turned his house into a curiosity he could show for money.

Anyway, at this stage, Frank stops reading the spy thrillers he once enjoyed. As a matter of fact, he stops reading all books that do not directly address what he sees as the "political dynamics" of the situation.

It would be foolish and untrue to say that all this is a substitute for education. When the truant officer finally catches up and screws Frank to higher attendance levels he lags badly in most subjects. But the social studies teacher, who counts the day a success if most of her class doesn't fall asleep, is pleased by his relative interest. She too is Union, Albert Shanker variety. She makes the effort of recommending Frank for a summer job at the Community Action Campaign, working to organize low-income tenants against the buy-out of neighborhoods by speculators.

One night that summer Frank drags Carbo to the Hallorans' kitchen. Dog farting fruitily under the table. Lou and Bendix of course try to gross Carbo out and make him drink dog-piss Chablis. Bendix feeds live mice to the rock python wound around his waist. Mrs. Halloran glares at Carbo, absentmindedly fingering the E-Z Off.

Carbo sits gravely and nods and treats Chink with great politeness even after Sam makes Chink scream by howling "incoming!" and setting off an M-80 under his chair. They eat boiled dinner. Frank after four Narries starts to unveil his theories as to how the bosses control The Prov and how he wants to change it somehow. Of course Bendix and Lou taunt him but to Frank it does not seem that they attack with their usual lack of mercy and he feels good, sure of something in him that will not be swayed. More than that: he is excited by the surge of life in his gut and groin, by the gleeful slamming of his heart, in the possibilities he is beginning to sense, even here in Central Falls that usually is defined by its crumbling chimneys, its locked community halls.

Another night a few months later, he walks over to Carbo's. A pair of not-very-clean long johns flaps from the east-wing pole. The neighbors are seeking an injunction against the junk in the yard and the subcode additions. The Hallorans have legal difficulties as well; Bendix is up for armed robbery after walking into the Roger Williams Club with a live rattlesnake and demanding jewelry from the guests.

Carbo takes Frank to the basement. "Dey von't let me use my yard," he says proudly. "Let me show you something."

Carbo has sunk a shaft fifteen feet down into the clay. From there, using a jackhammer, he has dug an adit, horizontally, forty feet to the south. The tunnel is ventilated by stovepipe and fans and shored by thick timbers scrounged from the electricity plant wharf. A Jabco bilge pump takes care of seepage. "Already," Carbo says with satisfaction, "I am twenty feet past de neighbor's line." And he starts laughing, his face going red as lingonberries from hypertension and drink. And Frank starts chuckling too, thinking one day Carbo will tunnel his way right under City Hall; and they hang on to the damp tarred supports and shout from the vigor, the daring, the sheer fuck-you power of this bandit brilliance while the politicos bargain and speculators deal and the good, proper citizens of Central Falls snooze on either side of them, sated, insensate, deaf to the Saturnic anarchy going on beneath their very feet.

forty-four

You checked your watch for the fifteenth time and found at last it was time to go.

You bent low over the cheap suitcase so as to gain a good perspective of the alarm clock. You felt with your fingers for the stem on the clock's back panel that set the time. The knurled brass knob twisted hard. This was good because you did not want it to swing wildly. You turned it in very gentle fashion, using index finger and thumb. The hour hand moved back across the metal face a fraction of a millimeter.

You took a breath. In these circumstances sometimes you had to remind your lungs to work. If the hand moved too far, skipping the difference in time, and made contact with the wire sticking through the protective plastic; if for some reason the wire had kinked and touched the metal face; if it even got just a tiny bit too close to the metal and shorted out with the ground—

You did not think about that. You were a technician, you took precautions, these things would not happen. You always set the time after wiring up; it was the only way to make sure the connections were secure. You dried your face with a corner of cotton shirt and slowly, even tenderly, set the hour hand to the current time, as exactly as you could given that you had no minute hand to fine-tune with. 12:55. That left forty-eight minutes till detonation, with perhaps three minutes' margin either way.

Nothing happened. Cars rushed by, a pigeon cooed. The wires were tight. You closed the suitcase, locked the hasps, and set it upright.

Now you went to the telephone and punched in the number you had been given. The other end picked up on the second ring. You could hear traffic loud over the wires. The voice gave you the necessary confirmation—time, place, sequence—and then the client hung up.

You stowed your tools, hung the kit bag on one shoulder. Picked up the suitcase with your other hand, and left the apartment. Only once you had locked the door did you take off the latex gloves and put them in your pocket. Walking carefully, making very sure you did not bump or jostle the suitcase, you found the rented car, delicately placed the case on the passenger seat, and got in.

Luckily these medium-sized towns outside the snow regions of northern Europe had smooth roads. You drove with care, braked gently, and parked in the station forecourt. You picked up the suitcase and bought a round-trip ticket to the next town. You checked the arrivals panel and walked out to platform number one. It was a bright clear day and the dry air seemed to deepen the gravid silence of a station waiting for a train. A thin man dressed in work clothes stood and fiercely watched the big station clock. You noted the composition of the train on the relevant panel and sat down on a bench under a small marble plaque that read "*À la mémoire des Agents de la SNCF Tués par Faits de Guerre.*" A metal pin held a fresh tricolor ribbon and spray of purple foxglove.

You wedged the suitcase carefully between your legs, and waited.

forty-five

On a diminishing six-eighths beat the train left the loom of hill and followed a wide valley opening to the northeast. A field of sunflowers bled cadmium, blooms opening south and west in the early afternoon sun. A pastry of imperial architecture came into view on more-distant high ground to the left, stubbing the horizon with columns and pediments. "It's a monument," Rohan told Frank and Eva without much interest, "Côte 204. There was a lot of fighting here in the 'fourteen-'eighteen war." The train slowed further as they passed silos and warehouses. The carriages came to a series of individual stops based on differently worn brakes. "Château Thierry," the station tannoy called, *"une minute d'arrêt."*

In the shock of silence they looked out the window at a station like a thousand others in France. Laval-era ticket offices and waiting rooms, built of brick. The "Hôtel de la Gare," the "Bar *Le Terminus* Tabac," an arch of Bastille Day ribbons. A man kissed a girl goodbye and handed up a string bag of leeks to her window. A dumpy woman with the almond-colored face and black clothes of Iberia fluttered like a bird on the platform until she realized this was not the train to Paris. Eva said to Rohan, "You didn't keep in touch with Leila, did you? After the hotel."

Rohan's face snapped toward her. His hands opened and closed.

"Why do you ask?"

"Because—" Eva pulled one bracelet free of another on her left wrist. "Oh, you were—close, no?"

Rohan stared at her. Frank picked a piece of *forrás*-paprika chicken from a package on the seat next to Eva, and took a small bite to disguise his interest.

"In a way, yes. In a way, well, I didn't know her at all," Rohan answered finally.

"Oh, come on," Frank said.

Rohan turned to face him, his hands taut now.

"You had something going on, you two," Frank continued.

"What does that mean? 'Something going on'? 'Close'? What are you trying to say?"

"It doesn't mean anything, Ludo," Eva said, seeking to mitigate the odd emotion in him. "I was just asking."

"She was a stranger to me," Rohan said after a pause, speaking to Frank, "ah, in all the important ways."

"So you didn't keep in touch," Frank said, "to answer the question."

"Why do I feel," Rohan asked, composing on his face the same monkey-code grin he had used in the Gare de l'Est to indicate this all remained on the level of talk instead of fight, but the color of his eyes had changed like coast water deepening to serious sea, "why do I feel almost like I am being accused of something here?"

Frank chewed slowly, though he had already swallowed his piece of chicken. A fleck of *forrás* was caught in his teeth and he sucked at it. Eva looked hard in his direction, then smiled at Rohan.

"It's OK," she said, "even if you cared about someone, how could you keep in touch? Under those circumstances."

"I wasn't accusing you," Frank said. "It's just—"

"It's just that *you* liked her," Rohan finished the sentence. "Didn't you? You fancied her. That whole time. There is nothing wrong with it—"

"Huh." Frank flicked his moustache to dispose of any remaining pieces of chicken or pastry. "Interesting you should say that."

"I remember, Frank," Eva put in. "I remember the way you looked at her."

"Yes," Frank admitted, "I thought she was lovely, and I thought she had guts. I mean, I would have tried to find out what happened to her, if it had been me."

"It *was* you," Rohan said. "You were there also. You could have tried to find out."

"*I* didn't sleep with her."

"Is that the only responsibility?" Rohan leaned forward. "What, the obligation of sex? The debt of semen? You seem very old-fashioned to me, Frank."

The loudspeaker crackled. A conductor sounded his whistle. Eva, looking out the window, began to hum, a lilting air full of the arpeggios and catches of flamenco. Though soft, it came clearly through the thinned air of expectation and departure.

The train jolted, gently. The bar/tabac, the station buildings, pink roses in a raised bed by the parking lot, began to slide past their window with the strange, heliocentric smoothness that caused passengers to think it was the world around them moving instead of the train.

"Remember that?" Eva asked quietly, "Remember that song?" She hummed again, seven notes.

The two men looked at her with expressions of disengagement. Rohan's left hand touched through his shirt the ring that hung on a chain inside.

"It was what she was playing," Eva explained, "the Dutch woman, the one who played guitar. Remember that recital, the night before the Gardia moved in? This was the last song she played."

"How can you remember that?" Frank's eyes had thinned to slits. "It was twelve years ago, you can't remember that detail."

"It's Spanish," Rohan said, "or South American or something."

"It's Manuel Ponce," Eva told him, smiling a little in her confidence. "Mexican."

"But I seem to remember," Rohan objected, "I thought she played European music, I mean Northern European. She played things like Purcell, Ravenscroft, I'm not sure they were that but I know she played only Renaissance things. I was surprised, well, my memory is not that great but I remember, I thought exactly that; she should play Spanish music, because of where we were."

"It was the only Hispanic piece," Eva countered softly. "Maybe you forgot. But I remember she began it with that radio playing 'The Revolution Show,' oh, the Spanish voices. Rebel radio."

"Maybe you got that wrong, Eva."

She shook her head.

"Not you? You can't forget?"

"I have an eidetic memory," she replied, "I forget almost nothing. Sometimes I wish I could forget more. Memory is supposed to work like that," she continued, hiking up a side of her blouse that had got wound up in her gestures; "not to remember because, oh, you would remember everything, too much; but to carve out the important details, like a sculptor chisels off most of the clay" (she glanced at Rohan) "to make an image of what you saw. That is what I don't do. I think I wish I could."

"What would you forget," Rohan asked, "if you had the choice?"

She did not reply at once. Her face muscles did not move but it seemed as if they did. The fingers of her right hand rose and fell, rose and fell; sequentially, just this side of perception, to a three-four beat.

"Things that hurt," she answered at last, "of course. It would be easier if you could forget the things that hurt."

"You would lose most of history," Rohan said.

"You would lose most of life," Frank agreed.

"I know," Eva said. "But when life hurts, oh, you want it to stop. The hurt, I mean. Don't you think?"

She turned to look out the window, then pressed her forehead against the safety glass.

forty-six

Unbridled pain, as Eva suggested, is something she remembers all too well. Even in the relativity of dysfunction in other parts of the body it lives unscreened in her Penfield areas and associated neural networks, beautifully organized and triangulated, every sequence and line-of-position worked out and programmed so that when the catalyst comes up, the code for "most pain," the hippocampus clicks in the relevant coordinates and she finds herself in the Cirque von Andau once more.

Those gears and wheels already greased, of course, by of the proximity of her last swing through these synaptic pathways.

They are in Kitzbühel, a third through the circus's route, and Eva by now has got used to the life of the road. Actually she has never felt happier. This, she later supposes—given the law of averages—must in itself constitute a warning.

She has subscribed fully to the myth of the circus, the illusion that this little world can exist sufficient unto itself. Its politics and society are hers entire, she runs her life by their sway and flux. She follows, in an organic way, the feuds and pacts of the tentmen, split as tradition dictates between Rhinelanders and Bohemian Czechs. The Germans struggle to get the left side of the tent up before the Czechs can erect the right; each set-up and strike triggers a European war in miniature. She tracks the screaming matches between Fredi, the Pole, and Haleytey, the Ukrainian Sioux, or between Fredi and Madame von Andau—to whom he once, in a fit of vodka, got married. Above all she studies Madame herself, whose fugues and passions form the strong isotherm of this facsimile planet.

Madame is bitchy and mean and remembers literally every forint in and pfennig out. Along with Fredi, Madame also lives with Kurt, a tame jackdaw who is her real mate. The bird, croaking Plattdeutsch, adopts attitudes of couvade and territorial defense against the hapless clown. Kurt tries to feed Madame worms, and she laughs. Madame resembles Pablo Picasso in his sunset years. She wears a tigerskin scarf and tinted glasses. Her laughter sounds like a drain choking.

Eva has cobbled together a clown routine. She set it up according to the precepts of Belov, of the Moscow Circus, by creating a character for herself. His name is "Pipa." He is curious and clumsy, alternately shy and tight with bravado. She makes up a whole history to explain this odd behavior. He wears oversize corduroys and a top hat stuffed with cotton-wool and alcohol that periodically bursts into flames. Fredi allows her the entr'acte, it gives him time to get a start on his drinking. On her first night the trick car she relies on as a prop malfunctions and she has to improvise. She waddles up to the bandleader's microphone and mimes a passionate speech, pretending not to notice the mike is turned off. When she does notice she walks around the equipment, getting her feet tangled in the wire. And so on. Pipa does not bring the house down but there are no catcalls, at least.

The first sign of grave change comes in the aftermath of the accident. Tamas's arm heals fast but presumably because of the blow to his head he remains subject to frequent migraines. His moods alter without warning or pattern. He is often irritable and sometimes flies into flash rages that make the horses skittish. Hansi, the circus's ad hoc vet and, by extension, medic, forbids Tamas to ride. However as soon as his arm is sufficiently healed Tamas goes back into the ring. Hansi thinks his balance centers have been affected. Others believe he has lost his nerve. At any rate Tamas starts to fall off quite often and his headaches increase in severity with every fall, to the point where even he decides to call it quits for a while. Haleytey takes over the horse act but her skills are minimal and she is sometimes booed, and when this happens the tentmen square off, and Fredi and Madame, Eva and Tamas, quarrel separately, deep into the night.

Eva takes over Haleytey's rocket-girl act. It burns every gram of courage she possesses the first time she lets herself slide down the barrel of the rolled-metal "cannon" — compressed air hissing from leaky gaskets. She is wearing sweatpants and a T-shirt because no one has told her different. "You keep your knees locked, your back straight," Haleytey reminds her in urgent Russian. With a sick-making jolt the charge is triggered. Eva's ears ring as the shock wave hits her. She is shot fifty feet through the air in an ungraceful arc, arms and legs flailing wildly—and lands in a net that has been greatly widened to allow for problems. She looks up, grinning in relief, to find Haleytey and half the circus rolling on the tanbark. For she is sitting stark naked in the net, her sweats, shirt and underwear torn off by the force of compression and the barrel's friction.

She wears a leotard from then on. After the seventh or eighth time Eva starts to get the hang of it. She gets hooked on the crash of applause when she shoots from the cannon's mouth at sixty kilometers per hour; she never loses her panicked thrill at the surge and feel of flying, albeit briefly, kids' faces opening like wildflowers below, and always the sharp wonder: will the net materialize under her at the end? She is still young and dying remains an abstraction.

But what is happening to the circus is no abstraction. The loss of Tamas, temporary though it may be, hurts the gate and lowers morale. Also—and this has been happening over several years already—audiences are declining generally. It may be due to the spread of television which, providing bread and circus on the small screen, lowers the motivation to go and seek it out for real. Whatever the reason this year's attendance was down even before the loss of Tamas, and the year before the gate was low relative to the preceding year. In Altkirch, Radetski, who never got over his hurt at Tamas's affair with Eva, quits, taking with him the Kazakh stallion and the three other horses he owns. Hansi, whose medical role sometimes includes that of psychologist, sits with his bear trying to comfort Tamas, who is wound up in a cycle of deepening despair. "*Sei rühig, Bub'*," he counsels, his Falstaff features wrung in empathy, tapping Tamas's knee with one finger while the old bear scratches and goes through Eva's pockets. "Be calm. Everything can get better."

Like a Polar explorer expending vital supplies in the gamble that she will find a cache at the end of her run, Madame von Andau pushes harder and farther than ever but her cash reserves are almost gone and fuel and food grow ever dearer. They cross the Spanish frontier for the first time in the troupe's history.

In Badalona, after a particularly disappointing performance, she calls everyone together and tells them the circus is breaking up.

At the farewell party the following night Fredi weeps without pause except to drink. Tamas brings his last horses into the tent and mutters to them all evening, his hands wound tightly in their white manes. Eva serves *paprikacsirke* to Bohemians and Rhinelanders who embrace openly, feuds lost in the greater damage. Kurt the jackdaw whistles his repertoire of boos and catcalls, his insults in a dozen dialects.

The next day the people trail off, leaving their animals to be sold if, as is the case with Tamas's horses, they belong to the circus. Like most of the animal acts he and Eva have spent their little money on vets more qualified than Hansi and they possess nowhere near enough for a train ticket home. They team up with Hansi and Bobo, who are similarly skint. When Eva leaves the stable square, the old bear shambling along in her wake, she feels like she is part of a handsome but tragically flawed race that is going into exile and will soon be extinct.

Paradoxically the first part of their trip north is pleasurable; and maybe this is the hallmark of real tragedy, that it be framed in the what might have been, the well-worked, the sound. This autumn is a gentle one. As the toasted plains of Catalonia give way to the foothills of the Pyrénées, Hansi and Bobo, Tamas and Eva are washed in a clear warm light that feels like a promise of redemption. They are offered rides on farm trucks, the drivers gurning like fools in the rearview to watch the bear sitting on the flatbed with the wind combing back his gray whiskers. They walk a great deal. Tamas's headaches slowly dwindle. In villages like San Agustin de Llusanas and Alpens they enter alone but by the time they reach the other side lead a procession of the curious and more often than not are given tortillas and a place to sleep, a hayloft or a stable, partly in thanks for the mini-circus they have offered the place, partly because in the villagers' subconscious they are reenacting a Middle Eastern folk tale with Eva and Tamas playing the parents, Bobo the miracle infant and Hansi, perhaps, filling the role of a Balthazar or Melchior. In bigger towns Bobo executes slow somersaults or clumsily waltzes with Hansi to bring in extra cash. In Ripoll they buy tickets for the French frontier on a train so ancient and creaking and used to livestock that no one thinks to evict Bobo or even complain as the bear goes through the conductor's pockets, scattering torn stubs like snow over the wooden floor. "*Mira el osso,*" the passengers yell, or "*Olé!*" as at a bullfight. The peaks of the Pyrénées rise somber, trailing freeze-dried flags of truce.

In France the conductors are stricter, the truck rides less frequent. They grow tired. To top it all the weather turns cool. Sleeping in a meadow near Lombers, sandwiched for warmth between her skinny, restless lover on one side, and the snoring brown bear and his fat old man on the other, woken up by bites from the fleas all four now share, Eva looks up and sees the sky whirling in a familiar manner over the spearpoints of cypress, stars tracing patterns on the woman-forms of the Tarn hills. In this land Cro-Magnon drew petroglyphs of the Great Bear, under this sky Van Gogh went mad. In these hills Tamas and Eva quarrel with ever increasing bitterness and frequency. They walk back-roads, keeping Big Dipper over left collarbone, heading north and east. Hansi, who reads astronomy columns in newspapers, claims this direction is illusory in the big picture since the earth, and the galaxy it inhabits, are headed in a separate trajectory, toward a spot somewhere between the constellations of Hercules and Lyra; but Tamas and Eva do not care about the big picture at this stage and apparent directions remain important to them.

After three days of rain Bobo starts to breathe hard. His snout is hot and dry, his fur perpetually damp. He eats less and less. Hansi tries to see a vet and is threatened with jail for owning a dangerous animal. He sits behind a hedge, cradling the huge bear as if he were a puppy, crooning to him in German, trying to get Bobo to eat the herbs and berries he has gathered to make him well again. The bear looks around with his child eyes and puts his paw gently on Hansi's head.

They are in the Loire valley, near Roanne, when Bobo dies. Hansi continues to hold him, lying next to the bear, his white hair mingled in the brown fur, trying to keep the animal's body warmth up with his own. Tamas sits beside Hansi, his good hand clutching Bobo's ruff. Eva hugs the old man and cries so hard she feels like she is turning inside out. Dimly she is aware that as in all grief she mourns not only the death of a single love but what that represents for love everywhere; for creatures past and as yet unborn. She mourns what is happening between herself and Tamas because although her conscious brain has not yet accepted it already she can sense in them that shift in the period of inner swells, the change in tides that will force them apart. She mourns the death of the circus and the community it sheltered; she grieves because the imagination of children in smaller towns will be deprived of its wondrous animals; she grieves for herself as a child, for the children she and Tamas will never have. She stops crying only when her strength is finally gone.

They leave Hansi in Roanne. Eva has decided to go to Paris. Her sister lives there, married to a French-American, working in computer programming. Tamas accompanies her, by default, for he can think of nowhere that he could both afford and desire. Anna accepts them both and loans them what cash she can. Within two months Eva, revived by the pulse of a great city, has got a job *au noir*, under the table. By Christmas she has enrolled in medical school. She knows, in a corner of her, that this is in some fashion a direct effect of her sobbing with Hansi and Tamas over the body of a clapped-out circus bear.

Tamas knows only horses and there is no horse work to be had. He adopts as his own the hackneyed spiral of drink, and anger, and more drink. When he has slapped Eva around two nights running Anna orders him to leave and Eva lets him go. Eva continues to see him outside the flat but days, then weeks, go by when she has no contact with him at all.

She is at a party when the call comes in: Hansi has been discovered, still in Roanne, dead on the banks of the river. The cops found Anna's number in his pocket. She tries unsuccessfully to get in touch with Tamas. On this occasion he is out of touch for three weeks.

Her sadness is less agonizing than before. Already the circus has faded. Despite her memory for detail, its colors and dances have gone slightly less sharp than even a few weeks ago.

She sends money for Hansi's burial but cannot attend herself, because of work.

Still it is years before she can think of the circus without feeling an echo of pain in her chest, and longer than that before she can listen to the overture to *Der Zigeunerbaron* without her throat knotting. And she will never be happy if bears are around, on television or in books, or in any form at all.

forty-seven

The German attack in Champagne slows as the sun of July 15 passes overhead. East of Reims the German Third Army takes severe punishment from well-sheltered French artillery.

The American 38th Infantry Division, dug into cornfields by the railway line in Les Evaux, puts up a game resistance.

The sixteen-year-old private who earlier had trouble aiming by this time has shot at a round dozen gray-uniformed Prussian grenadiers and seen four of them drop. Yet the Germans keep coming. A 105 cm shell explodes twenty yards to his left and the hellish concussion bounces three of his messmates into silence and immobility. A lieutenant from Attleboro—this is largely a New England regiment—yells "At 'em now!" and the private, proud of his increasing lethality, fooled by his hundred-percent record in breathing thus far, follows the line of men advancing toward a German machine-gun position near the southern bank of the Marne.

The machine gun the Germans use is an Austro-Hungarian Maxim-Nordenfeldt recently released from the Eastern Front. It was originally sold to the Imperial Army by a British arms merchant named Basil Zaharoff. The private barely hears the Maxim rattle before he is knocked flat by what feels like two pile-driver blows to his chest. He tries to get up but finds he lacks both energy and interest. He is surprised that the smell of loam and maize still exists amid all this dying, that the blue of the sky is so like the sky in Rhode Island, and he dies quickly amid that wonderment.

At 4:45 P.M. Pétain once more asks Foch to postpone Mangin's flanking attack but the allied commander refuses to yield. At 5 P.M. Gourand announces that the line east of Reims has held. The French Sixth Army has stopped the enemy near Château Thierry and reports from the Fifth Army indicate the Germans are flagging.

At the headquarters of the German forces, Luddendorf is beginning to feel anxious. He calls off the action for that day with an order to resume the following dawn. Kronprinz Wilhelm is even more nervous and he restricts the attack to two army corps only. July 16 passes in ragged though lethal back-and-forth skirmishes that do not alter the line much.

In the meantime Mangin's Tenth Army has been moving quietly into position in and around the forest of Villers-Coteret. His troops include units of the Foreign Legion, the

U.S. Fifth Marines, and a regiment of French mounted dragoons. More importantly, as it turns out, the Tenth will move into action with the support of several hundred tanks. It has started raining heavily. At 4:35 A.M. on July 18 allied artillery lets loose a barrage on the western flank of the Kronprinz's army and Mangin's men advance eastward. A stretcher bearer named Teilhard de Chardin later writes of the battle: "On all sides great bursts of smoke appeared, white, black, dirty-gray in the air and on the ground. Over all this there rose the sound of a continuous light crackling and it was a shock to see among the ripening crops little blotches that lay still forever. Here and there a tank slowly made its way through the tall corn followed by a group of supporters like a ship sailing through seas."

The twenty-four allied divisions driving from the north push back the eleven German divisions like a train bunting a truck off a level crossing. The Kronprinz, seeing his troops heavily pressed along his right flank, orders, first, resistance on a northwest-southeast line between Château Thierry and Soissons; then evacuation of the Marne bridgehead. Hindenburg suggests a counterattack on Mangin's flank but Luddendorf, who is drawing heavily on reserves, refuses. Twelve German divisions by now have been knocked out or heavily damaged. Luddendorf already is doing what he aimed to force the French to do; that is, call in fresh troops from the Flanders front.

forty-eight

Around Blesmes one of the great fluffy central France clouds that seemed made to conceal armies of Renaissance putti, nymphs and centaurs slipped its vapor shim under the edge of sun. The land trundling by alongside the train darkened in tone, the way an embarrassed woman blushes—not fast, but deeply.

Rohan saw this happen out the train window and felt the usual microscopic drop in spirits he always associated with an overcast in central France. At this stage the effect on him was light and nonspecific. Because he had trained himself to fight this effect, even at its most innocuous, he took the opportunity to get to his feet and take his doctor's satchel back off the luggage rack.

"I almost forgot—I brought something," he grunted, "as well."

Frank squinted at the satchel. Eva asked "What did you bring?" with no great interest, and folded her lips inward as if to smoothe her lipstick. Some of the clear lines in her face were no heavier than usual but they seemed to have tightened, the fields of force they represented grown more active.

"Duck paté." Rohan picked the items out of his bag. "Spanish sausage, it's hot: *choriço*. Bread, of course, no Parisian can eat without bread, this is *pain brioché* from Boulangerie Monge, the best. And Cendré des Riceys cheese." He smelled it appreciatively. "This one is perfect." He unfolded the copy of *Le Monde* Eva had been reading and laid the items upon the paper. Grease made the newsprint transparent. An article announcing lesser reporting requirements for large EC firms became one with a boxed feature on anti-immigrant riots carried out by neo-Nazis in Lyon.

Frank leaned over to sniff at the *choriço* but he did not eat, nor did Eva. Rohan sat down and looked out the window once more. The train ran parallel to a ridge. The topsoil had been eroded off the ridge's crest, exposing the chalk beneath so that from this perspective it looked like a distant mountain chain with snow on the peaks of it. Underneath, and closer, a twelfth-century church tower reached its anguish to the sky. Before that, a white horse stood quite still in a field of light-yellow grass.

Rohan looked at the horse.

The horse, impassive, watched the train.

Everything else was different, wrong, but that combination was so specific in Rohan's mind that whenever he saw it he would always remember, consciously or no, one field in a particular place and that place would always be Samothrace.

forty-nine

Blowing on the southern flank of the Fengari Oros the Sirocco wind carries a long riff of humidity sucked up on its passage through the Mediterranean and dumps it, not in the form of rain but in spits and curls of clouds combined with thin bars of sunlight hanging off the ochre peaks of the island.

Rohan hikes with Marie up the dirt track from the road leading from Kareomatissa to the principal Hellenic ruins at Palaeopolis. In early December this rack of rock in the northernmost corner of the Aegean is not warm. Climbing around a wedge of olive grove they come upon a small field of winter rye carved from the igneous soil. In the middle of it a horse of pure ivory stands cropping the stalks. The wheat is thin and meager and so is the horse, but one of the bars of sun chooses this moment to roll across the field and in the grace of that coincidence the horse raises its head and it looks like a creature of legend, noble strong Pegasus, and the grass appears to have been spun by some chtonic smith from paillettes of cleanest bronze.

Both Rohan and Marie stop in their tracks and watch till the sun is gone and the animal, thin nag once more with fetlocks and tail yellowed by its own manure, goes back to grazing the outlaw corn.

Higher up they tread the ruins of the ancient shrine.

They came to this isolated island in an unfashionable season ostensibly because Rohan had research to finish here but really in order to decide what to conclude or shape from their growing indifference to each other. It has become clear rather quickly that, not only will the research Rohan is doing never be published, but the setting of targets for their relationship has inexorably defined the limits rather than the possibilities thereof. They sleep in the house of the mayor of Kareomatissa and come up here to quarrel, or lament; a tiny, encapsulated tragedy among these rocks from which Zeus was said to observe the fall of Troy.

"I think I've decided," Marie says, drawing a shawl close around her head. "I'm going to take the job with George Bass, in Kos."

"It's a good offer."

"I'd work with you, Ludo. If you came up with something."

"It would be better not. We agreed. Besides, well, George is the best."

Rohan is kind, understanding, rational. It makes them both want to scream.

The ancient shrine of Samothrace was built along two streams running southeast down a ravine to what was then the shore. It once must have been a graceful glade shining with marble and neat groves of olive and orange blossom. Now the hairy growth of garigue as well as cypress, rogue olive, and wild mint have crept up on the broken walls and columns of the temples. Under this gray autumn sky the harmony is less planned, a function of random growth, excavation and decay. Still you cannot help but feel the power of the Hellenistic ideal, the considerable half-life of this aesthetic: that it should, even in the destruction of what they cherished, achieve a certain balance, between the works of man and those of nature, that was the essence of what they believed in.

Marie touches his shoulder then digs her hand back in her coat pocket.

"You love this," she says, looking at him from under her shawl. "Please don't—" She does not finish.

He knows what she means to say. It is not just the site, but the reckless glory of those ideas, it is the sheer chutzpah of people who sailed in boats of pine lashed by rope with only folktales and stars to guide them across the faithless, monster-ridden seas. When he thinks of it, when he looks at what they did despite their fear, his chest hurts from the excitement in him.

Finally, it was always the ideas he loved best.

Rohan clambers farther up the rocks of the eastern hill. To the northwest the sea seems to climb with him, dark as a bruise, and the wind rises in strength. It is a white-squall wind, he thinks, the kind that scales one side of the mountain then, drunk on pressure, falls on the lee side like a tornado. It's the kind of wind that might well have sunk the ship at Edremit.

He enters the remains of a rectangular structure. An olive tree, crippled branches held up by crutches, itself props the walls of crumbled stone. This building formed the setting for the first stage in the binary rite of the Samothracian mysteries. The ceremonies always took place at night. First, initiates were warned about the deathsome secrecy of the cult; then they were led here, to the Anaktoron, to change into clean robes in a separate chamber. They were given an oil lamp—he walks the scrubby path himself—and led around to the northern entrance, here, guarded by two Bacchic statues. Inside the main chamber the first mysteries were revealed. Rohan believes they mostly consisted of spells and recipes for safe navigation. The principal protection afforded by the Samothracian mysteries was against maritime peril. The initiates were guaranteed safe landfall as long as they kept their thoughts clear. Many of the *mystoi* whose names are inscribed here were seamen.

Yes, he loves this, as Marie says; and, like Marie, it is going to be taken away—or more accurately, his ability to make a living at the piecing together of stones and bits of old ships is slowly being denied him.

It's because of Sanders, of course. Yet he has to admit that the catalyst in the process was himself. It is true that he was working with Sanders on the Edremit Korfezi wreck and he had promised not to publish before Sanders had a chance to review the data. But because the site was unique and, more dangerously, because it was the oldest; because it contained human remains in recognizable shapes and poses; it possessed elements that attracted like bears to menses the vast entertainment engine that Western civilization had become. Already news had been leaked to an Italian TV crew and everyone on the team was being assaulted with calls and requests for interviews. "This is *sexy!*" Rohan remembers an editor telling him, "really sexy." The throb of lust lay naked in his tone. Rohan did not want the site defiled by the incursion of a press bent on selling advertisements. He wrote a cool preliminary article for *Journal of Marine Archeology* describing the data and the possible conclusions one might infer from them. It contained pictures of the site, of *Karayel*, of Marie even.

Now Rohan, head thrust into the wind, trudges back downhill, threading the ravine. Marie is huddled in the lee of rocks, reading an inscription: μέσ[ον ἐντὸς] διαθέματος. Rohan believes that the *mystoi* who wanted to graduate to *epoptai*, the next stage, would have gathered here, outside the underground chamber. Gravy-boat lamps and the bones of birds have been found in great numbers. Rohan kicks a stone around a pit that is all that remains of the chamber.

Sanders's counterstrike to the *JOMA* article was not long in coming. In a letter to the editor he chastised Rohan for hasty and misleading interpretation of the data. Rohan, he charged, nomothetically had fitted facts into his preconceived ideas. Rohan fought back with vigor, defending his

dig in *JOMA*, at various symposia. He believed he was successful. After the Throckmorton Prize came his way he was
offered the directorship of a planned Center for Naval Archeology in Murcia. A British publisher advanced him cash
for a book he would write, based partly on evidence from
the Edremit wreck, on early Bronze Age navigational cults
in the Eastern Mediterranean.

But the following summer it became apparent that Sanders was pulling strings behind the scenery. Less money was
available for the salvage. They had to cut corners tighter
still. Rohan decided to haul the wreck up early, before reserves ran dry. The tunneling and laying of slings under the
argosy went surprisingly well despite mechanical problems
on the cut-rate salvage barge they had leased. Then, one
day, as they were lifting the ancient hull carefully from 140
to 130 meters, the brake-pawl on one of the winches
slipped. The hull cracked, broke apart and fell in a shower of
priceless ruptured patterns to the peace of the abyss south of
Cape Borobabo.

Marie calls to him. She is getting cold. He shouts back,
"One minute more," and retracing his footsteps makes his
way to a fault line of chert beside the Anaktaron. Here he
crouches beside the rocks.

These are lines more of concept than stone. Yet this is the
heart of the site. On this spot Von Linde found the shrine of
the original early bronze age inhabitants of the island. It was
an altar dedicated to Axieron, the "Mother of Rocks." The
center of it was a lodestone, a magnetized boulder.

Beside this stone they dug up a number of rings and seals
made of magnetized Samothracian iron. Two of these bore
the same trio of symbols as the ring he found on the wreck at
Edremit Korfezi.

Rohan has hired a silversmith in Piraeus to fashion a duplicate of the Edremit ring. He has carried it in his pocket
for five days, meaning to give it to Marie at the right time.
He is not sure now if he will give it to her. It is after all only

the symbol of something dead. He knows another who would appreciate it more.

• • •

Rohan and Marie walk back to Kareomatissa. The next ferry to Alexandropoulis is due tomorrow morning.

That evening they dine at Aristotle's *taverna*, by the northern breakwater. It will be their last night together. They make a determined attempt to avoid the irrelevance snuggling like a lonesome Saint Bernard between them. A trio of drunks from Sidcup insist on doing "Greek" dances in the middle of the floor. "Zorba," they call out to the lone bouzouki player, "*Zor*-ba!" The floor is tiled with ancient potsherds dredged from the bay outside. They eat olives, and greasy mutton flavored with mint leaves, and drink, from a tin pitcher, wine that tastes like a pine tree pissed in it.

Rohan looks out the small window where the sea is being whipped to bitter fury by the wind. If he stays here on the money he has saved he could live well for three or four years. But eventually, he believes, in the winter, the things and people that are shut from him would crowd in too close, and the only solution to that shutting might well be the cold openness of waves. He would wade, scuffing the sunken pots with numb feet, and then swim until he could swim no further. It would not take long.

A thin Athenian with a lupine nose and red-rimmed eyes talks to Marie. He is in his eighties. He wears a black silk suit. A woolen muffler twists around his scraggy neck. Aristotle has told him who Rohan is.

"I have read your articles," he tells Rohan in English. "Your 'cult of navigation,' *nei*? Where was it?"

"It's hard to say," Rohan replies, "I am sure of so little." The retsina makes him more afraid of silence than words. Marie's moss-green eyes watch him calmly and that makes him talk more as well. "The triple symbol has been found here, and at Edremit Korfezi—on a 300 B.C. wreck at Anti-kythera. Also a third-century ship near Béziers, in France."

He believes that the gods of sailors—the Kabeiroi, the Dactyls who live on the mountains near Edremit, the Dioscuri—were syncretized into one cult centered on the shrine above them. For now, of course that is impossible to prove. He shrugs.

He does not describe his belief that the cult may have been grafted onto later Christian heresies. The links are diverse but strong. Iason, the mythical founder of the Samothracian cult, according to Pliny was also the tutor of Zoroaster; and Zoroastrianism was the direct forebear of the heresy of the Bonshommes. The points of the compass were vital to all of them. The great Cathare sanctuary at Montségur is oriented, like the shrine above them, toward the rising place of the sun at winter solstice. The old Greek is not really interested.

"It is a theory only, then. It is not true."

Rohan shrugs once more. "There is nothing wrong with theories. It is wrong to think you can restrict yourself to facts only. Facts are nothing without a theory to bind them. Like landmarks with no chart. Like grain without yeast or water, like—" he looks at Marie. Her eyes are lit with tears. He swallows.

"The art," he finishes quietly, "lies in finding a balance."

"You never found that in yourself," she tells him in French, "between what you dream, and what you can get?"

"Find what?"

"*L'équilibre.*"

Something turns in him. He seldom lets himself go, there is too much of his father in him for that, but now a catch is released and he finds himself shouting at her, "Don't you see that is *all* I ever desired? In me? In my work? In you?

"The balance," he continues, more quietly, flexing his hands out of their fist shape. "Or, at least, an imbalance I can live with."

The old man looks back and forth between them, grinning. "Love," he says, "or chaos, *nei?*" His fingers mime things coming apart. "I remember now," he adds, "the Turkish terrorists, the 'Gray Wolves,' they threatened you. They wanted to blow up your ship, you were stealing their history." He coughs approvingly, lobbing spittle into their wine.

"Zorba!" a drunken Englishman yells and, kicking his legs too high in what he fondly imagines to be a dance step, collapses into one of the tables, scattering pitchers of resinated wine and plates of mint-flavored lamb across the restaurant.

The original mint, or *Minthe*, was a nymph who fell in love with the god of the underworld, Pluto, and with whom Pluto cheated, serially, on his wife. When Persephone found out, she killed the nymph and stamped her vengefully into the ground, where Minthe became a weed whose leaves defiantly give off sweet smells when stepped on, and whose roots burrow deep into rocky soil, still seeking Hades.

• • •

That night Marie says, "It's your fucking theories. I always had the impression there was someone else, but I realize now—*she's a theory too*. And the nice thing with pure theories, Ludo, is you can manipulate them without fear of correction."

In the morning he sees her off at the quay. The squat, black-hulled ferry gives Cape Akrotiri a wide berth. Her skipper takes a bearing from the peak of the Fengari—in the same manner as the skipper of the Edremit ship must have done from Lesbos, 3,800 years ago—and lays a course to the northward, for Thrace.

•

fifty

A sun the color of ripe persimmons rises in the crotch between the eastern volcanoes.

A vulture circles on the fetid air rising off the packed slums of Xelajú. Churchbells ring, abstract and tinny. Gardia loudspeakers outside the hotel greet the dawn with a Souza march.

It is the morning of the ninth day and for the first time the Indian footsoldiers of the Armed Front for the Liberation of Los Altos are beginning to act jumpy. They play with their safety catches and recheck ammunition slides. The man assigned to guard the grenade bombs keeps one fist closed tight on the trigger wire as he flexes stiffness from the other. Lieutenant Suchil's shouting has the beginnings of a tremor in it. One of the Indians, confronted by a bitching guest, listens for all of five seconds before bashing him in the kidney with the butt of his gun.

The frogs seem to have taken over the entire hotel. They thrive on a diet of mosquitoes and flying beetles. Their constant croaking drives beautiful men and tough women to tears. Six hours remain till the deadline and the manager has taken refuge in a form of autism; the dismantling of his office to construct a barricade in the back hallway does not elicit from him even a groan.

Many of the guests, too, seem to have retreated into shock. They do not touch the tins of *hierba-buena*-flavored quail that Eva and the Dutch guitarist and an American shoe manufacturer pass around for breakfast. The ballroom as a unit holds its warm and halitosic breath. The growing fear is like a sheet of black ice; once in a while someone breaks and sobs and then, with an explosive sound that emphasizes the brittle nature of their collective emotion, it spreads instantaneously among the bodies lying in "Wreck of the *Hesperus*" attitudes across the room.

Frank thinks that the once-grand ballroom now looks like the set for a Kevin McCann horror movie. Flying beetles bumble like transport planes in the putrid air. Sodden panels peel from the ceiling and walls, wires droop like poisonous snakes from I-beams. Even in daylight the room is swamped in a microclimate of mist and odor in which here and there clusters of couches or chairs covered in sweating bodies rise from the miasma. These islands are marked by a single lamp or candle that reflects dully on the black, virus-ridden water surrounding. Every thirty seconds or so a frog plops from some clump of insulation to an empty tin or other object, causing ripples to spread in the Stygian liquid.

The fat man, Calderón, alone seems impervious to the dynamics of siege, perhaps because he manages to steal enough booze from the bar to keep himself at least halfway drunk on a permanent basis. He splashes over to their corner the morning of the deadline and offers them Metaxa. The brandy makes him talkative. He waves his bottle at the bomb guard, the lieutenant, at the Mexican chargé d'affaires now whispering intently in the frieze-protected doorway of the bar—at Leila who sits alone on the piano, cleaning her .44 with hotel napkins.

"You gringos," he says, "always think this is new, no? That you are the first it happens to. But you see, this started a long time ago—in 1847. That was when the Indios took over Spanish farms. They sold the coffee in Belize to buy guns, mostly Mausers. They were winning that war but the stupid bastards made two mistakes. *Primo*, they stopped fighting when it came time to plant the corn. *Segundo*, they listened to the priests . . . the church had come out against them, you see." Calderón peers around carefully, leans closer to his audience.

"Then one of the chiefs had a great idea. He hired a *ventriloquista*—a ventriloquist? He took his people to a little *cenote:* a well, deep in the jungle. A tree with a small cross carved on it growed by this well. The ventriloquist made it speak. And the cross it said, 'Fight the government, fight the Spanish, and you will win.' And they did. The Indios called themselves the 'Cruzob,' this means 'People of the Cross.' They dressed the trees with the clothes of women. A town arose near the *cenote*. The Indios took white prisoners and made them work the fields." Calderón chuckles, and stops to take a swig of Metaxa. The spirit leaks from one corner of his mouth. Frank unconsciously wipes his moustache. Rohan lifts himself on one elbow.

"So what happened," he asks the fat man, dully. "What is the point of all this?"

Calderón shrugs. "Well. In 1895 the English did a deal with the government. They sealed off the Belize border, so the Indios could buy no more guns. The Mexicans sent troops with repeating Winchester rifles. It was over." Calderón automatically fishes for a cigarette but finds none. Frank wonders with a slight burn of fear if all this talk of armament is not some kind of coded warning; perhaps his cover has been blown. Later on he decides not. Guns, in this part of the globe, in most of the world he deals with, are a living factor, something to rely on when faith is gone. It is normal to discuss their movements and whereabouts.

The Canadian sings "Ru-uby, don't take your love to town," in a voice of heartbreak.

Five minutes after Calderón has finished his story something happens.

Softly behind the plop and piss of water and the caretaking sounds of misery and the rooster squawks of the Air Force radio outside they hear a roaring start at a frequency so low it is at first more of a physical tremble than a sound. It swells in volume and lifts in tone and adds clanks and squeaks to its repertoire. All other sounds, even the frogs, stop as the tanks take up different positions close to the other side of the compound. Leila stiffens, and quickly snicks her pistol back together.

"They will learn now," Calderón says, and raises his bottle toward Leila. His eyes burn with black joy. "Stupid Cruzob *puta!*"

"Get out of here," Rohan tells him calmly, though his stomach feels like a caravan of fear has taken up camp there with big tents and rugs and camels.

"Yeah, fuck off, Calderón," Frank says in a louder voice.

No one else notices. Calderón hands around business cards and, when they are not accepted, lets them fall into the dark water. He smiles and sloshes off, clutching the brandy. Eva realizes she is hugging herself in utter panic and laughs shrilly without finding anything funny. Her clasped arms hurt her breasts. Her abdomen locks in a furious spasm. It astonishes her that her body has chosen this of all times to subject her to premenstrual distress. It is true that the body's hormonal feedback system functions like a form of logic and may be making a rational choice here based on the schemes and wonders of data available. On the other side of the ballroom a woman sobs. A man shouts in a Glen Ridge accent "Somebody has to *too-alk!* Can't we *too-alk* about this?"

The tank engines idle.

In the bar, the telephone rings.

The man who wants to talk thinks better of his advice. Everyone is silent except the Canadian, who has gone back to *Ballad of the Green Beret.*

> *Put silver wings, on my son's chest;*
> *Make him one . . . of America's best. . . .*

The Indios stand like stelae, watching the movement outside, their machineguns still and aimed for business.

Frank stands on a couch to see better.

"What's going on?" Eva asks him.

"Shut the fuck up," Frank snaps.

Now the Mexican chargé d'affaires comes out of the bar and nods. Calderón walks over to the lieutenant's side. They talk briefly. The lieutenant shouts *"Andalé!"* Five Indians move from their positions to a web of people draped in the lee of a big armchair on the other side of the room from Frank, Eva and Rohan. Leila stands very still and straight and then without other warning lets out a shrieked *"Nooo!"* She sprints toward the rebels who are pulling a thin man with a face of sleepy haunting from the group and holding him tight against them: Julián. Another two of the Indians obviously have been detailed to keep an eye on Leila and they grab her by the waist and elbows and pull her away.

"Traidores!" she screams, splashing water with her flailing feet. *"Lo vendión!"*

"You don't understand," the lieutenant tells her, in Spanish, "they already knew. From inside. Someone told them."

"I don't care," Leila shouts.

"They called him *'capitán,'*" the lieutenant continues, wearily, "but they knew."

The other rebels, all once more wearing combat boots, line up in rough order against the office wall under a bizarre wooden representation of the Mayan calendar cycle. This is a double ring of geared circles, meshed internally and meshing also on the outside with a much larger cycle, creating in those differentials fifty-two years worth of unique and holy dates.

No one in the Continental Hotel is thinking in terms of fifty-two years, or even fifty-two hours. For once, every person is fixed solidly on this minute. Eva has sunk into herself and her hands, like predatory insects, move jerkily. Leila still shrieks and curses and wrestles. Her glossy hair tosses back and forth over the Indians holding her. Rohan and Frank glance at each other. Each struggles with his own dread and timidity weighed against what is left of human concern in a situation of tanks and bullets. One or the other moves first, neither remembers which, for the movement always depended on a corresponding sign from the other. They walk together halfway across the ballroom. Immediately three of the rebels detach from the main squad and stop them with the muzzles of their guns.

"*Déja-la quiéta,*" Rohan calls ineffectually, his voice rasping in a dry throat.

"What are you doing with her?" Frank chimes in, and fights off an inexplicable urge to giggle.

They can go no farther. Their sweat makes circles in the water around their toes. Rohan swats from his face a beetle that seeks to climb in his nostril and lay eggs. He feels a hollow opening in his bowels, and wants to shit.

Several more Indians move warily into the courtyard. Car engines race. The courtyard gates are pulled open and a Gardia major walks in, holding himself like a bullfighter. He turns and beckons. A few minutes later a yellow schoolbus, a 1974 GMC, reverses through the open gate.

One of the Americans reacts positively to the sight of the bus, which looks exactly like, and may even be, the bus that ferried him to and from the same country day school every weekday of his early life. "They're going to let us go," he cries. "Thank you Jesus!"

The Gardia major stalks into the entrance hall and stands beside Julián, his face drawn in a snarl of contempt that has the behavioral side effect of curbing the fear in him. The Mexican signals to Lieutenant Suchil. At a sign from the lieutenant the Indian guarding the grenade bomb carefully removes the wire that links the firing pins.

Then the rebels file slowly into the courtyard, blinking at the white sun, their fists still solid on the trigger handles of their rifles. They half push, half carry Leila but leave Julián standing by himself in the lobby. "*Assassinos!*" Leila wails. The rebels board the bus, looking suddenly like a bunch of ghetto schoolchildren leaving for a daytrip they have been somewhat nervous about.

The chargé walks toward the bus. Frank shouts, "Wait, you, hey—where are you taking her?"

The Mexican turns.

"She is free," he says shortly. "She will go with the rest. They have all *laissez-passer*."

Rohan shakes his head repeatedly.

"But where can we—she's a—a friend . . ." As Rohan says this last word his voice drops involuntarily. But he says it; he says it.

The Mexican shrugs. "They will go first to the embassy. Then to Oriente, in the mountains. My government has guaranteed this. After that—" he shrugs again, turns away. Rohan and Frank stand in their puddle of water. Eva, who got to her feet when the two men betrayed their group's immobility, sags back against the wall in her corner of the ballroom, leaning against the plaque that captions the mold-blurred artwork overhead.

"After he fled the trap of Gumarcaj" (the plaque reads) "Alvarado resolved to pay back the Indians in their own coin. He invited the chiefs of the Maya-Ki'iché to his camp under the protection of a flag of truce. When they accepted he waited until they and their escort were well within the precincts of his camp and then signaled his soldiers to encircle and disarm them. Alvarado and his priests were well versed in the arts of inquisition. They tortured the Indians with fire and white-hot swords until the chiefs confessed the trap they were planning for Alvarado in the mountains."

The former hostages are beginning to stir. They stand or kneel to watch as the bus full of rebels roars in neutral, then shifts into gear. It rolls slowly out the gates, past the tanks guarding the entrance to the hotel compound and disappears down the hillside. Someone claps shakily, one-two-three, one-two-three, but no one takes up the rhythm. Calderón sloshes calmly toward the entrance and stands in front of the Gardia major and Julián. Without uttering a word he leans in at the right shoulder and punches Julián under the sternum with all his might. "Vent'uno," he says, with no inflexion in his voice. Eva groans and closes her eyes. Julián doubles up, retching. The Gardia major chooses a cigarette and lights it. Then he shoves Julián, still jacknifed in pain, through the courtyard, out the gate.

Eva watches him go until he is lost from sight in a clutch of green uniforms and armored cars. She has grown so used to not thinking about Julián that his physical removal does not affect her much. What she feels, perversely, is disappointment, because the rebels have left. It offends the Magyar in her that after nine days they should have departed without formality, or an empty gesture even.

From the southwest, toward the airport, comes a series of dull thumping sounds.

A slight braid of smoke lifts into the placid sky and is carried toward the Pacific with the prevailing wind.

fifty-one

Lying a little further to their left now the spine of white chalk rising over the steep hillside ascended to a peak and then collapsed into the velvet greens, browns, and yellows of the summer countryside.

Frank followed this feature with his eyes. He was used to different geologies and he knew limestone when he saw it, but the white crest rising over green-brown slopes reminded him of high-altitude snow and he allowed himself to be fooled for a second or two.

He had spend three weeks once moving through snowy faults and synclines and all the rest of the crystalline obstetrics of mountain building. His thoughts brought to the foreground a hint of that place. Vague and short-lived as it was, this wove an electricity of substance into what Eva would have called the story areas of his brain.

...

Frank, at the close of his career as a munitions merchant, tries to stay away from the arms in general, and in particular since that last trip to Bahr-el-Ghazal. Although or because they constitute the practical culmination of his work, directly handling weapons can be messy and dangerous and he is better at contacts and organizing.

Nevertheless at times he has no choice. Specifically, four months after leaving Colonel Hakim's newly declared republic he finds himself on the wet end of a "munitions transfer" involving PETN explosives, Swiss 60 mm mortars and shells F.O.B. for the Nooristan Islamic People's Army in the northeastern marches of Afghanistan. He came to Kabul two days ahead of the shipment, flying into the brown plain of the Koh-I-Damal for once mercifully clear of civil war and rocket attacks. But, meeting the Franciscan in the airport transit area, he learns that the army colonel they paid off has been transferred out of the capital, which means the highway is now too risky and they will have to run the cargo north via some other route.

The Franciscan is dusty and worn by Asia and a taste for poppy sap the way an old phonograph record is made scratchy by the rasp of needles. Frank waits with him, playing poker for *afghanis*, in a Quonset hut in the free zone. The Franciscan drinks vodka and trembles. He cheats well and wins consistently. The first time they met, several years ago now, he gave Frank a book by a twelfth-century Franciscan monk named John Duns Scotus. Now he quizzes Frank on Nominalist theory as they play. The temperature is 102 degrees. They hire a cadaverous Tadzhik to truck the cargo north when it arrives but Frank does not trust him. The plane, a twin-engine HS-748, flies in from Trabzond on a day of brown and sidewinding wind. Frank, assaying the mortar shells with a small magnet, finds that a third of them are cheap, dangerous Chinese refills and will not take delivery of these cases. The customs crew, well bribed by the Franciscan, turns blind eyes to the truck leaving the free port. The Tadzhik uses side roads, avoids checkpoints. One hundred and twenty miles northeast of Kabul through the acrid towns and poppy fields the truck runs out of road. Fifteen NIPA guerrillas with packhorses outfitted in gaily painted harnesses and wooden packsaddles wait beside a boulder near a spring. The crates and mortars are loaded on the horses. "You will have to come with us," one of the Nooristanis tells Frank. "Your friend has been taken by the police and you cannot go back to Kabul now."

For the last three or four months Frank has felt as if he lived on a planet that had visiting rights with the solar system but did not move in any recognizable orbit in relation to the sun. As they proceed east into the ascending blue ridges of the Hindu Kush that feeling grows stronger. Fields of yellow flowers dust the men and horses with pollen as they pass till they resemble a column of golden creatures from Persian myth. The path winds up arid riverbeds, past the rusted hulks of tanks and half-tracks around which holly-like trees have taken stubborn root. They spend the night in ochre forts while the wind scours spittle-snow from the sky. He can hear women in these forts but he never sees them, not once. At night, drinking through chemical filters water he has purified with chlorine tablets, Frank opens the book by Duns Scotus. He reads: "The prior, according to the essence of nature, is that which is able to be without the posterior, although the opposite is not true. I understand this in the following sense: though the prior of necessity causes the posterior and therefore is unable to exist without it, this does not mean that it needs the posterior in order to exist, but rather the other way around. For if one assumes that the posterior does not exist, the prior nevertheless will be; and there is no contradiction in this." Outside, shooting stars fall, bright into dark, as if the sky were a pool and on top of it floated a boatful of monkeys shelling peanuts of light and dropping the shells into the still black water.

On their third day into the mountains they pass through the ruins of a village. The houses are smudged with fire. The tomb of a fourteen-year-old boy is oriented west, where the sacred dog al-Borak will ferry his soul. The Nooristanis speak of Hind helicopters and napalm. Trudging in thirst, fatigue and painful Kabuli sandals Frank remembers when he was fourteen and his father took a job in Newport tending the grounds of a private school. A few of the boarders were friendly, and one of them, a comely girl named Stacey Quinn, by some miracle "went out" with him; but the rest made fun of Frank. They had grown up playing expensive sports and they taunted him because he could not sail or waterski well. Ultimately Stacey dumped him for similar reasons.

It makes no sense that napalm and burnt earth should remind Frank of that pretty school with its gardens soaked in green and water. Although it is true that Frank, now as then, is not in great physical shape. I should exercise, he thinks. He promises himself—groaning, sweating, complaining bitterly to no one in the column's rear—that he will take up cycling again.

They climb steadily but the mountains only grow taller to compensate. Thunder like a shy giant crumbles sound in the distance, never comes closer. In the clarity silver falcons turn. Small gray wolves watch unseen from cover and yip when evening comes. The ridges, shining with ice and new rock, repeat each other in shades of purple and tan into the ascetic gloom of the ionosphere.

The air is very cold and now Frank wears a blanket around his shoulders as they climb. The Nooristanis joke and run up steep trails like goats and target-shoot their AK-47s. They ask if he is a believer in Allah. Frank tells them he was brought up Catholic and has a cousin who is a priest. That is all right, the men say, for Nazarenes and even Jews are cousins, therefore they are not necessarily to be killed, they may even be tolerated, according to the Koran. Frank believes the mountains, as they grow higher and colder, start to take on facial features that reveal their true natures. Some of the peaks smile and some are angry. Most look like they could not give a shit about men and their pathetic needs and schemes.

The texts he reads at this point now speak of the character of "thisness," using the meaty precision of Latin and the confidence of new logic. Duns Scotus did not believe that you could fully describe an object or a man by lumping him into a general rule or class. Each person or thing had a thisness which was particular to it as an individual. The scholastic's words ring of rock and purity. To Frank, each facet and character of the mountains around him, like the wadis and tracks of the Sahel, possesses "thisness" in a unique and powerful way.

They reach a pass where the wind cuts ice from a glacier into blade-like shapes. In the valley and base camp below the mortars are stashed in a cave. Frank is paid the balance of his fee in dollars and deutschemarks. Five men are assigned to lead him over the eastern passes to Chitral, in northwest Pakistan. They walk at speed down winding gorges, wary of ambush. Frank is well aware that his escorts, for private or for policy reasons, could kill him and dump him down a gorge and no one would ever know what happened to him, but, oddly, he is not concerned. In these mountains standing strong and timeless as a philosophical proposition, in a way that is as much visual as intellectual, he understands that, as Scotus insisted, all causes must exist at the same time as the events they triggered. This—so Scotus said, more or less—was the prerequisite for free will, for if everything could be led back through its infinite complexity of actions and reactions to an initial condition of God, free will would not exist, nor would God have to be present now.

Frank, under the looming storms, shadowed by ridges and rocks that each could conceal a sniper, guided by men who would happily kill him for an assortment of reasons, carrying money that would make each or all of them princes in their own land, feels as far away from free will as he ever has in his life. Perhaps it is this situation in itself that makes him aware of the myriad turnings in his life that have brought him exactly here, to *this* ravine, *this* mountain, *this* day and hour and minute.

He thinks, There is nothing I have ever done that fully justifies my being here. He thinks of the village in Bahr-el-Ghazal and the blind man lining up the bodies of his family and he knows that the affect still is cached inside him, shiny and hard as nickel ore. He also finds the altitude has anaesthetized him in the classic way: by cold and lack of oxygen, by cutting off pain now in the promise of pain to come. He starts to sing as he walks, old AM radio songs: *When I Die, Lucy in the Sky with Diamonds.* The Nooristanis watch him in pity and alarm. The moon grows and converts the mountains from rock into frozen emotion.

Frank reflects, without feeling good or bad about it either way, that it is a very damned convenient logic that can sever the link between the tomb of a fourteen-year-old and an initial condition of his creator.

They cross the border into Kafiristan on the twenty-second night. Full of a sudden, almost biological affection for his guides, Frank turns to thank them, but they have already disappeared, their spent breath hanging like birds of mist in the thin air.

fifty-two

A sudden cant in the track, which was banked for expresses and other trains of much higher speeds than the Bar le Duc local, took Eva by surprise, and a portion of her wine slopped from the glass she was holding.

Muttering a curse she mopped the spill off her jeans with a paper napkin and refilled her glass. They were well into Frank's bottle of Lynch-Graves now. Soon they would be ready for the Tokaj and she looked forward to that. The taste of Tokaj always brought a feeling of calmness no doubt associated with other memories linked to times when that wine was a definable part of her life.

She licked her lips, appreciating the residue of tannin upon them. The Lynch-Graves was making her movements a little loose, and she was starting to feel better. For some reason her thoughts had turned dark there for a spell.

It felt good, too, to ride with these men, it gave her a feeling, illusory no doubt but nevertheless strong, that the hours and days rolling out behind her like sleepers under the train might not be forever gone—that they could, in fact, come back, prompted by coincidence, as her memories of these men had returned, to thrill or haunt you with almost the same force as the actual event, at any age or stage of life.

Of course she might well have met up with Rohan anyway. He lived in Paris now, it would not have been so unlikely.

"How long have you been here, I mean, in the city," she asked him, bracing her glass more securely against the motion.

Rohan stared at her. He seemed far away and, now she thought about it, not overly anxious to chat.

She repeated the question. He told her two and a half months. He had been in California before that. She pressed on, ignoring his dearth of enthusiasm, asking what he did at UNESCO.

"I am coordinating a film project," he said, "it is on marine archeology—we'll be telling the history of the discipline, interviews, we'll film some of the big sites and so on. Well, I thought you read about it, you said—"

"I told you, I read the announcement in the *Courier*," Eva replied, "but I wasn't sure."

"Anyway." Rohan waved a hand. He seemed anxious to

change the subject. "And you? I mean, apart from transplanting brains and so forth."

"I have my research." She looked at him curiously. It was as if he knew that there was something else. She remembered now he'd always been attentive to subtexts and inflections. "As it happens, I also run a small publishing house, my husband left it to me."

Frank, who had been looking out the window though his eyes no longer followed the scenery, turned his head at this.

"That sounds like fun, Eva, that sounds—huh. What kind?"

"Books."

"OK." He frowned. "I meant, what sort?"

"Poetry, mostly." She smoothed her lips with one finger. "Right now I'm doing something I always wanted to do, I am putting out a volume of Attila József, translated of course, he was the best modern poet in Hungary I think." She rummaged in her bag and produced a thin red-colored volume. The cover bore a photograph, black and white: a face with a widow's peak, a pronounced chin, Nosferatu eyes, a dark moustache. *Medvetanc*, the title read.

Frank continued to watch her, preventing his own features from reacting. She placed the book on her knees.

"What's wrong with that? You look—"

"Nothing."

"But you—" She replaced the book in her bag, protectively. "You looked almost like you were, oh, *dégouté*, how do you say that?"

"Disgusted," Rohan offered.

"Disgusted," Frank repeated. "I didn't mean to—well, maybe once I would have disapproved, I guess, but that was long ago." Their looks were expectant. Frank sighed. "Long ago, in my, um, you could say fire-breathing political days, I only read things I thought were committed; you know. I mean, things that had an effect, that did something to the world, to society—"

"How on earth," Rohan asked him in a placid voice, "did you determine that? What was 'committed'?"

"Huh." Frank tapped on the armrest, three nervous rolls of his fingers. "By the trouble it caused, usually," he admitted. "If the fat cats tried to sue, if the big chains refused to sell it, if the *Providence Journal-Bulletin* studiously ignored it in their usual fucking supercilious manner, like, if they don't pay attention to it, it don't exist—"

"But now," Eva told him, thinking the Ermisen book surely fitted that category, it had been rejected, condemned, rusticated by everyone before success made it acceptable. "You are not sure of your standards, no?"

"It seems naive to me." Rohan took a gulp of wine. "So *soixante-huit*, to judge that way. If you don't mind me saying this."

"Maybe." Frank smoothed his moustache. He was not aware of the gesture. "I mean, I hope I've learned something over the last few years. I know you can't easily figure out just what the hell's going on around you in the world. And it's even harder to know how what you do, or try to do, will affect things."

"If you read history," Rohan said, lifting his chin a little, "you learn *nothing* can be affected, well, in a predictable manner."

Frank chewed softly, though there was nothing in his mouth.

"All you can do," Rohan continued, looking down with eyebrows taut at the compartment floor, "you try to get a balance of facts; well, you make a list, after a lot of research, of the three, four most likely scenarios for what happened. So, one day, maybe you will be in a similar situation, and you will know what your options are."

"Huh," Frank said, and his hands stirred slightly, as if he was moving a chess piece. "Sounds pretty *soixante-huit* to me."

Rohan looked up abruptly, his eyes locking on Frank's.

"You have a better idea, Frank? Teaching to rich middle-class American kids, that will have some positive effect?"

"More than history films," Frank replied quietly. "Who does history know, where does it eat lunch?"

You cannot stop men from going through their stiff-legged, teeth-baring, asshole-smelling tropisms, Eva thought. All you can do is distract them at the right time. "You two are putting a lot of energy into this," she commented brightly, and took a pen out of her bag without meaning to. "Do you have any idea where that comes from?"

Rohan shook his head; this was not meant as an answer. Frank stared out the window again but he could see her reflection in the glass. Both expected a fashionable theory, a post-situationalist twist on F. W. Rohrich, disguised as charts of their individual libidos. Both were slightly taken aback when Eva continued, doodling with a felt-tip on the greasy wrapping paper beside her, "It's simple. At some point you go over a limit, a threshold—it's usually age, though not necessarily, maybe illness of yourself, or a parent—but when you cross this line you see time shortening all of a sudden, and then, the trouble is, oh, you have to justify your time, the time you have lived, to yourself."

"My god," Rohan muttered, "the woman calls for justification."

Frank replied in measured tones, "I don't have to justify my time, nobody does, it speaks for itself."

"So the answer," Rohan turned on him, continuing in a voice just as flat, "coming back to the question earlier, which by the way you never addressed, the answer is Yes, your guns have helped people? When you were dealing in guns?"

Frank's jaw moved slightly. He could feel anger rise in him like lava bursting through the crusted slag of the day but he pressed it down.

"There were four, probably five situations," he said, even

more softly, "when my 'guns' as you put it did help to make a better situation for the people involved. Not the colonels, not the rich planters or, or the bankers. Just normal people trying to survive. An', an' I would never have affected those situations if I was simply digging up bones in the desert."

"I don't dig up bones." Rohan's left hand went to his chest and touched the ring beneath his shirt. "I analyze. I research. I interpret. I—"

"I thought, all you do now is make *movies?*"

"I thought all you do now is *teach.*" Rohan's voice was hard as the lip of a steamshovel. He leaned back in his seat. He put his fingers to his eyelids and massaged them. His fingers, to his astonishment, trembled with rage.

The train, running alongside a road, passed a small "routiers" restaurant on the flank of that road. A blue twelve-speed bike stood propped against the door. The tiny garden with its *rosae mundi* and red Byrrh umbrellas had been lined with fake, shattered "amphorae" to give it an Attic look. The name of the restaurant was "Le Relais du Cirque," and on its small sign was painted the stock symbol of a dancer pirouetting aboard a prancing, cockaded stallion.

Frank forced air out of his nostrils and looked outside once more but he still saw nothing and did not notice the restaurant.

"Listen," Rohan continued after a pause. "Frank. Everything, all we do is theories. What worth our work has—well. But what I try to do, even filming, I try to find out what really happened in a particular place, a particular time; what their 'certainty'"—he put quote marks around it with his intonation—"might possibly have been. It's all I can do."

"What you call 'certainty,'" Frank said firmly to the window, "is a luxury. It's a tale told by a rich man, full of false assumptions, signifying nothing. In most of the world, the certainty is, who is holding a gun to your head. You fuckin' *know* that, Ludovic."

"Oh, look, an *archetype*," Eva put in, looking from one to the other of her companions. "The one who is prepared to accept belief, versus the doubter. No?"

Rohan started a gesture with one hand that was cut short when Frank interrupted, pointing his words at Eva now, his voice stinging with annoyance at what seemed like her siding with Rohan, "And I suppose, because you're a scientist, you have to pretend skepticism, when you're really desperate to believe, oh, in *one certain thing*, one Grand Unified theory that will—"

"That's not true," Eva interrupted.

"—one incontrovertible fixed equation—" Frank, referring back to sixties *Twilight Zone* episodes, could not keep the sarcasm from climbing in his tone—"that will *serve mankind*"—

Eva took a deep breath. She waited, holding it in, till Frank's body had settled, signifying he was climbing down from active riposte to a more maintenance level of defense. She had felt the anger swelling in her, and tried to remember the yoga rhythms she had learned, when she was in med school.

Another long draught of air, to the pit of her abdomen, slowly released to dissolve that node, that fulcrum.

Shantih.

"To be honest," she said at length, and her voice now was only just high enough to be intelligible above the drumbeat of train wheels, "I can't answer that. I don't know what certainty is. I know, because I can locate your memory, I could hook you up to my instruments and we could make you think of the quality of 'certain' and for twenty seconds you would see everything become, maybe, a 'certainty.' But to me the idea of certainty or anything else does not help unless you can use it to help someone you love. I have never been able to do that, with science, or poetry books, or anything else. All I have is a hope—I hope maybe I can. I hope I am given time to help. Maybe even to help you, Frank." She smiled. Frank, looking at the equipoise of that smile, the graceful script of her lips, felt his anger turn in on itself, shrivel into powder and blow away, mostly. "Or you, Ludo, as well."

Rohan said nothing. Eva's hands were folded in a strangely hieratic pose, the practical fingers as suited for blessing as for hard labor. She had put away her pen. On the wrapping paper he could make out a bird-like creature with gawky wings and wide eyes and feathers sticking out every which way. The train, like a doubtful suitor, continually drew close to, then pulled away from, the Marne. Now it was rolling nearer once more. On their left, cypresses in protective rows stood guard over willows drooped like girls washing their hair in the olive water. They passed a lagoon of cadmium blue with docks and river punts and duck blinds. Behind that, wheat fields drew away toward a ridge marking the northern horizon.

Cypress and willow and the cheap symbolism of rolling water always meant something specific to Eva, but right at that moment she was too wrapped up in the weight of what she felt to let the association follow through. Her breath juddered a bit on its way in and out of her lungs. There had been too many of them, people who needed her help, people she had been unable to touch at the right time.

However the circuits of memory are programmed with a fail-safe that forces one off a given track if the intensity is too long in duration or too strong. The body imposes its demands, the world of the present thrusts itself upon that which lives in areas of recall. She pulled her hands apart in exact though unconscious replica of the way energy and neurotransmitters were being diverted from certain neural centers, and glanced outside. Her bladder was filling again, and at the same time she felt thirsty. I should open the Tokaj, she thought.

And finally it was this, in a curious time delay, that threw the next switch; the short-term impression of water world coupled with her previous thought and the anticipated savor of a liquid round in fruit sugar and the keep of springs.

fifty-three

Now Eva's thoughts resolved, without her being fully aware of it, into a picture of a scene she could not immediately put a name to.

For to her, at that point, the memory *was* a picture—a holiday snapshot full of color, meant not to win composition prizes but to serve as a catalyst to further memory. Like a snapshot it could be seen on the surface—gestalt, a whole—or analyzed more carefully, holding the loupe over, here a face, there a tennis racquet or shoe, that in turn gave rise to another link of recollection.

fifty-four

Coming to rest, therefore, on a small cottage less than one kilometer from Lake Balaton, in Transdanubia, west-central Hungary.

The cottage is built of stone and lime with a roof of orange tile. Eva's uncle, to whom it belongs, has raised a grape arbor on one side, and dozens of pots of day lilies and candy-striped geraniums sit on a shelf between two deeply inset windows. An empty wooden birdcage hangs by the door. Flowered bushes and a stone wall surround the house, which is set on a low rise. A ridge with other rooftops, cypresses, limestone outcrops covered with *calluna* and, in the distance, the towers of a disused monastery form the backdrop.

The door and window of this cottage are thrown open, though wind rinses the trees and the sky is full of clouds; but that is normal weather near Balaton, on this plain originally formed by winds sweeping forever out of the continent's heart. Through the window of the bedroom one can make out the shape of a heavy wooden bed with thick, straw-filled ticking.

This is a period of cusp for her, planets crossing, holding their breath. She has just, after a year of mind-wringing preparation, passed her neurology *internat*. She married Serge six months before the exams. Her mother—to square out the roadmap of her recent life—died eight months before that. Eva is exhausted, pale, underweight, subject to chronic bronchitis. She wires her uncle to arrange rent, then tells Serge she is taking off May and possibly June to rest here, near the big lake. He is accommodating, as always. She takes the "Bartok Bela," the night train. In Pesht she visits her father and buys a trunkful, quite literally, of books. She rides the Balaton Express and hires a taxi from Polgardi and halfway to its destination the creaking Wurzburg breaks a spring from the weight of her books.

When she first arrives she stays in bed almost without interruption for a week, watching the clouds march like Magyar nightmares, dreams of the seven hordes, out of Russia. The mattress enfolds her like a fat lover and the blankets are thick and warm. The scent of rain, of geraniums and flowers she doesn't know the name of, washes in and out of the cottage. Only on market days does she get up and leave the cottage to shop in Polgardi. This is a period of transition for Hungary also, a few years before the collapse of the Party, when the gothic stalinism of Janos Kadar is giving way to "goulash" socialism; and one can eat quite well, though she rarely takes the trouble to fix anything more elaborate than cucumber salads or leek soup or sometimes chicken roasted with paprika in the small stone oven.

Deep in the shadows of the bedroom, almost out of reach of snapshot detail, the shelves sag from the weight of the long Russian and Hungarian novels she bought. Once she has got over her deep deficit in sleep she starts to read. She does not have to get out of bed, she simply reaches over and picks up a volume, delighting in the massy thick feel of books that have never been opened, working indiscriminately from the left end of the shelves to the right, all the books she meant to read from school, college, university but never found the time for: some Russians, Turgenev, Dostoevsky, the odd German (Mann's *Magic Mountain*), but mostly Hungarian novels from the nineteenth century, usually about the country; the kind that spend the first 150 pages introducing the cast of characters, everyone from milkmaid to magnate, with genealogy attached, depicting the houses and flowers and the rotation of crops.

These novels are, in fact, so placid and laborious that you might say they simulate rather than describe rural life. They are books where you could slog through a hundred pages, and several years, and find you are no farther along in the linear plot than you were before; volumes the reading of which involves real aerobic exercise just to hold them in the light; where old characters constantly return, unexpected and unwelcome as the 'flu; where you fall asleep in the middle of the chapter and wake up feeling as if the book has, through sheer weight and inertia, actually dragged you backward down the timeline, so you have to pick up earlier than where you stopped just to hold your own.

She cherishes these cheap, yellow-paged paperbacks, she lives in them. Simply through long familiarity the characters become more real to her than most people she knows. The long, dream-like stories of Jokay Mor; the exhaustively analyzed character operas of Kemeny Zsigmond, like *Fergesno*, or *Husband and Wife*, where the genesis of each person's ultimate and individual ruin is pinpointed down to the smallest splinter and cough; above all the grand landscapes of Eolvos József, like *Hungary: 1514*, whose subject is the failed revolt of Dosza Gyorgy; each book contains a family tied to her with verbs in the place of blood. She reads late, usually by an oil lamp, for the electricity here is weak and unreliable. When she gets to a passage she particularly loves she will recite it aloud, dramatically, the good Magyar vowels cracking from her lips, her arms making black griffin shapes on the whitewashed walls.

When the novels start crushing her by their sheer weight and depth of life she can always turn to the other József, Attila, who lived and died not far from here. One of her rare outings consists of taking the bus to Balatonszárszó and visiting the shrine they made of his sister's house and walking along the railroad line where the Balaton Express runs, down by the shore where the willows look like they want to drown themselves in the deep green water, this place of cool shadows and reed and shifting light where Attila József lay down on the rails in front of the evening freight on the third of December 1937. This makes her melancholy, in a cheerful way; she is, after all, Hungarian. One of her favorite actors, Latinovics Szoltan, committed suicide under the Balaton Express in deliberate resonance with the manner of József's passing.

She feels empathy for their feelings but not their deed. The shift in emotions and the unexpected vacuums that result from her mother's dying sort themselves out within her like loose *forint* pieces settling in a coat pocket. She is not consciously aware of it then but this is a time of actual pleasure for her, a period that does not draw attention to itself with cheap displays of happiness but that, looking back from a vantage point of years, seems a sheltered and tranquil cove on a waterway usually lashed by quick conflicting winds.

On one of those visits to Balatonszárszó she is walking along the track in the afternoon when, daylighted on a nearby ridge, she sees a line of horsemen riding, black figures made noble and interesting by the multitude of riders inhabiting the books she reads. They are probably only vacationers from a summer camp astride useless and ungraceful hacks but she stands and watches them till they file out of sight into trees. That night she dreams of hooves beating in the night, of Elizabeth Bathory bathing in the blood of men, of wolves in silent hunt.

> *The green lizard shines.*
> *Wheat fields cast out seeds; if a stone should drop*
> *The lake takes me in. And the graves,*

Attila József writes.

If you approach the cottage from the front gate you will see a bulkhead set in a brown-painted band along the base of the house. This leads to the cellar, and the bins of Tokaj that Uncle Arpad preserves in dark humidity. She opens a bottle every other night and drinks the rich wine, savoring the flavors of fruit and mineral, first at the white-painted table, eating her simple salad, with the single unshaded electric light overhead; later in bed with the wind nibbling at the leaves and bringing different smells for her nostrils to pick up or leave alone and the clouds scudding across dark of night or silvered moon.

> *I live near the tracks. Trains come and go*
> *With glistening windows. They are the rush of lighted days.*

The geraniums and day lilies in Arpad's flowerpots die despite or because of her care. She will have to buy new plants when she leaves. On a walk by the shore she finds an infant black-headed gull and tries to keep it alive in the bird cage with strips of raw fish, bacon, and milk dripped down its beak, but it too dies after a brief period. In an irrational way this confirms in her an earlier decision not to have children. In any case Serge does not wish to be bothered with kids.

She gains weight. Her cough disappears. The mass of facts and discipline, all the anatomy and clinical neurology that she has learned over the last seven years does not disappear but the body of it is absorbed better, her brain trimming the data with beta waves, rearranging some definitional categories, discarding others; fitting larval ideas, perceptions, angles of thought more comfortably into the elaborate cloisters of her long-term memory.

Serge comes to visit for ten days at the end of her two months, and while this is pleasant and she is glad of the company, it is the time spent alone with the Tokaj and the scores of characters from impossible novels that will stick out for her in the future as most precious, like a rare stone found once and almost immediately lost again, when she recalls that part of her life.

fifty-five

Early in 1842 is when development of the Paris-Bar le Duc railroad line—or at least the concept of a line that will link Paris to Strasbourg—acquires official shape. It comes under the guise of a government charter that hands over the concession to the financier Cubières. The government is to be heavily involved both in capital arrangements and in establishing the right-of-way by eminent domain.

The first big issue to resolve is what route the new railway will take. The two principal options are to run around the hills of Brie and the ridges of Champagne through the more densely populated but sinuous valley of the Marne, or else cut directly to the north over the Troyes plateau.

In early 1844 a new corporation is formed to take over where Cubières left off. It includes Molé, a powerful political ally of King Louis Philippe. As usual in rail projects of this era the British grab a lion's share. Robert Stephenson, inventor of the "Rocket," will be the project's engineer. British financiers put up forty million francs of the private money, as opposed to thirty million from the French banks of Rothschild, Fould, Hottinguer and Mallet. Rothschild and Fould also are allies of the king and his cabal of *haut monde* moneymen.

The corporation, with government backing, opts for the Marne valley line as opposed to the Troyes plateau. However by this time other financiers, like hounds smelling garbage, crowd around the new project. Cliques of bankers, Englishmen, generals, Second Empire aristocracy and steelmill owners growl and hump for their share. A third of the stocks in one of these companies is held by a partnership newly formed to finance Teesside steelmills and a rifle manufactory in Connecticut. It is called London-Erie-St. John.

The situation overall is chaotic and untenable and in the midst of it Cubières is indicted for bribing a government minister. A series of secret negotiations led by James Rothschild results, on December 17, 1845, in the fusion of these multifarious corporations into one single organism that eventually is to mutate into the Compagnie de l'Est.

The revolution of 1848 shakes the apparent stability of the new alliance, but not for long. The right-wing republic that follows is anxious to accommodate the financial barons, and the Catholic right kills a proposal to nationalize the railroads that year. Although a bill is passed by the National Assembly to prohibit secret mergers such as that which formed the cornerstone of the eastern railway, the coup d'état by Louis-Napoléon in December of 1851 changes the political map back in the barons' favor. And in March of 1852 Louis-Napoléon's government rams through a prohibition against the earlier prohibition, allowing back-room mergers to become once more the order of the day.

London-Erie-St. John creams capital off the lucrative Compagnie de l'Est until 1908, when it sells its shares and with the profits takes a minority share in a subsidiary of the Thyssen Group, and a majority interest in Banque Atlantique.

fifty-six

"... *does not help unless you use it to help someone you love, to me the idea of certainty, or anything else does not help* ..."

Rohan closed his eyes once and once more massaged his eyelids with his fingertips.

The train was slowing gradually from its already bush-league speed. The conductor swung, an understated ape, down the corridor, repeating "Dormans, Dormans."

For Rohan the anger at Frank had crested and subsided somewhat but still left at the high-tide mark a wrack of aggressions and insecurities.

None of that mattered however compared to what Eva had said, in particular that sentence of hers now looping through Rohan's brain—*use it to help someone you love.* Nor could he put out of his mind what had followed;

I've never been able to help, with science or anything else.

It was more or less what Dominique had said when he'd heard the news about Nathalie, three years ago, in their bedroom hidden in the overgrown mimosa that surrounded his bungalow in Venice.

fifty-seven

She is fast asleep, they are both asleep. Even the sirens are silent. Chloé sighs gently in the next room. The Pacific breathes in and out fifty yards away. They have been content without knowing it. Their days are scented with mimosa. The news comes as such news always does, in a scream of bells alarum up from the narcotic night, the digital clock announcing in senseless precision 0340 A.M. Grasp the Bakelite nettle. His father's voice, racked by satellites and the effort of holding everything in, which is how he usually sounds on the rare occasions they talk on the phone. Only tonight it comes across even more constrained.

"J'ai de mauvaises nouvelles, Ludovic. Ta soeur est morte, un accident d'avion. Elle suivait des cours de pilotage, elle ne m'en avait rien dit."

Rohan puts the receiver down. After the first wave of refusal passes he circles his arms around his knees and starts to rock, hard, harder. He has an idea where such behavior comes from but the origin is not important. Moaning *"Merde, merde, merde"* until the convulsions of the bedframe pull Dominique from sleep again.

"Ludo—what is it?"

He cannot cry. His body wants to scream and ullulate like a Bedouin and thrash the wall with its fists. He starts throwing clothes in the leather doctor's satchel. He will go to LAX and wait for the first plane to France. That's when she tells him he cannot help Nathalie anymore, not with love not with his logic is how she puts it. She only says it to calm him, to prevent his looping closer and closer to a kind of madness, but the words feel like a hot spear thrust into a preexisting gut wound. He puts her down with something cold, and he knows exactly where that came from. "I'm sorry," he says, holding her. He goes in and sits beside

Chloé's bed for a while; just listens to the child breathe. Then he calls Supershuttle.

He is lucky; there is room on an Air France flight at 1 A.M. The flight is zero, nothing, wasted space sucked in by Pratt and Whitneys, converted to orange torch. They cross Greenland and the fields of ice under stars are the only thing he can look at without experiencing agony. His entrails feel like those of the Spartan boy the Jesuits taught him about, the one who during endurance trials caught a live fox to eat. The boy hid the animal under his tunic and it started to chew out his stomach but he said nothing because of the shame of being discovered. The fathers seemed to consider this good form.

Rohan arrives in Paris at 5:20 the next morning, French time. The accident happened not far from Béziers, where Nathalie bought a house with the money Pé left her. He calls the contact number his father gave him, then changes to Air Inter, landing finally in Montpellier at 11:30.

In Montpellier on July 15th, 1209, Arnaud Amalric, leading a crusade against the Bons Hommes heresy, rejected the peace offerings of the Viscount of Béziers. His army took that town six days later and slaughtered the 30,000 inhabitants. "Kill them all," Arnaud was quoted as replying at the time to a lieutenant who had asked whether to spare the women, the children, the infirm. "God will recognize his own."

Marielle is at the airport to meet her son. Her hair is quite white. She wears a frumpy black dress and looks like something that has been repeatedly rolled and digested and spat out. She hugs him fiercely, and this is unusual. Tears leak continuous from one eye only, like water under a worn washer. She talks about practicalities, the autopsy, the funeral, what to do with her cottage. He says little.

The place they aim for actually is closer to Montpellier, near Aniane. From the road he can spot the hills of Montagnac, where their grandfather's house stood; the pimple on the horizon might be Tour Guillem. When Pé died the *marais salants* became a resort and the villa was sold to become part of a separate holiday camp for Dutch people. After fifteen minutes Rohan stops and gets out of the rented car and donates airline chicken to the road's unsympathetic shoulder. Ten minutes later they reach the site.

A gendarmerie car stands by a gate at the foot of a hill running northeast from the coastal plain. Further up he can see a van and another cop car and a small truck lying around what looks like junk metal scattered on a sweep of slope. Rocks and wild catnip and the tough dry plants of garigue cover the rest of the hillside. In the bounty of summer tufts of goatgrass and clumps of wildflower also spring from whatever is not rock. Through a saddle to the left one can distinguish the sapphire ocean between the towers of a distant casino. Rohan notices, a few hundred meters to his right, a shepherd's hut crumbling beside an ancient wall. The police car's lights flash blue, inane, repetitive. His mother stays in the car. As he approaches he can hear the spatter of radio. Voices raised in argument fall slowly silent. They have been waiting for him. Henri Rohan shakes his son's hand and introduces him to a gendarmerie captain, the director of the Cap d'Agde flying school; also, an insurance adjuster, and an inspector from the ministry of civil aviation.

The old man seems more cable and tendon than usual and can only hold himself erect for limited periods. The briefcase, worn and patched and, as always, locked, remains firmly gripped in one hand. The captain explains for the fifth time the facts of the matter. No distress call, no warning. It was her second solo. A witness said he saw the plane fall into a dive. The angle of the Cessna at impact was roughly forty-five degrees, or straight into the hill. She was killed "instantaneously"—they all repeat this, as if it is some kind of novocaine for his missing her.

He leaves the captain in the middle of a description of how the plane flipped on its back as the wings were being sheared off by stress. He is drawn to these pieces of lustrous structure that now are all ripped and chewed and in some cases blackened by explosion but that in their chrome bits and incongruity speak only of what they once represented, a pattern of function, a machine to fly.

A section of wing is stabbed into the dirt to his left. A wheel from the landing gear, torn panels, wires lie nearby in seemingly haphazard patterns. Strings, marker ribbons guide the investigators.

Here it is hot and quiet and perfumed.

It reminds him of a dig. The idea is the same, after all: to trace in clues the site provides what occurred in another time.

The biggest recognizable chunk of aircraft consists of the after fuselage. Half the tail, one of the tail elevators. The epicenter of the crash must have been this carbon-colored hole dug out of the ochre with lengths of aluminum pipe and a rather large piece of cracked windscreen.

Rohan walks straight and slowly toward the hole. In all this mess he seems to know exactly where to find her.

Beside the tail a small patch of dark brown that could be blood. When he bends down to touch it is bone dry. A smashed card from an aero compass lies nearby. He can read a portion of it: 115 degrees-120.

Walking around the broken aircraft, his feet scuffing multicolored wire trailing from every control surface, he thinks, without logic: the Cessna was bleeding too.

A good ten feet from the patch of blood he finds a fresh tampon, only lightly stained with red. It is flagged with a little orange ribbon. The force that could rip this from inside her and throw it so far takes his breath away. A few feet from the tampon, also marked with ribbon, he finds the ring he gave her, the replica of the artifact from Edremit.

Right next to the impact crater, completely unscathed by fire or collision, a clump of *digitalis purporea* shivers in the strong southeasterly wind.

He wants to scream the way someone who has swallowed salmonella wants to vomit. He feels turned inside out anyway, as if everything solid within his psyche had been sucked out. Once in a while, as he walks around the hillside, he understands for a thin moment that he will never make her laugh again, never fall for her velvet blackmail, never see her dark eyes narrow with pleasure at his approach. "I didn't know you were coming, you bastard Ludo." Never again spot her slight, driven form whipping down a street or throwing back the hair that tumbled loose over her eyes.

He finds himself growing furious, the classic response, wanting to yell at her for abandoning him in such a common fashion.

The man from civil aviation walks over to him. He is small with a round face and tinted glasses, a hedgehog nose, mongoose paws. "You mustn't disturb anything," he says in a high, scratchy voice.

"I know," Rohan replies, "I'm not a schoolboy. But I do want that ring, when you're finished with it."

"I can't guarantee it," the inspector says.

"If you don't guarantee it," Rohan tells him levelly, looking him right in the glasses, "I will take you to court. If that doesn't work I will find you and kill you with a blunt knife."

"It's so hard," Nathalie observed the last time she phoned. "I thought it was supposed to get easier as you got older."

A trio of black-headed gulls floats almost immobile on the thermals rising off the northern slope.

Rohan rejoins the group of men by the truck. Marielle has come up the hill and stands xanthic in its shadow. Was it always me and you against them? Rohan wonders; he is not talking to his mother. He feels mugged by the brutality of this dense earth. His father is stiff and pale with fury. The little inspector bobs like a bird, glancing angrily at Rohan. "You can inspect all you want but you are going to find it was pilot error, or mechanical trouble," Henri Rohan says.

"*Not* mechanical trouble," the owner of the flying school

objects, "that plane was perfect. The pressure differential over these hills—"

"The indications are there," the insurance man says. "I have seen cases of suicide—"

"She was not *meant* to fly!" Henri is shouting now. "There could have been a heart attack, or, ah, she may have been lost, her navigation was probably poor, she was always bad at math. You cannot *know*." The old man's features have blurred with age. He holds the locked briefcase like a rifle.

"The nav systems worked," the flying school man yells in reply.

"What the fuck difference does it make," Rohan tells them.

Henri Rohan glances at his son. The glance is brief but it registers solid as a bas-relief whose sole motif is contempt. Marielle walks toward the wreckage. Supporting herself on the tail section she begins bobbing faster even than the aviation inspector. A curious rhythmic wail comes from her throat, rising warbling in the hot wind. The rhythm of the alien words seems to Rohan to meld with the desert wind, the dust, the death of this place. It expresses in him something words cannot begin to touch. *Kaddish.* The old man, who does not hold with such Jewish hysteria, moves to stop her but for the first time in his life his son physically stands in his way and will not be shoved aside.

He thinks of her singing, in the hills west of here, the dry verse of this land.

> *Alas, how I thought*
> *I was practiced in love*
> *Something I really*
> *Knew so little of*
> *Since I could never*
> *Stop myself loving*
> *Someone from whom*
> *I would gain nothing.*

Bernard de Ventadour.

The funeral, of course, is Catholic. She left a will, anyway, specifying a cemetery in Béziers. There are Aleppo pines and the ocean glints merrily not far away.

Nathalie's husband P. shows up for the funeral. He is slim and elegant as a Spanish curse. Rohan refuses to talk to him for he thinks he can spy in the man's correct mourning, in the somber but elegant clothes he wears, every detail of the raw indifference she suffered from and that in the long run killed her.

As it turns out, he is wrong. When he returns to LA Dominique hands him a letter from Nathalie postmarked "Béziers" the day before she died.

"Don't," Dominique says, looking at him carefully as she holds him, "don't let her manipulate you with that, too."

Rohan does not answer.

He waits a full twenty-four hours before going to the beach and opening the letter. This is the last he will hear from her; by waiting he can keep her a little longer. The waves cracking against the sand after a 6,000-mile run from Japan provide a meter for her words that like Kaddish, like the old songs, seems to flow in exact time to the present circumstances; her lilt in talking, her neat schoolgirl hand.

Béziers
la St. Olivier
Dear Ludo;
What I love in you is that never will you comprehend that one can feel so alone and so exhausted that finally death seems like a gift. But I assure you it is so.
I'm sick and tired of my life. It has always weighed heavily on me. P. is not unkind but he and all the others bore the shit out of me — yes, forgive the poor play on words — they bore me to death. The law-cabinet bores me. As you know ever since I was a kid I always wanted to learn how to fly but the real reason I started to take lessons was to do what you now know I have done. The irony

220

of it all is, flying is the only thing that has given me pleasure in the last three months. Still, piloting Cessnas is not enough for a lifetime.

You know, it's you I love, whom I have always loved. I don't say that out of despair or drama. It's simply true, the way it is true that the sun rises, or that simplicity does not make up for emptiness, or that even simple things no longer excite me. Anyway, you knew all along. It's not because of you but despite you that I'm going to put a stop to all this.

Nothing more to say.

Nathalie.

P. S.; take care of Marielle, you know Henri will blame her.

He sits on the sand for a while. He thinks that the letter is full of things said with exaggeration, to excess, and this makes perfect sense for it was always when she was saddest that she was most loud. He strips and walks into the sea. The water is cold and not very clean. The undertow is a giant hand tugging you further out. He stops swimming for a moment, letting himself be tempted as she was. He remembers imagining something similar for himself a few years ago, in Greece, when he was upset because of Sanders, because of losing Marie. He feels his muscles losing strength as the cold draws energy from his body.

> *In this my lady*
> *Is like all women*
> *And I reproach her for wanting*
> *What she must not covet*
> *And desiring what is forbidden.*

The meter of the *lai* meshes with the waves as they crash, and suck, and crash again.

His hand touches something in the water. A disposable diaper. He recoils in disgust, and starts swimming again almost immediately.

If he were to drown now, there would be no one to remember Nathalie the way she really was.

If that were to happen, Henri Rohan would have won.

Also, he is supposed to pick up Chloé from school at three. If he lets the Pacific take him she will wait there alone. After a while she will grow unhappy, even scared.

He still cannot cry but in a way he cannot explain to himself the freezing polluted water now takes the place of tears for him, tears on the outside of his body instead of in.

He fights the water more than he really needs to, pummeling its cold salt slickness with all his strength toward shore.

fifty-eight

The train was on time, almost to the second. The aging BB locomotive roared dramatically as it pulled its *rame* of obsolescent carriages into the number one quai. The Tannoy squawked, doors banged. Greetings, farewells, the hurry of feet gained precedence over the noise of declutched turbines.

The carriage was where the voice said it would be and also where the *composition des trains* board said it should stand and you appreciated this accuracy. It felt better to work with professionals, it gave you more of a sense of mission. You climbed the steps of the car, holding the suitcase high in front of you. You moved quickly but not hastily, earning a glare from the thin priest in work clothes both for getting on ahead of him and for not helping with his many bags. You counted the compartments down, as they had instructed, stopping at the fifth from the front of the carriage. You slid the door open and entered.

There was no one inside. That made everything cleaner. You could hear voices in the next compartment forward. You lifted the suitcase to shoulder height then, with almost sexual care, pivoted it thirty degrees on the vertical axis so that it hung parallel to the downward slope of the luggage rack, closer to the window since passengers normally chose that end. You laid the broad flat side gently on the lip of the rack and let it slide as if on eggs till the suitcase's bottom came to rest against the bulkhead separating this compartment from the next one forward. You took a deep breath, and dropped your hands.

Doors were slamming again. You went out into the corridor, not hurrying. The thin priest dragged his bags into the sixth compartment down. You were not sure that would be far enough away to ensure his continued well-being, but it was not your affair. You walked up the corridor toward the front, casually, like a new passenger ascertaining for future reference the position of the toilet. You were aware of movement in the compartment just forward of the one you'd left the suitcase in but you did not turn your head to look. The faces were unimportant, the people did not matter anymore. You could hear the loudspeaker as you climbed down the steps of the train. "*Attention au départ.*" The conductor did not even glance at you as he strode officiously by, slamming the door you had just exited. A whistle blew. The train jerked and, in slow motion, accelerated down the quai. The faces in the windows seemed already ghostly against the reflection of station and sky.

You watched the train pull out of the station and disappear down the tracks. The red light on its last car was a friendly, innocent eye. You felt a brief surge of loneliness for the departure of such a powerful object.

What you liked in explosive devices was that they restored importance to objects. All their lives people depended on inanimate things, used them, discarded them without gratitude or any sense that such objects had an existence of their own.

But an explosive device for a brief fraction of a second

allowed objects to have an impact on people instead of the other way around. It reasserted the balance of things; for there were after all many more objects in the universe than there were men and women.

You were surprised by these thoughts. Normally you avoided such speculation. You checked your watch against the electric clock and walked out of the station, still not rushing, like a person who had just put a relative on a train and was now returning, without great enthusiasm, to the placid stream of his daily life.

fifty-nine

Once, when he was younger and a little looser in his curiosities, Rohan had tried to determine if you could completely think yourself into the past.

This was, he believed, part of the discipline of being a historian—or an archeologist, which was just a historian with an anal fixation for silt. The attempt took the form of an exercise for old Mortimer Wheeler at the Institute of Archeology at the University of London; he had gone there after finishing his year of military service.

So he had thoroughly researched a period, a place, a stratum of people who existed in the thirteenth century. He set himself up in a dark room, surrounded himself with props: pictures of period household implements, engravings of a ship of that era, woodcuts of wimpled noblewomen and rough peasants, a borrowed reliquary; all lit by candles whose shadows cut out everything else in the room. He put a looped cassette of plain-chant on the tape deck. Alternately reading texts from Peire Cardenal, and closing his eyes, he tried for two hours to dream himself into another time.

Now, as on the left side of the train the buildings of Dormans pulled away at an increasingly rapid rate, then gave way to a gravel pit, a field hemorrhaging with poppies, Rohan found that he had been pulling slowly out of the part of him that remembered, that *was* Nathalie's death. But the field of poppies slapped him into relapse, the way an overlooked prop might pull him back into the stageset he'd just struck. Again he was reminded of that lonely tampon dried on the sterile hillside. He had been thinking of saying something. Now his mouth closed on the potential phrase.

Eva had glanced toward Rohan when it seemed he was about to speak. When he shut his mouth she turned to Frank. The echoes of their earlier words, the reverberation of the tension behind, had been moving around inside her, irksome, intrusive. She knew the words she spoke had not been overtly aggressive but she wondered whether the timing and tension in her had not been out of synch. Perhaps she was more directed than she thought; perhaps, in the roiling of emotions and memories that these men, this trip, had conjured inside her, against the overarching background of her bodily fear, she had unholstered some hostility and aimed it at Rohan and even more at Frank. Impulsively she leaned forward and to one side—she was at the window, and Frank sat diagonally across from her—and put her hand on his arm.

"I agree with what you said, in a lot of ways," she told him. "Even though I am a scientist."

He looked at her in mild surprise. His face was pulled almost into a frown. Then it cleared, and the creases around his eyes deepened. The ledge under his moustache stretched. He placed his hand over hers.

There are more nerves and blood vessels per square millimeter in the fingers of the human hand than in any other part of the body.

Frank's fingers did not constitute a second brain, they acted very much in concert with the frontal lobes and motor centers; however the way they traced, in that one brief touch, the topography of Eva's hand, registering the warmth, the size (a little bigger than Jodee's), the texture (somewhat softer), made him feel as if his hand was in this truncated instant actually doing the thinking for him, drawing up an image, comparing it to other stored images in data banks accessible to his palm and thumb, coming up with a perfect match that was, and had to be, the first time his hand touched hers, in the depths of that smoking church by the Santo Tomas market in Xelajú.

sixty

Rendezvous of the clandestine variety are notoriously difficult to pull off. In any case Frank, since Bahr el Gazal, has grown tired of the infantile strictures of stealth and misdirection. As a result he has approached the scheduled meeting with the army agent in Xelajú a little wearily, certainly without enthusiasm, and he is all the more pissed off when it comes to nought.

The whole point of this exercise is for the army to sell off surplus stock without the parliamentary audit committee knowing about it. That arrangement means the colonels will ask a low price but keep a hundred percent of it, instead of seeking market value and only putting a fraction of the sum in their own pockets.

But the army agent never shows up. He knows what Frank looks like, he is aware that Frank will be clutching a copy of a book called De Primo Principio. The agent is supposed to be wearing a lapel pin from a local soccer club and he is to "stumble" into Frank and then lead him to a safehouse in a nearby alley.

Another problem in dealing with these police states, Frank reflects, is that they are locked into the outmoded tradecraft of the Cold War era. And their security is a joke. Santo Tomas market probably is crawling with rebel sympathizers; two grenade bombs went off in central Xelajú only last week, to the great consternation of white people, none of whom were hurt.

The second bomb killed three Indians.

Frank moves unhurriedly down the stalls of the market toward the half-ruined white church crouched on vast stairs that were deliberately shaped, in the wisdom of the early Jesuits, to resemble a Mayan temple.

Nine out of ten of the faces here are pure Mayan. Some of the women still wear the color-soaked *huipil* blouse whose patterns, they say, assuming you know how to read them, denote not only the village and caste but also intimate personal data concerning the wearer. The Indians bargain over fruit and nylon hosiery and their flow solidifies into a stream converging on the church steps. He does not mean to enter the sanctuary but he sees a woman hesitating on the steps, staring up at the white towers broken in their attempt to reach a god who might make these brown people a little more compliant than would mere force of arms. She is European or American, in her early thirties perhaps, with a calm face, a short, retroussé nose, and long dark hair drawn up in a bun. He recognizes her vaguely. She is staying in his hotel, he has seen her in the restaurant. He is surprised that she is here alone, for the market is off the beaten track and generally avoided by tourists because of its thievery and smells. When she makes up her mind to enter the church he follows. He has no real motive other than idleness, curiosity; a slight interest in her looks, a slighter concern for her safety.

The inside of the church looks more like hell than heaven. Rank clouds of incense rise from thinly disguised Maya-Ki'iché idols at the entrance. Although she is taller than the Indians he almost loses her in the smoke and confusion. When he finally does get close he reaches over to touch her shoulder and she whirls, eyes blue-white against the shadow. He makes some excuse, asking a transparently fake question about the church. To his surprise she provides him with an articulate answer, spoken offhand as she looks behind her.

She says she is not sure how to get back to the hotel and he offers to guide her out of the market. He remembers holding her around the waist, hands so thick against her silk, supporting her through the crowds as they fray a path in the umber fragrance of the slums.

He never does hear from the agent, though the army knows where he is staying. Frank is in the Continental's dining room, eating steak and drinking Alvarados, when a growing confusion and din of voices announces the revolution, or at least the attempt to light it off at the Continental. That is his first sight of the Sturmgewehrs he came to Xelajú to buy; the guerrilleros herd everyone into the ballroom, the outdated blue-black weapons cuddled comfortably in hands and elbows. Huh, Frank thinks, no wonder they never contacted me. He does not know, nor does he ever learn, why the army did not simply send a message notifying him the weapons were no longer for sale.

He spots Eva standing behind one of the couches and makes his way through shocked tourists to her side.

It is precisely in that instant, as his movement toward Eva brings him in a half-circle around the podium, that he first spots Leila. The sight of her alters the mild Lothario impulse he has been feeling in regard to Eva. The *mestiza* is much more exciting to him visually. He watches her tense, move, and relax. He feels, in the syncopation of her movements, in the hooded, cheetah quality of those blues-bar eyes, a power that will open to both of them a channel into each other's secrets, into the smoke at the base of sex, to the very heart of their difference.

228

Later on Frank will understand she possesses something more, for Leila contains in uncured form a quality-of-being Frank once had: of putting herself on the line, of gambling all she owns in order to win a goal for which she cares desperately. Political and economic security for the *chulos*, a release from bondage to the cross-border banks whose interests the army represents, the details of the goal do not matter; it is that knot of raw yearning in Leila that Frank is drawn to, with all the strength by which he measures its passing in himself.

But Leila is one of the rebels. The roles they assume have made them, to some extent, competitors. When the *indios* tell them they can return to their rooms he gives Eva his room number and this time it is because of a certain clear, though possibly superficial, gentleness he sees in her— linked to the fact that, in the core of him that is still untwisted and clean, he is willing to put himself out to protect that quality in Eva, as an abstraction if nothing else.

The detonations, he finds, do not surprise him. He knows something about the "Frente Armada para la Liberacion de Los Altos" and he is aware they possess a stock of RPG-7s probably funneled to them by the Colombian M-21 via Cogswell. The army of course possesses Milan wire-guided antitank weapons they could easily use on the hotel. And the rockets boom and whistle and glass rattles but he has the impression that very few of the rounds are aimed at anything. This is merely a skirmish laid on by the military to test how serious the rebels are about the whole affair; rather like the first dance at a private-school ball, to winnow out the wallflowers. The volume of fire, he thinks, if not its accuracy, should convince everyone.

As his body learns to live with the racket he remembers Eva. At some point—later his memory is not very clear on this, but he thinks it's within five minutes of the first warning shot—he decides to see if she is okay. He walks carefully down the corridor to her room, feeling the floor shake under his feet. He finds her under the bed, quaking with fright in a syncopation roughly tuned to the explosions outside. He slides under the bed with her and she grabs his hand—in relief, he thinks, even in desperation. They watch the tracers together for a while, holding hands.

Later he will not clearly recall who made the first move, or why. He believes it was him. At first, in the confusion, he is not even aware that their thighs are touching, hot under the furniture. They are still watching the tracers fracture the sky into roseate cracks over the mass of the volcanoes and it could be the exiguous beauty of those patterns coupled with the underlying sense that he and Eva might within seconds see the glass smash under the nose of a rocket-propelled grenade and find their circuits cut before they are even aware of it that pushes him to take the next step: the hand moved to her waist, a wriggling close; seeking the prime alliance of skin under stalagtite box-springs.

Whatever the reason, they know exactly how to communicate urgency to each other without the use of words. They bite gently to make the kisses more potent and pull at each other's clothes with the strength of panic. She is soft and warm and very wet and without the slightest forewarning he feels a pulsion of tears break from a cage in his chest to rise through his throat to the eyes. He is trying to hold back tears when he goes into her but entering only helps the tears break free. She pulls him deeper into her body, muttering something in a tongue that is not English, the machine guns let up for a spell and he lets himself come, quickly, without asking about the status of her womb, nor worrying about the contentment of her clitoris, aware only of the preference to live a little longer. In the darkness of his coming he sees, not Eva, not even the cheetah girl presumably letting her Sturmgewehr rip at the army below, but simply colors: reflections of places he has seen. The blue harbor of Jamestown, a snowy mountain in Nooristan, the blaze that inhabits the maples of Vermont in early autumn.

He has no idea why he started to cry. It has never happened to him before this way, and it never will again. The tracers fly once more, followed by the hooked-up booms of the automatic weapons he came to buy. "I hate this," he remembers telling her, and it is clear to both of them he refers not only to what is happening outside but—something she can only sense—to a growing disgust at his way of life, the parched cyphers, the uncertainty of effect.

She touches his face and he senses her looking at him in the fibrous and flickering dark but neither makes a comment. When the firing finally stops and stays stopped they climb up on the bed and slide under the sheets. They spend most of the night holding each other. They do not make love again.

sixty-one

"You've finished that," Eva told Rohan, referring to the wine Frank had brought. Fishing around in the growing confusion of discarded wrappers, scraps of uneaten bread, and wine containers on the seat beside her, she picked up an amber bottle with a label showing a sapphire lake surrounded by green hills. Rohan pulled out his fisherman's knife, which was usefully equipped with a corkscrew. He drew out the cork and poured a draught into each of their glasses. Eva, leaning forward so he could fill hers, touched his hand also. The gesture was less impulsive than the one she had used with Frank but it was meant as a continuation of the same sensibility and she could see that Rohan took it as such by the way he glanced up at her and then nodded, a little self-consciously.

A man pushing a cart laden with ham sandwiches, beer

and chocolates knocked on the sliding door. They all glanced at him, made negative signs or looked away, and he continued toward the next carriage.

Rohan took a cautious sip of the Tokaj. He did not normally care for sweet wines but this one had an unusual quality, a clear taste, rather like the one you experienced touching your tongue to an alkaline rock, underneath the crowd of fruits and tannic acids.

"Do you like it?"

"It's not bad."

"It's very good," Frank said, "it's great."

"I think I'm getting a little tipsy," Eva remarked, and crossed her legs in a way that shut the gates of her bladder more tightly.

They were rumbling through a village. A sign on the empty station platform read "Troissy-Boquigny." On the outskirts, a glue factory and mechanical workshop, then willows and other hardwood on the riverbank. Vines climbed the surrounding hills in precise rows marked by bright orange plastic markers. Crows preached disaster from sullen trees.

"It reminds me of Hungary," Eva said, touching the Tokaj to her mouth, feeling her lips with the tip of her tongue. "Oh, this area, near Balaton Lake, I used to go there for a vacation. The limestone on the hill, these vineyards."

"I was thinking earlier," Frank said after a pause, "it reminded me of Vermont. Because of the hills." He pointed at the label on the Tokaj. "I used to take Jack to a camp, near Warren."

"How old is he, you told us—"

"Eight. Nine in November."

"Does he look like you?" Eva asked.

"Of course." Frank smiled and rubbed his moustache. "Jodee's family thinks he looks just like her but what do they know, they're just a bunch of no-count Fall River fourflushers and they'd lie about it anyway.

"And, because I know you're gonna ask," Frank continued,

"he's brilliant, a straight-A student, also he's very good-looking like his dad, he's already a talented computer programmer too; he's, umh, he's responsible, helps out at home *all* the time, good with dogs and little kids . . ."

"Of course," Rohan said, glancing at Eva to see if she'd noted the stain of defensiveness behind the irony.

"Actually—" Frank unfolded one palm and looked at it as if surprised to find his callouses and lifelines still present. The smile continued to live behind the moustache but weaker. "Of course I'm joking.

"In fact he's becoming somewhat of a problem. I mean I know that Jodee and me—because of the divorce, obviously that's somewhat to blame. He is a good kid but—"

There had been the blockade incident, the virtual-reality masks. Frank described it quickly.

"But that's interesting, at least." Eva pulled down a corner of her mouth with one finger. "A new way of causing trouble, no?"

"He's not doing the same boring things, like just trying to sneak out of classes," Rohan added, thinking that Chloé had liked school, although girls were different and in any case a French Montessori school in Topanga Canyon probably did not provide a fair basis for comparison.

"He's original, I grant you that," Frank said, feeling without wanting to the automatic burst of pride sparked by praise, even left-handed praise, for his kid. "It's not like the gangs I used to run with. What worries me is, he hides it. Lies about it, even."

"Kids lie," Rohan remarked. He took out his pack of cheroots, but he had been too long in Los Angeles to light up in company without absolution. Changing his mind, he slipped them back into his pocket.

"It's part of their development," Eva agreed. "If the facts don't fit your story of what you want the world to be, oh, you make up a different story. Jack will stop, at some point, if he is healthy in how he thinks."

"I ought to take him to Vermont," Frank took up more slowly. "I think I'm gonna have time to, soon. We could rent a cabin . . .

"You ought to come," he added, looking at Rohan first, then at Eva. "It's nice around there. A lot of Russians live near Warren because it reminds them of home. There's birches, pine forests. Mountains."

"It sounds nice," Rohan said.

"But seriously." Frank was frowning a little as the thought bit. "It would be great for Jack to meet some interesting adults, as opposed to his parents. You could come for Thanksgiving, maybe we'd go up there then. The fall's the nicest time of year, it's not bitter cold yet."

"I would love to," Eva told him. The smile on her lips was slight and fixed. She put the glass of wine on one of her crossed knees, holding it there against the train's sway.

She had fooled herself, out of habit and for a fraction of a second, into taking him seriously, into thinking that maybe, just maybe, she could steal a week or ten days in the autumn . . .

Whereas the reality of course was very different.

She had managed to put him out of her mind for an astonishing length of time already but now there was no turning away the thin black messenger when he presented himself so baldly in her thoughts.

In the fall she would be otherwise engaged.

sixty-two

On a good day Paris can remind her not only of her mortality but of the relative unimportance of her ever having lived.

This is not a good day. Nor is it particularly bad, as far as weather goes. The sky is drab and full of the threat of some Atlantic storm that may or may not irrigate the city with a solution of moisture that is too thin to be called rain and too thick to qualify as mere humidity.

It is the day of her first appointment at the Clinique Nicolas Bourbaki.

Where the old stones have been spared by Cogédim, B.A. Constructions, Bouygues and other real-estate barons, they speak of a thousand years of people with every justification dreamed by man to go on living—empire, beauty, intelligence, sheer bloody-mindedness—qualities that should weigh in the balance, if such a balance existed, to cheat the clueless mediocrity of death.

She knows before she ever crosses the stone lintel that this is going to be bad. The hemorrhage that signaled the problem was hardly a good sign. She is competent to do her own rough internal and has found a hint, already, of something that was never there before and should not be there now. Two small flecks of gristle merely, almost beyond the reach of her fingers, where it should be smooth and soft as an oyster's stomach.

You try not to panic, she reflects, but in one instant of clear probability every microgram of scientific detachment and hard-won perspective is blasted aside like a fungus on a mine face; as if, deep in the cave where fear lived, you never really got past the age of five.

He cannot tell for sure from the first scans. She will have to come back in ten days, 7:20 A.M. sharp, having taken no food or drink for twelve hours beforehand. Doctor Makabeus records the appointment for his secretary on a machine that looks like a chunk of polished marble. He sits there in his black granite office reading printouts. Even then, he reads printouts. She simply has not got used enough to the idea of such emergency to make jokes but she does wonder vaguely what he can discern at this stage in the insanity of detail his scanning software generates.

She leaves the clinic clutching a sheaf of data on the Bourbaki techniques. The front has passed overhead while she was inside that cool bright microclimate but the drizzle is not heavy and the streets are full of people leaving work. They walk with the open closure of the Parisian, smallish steps, hands and arms pressed tightly to their sides, eyes alert as a fox for difference. She has learned to walk as they do. No one seems to notice the difference within her. She lets herself follow, vaguely obeying the complex dynamics of traffic flow, looking at the windows of pharmacies and pastry shops without seeing anything, up Fer à Moulin then right at Gobelins to La Mouffe. This is the second oldest part of Paris, where Pierre Esbailard came to teach logical rigor to virgins away from the iron clutch of the island church. Down past the old Polytechnique buildings to St. Jacques. Past the bar she visited on her first night with Serge. She turns right and enters the park of St. Julien le Pauvre. She loves the unassuming grace of this church. Inside, the Greek archimandrites burn the same copal resin as did the Indians of Xelajú. She used to wonder if there was any connection (the Mayans painted their tombs with red cinnabar; so did the ancient Chinese). She and d'Abruzzi liked to come to Saint Julien for baroque chorale concerts. Amid the clarity of those organic arches, in the sweetness of boys' voices, she could lose, almost without reservation, her abiding sense of separateness.

Cutting across to Cluny she passes the Grand Hôtel de la Loire where she stayed with Tamas. It was after the bear died, when they first arrived in Paris, before she had managed to locate her sister. In those days the Loire was a student hotel charging forty francs a night and Monsieur Victor locked the door at eleven P.M. so you had to free-climb up ridged steel shutters to the second floor to get in late, risking Victor's wrath. Now it has been renovated; a sign warns that the cheapest room costs two hundred euros. She sees a yellow circle of light on the ceiling of their old room. The plaster mouldings appear unchanged.

The walking does her good, it serves to cut the fear. On one level she feels a sadness—sharp but not as powerful as it would be were she standing still—that all this weave of grace and memory might be taken from her before she is ready to go. On a second level the exertion allows to rise inside her that inane and circular tautology, which, she believes, is part of every living creature and in fact the wellspring of religion: that I am living and therefore it is impossible, given the principle of exclusion, that I should simultaneously be engaged in dying. No one could live without this drug, she thinks, and wonders briefly if it might not in fact *be* a chemical, a particular configuration of serotonins or dopamines so basic it has never been identified.

She has not eaten for over twelve hours, because of the tests, and she decides to stop at La Coupole on her way home. They seat her in the middle, near the marble fountain. She feels stupidly flattered because it's the fashionable area to sit. She orders pickled herring with cream and a *pied-de-porc grillé Sauce Soubise* and a bottle of Nuits-St. Georges from an absurdly youthful waiter before she opens the folder given her by Dr. Makabeus.

Statistics again, right from page one.

The reason she went to the Clinique Bourbaki to begin with lies, of course, in her suspecting she was going to need radical treatment immediately and also in the clinic having a good reputation and her being able to get a fast referral; but none of that weighs as heavily as the fact that she finds in Dr. Makabeus's techniques a substantive echo of her own ideas and lines of research. They are technically exciting to her.

Intellectual excitement, she knows, is her defense mechanism. It is her grail and her religion. Even blasted by the storms of trial-and-error, experiment and disappointment, it provides her with a structure to wield against the night.

She is too honest to deny that in twenty or even ten years new theories and discoveries will invalidate three-quarters of that structure, making a joke of her belief system. But in a sense this is not important. The excitement is what counts; it is what she wants to be, and therefore what she is.

Dr. Makabeus's theory is this: The cellular system works as a complex information-processing mechanism that feeds back and makes adjustments based on short-term data and also works according to deep, fluid structures that only come into evidence after exhaustive analysis. In particular—and this is a sentence she underlined earlier—"the Bourbaki technique treats cells as a functioning intelligence based, as classic intelligence must be, on the healthy selection of [cell] memories. A healthy cell will 'remember' to grow in a certain way; at the right time it will forget that command, and recall a second order: to kill itself, to die. A tumor cell will 'remember' the first command but not the second. It is our job to restore the balance of cell memory, not only by targeting the rogue cells but by replacing them with a cytosystem whose mnemonic triggers are correctly selected and tuned."

She looks at a four-color separation of the processing system they have built at the Clinique Bourbaki, noting with professional envy the ports for a Mitnal-Uragiri 3-D hookup. Although it appears much neater and more high-tech it is not unlike her SEM in its basic function. Instead of working exclusively with brain activity however the computers are linked to a real-time gas chromatograph, which, through IV hookups, monitors endocrine levels and hormones, glands and salts. They will be able to plot what her cellular system is doing in different areas of her body and calibrate the overall rhythms from these data. To some extent they will channel activity to the place it is needed—sending the prescribed hormones, the genetically altered white cells paddling upriver to find those agents gone native in the heart of her body's darkness.

It is getting on for nine o'clock, and the single vast chamber of La Coupole feels like a pan spilling over with a sauce of noise and cigarette smoke and movement, smells and bright colors. Joe Lanner waves as he comes in with Lambert Simnel from Editions Cocytus. Here as well she used to come with Serge, in the days when old man Lafont and his son sternly patroled the place in black suits. The restaurant has since been taken over by a chain of brasseries but, while the quality of food and service has slipped and a modern office block has been built in the air space overhead, for once the government did not allow them to alter the physical space. In that corner she and Serge spotted Perec and Derrida arguing over ratios and a plate of belon oysters. Over there, by the bar, Serge once accused the saurian deputy-minister of housing, Jean-Louis Méleux, of constituting a "revolving door" between de Broglie's slush fund and the coalition government. Even now she recognizes the oldest clients: Leopard-woman; an octogenarian poet in a homburg; people who have been coming here since the Waffen-SS got the best tables. The talk ebbs and flows around her in accordance with its own currents. A man complains loudly that EU hygiene regulations have made true Cendré des Riceys illegal. She realizes why she chose La Coupole: because it is and always has been full of life.

She feels a wave of longing to be with people, even more than the promiscuity of this restaurant will allow. What she really wants is to sleep with a man, to hang her solitude on someone else's coatrack for the night. But La Coupole has a reputation as a rendezvous point where gigolos pick up lonely women. Her color rises slightly at the mere thought. She goes downstairs and uses the bathroom then, on impulse, unfolds her mobile and phones her sister.

"Allo?"

"*Yo estete.*"

"Eva? Just a second."

Kids roister in the background. Anna and Caleb have no offspring but Anna craves a child and she is going through a phase of taking care of her neighbors' children to compensate, much to her husband's disgust. She yells for quiet. This does not work.

"Eva—I'm sorry, it's madness around here, we're just fixing supper—"

"I can—"

"Do you want, is there anything—?"

"No, ah—I just wanted to say hi."

"Call back later?"

Eva hangs up, goes back to her table and orders dessert. Profiterolles; after all there is no point in worrying about her weight at this juncture. She feels the tears oiling up behind her eyes and presses them firmly away. She uncaps her felt-tip and doodles birds on the paper tablecloth.

She remembers a man crying when he made love to her. It only happened once and for all the steel accuracy of her memory she simply cannot recall who that man was.

Thirty-two-point-sixty-eight percent, Makabeus said, subject to test results of course; she has a thirty-two-point-six-eight percent chance of surviving the next eighteen months and going on to full remission under his regimen.

Without him, of course, her chances are close to zero.

Eva realizes that the walk has served another purpose. Amid all the vague thoughts and feelings she has decided what to do.

She will give Dr. Makabeus nine months to work his miracles. If a marked improvement is not detectable by then she will put her affairs in order. She will go on a long trip and see everything she always wanted to see but never had time for. The Zambezi smoking over Victoria Falls. The white horses of the Camargue. Pilgrims bathing at Benares. Macchu Picchu, Qasr Hallabat, Namrud Dagh. She will visit her father also, in Pesht.

Then she will return to her apartment. Late one night when everyone is asleep she will tape a note on the concierge's door asking her to call the SAMU ambulance in the morning. She will bathe and change into her best dress, the long green Tamara de Lempicka one. She will drink a bottle of Tokaj, and another if she feels like it. Finally she will take out her kit and inject herself with 30 cc of sodium pentothal and lie down on her bed with the *Diabelli Variations* and *Aufförderung zum Tanze* and the third movement of Tchaikovsky's Fifth stacked up on the CD player, the kind music washing over her like a river.

She will not go through the bitter humiliation of watching herself die alone and in ever-increasing agony. She has seen it happen. She has the knowledge and means to avoid it. It is as simple as that.

Looking at the birds she drew earlier, she sees she has written under them the words "shot while escaping." It's what the government said happened to Julián, four months after the incident in Xelajú. Yet she does not think she wrote down the phrase in reference to Julián. She has a strong feeling that she wrote it about herself.

The waiter breaks her unfocused gaze by placing a snifter of Walsin-Esterhazy in front of her.

"I did not order this," she tells him.

"*C'est de la part de monsieur,*" he replies, jerking his chin to her right.

Diagonally across the aisle a tall man with a brindled beard nods gravely at her over his own Cognac.

She stares at him for ten or fifteen seconds. The waiter shrugs, disappears. The man is dressed in a worn corduroy jacket. He looks too intelligent, too nervous, and frankly too odd to be a professional. He smokes cigarettes that bear the golden band of Silk Cuts.

She takes a deep breath, picks up the brandy, and nods back.

sixty-three

For nine hours Mangin's Tenth Army has been advancing steadily against heavy resistance. The attack has succeeded in busting through the Germans' right flank but by now the allied troops are exhausted.

Near Les Granges the French 23rd Mounted Dragoon Regiment has shuttled back and forth in response to conflicting orders directing them to support tank assaults to the north, then to the south of the village of Louatres. One of the dragoons, a private from Morbihan, slopes off with his horse into a copse and dismounts to urinate. He is relatively new to combat. The shaking, spleen-crushing fear that accompanied the first hours of the dawn assault has given way to weariness and impatience. Even the prospect of imminent death, he thinks, has got to be better than the boredom of confusion, of stupid orders, of mindless noise. He takes the time to light a cigarette and has just got it drawing efficiently when his sergeant gallops up and furiously orders him back into the line. The dragoon remounts, takes one long last drag on the cigarette. Then, automatically checking sabre, carbine, and girth buckles, he canters back toward his platoon.

The regiment, yet again, has new orders. The American First Division and several battalions of Foreign Legionnaires have been hung up on the lip of a ravine near Vierzy. German troops have dug in a number of machine-gun nests with interlocking fields of fire that are making hash of infantry assaults. A colonel at divisional HQ has decided this is where mounted troops might finally make a difference. The 23rd is ordered to form up to the east of a wood near the ravine. Pennants flutter at the tips of lances, sabres glint in the occasional sun. Horses, sensing their riders' anticipation, whinny and buck.

Then, at a signal from the captain, the dragoons charge.

The horses are handsome, their gallop graceful, their order perfect. They overrun a couple of German positions, firing carbines from the saddle. Their charge continues, full of smoke and rhythm, speed and mettle, scanned by a thrill of trumpet. The private from Morbihan has never felt so proud. He is one with his horse, with his regiment, with France.

A mortar round explodes to the left. And now the machine guns open up. Three dragoons to the left of him fall immediately in a dreadful concatenation of stumbles. The horse to his right goes down. No one from his squad rides near him now. From behind, the trumpet repeats the call to charge. The private feels desperation rise inside him like bile but the backdraft of the feelings he experienced just a few seconds ago will not permit him to falter or turn around as yet. The machine-gun bullets howl and flutter but he is untouched. He spots a machine-gun nest to his left and is nudging the horse in that direction and holding his carbine ready thinking maybe, just maybe, if he has got *this* far, when the mortar shell explodes beside him. The shrapnel pierces his knee and the side of his skull and he sags limply from the saddle and is dragged thirty meters in a circle by one stirrup before the horse is brought down by scything rounds from the muzzle of a Maxim.

Late that afternoon Mangin sends Pétain an urgent request for fresh troops. Pétain, who always grows nervous on the offensive, denies the request. Mangin resolves to press on with the men he has.

Fifteen tanks roll up to Vierzy and under their shelter the Foreign Legionnaires and the American troops clear out the German machine-gun positions.

The Mangin attack continues despite heavy losses on the 18th and 19th. On the 20th Luddendorf is forced to cancel Operation Hagen in Flanders.

Finally, on the 22nd, he orders his troops to withdraw from the Marne. He opens the drawer of his writing table, removes his prayer book, and reads the passage for July 15 to Oberst Metz von Quirnheim.

"You know," Luddendorf remarks afterward, "I never had much faith in July 15th."

sixty-four

The tracks straightened up as the alluvial plain around the Marne widened near Mareuil-le-Port. The engineer running the Bar le Duc local pushed the throttle lever forward, boosting speed to ninety kilometers per hour. The passengers in the fourth compartment of the second-to-last car registered the acceleration. All three once more and automatically glanced out the window.

The Marne was close again on the left, and to their traveling eyes the northern hills appeared to have pulled away from the river. Now they were well into Champagne and vines covered most of the south-facing slopes. Apple orchards stippled the river banks. To their right, unnoticing, they passed a warehouse filled with over a quarter million bottles of sparkling wine.

Rohan looked up the northern ridges and saw a monument that he recognized from earlier trips on this line. It looked like a man in robes with arms upraised in benediction. He assumed it was either a monument to the monks who invented the local brew or a war memorial but he did not know for sure. It probably had something to do with a monastery because to one side of the nearby village stood a hybrid of church and palace that indicated this place once lay under the sway of a religious order.

Rohan's memory was no better or worse than the average for a man of his age and it worked the way other people's did, organizing and sequencing data according to principles that were not always obvious to the conscious brain. For instance, he did not directly associate the sight of a church, the statue of (possibly) a monk, or the idea of a monastery with his own first communion.

What did bridge the gap, however, was color; the grizzle of old stones and the architecture of the monks' palace with its buttresses and towers that represented, depending on your outlook, either a magnificent stretch toward heaven or an agonized tension aimed at denying everything warm and normal below. Such a pattern of stones and towers and the dun shadows they spawned tended to open in Rohan a channel straight back to the Lycée Erasme and the church of St. François d'Assise to which it inextricably was linked.

sixty-five

He lives as an only child from the time Nathalie is born to the age of eight. This is because of an episode that is never adequately explained to him as a child or later. All he ever knows is that Marielle and Henri Rohan live separately for that period, with Marielle taking the infant girl and Henri assuming care of their son.

It is not long after the end of empires in Indochina and North Africa, and the absorption into the foreign ministry of the *service colonial* in which Henri Rohan served as an officer. He is making the difficult and humiliating transition to the Quai d'Orsay where colonial functionaries are scorned, often with reason, as mediocre cousins, as *pauvre types*. The transition is not made any easier by the fact that Henri Rohan's wife is half Jewish. Partly in order to further his career Henri Rohan rents and then purchases a neglected, overpriced nineteenth-century house built of porous, saffron-colored Île de France rock in the least posh area of Passy. The rooms are choked with molding drapes and sagging beds. Their high ceilings are hid in damp and gloom. The garden is dominated by twisted yews and monster cedars that darken the house even when the sun is shining. Crows sit in the bosky murk and complain like old men.

When he is five Rohan looks forward to going to school, only to find that the local school makes home seem cheerful. It is part of what before the revolution was a Franciscan monastery and teaching college, since converted to a government lycée with an elementary school alongside. The church remains a church. The separation of church and state, like that between Marielle and Henri, only underlines the grim connection between the two, for the French educational system has absorbed entire the Catholic logic of guilt, discipline, and transcendance.

As for Marielle, it turns out she is permanently linked to her husband by an absence they have in common.

At school Rohan is a slow learner and lazy. In the playground the kids from the swank half of Passy, boys whose fathers are ministers, or wealthy, or real diplomats, like to taunt him; "Ludo," they yell, "*cul d'eau!*" He has a few friends and they are to a man black-hats. He remembers class as a farago of humiliations small and great. Home is a system for mirroring his failures at school. His father spends the evenings forcing him to write out "dictées"; the single goose-necked reading lamp makes a death's head of the gaunt features of Papa. His foot taps in a crescendo of annoyance at what can only be his son's stupidity. Nights are an arena of apprehension and guilt because Rohan has forgotten or has bungled his homework. Already he takes refuge in the wrong books: stories about Breton corsairs, or knights who tie the scarf of their damsel to their lances as they ride, shining and clanking, into the lists.

One spring Marielle and Nathalie return. Nath is seven, a

year younger than Rohan but smarter in all areas. After the first shyness and jealousies are over, Rohan and Nathalie discover in each other an indispensable ally against the shame they have been made, quite unconsciously, to feel in respect to their parents' parting. A month after what was for all practical purposes their first meeting they are already inseparable. They play and walk to school together. Rohan will always remember her in some part of his mind, knees stained and wide mouth grinning maximum over buck teeth as they bury Philippe Samory's plastic soldiers up to their necks in Maman's peppermint patch, as part of a longstanding campaign against the platoons of the kid next door.

In the schoolyard Nathalie is faster and more agile than most. Rohan's friends, respecting this, partially exempt her from the role-defining gynophobia of preadolescence. In school's jungle society Rohan comes to be seen no longer as a glum and troublesome loner, but as a boy with connections. Even the elegant kids give him less flak. He does not mind if Nathalie sometimes, through douce cajoling or subtle argument, tricks him into doing things he would not otherwise have done. His new ease brings down other barriers. His marks improve from terrible to poor. He starts to enjoy some of the classes: natural science, history, drawing. At home their mother says little and walks around, pale as a poltergeist against the rooms' darkness, closing the heavy drapes against the chill. She scrubs the floors without pause or mercy. In the dining room she hangs up photos of her parents, who were picked up in the *rafle du Vel d'Hiv* and deported to the camp of Drancy and then to Auschwitz, where they were employed as slave labor by the Thyssen Group.

Henri Rohan seems more relaxed. They fell one of the cedars, open up the hallway into the dining room. More light enters the house.

One aspect of school that even Nathalie's arrival cannot change for the better is catechism. This, paradoxically, is the one class they share. Twice a week it is convened by Père

Bellearmine in one of the smaller classrooms near the roof. Outside the grimy windows one makes out the limestone necks of gargoyles straining to dump runoff on the street beneath. Père Bellearmine is a Franciscan; he is tall and abstract looking. He exclaims "Hah!" repeatedly. His nose hairs measure at least two centimeters. He maunders on without end, using a tone for which soporific would be too thrilling a description. He awards gold stars for memorizing prayers. Nathalie wins dozens of stars, Rohan not a one. He makes trouble in the back of the class and is forced to copy the prayers two hundred times as punishment. Père Bellearmine attempts to demonstrate how the scriptures point to Truth in all circumstances, using examples and arguments culled from various fields and epochs. Later Rohan will realize that the elegant form of thesis–antithesis–synthesis employed by the priest is endemic not only to catechism but to every class in every lycée in France. Much later he will understand that this is because French learning, laic or religious, is a series of streams that all flow down the same watershed. This watershed consists of the scholastic logic of twelfth century monasteries, of monks bent over dim parchments in towers overlooking church properties; of Esbailard, Erasmus, John of Occam.

For the time being however he can only register distress at the sophistries that clash with a kid's sense of fairness, which in turn is garnered from children's fables much older than the Scholastics. Why do humans go to heaven but not animals, like the Samorys' dog Bob, who seemed so much better and more innocent in every way? How can one allow wars while proclaiming "Thou shalt not kill?" Père Bellearmine has pat answers that he pulls out like trick rabbits. Rohan snickers at the priests "Hah"s and trades yo-yos in the back of the room. A thin metal Christ hangs hopelessly from a cross over his head.

From 1942 to 1944 monks of the Franciscan order ran the concentration camp of Jasenovac in northern Serbia that exterminated over 60,000 gypsies, Jews and communists. When the British army entered Yugoslavia many of these priests fled and were offered asylum in Argentina.

Père Bellearmine knows nothing of this history.

On Sundays they go to the church of Saint François that once linked the elementary school to the lycée and now theoretically stands alone. The anvil against which Rohan's distress is sometimes hammered consists of his believing, with all the pent-up emotion of a normal, that is to say half-miserable, child, in the redemption of his sins by the fables of lambent virgins, somewhere deep and unspeakably identified with girls, with Nathalie, even Marielle. So his final rejection is not undertaken lightly.

Nevertheless, on the initial day of catechism in his Confirmation year—a day when summer still rules and the windows stand open and even city air smells of burdock, lust and crossroads—when Père Bellearmine asks who is opting, with parental permission, to drop out of catechism, Rohan raises his hand though God knows he has no such dispensation. No one queries him. Nathalie is in awe of his daring. Rohan even gets out of the problem of how to sign up for Confirmation by going independently to the retreat, which is organized outside of St. François. He thinks he has been very clever until one Sunday in spring. The congregation, leaving church, files in front of the priest shaking hands Vatican-Two style by the main doors. Henri Rohan remarks, "It must be almost time for Ludovic's Confirmation." Père Bellearmine looks blank, he has not figured it out yet.

"But, hah," he says finally, "Ludovic will not take Confirmation this year."

"No?" Henri Rohan asks. "Why not?"

"Because," the priest tells him, "you gave permission for Ludovic to skip catechism. Didn't you? Hah?"

Rohan is behind Marielle trying to drill himself like a tungsten bit into the granite steps. Their father looks around at the crowd of parishioners to check whether anyone from the Quai d'Orsay is within earshot. He is silent as they drive home. He takes Ludovic into the dining room and slaps his face three times, very hard. His father's silence is worse than the blows but somehow what is worst is the fact that Henri Rohan refuses to believe that Ludo went to the retreat, that he *wanted* the sacrament, only without the red tape surrounding it. "Liar!" he yells, not moving at all in the force of his rage, "you're a liar." The crows chuckle. Marielle comes in but does not intervene and in her eyes is the blankness of the worst abandonment: an opting for safety, the jettisoning of a belief in what is finally most fair. Above Henri's head the eyes of Rohan's grandfather, who was killed in the Great War, and those of Marielle's parents, who were arrested while Henri Rohan was on duty in Djibouti and she was hiding in Lyons, look over the scene with all the indifference of those no longer at risk.

Late that night Nathalie comes into her brother's room, although she has been forbidden to do so, and finds him kneeling by the damp and sagging bed. He is crying and mumbling "Hail Mary"s at the same time. She comes back an hour later and finds him in the same position. She kneels beside him, puts one small fist on his shoulder.

"Why are you praying, Ludo?" she asks.

"Because I don't want to be scared."

"Are you scared of going to hell?"

"No," Rohan tells his sister. "I know I'm going to hell. I just don't want to be scared of it anymore." Even at that age he has seen the fear in his father's face and taken it as his own.

• • •

Of the 12,884 men, women and children ultimately deported as a result of the Vel d'Hiv roundup, only thirty survive.

None of them are children.

sixty-six

Eva, Frank, and Rohan stand on an empty platform, waiting for a train that does not come.

The platform is of beaten earth, slightly raised to distinguish it from the track bed. The single track runs alongside on cracked cement ties. Although the train is said to run every two days, in this humidity the rails always carry an orange scurf of oxidation, and the earth around the ties is thick with weeds and tiny roseate orchids.

Beside the platform stands a small adobe building with a tin roof, a blocked window, a door. A sign next to the door reads "San Cristobal—FNX." San Cristobal is the name of the station; FNX stands for Ferrocarril Nacional de Xelajú, or Xelajú Railways.

A little farther away a rusted mobile home painted with camouflage stripes is propped on ironwood blocks. From a flagpole beside it the national colors droop in the lack of wind. A sign on the mobile home reads *Frontera—Gardia Nacional*. The border lies half a mile away.

Around the station and along the dirt road leading here the jungle poises like a silent giant. The raintrees and vines hang, dark-green and moist, all over the little clearing, the tracks and the road, waiting for just one week of inattention to claim it all back. Behind the station and the jungle rise the dramatic mammaries of two recently extinct volcanoes, their upper slopes still blistered from lava. The volcanoes' official names are those of Catholic saints but the Indians around here have different terms for them that refer back to Balatikun and the nine gods of the Mayan underworld.

In local folklore these volcanoes are the on-ramps to major highways leading to the country of the dead.

Eva, Frank and Rohan got to San Cristobal this morning on the day after their release from the Continental Hotel, following an all-night bus ride from the capital. Under ordinary circumstances they along with the bulk of the gringo hostages would have gone straight to the airport; however the runways were closed by a ragged mortar attack unleashed by the rebels fifteen minutes after their forces—with the signal exception of Commandante Vent'uno—made it out of the compound to safety.

Already the rebel radio is proclaiming Julián a martyr to the cause of freedom and justice for the people of Los Altos.

Eva and Rohan slump on their luggage, which is piled up in the shade of the station wall. It is very quiet in San Cristobal. After nine days of drips and sobs and the croaking of frogs and the buzz of spotter planes, not to mention the previous night of bus diesel, their ears are continually amazed at the silences of the jungle here. Noises in fact exist; a bird calls, a frond falls; but these are so tiny that they only have the effect of amplifying the surrounding quiet.

Behind the adobe building a fat Indian woman sleeps beside a basket of warm beer and cold *pacayas*. Rohan wakes her up to buy three bottles of Alvarado, which he opens with his fisherman's knife.

"*Tu quieres?*" the woman asks, tugging at her huipil.

"*No, gracias,*" Rohan replies politely.

The woman shrugs.

A card falls from Frank's wallet. He picks it up and reads it idly. "Sebastian Calderón de la Barca," it reads. "President, Industrias Calderón—a licensed subsidiary of Hun Hau Holdings."

Frank lets the card fall back to the ground.

"Where will you go," he asks Eva on the other side of the station building.

"After?" Eva refers to the capital of the neighboring country, which is the destination of the train they are waiting for.

"Of course."

"I'll fly back to Paris." She already has called d'Abruzzi, who was unaware she was a hostage, since the medical conference was held in a different hotel. In any case they rarely

252

keep in touch by telephone when they are traveling. It is part of their arrangement.

"And you?"

Frank shrugs.

"I don't know."

"Well—but you must live someplace, no?"

"I have an office in Nicosia. I stay there when I'm not traveling." Frank sniffs his armpit and makes a face. Eva laughs. "I might stop by the States, though, see my brother."

Rohan squats beside them and hands around the beers.

"Where will you go?" Eva asks him.

"To my job." Rohan takes a swig of the brew, then another. "This wreck, off Cuihoga. If they still want me. Maybe not; I am ten days late for work."

"But you are justified, no? It is not your fault."

"Yeah." Frank gives a short, explosive laugh. "The rebels ate your homework."

Rohan looks at him without comprehension. Then he grins. The grin makes his face look almost ugly.

They sit in a row against the wall and drink. Frank dozes off for a moment, then wakes with a start, thinking he is back at the Continental and a squad of rebels is lining up, MP-40s at the ready, in front of the wall he leans on. Far away someone beats on a hollow log; "TUM-da-da. TUM-da-da . . . Tum."

"You sure she got the message?" Frank asks at length.

Rohan shrugs.

"You were there when I telephoned, Frank."

"I know, but."

"I talked to the chargé d'affaires's secretary. The same one. The second time, she said she talked to Leila in person. She said she could meet us, maybe later, over the border. I repeat, 'maybe.' *Quisias*, in Spanish. That was Leila's message."

TUM-da-da . . .

"Maybe I should have gone with them," Frank says. He means the rebels, he means Leila.

"Don't be stupid," Eva says sharply. She puts down her beer bottle. "It is not your fight. Besides, we know they got out of the city, they are safe."

"We can't know that. We can't be sure about her—"

Eva shakes her head.

"She is tricky, that girl. Don't worry."

"Not so much tricky," Rohan replies, "but lucky, I think."

"I believe she got out," Eva insists. Because of the exhaustion her voice is as rough as if she had spent twenty years drinking cheap whisky.

"Maybe," Frank says. "But why couldn't she meet us at the bus, then? Or here?"

The drums fade from hearing. In the rain-forest a bird calls, a trio of experimental notes; Hi, this is my life, my territory, anyone listening?

The Maya-Ki'iché language is unusual in that its syntax rarely distinguishes form from function.

"I don't understand," Eva says softly, "why she would want to come with us, anyway."

"Maybe she does not." Rohan set his empty bottle on the hard earth. "Our message said this only: 'You will be safe with us, they will not hurt you with us, if you want to leave for a while.'"

"They would have taken her, if they wanted her," Eva adds.

"She should just take a break," Frank adds. "Being a guerrilla can get real boring."

They sit in silence once more. A burro brays in the valley. High above them a vulture circles the lower slopes of the nearest volcano.

"When is that train due again?" Frank asks.

Eva looks at her watch.

"Four hours and fifty minutes ago."

The beers taste good and they have already finished them. Rohan buys another round from the Indian woman. A dragonfly buzzes slowly down the platform, hovering, darting, hovering. Eva looks in the station building but sees no toilet so she walks carefully down the track and squats behind a clump of tall weeds. I hope the train does not come right now, she thinks, remembering Attila József and Latinovics Szoltan. No one will believe I was not playing Anna Karenin. She almost giggles at her own joke. On the way back she notices grass twitching and spots the red-black chevrons of a snake greasing easily back into the bush. When she sits down beside the station building she finds she is trembling.

A half-hour later the sound of gears whining under a gasoline motor intrudes and grows behind them from the direction of the road. A jeep pulls up behind the station. Three Gardia troopers and one lieutenant get out and circle the station like dogs looking for a hydrant to piss against. The lieutenant walks over to their group, clicks his boot heels politely, and asks for their papers. The troopers deploy in textbook fashion, standing guard at three points on a perimeter whose center is the station. Frank feels his mouth go dry; normally he is used to soldiers and their games but his defenses have eroded over the last week. However the lieutenant merely hands back their passports, clicks his heels again, and walks off to open the *frontera* post.

The shadows lengthen slowly. The purple volcanoes take on sable tones and collect clouds. Here and there fibers of lightning begin to knit together the mountain and the evil-looking sky.

"Now I almost wish we went to the Maya-Excelsior," Frank growls over his fourth beer.

"I thought you were tired of hotels."

"I am. But I would kill my grandmother for a shower."

"You would not have to," Rohan says. "She would die if she smelled you."

"Water," Eva murmurs, dreamily. "Hot hot water and soap. Avocado soap."

"I wonder if they grow avocados here," Frank says.

"Maize," Rohan tells him. "What you call corn. That is all they ever grow here. They even have a corn god."

"Yum Kax," Eva says suddenly. "That's his name. Yum Kax."

"How do you know these things?" Frank asks her.

She does not reply. Rohan looks at her, then looks away.

"Rain," he says, "also. They have a god for rain: Chac. Chac, he's the lord of the four directions. Each direction has its own ceiba tree, and its own color. If green is north, then the north tree has a green bird in its branches. And so forth."

"My," Frank says sarcastically. "I guess those nine days weren't wasted after all."

"You're tired, Frank," Eva tells him crossly.

"Be quiet," the American replies. His fingers tap nervously: "Shave and a haircut, six bits"—a rhythm originally based on a Yoruba ring chant sung by American slaves who were allowed no other means of expression.

Eva sees in a corner of her mind the figure of Julián standing straight, thin, and quiet as the Gardia captain stood beside him. She bites her lip, hard, trying to wipe out the image, but this time it is like trying to drown a balloon, round parts of the memory keep bobbing to the surface. The last piece the Dutchwoman played, the modern one, the fourth movement of Ponce's *Concierto del Sur* for guitar and orchestra with its sad, weightless arpeggios and trills, runs in the back of her mind like a dirge.

A handful of mountain Indians appear out of nowhere and squat on the station platform.

The dark brought by the clouds around the volcanoes slowly joins forces with the decrease in light coming in from the east. Behind the station the sun lays out a shallow picnic of yellow and red colors along the jungle horizon. Cicadas begin their ratcheting duets.

"I'm sorry I yelled at you," Frank tells Eva, "back at the hotel."

"Don't be silly," she tells him. "We were all frightened."

"It was an *emergencia*," Rohan adds, softly, and rubs his chin.

Only a fan of light is left to the west when a distant rumbling too treble for thunder begins to erase night sounds from the east. A whistle sounds faintly. The rails ping. A round yellow light that is not the moon appears well down the track. The Gardia lieutenant comes out and stands next to the rails, whistling *Estrellita* between his teeth.

"Jesus," Frank says, "I don't fuckin' believe it."

"There it is," Eva says simply.

"I don't know," Rohan says, "now they will probably say we can't get on because we do not have tickets."

But no such problem arises. They load their suitcases and sit on hard wooden benches surrounded by the bags and baskets of Indians who do not look at them. Their sweat drips on the wooden floor. The diesel mumbles and chuffs for five minutes, then, laboriously, climbs into gear again.

Frank gets up and leans out the window. Black trees appear to move past the carriage he is on, changing the view before him. The last finger of sunlight touches the tips of the volcanoes. The breeze of the train's motion fans his forehead and for what seems the first time in ten days dries the sweat accumulated there.

After his inquisitors had tortured the truth of their bungled treachery from the Maya-Ki'iché chiefs, Alvarado decided to teach the Indians a lesson. He built bonfires and burned the chiefs alive. Then he marched his soldiers to Gumarcaj, the mountain city that was supposed to be the scene of Spanish defeat, and burned that too. Because the Spanish needed the Indians to work plantations Alvarado did not try to kill them all, but he set up strict rules so the Indians would know their future place in a Spanish Catholic universe. They were forbidden to use their calendar and were flogged publicly for failing to produce a child within one year of marriage. They also were barred on pain of death from riding a horse, or using their knowledge of the stars for any purpose whatsoever.

sixty-seven

Settled now at a steady 110 kilometers per hour the Bar le Duc local ambled on toward Epernay. It used the same track that the world's first international luxury train, later dubbed the "Orient Express," traveled on during its maiden voyage from Paris to Vienna on June 6th, 1883. Frank, propping one elbow on the armrest and holding his glass with the other hand, sat back in the seat and stretched his legs out diagonally against the seat next to Eva.

The wine was loosening him up. He had not realized how tense he had become. He could feel a knot in his stomach slowly untying. Part of it had been the simple strain of travel and fatigue and jetlag. A lot of it was PISR. Much of it was Jodee, god rest her complications. Some of it was Jack.

The idea that had come to him earlier played in the spaces wine was digging out between his preoccupations. He was pretty sure Jodee would let him take the boy to Vermont. For all her insecurities and resulting bitterness she was conscientious about custody obligations and fashionably aware of Jack's need for a father figure. Also she was finishing up her master's in social work at Kenmore, and would welcome the free time.

So they could go up to Vermont. His thoughts had not progressed far beyond the nebulous image of a cabin built of rough pine boards in a stand of birches on a hillside not unlike the slopes moving past this train's windows, though the reality was more likely a time-share in Sugarbush.

Frank took another sip of the wine Eva had poured. He

was not an expert and he enjoyed without embarrassment sweet stuff like this. Though he had no time for fad oenology and its *bourgeois gentilhomme* aesthetics, he particularly liked the variegated tastes like apple and chalk in the Tokaj. He appreciated the way images and thoughts curved freer, more relaxed under the wine's influence.

Jack might protest the idea of going to the hills. He would want to bring his video games, his Mac, his virtual reality masks and hookups. He might resent leaving his cronies.

This was one of the objectives of the exercise, to get him away from the gang he was running with. A boy needed a change once in a while.

And if Rohan brought the girl there would be another child around. Younger, of course, but at least she would be someone who was not an adult—someone acceptable, in the freemasonry of kids. Jack, when subtracted from the pressures of peer group and the extreme male role modeling they brought out in each other, could be surprisingly patient with younger children. Frank did not remember her age—seven, eight? He looked over at Rohan, about to ask, not sure he didn't prefer staying silent, enjoying the decompression of wine. Rohan, catching his glance, raised his eyebrows—

Frank, half automatically, half because of what he was thinking, lifted one eyebrow in response—

Underneath them, the line of tracks was interrupted where the rail separated to allow, in other timetables, splitting off to a shunt line to Leuvrigny.

The brief gap in points on both sides changed the rhythm created by the interplay of regular welds and the roll of train wheels. The three-quarter rhythm broke, *tum, dada tum, dada*; held for a space; changed again (*da-tum, da-tum, da*) into an eight-twelve beat, the rhythm of Colombian ballads Frank had once listened to, an association so brief he never defined it fully. A short screech of metal as the train's weight shifted, rising E-flat—

sixty-eight

—E-sharp;
An interval without sound, and thus lacking meter, and time
Then the train settled into its previous, waltzing canter.
Rohan kept smiling, though he was no longer looking at Frank. Frank had a sudden, clear sense of different associations on the cusp of being summoned in his head—Barranquilla; Rohan; a boy at the school in Newport; Jack.

But the shift in rhythm had disturbed that process. It shorted out the current of immediately available memories, dropped Frank through levels of resistance and space to fetch up against a feeling of bleeding through layers, of utter desolation come from nowhere in particular.

For a second it seemed very clear to Frank that this feeling was somehow kin to the process of serial randomness that had brought him here.

It also resembled, he saw that now, the impression he'd had a few minutes back, when he recalled making love to Eva in the Continental, and sobbing like a choirboy in the midst of it.

Frank shifted weight from one buttock to the other. This sense of abruptly vanishing partitions was not a comfortable thing to experience in a slow provincial train after lunch.

He draped one arm on the seat rest, drumming his fingers. Rohan shifted opposite, as if Frank's discomfort had suggested a corresponding cramp in his joints and tendons.

The way Rohan thought, Frank mused, he would never let mere suggestion trigger action in him. More likely he would most carefully do the opposite. Rohan was like a lot of Frenchmen, he seemed to exist by what they called "spirit of contradiction," building bridges to what he wanted or believed only by first confronting the rivers of what he violently objected to. A nation of atheists who needed the church, of anarchists who required the state. The sheer effort with which Ludo had rejected his liaison with Leila was an example of this pigheadedness. So was his denial of the music Eva remembered: the modern Mexican piece at the tail end of the Dutchwoman's recital.

Frank shifted his legs. He had been sitting too long. What he should do now was get to his feet, walk up and down the train, start his blood flowing again.

But the lullaby rocking of the carriage, the gentling of wine, the digestive ennui of lunch, lessened the energy available for action. And finally he stayed where he was, letting thoughts spark off each other, wondering idly why Rohan's negative insistence seemed important now. Thinking maybe it was because it had come at a crucial time, that music, against the background of radio, the rebel radio—

Frank's fingers stopped drumming. They lay motionless on the armrest.

The *indio* who guarded the last working phone and listened to the only functional radio had come into the dining hall to listen to the guitar instead. Which meant that during those few minutes, for the only time Frank was aware of, the phone in the bar had been left unguarded.

A blush of discovery warmed Frank's insides.

It followed that—since it was the only opportunity to call out—this must have been the window of time during which someone phoned the Gardia to tell them who Julián was.

Frank looked at Rohan again. The pleasure of what he had figured out was an intellectual jiz, based on unexpected shuffling of ancient data into a recognizable pattern. It raised endorphins in the same areas that were stimulated by the chain-reacting logic of John Duns-Scotus, which in turn summoned less relevant flavors: of the Hindu Kush, of control utterly lost. But overall, after Tokaj, amid the much greater power of other memories and more recent concerns, it did not exercise him much. And as the train slowed he shifted his gaze to the left, to check what new countryside was coming up—and then, as Eva moved, shifted back to follow the line of her body as she unbent it, section by section, standing up, stretching with one hand on each luggage rack for balance, jingling as she moved.

sixty-nine

As the train slowed again, rocking—the tracks were curving east and south near Oeuilly—Eva realized her bladder once more was full. In fact she'd let it get a little over the mark and had to pee, now, without further breathing or delay.

She got to her feet carefully, muscles taut, grabbing the luggage rack for stability against the camber. The bracelets on her wrists shook down and rang. Frank glanced up. Rohan stood to ease her passage. She smiled at the two men. She felt no need for explanation this time.

She had the impression—not very logical, but still—that they had done more traveling in the last hour and a half than could be reckoned in mere minutes and kilometers. It had to do with the weight rather of what they did not say than of what they uttered; it had to do with what happened twelve years ago, and the release of this past like pure oxygen between them. It mostly stemmed, she felt, from the way they had lost touch and then met once more, as if their coming together for the second time had consecrated not only their mutual history and the years elapsed since, but all connections built over time, and all the people who formed the beam and frame of their separate memories.

There would be plenty of opportunity to discuss that over the next couple of days. She slid the door open and turned left, down the corridor, already undoing the buckle of her belt.

After she left the two men did not talk for several minutes. Rohan moved to Eva's seat, to be closer to the window. The wheels clanked and juddered across another set of points. Frank, looking left, watched a farm with wooden dovecotes slide past. In the unfolding of a tall wood he glimpsed a fretwork of stone, marble, and mansard. A sixteenth-century palace was swallowed up in the arc of its own perspective before he could utter a sound of surprise or admiration.

Rohan was taking advantage of the window seat by looking back at the country they already had passed. On the left a small campground receded into the distance. Slowly the Marne had swung north and widened. A snowy beach spread itself between verdant willows and emerald water. A stream disappeared in a field between the tracks and the river.

Rohan smiled, his eyes now focused short of the landscape. Then he chuckled out loud.

"What's so funny?" Frank muttered.

"Oh." Rohan rasped his beard. "Nothing important. I mean, it's the same as what we were talking about earlier; but the odd thing, I never mentioned it, because I am not sure at all—but I *thought* I saw Leila at UNESCO. Or rather, a woman who looked just like her."

Frank stared at him. Rohan lifted his eyebrows again, and spread his hands to strangle his own surprise. "It was two or three weeks ago," Rohan continued. "I was going to run after her, but she was already down the reception hall, and then she got on the lift. The fellow I was talking to said she was with the Peruvian cultural attaché."

"Did you ever find out?" Frank asked, hunching forward a little despite himself, smoothing his moustache with one finger. "If it was—"

"No. I did not get a good look. Now I know that was a mistake. Still—"

Frank leaned back.

"It's strange."

"I guess."

Rohan's gaze shifted downward. "Well, we talked about this before, but maybe this constitutes evidence, no? I don't understand it, but a couple of weeks after I think I see Leila, you run into Eva. And two days after that we are on a train—as we said. But you still don't believe in the hidden structures."

"Huh." Frank chewed at air, looking out the window again.

Rohan brought his gaze to Frank's face.

Frank's eyes moved around the compartment, avoiding Rohan's stare. He seemed to be collecting thoughts like thorny fruit, aware of the penalties. "Ah, hell," he continued in a quieter tone. "Sure."

"I mean," he went on, "the people I work with believe in that kind of thing. Like, the equation you use to describe how chemicals react in a Petri dish is *exactly* the same one that describes how wolves and caribou interact. Or, or how water moves through rapids. The way humans act in cycles that recur every fifteen minutes, or twenty under stress . . . But if you can't explain it—" he chewed again at his imaginary gum.

"It's just a pattern our lives make," he went on, "Leila or no Leila. Statistically, events *have* to group up. Like we were saying earlier about coincidence. It's only because it's our lives that we see special meaning in it. Or beauty, or significance.

"In fact—" Frank looked directly at Rohan now—"it has no more meaning than the pattern a spider makes when it's spinning its web. Or the ripples a heron makes, swimming in the water."

"You don't find a spiderweb attractive?"

Frank shrugged.

"Do you think—" a half-smile capsized Rohan's features—"do you think the *spider* thinks it has meaning?"

"No," Frank replied, looking back calm as a Siamese, "I do not."

The two men stared at each other for a full cycle of track rhythms. Rohan's smile widened to a wolf grin.

"You don't fool me, Frank." It was Rohan's turn to bend forward, leaning on the armrest to his right.

"You care. It's written on your face. Even if you don't believe, you *care*. It's like that spider, who doesn't believe in the pattern or anything. But he still wants it to be the best web he can build."

Frank kept frowning for a beat. Then he relaxed, amused by the solemnity of the man's theorizing. He had to respect his force, the sheer effort Rohan made, even if the results were bullshit. Because the beauty of discovery was surely not so great if you had crafted the web to begin with.

"That music," Frank said. "The *Concierto*—you weren't there, were you?"

Rohan did not change position.

"You were on the phone." Frank's voice was just strong enough to be heard over the trainsound. "I mean, *somebody* had to tell the Gardia. Someone who knew who Julián was. Somebody had to get to the phone while the *Frente* kid was gone."

Rohan's eyes were still locked on Frank, though the focus was different now, set for a longer depth of field.

"And who," Rohan asked finally, "is making pretty patterns now?"

"You're avoiding the question."

"And you are proving my point. But the truth is," Rohan continued—and he rubbed his face again, consciously raising noise from the stubble on his cheeks— "I simply have no memory for music. It is much more likely, well, it was the kid himself who called. Or someone else in the *Frente*. Or the government man—remember? There was a government agent among the hostages, Leila said.

"The most likely, though, is the guerrillas. The soldiers would have shot every one of them, otherwise." Rohan quit rasping his chin. "And we wouldn't have survived, either."

"But it wasn't the guerrillas, was it? It's OK," Frank added, "anyway," and slumped back in his seat. "You do what you have to do. You do what you *have* to do," he repeated, almost to himself.

A rattle, caused by sympathetic vibration between the wheels and the carriage chassis at this speed, made conversation impractical for a few seconds. The train's pace altered slightly and the rattle subsided.

"Maybe we are all guilty," Rohan said a little later. His voice was set at the same low volume as Frank's had been. "If we dare to examine history to understand how it happened. If we presume to visit a place in such pain as Xelajú, to begin with.

"I do not need quantum numbers to tell me," he went on, "that if you examine a thing, you inevitably change it. If you tell a story about an event, no matter how many facts you know, it will still be, mostly, your story.

"But Frank," and Rohan spread his hands, and he asked the question as if it truly were a question, with his voice rising to uncertainty at the end. "What choice do we have, in the end, but to tell this story?"

Frank did not look at him or respond.

Rohan, who had felt irritation at the American for his cut-rate inductions, for the many questions they ignored or did not answer fully, now felt the hostility subside. It was all so long ago, after all, and he and Frank were older.

In any case, Rohan thought, he was not wrong. Frank did love the patterns, even if he did not believe in them. In that lay a core that might underpin, if not friendship, at least a continuing alliance. A wash of light affection for the other man, liberated, or possibly formed, by his own definition of how Frank Duggan operated, touched Rohan's chest.

After this both men turned back to the window with relief. Electricity pylons marched across a cornfield parallel to the train. From his position facing forward Frank could see in the distance a rank of tall poplars forming a windbreak between the track and the river.

"What time do we get there?" he asked.

"Bar le Duc?" Rohan looked at his watch. "Three-oh-five. In, well, an hour and twenty-seven minutes."

"Huh," Frank remarked in a casual voice after a few seconds had gone by, "you may be right about trains—the slow trains."

"You see?" Rohan agreed happily, waving his hand toward the land and river on the other side of the Securit, "you get to really see the landscape, you're almost part of it."

They sat in silence again. The carriage made clanks and rumbles in a pattern that had to do with track ties and rail welds but also with the harmonics of rails and wheel bearings, all of which were made of the same high-tensile alloy from a mill in Mülheim, Germany.

The two men did not speak further.

seventy

Rohan thought of Dominique. Checking his watch against the schedule naturally had the effect of bringing to mind the goal of his trip, and this was as it should be. He had no desire, in any case, to dwell on the issues Frank brought up. Their complexity tired him. He much preferred to think of the woman waiting for him in Guebwiller. Part of Rohan's enthusiasm for slow train voyages stemmed from believing that the only point of travel was people. Those you left, those you left to find, those you met on the way.

He thought of other women he had traveled to or with or from, on slow and human-smelling trains such as this one. He thought of Leila, who had missed the train at San Cristobal. He imagined her now, for some reason, with a face like Dominique's. And in the loose sedimentation of memory he was beginning to see Dominique looking a lot like how he remembered Nathalie. Merde, they were all crowding around, he reflected, not very comfortably, squirming a little in Eva's seat. As he aged he was starting to feel that the women he had loved in his life were forming a continuum, a whole: becoming not one aggregate woman but rather a single mosaic of different ones who folded in and out of his consciousness even when they had been gone for three or nine or even twenty years. Marie, Anita, Leila. Which one happened to spike off the flow of memory had little to do with the length of time she had been gone; instead, increasingly, it seemed to depend on his mood, the places he was in, what he was eating or smelling or desirous of at that instant.

He winced a little at the idea.

He had been thinking about asking Dominique to marry him. The big impetus there was the mounting difficulty he experienced in being apart from Chloé, who to him contained and defined the entire relationship between Rohan's being and such forces as autumn, and jazz, and the punch of a good Margaux. The big obstacle in his mind had been the heft of these other women, and the fact that they never seemed to leave his mind for good. If you looked at it one way, that could seem a betrayal of Dominique. But you could also, Rohan realized, stand that argument completely on its head and posit, since all these women carried components of each other inside them, that they actually reinforced the position of the woman you were with *because she represented all the others*; because, in the end, she was the symbol of the impossible phantom female you had been trying to capture through them all along.

Rohan thought he could be happy with Dominique and Chloé. And he could live comfortable in that knowledge which, if not politically stylish, was at least, for him, the truth, or as close as he ever got to a personal truth. The memories of other women might drift in and out of the past like ghost ships, spectral schooners creaking from the fog and storm wrack at different points and phases of moon, depending on the conditions that were supposed to evoke them. Like all ghost ships, they would be significant less for what they had been than for the warnings and abstract devices they represented now. And they would not spook him, or Dominique either, because he would know what lay behind their haunting.

Rohan rubbed his eyes.

The analogy was apt. His last professional job, if you could call it that, had been to find a ghost ship. The memory was itself a specter of amperage and chemicals that touched his consciousness lightly—but this touch, like a hologram, contained every detail of fathom and uncertainty of his bizarre week in Ottawa. He let the touch please him because, as Frank had pointed out, it was part of his life, and for all the doubts and qualms it carried, it was nonetheless proof that he had lived.

seventy-one

Coming as it does out of thousands of years of men disappearing in tiny, fragile vessels on poorly charted oceans, the folklore of maritime peoples, Rohan knows, is packed with tales of ghost ships.

These ships do in fact have several further characteristics in common both with each other and with the various women Rohan has known over the years. They tend, for example, to be light and graceful. In the case of the ships they float like great birds just over the surface of the sea, or move through clouds, even over dry land. They are unpredictable, appearing out of, dissolving into, black of storm or bleach of fog without warning. They are often fiery, and burst into

269

flame equally without notice. At times they move in ways you do not expect, sailing backward, or moving with all sails set into the teeth of the wind, against logic: the way Rohan, in his deep lack of understanding, sees his women react.

More to the point perhaps, these ectoplasmic craft invariably are manned by skeletons from long ago hanging ratchet-boned in the shrouds, empty sockets frowning at the impertinence of your enduring ability to remain alive without them. Finally, there is always a moral at the heart of their haunting, some lesson of epic arrogance, some fault in your fundamental economy of life that has caused them to wander forever, miserable, unsatisfied—all, in a basic way, because of you.

Little Teazer, The Flying Dutchman, Skidbaldner.

Leila, Marie, Nathalie.

However *La Grande Chausse*, though she has created her share of legends, is more substantial than most such ships, which remain a compound of fear and legend where the historical record plays an incidental role at best.

For one thing this 300-ton Canadian steam coaster, once engaged in the Arctic trade between the Yukon and Alaska, actually existed. For another, she may have reappeared off Kap Marie Valdemar, rusted but quite corporeal, forty-seven years after she was supposed to have vanished for good in the North Pacific. A team jointly working for Triple-I Research and the Marine Oceanographic Institute of Falmouth, Massachusetts, stumbles upon her while doing secret ice-sonar tests for the U.S. Navy on the pack off eastern Greenland. There is speculation the craft may have duplicated the voyage of the *Octavius*, a ship manned by freeze-dried corpses that floated from Alaska to Greenland between 1762 and 1775.

Rohan, between films, is hired through people he knows at MOI to sift through paperwork and come up with details that will enable them positively to identify the Marie Valdemar derelict. He flies to Ottawa at the onset of the Canadian spring, armed with sheaves of faxes showing prelim reports and snapshots of the wreck. The nineteenth-century turrets and gambrels of this odd city are just starting to shed the brownish rime of winter. He checks into the Château Laurier and from the windows of his bedroom watches floes crack and drift down the Rideau River.

Then he walks up Kent Street to the Department of Transport.

The DOT is housed in a tall glass and concrete tower that makes the Dominion Tudor architecture of the rest of the city appear elegant by comparison. The Office of Ship Registration and Tonnage Measurement lies on the twelfth floor. A pudgy man in a houndstooth jacket looks at Rohan as if he were requesting conjugal rights to his sister.

"The papers," he asks incredulously, "for a ship that was registered in *1947*?"

"That was the last year it was registered."

"Is that all?" the man asks sarcastically.

"Well, I can think of more questions," Rohan replies, "if you're looking for extra work."

A small, crop-haired woman across the office cracks up into her computer screen.

The records are all on microfilm. The immediate trace of *La Grande Chausse* shows up quickly, where it should be, alphabetical: a 299-gross-ton coaster, steel and extra-plated for ice navigation, 145 feet long, reciprocating steam engine of 580 horsepower, purchased and registered by Winchester-Goodwin Shipping Ltd. in 1938.

"Records after that," the pudgy man tells him happily, "you'll have to go year by year, we don't cross-index and we can't do it for you now."

"I'll come back tomorrow," Rohan says. The crop-haired woman smiles at him as he leaves. He calls the Vancouver Port Authority from the hotel but they have no record or memory of Winchester-Goodwin Shipping Ltd., or of the ship in question.

The next day Rohan goes through the annual records. On his way out for lunch he takes the lift with the short-haired woman. Rohan asks her where to eat and she shows him a Chinese in Slater Street and they end up ordering boiled pork dumplings together. She is in her late twenties. She has warm hazel eyes, very black hair, a Phoenician nose, and a smile that lifts her face into prettiness. Her name is Hélène Bourgeoys. She comes from Trois Rivières in Quebec and Rohan tries talking French, but their accents make it difficult for both of them so they revert to English. She is working part-time for a degree in agricultural economics at Carleton University. She has never been farther afield than New York and is impressed with the places Rohan has seen.

The yearly records begin to show the ghost ship's spoor. A board of trade inquiry in 1942, a minor collision in '46; her skipper, a Dane named Fokke, charged with drunkenness and abuse in the same year. Nothing after 1947. This confirms the chronology of the legend at least. He leaves the office of ship registration and goes to the National Library. For the rest of that afternoon and all next day he searches through rarely touched volumes concerning the history of shipping in the Yukon and the ports of British Columbia. He finds one passing reference to La Grande Chausse, something about her notoriety, a detail of no use.

That afternoon he calls Ship Registration and asks Hélène to have dinner with him and she says, why not, she has no plans.

They eat in an Italian restaurant on Elgin Street. Hélène is still amused by the different "exotic" foods available in Ottawa. In Trois-Rivières, it seems, the coffee shops serve only white bread and stew. He drinks Stella beer and with every bottle her smile gets prettier, her eyes warmer. He recognizes the milestones on the road to seduction—the Cognac in a bar, the walk to her house, the last, late-night espresso—and hates himself a little for this knowledge but it is not enough to make him refuse the invitation to her flat, or to make him feel anything but frustrated when she stops him, at the last minute, pants flopping around their ankles on the futon couch, the tapedeck playing "Andean" flute music and a quarter-moon smirking across the Rideau Canal half a mile away.

"I have a lover," she says.

"What's that got to do with anything?"

"I want to marry him." Her skin shines like pack ice in the wash of moon. Her breath smells of spearmint.

Rohan snorts.

"Do this," she tells him, and for all his frustration and smarting vanity he is not too proud to let her handle him the way Nathalie did, in a penumbra different yet similar, so many years before.

Walking the wrong way when he leaves her flat he gets thoroughly lost and has to phone for a radio taxi to take him back to the hotel.

The Vancouver papers in the library archives include reports of *La Grande Chausse*'s loss but no further details or photos.

He stumbles across the University of St. John's' massive *Compendium of Sources: Canadian Maritime Folklore* at three the following afternoon. In the middle of the third volume is a photo of *La Grande Chausse* at anchor among a gaggle of coal barges in Victoria. The picture is old and fuzzy but he can distinguish the donkey engine on the forecastle, the single stack, details of bridge-deck and davits that will be useful in identifying the Greenland wreck.

He looks at the faxes sent by MOI but they show only a beat-up hull trapped in the heart of a floe under cliffs of sheer ice. The derelict has a straight stem, and a raised sterncastle, badly crushed under the bridge. Her after end blends so well into a drift of frozen snow that one cannot tell where ship ends and iceberg begins. Every inch of the coaster is covered with layers of corrosion and the ice around her is orange from rust. No other details are visible.

"La Grande Chausse" (the *Compendium* reads) "allegedly was sighted on four different occasions after 1947, always in poor visibility or storm, and when the ships involved were unsure of their position."

From a phone in the lobby Rohan calls his friend at MOI. His friend tells him the job is over. The MOS/Triple-I team returned to the derelict the previous day, thinking to use it as a calibration base in their sonar work; they were having problems with the sensitive electronics used to pick up metal hulls in an area not far from the north magnetic pole. But the floe in which the wreck was embedded apparently had hit a rock and broken. The derelict was gone.

Rohan dials Hélène at work.

"Found it," he tells her, "but too late." He describes what he has learned.

"So you will go now. Back to Los Angeles?"

"Yes."

"You're lucky."

"Will you have dinner with me?" he asks, adding hastily, "just dinner, before I go." He does not want to pressure her, nor does he want her to think he was using her for entertainment merely. But she is far ahead of him on both counts.

"It's all right, Ludovic," she says, "really. You don't have to make a big thing. It was a small—contact, eh? But even a small contact is nice."

"Send me a postcard," she adds, "from California?"

As he hangs up the phone he feels an automatic sense of relief because she did not make more of this affair than was warranted by their "small contact." But on the heels of the relief comes a feeling of disappointment. And he realizes, suddenly, for all the brevity of their coming together, he has grown attached to Hélène—the grin, the unabashed curiosity, even the pallor of her. The realization leaves him feeling used, and this is a sentiment with which he is unfamiliar.

• • •

It is too late in the day to fly back west. For dinner he returns to the Italian restaurant he ate in with Hélène. The waiters are small and dark and not too friendly. They speak in the hollow dialect of the deep Mezzogiorno. He orders saltimbocca with a pitcher of rough Orvieto. After he has finished eating he orders a second pitcher. The waiter leans over to bus the dirty dishes and his red jacket gapes open, allowing a small iron medallion suspended around his neck to turn in its brief release from clothing. Rohan sees inscribed in the cheap metal a trio of symbols that ring in his mind as clearly as if a bell had been struck: a star, a stylized bird, and a fish, or more likely a dolphin. The dolphin appears to be drunk.

"Where did you get that?" Rohan demands.

"Wha'?" The waiter stands straight, clutching the encrusted plates.

"That, ah—*médaille.*" Rohan forgets his English. He points at the waiter's chest. The waiter touches the medallion through his clothing, much as Rohan has taken to touching the ring that hangs on a thin chain around his own neck.

"Oh. Nothing. Family."

"What family?" The waiter looks at him suspiciously. Rohan is clenching his fists and leaning forward in an excitement that must seem out of place. He loosens his hands and forces himself to relax.

"My gran'fath'." The waiter shrugs. "It is for *buon' fortuna,* he says."

"Luck. Is that all?"

"That is not enough?" The waiter looks around him with a sarcastic expression, as if to say he will need all the luck he can get to escape this crummy job, and turns back to the kitchen. Rohan takes a swig of Orvieto and shuts his eyes. In empathetic reflex he touches the magnetite ring that he found in the wreck of Nathalie's plane and thinks back, as he does so often these days, to what the ring evokes.

In the years since the wreck at Korfezi and since he visited with Marie the shrine at Samothrace Rohan has continued to research on his own account the cult of navigation that he believes was centered there.

Over the years he has reached two conclusions. First, the navigation cult survived in Asia Minor and then spread via Zoroastrian mariners to the Bonshommes cult in southwestern France. Second, the cult's pivotal mystery may have been the first use in Europe of the magnetic compass. He has evidence beyond the lodestone and the rings found on Samothrace. For starters, a passage in *The Odyssey* seems to describe the use of magnetized iron for directional purposes. Also, in 1205, well before the compass was supposed to have appeared in Europe, the troubadour Guyot de Provins, who worked for Cathare noblemen, wrote that mariners "have a contrivance (with) the qualities of the magnet . . . they stick the needle in a straw which they float on the water, then the point turns directly toward the (Pole) star, with such certainty that it will never fail."

Rohan takes Nathalie's ring from under his sweater and stares at it. Even its association with his sister and her manner of going cannot quench the silent yelps of excitement rising in him.

What if the cult still exists? What if there are still seamen bearing the triple symbol, in this era of GPS and computerized azimuths, still learning rites that the men on the Korfezi wreck practised over three millenia before?

Later on, when the restaurant is less crowded he will quiz the waiter further and find out that his grandfather was a fisherman from Lampedusa, near Malta, and that no other meanings or legends were handed down with the rough heirloom. But Rohan has never lost his capacity for idle associations. During the rest of the evening he finds himself thinking of missed opportunities, of roads that seemed to be level and open, which soon turned into narrow tracks and finally were blocked altogether; of men and women who know each other only as representations, as stories of what they were or might have been; of shades whose final curse is not apparition but absence.

Finishing the second carafe he finds himself almost grieving for *La Grande Chausse*. His friend at MOI says that Banque Atlantique (which controls Triple-I) was ready to finance an expedition to examine the derelict. If she was indeed the same ship, then she survived half a century of being shunted round and round the slow tidal gyres of the Arctic, drifting in loneliness, cold and rust the length of the Canadian and Russian coasts—only to sink within days of her voyage being catalogued and understood.

He thinks, more than is called for, of Hélène. And this turns his thoughts, in the sympathetic logic of betrayal, to Dominique.

Clouds roll across the prairie and sprinkle a little snow on Ottawa. People come in from the movies and order foccacia and spaghetti, laughing about things that are quick and warm and far from the bitter seas off Kap Marie Valdemar.

It has been a long time since he has talked to Chloé. He decides to call them as soon as he gets home.

seventy-two

Hour hands in most clock movements do not function independently but are part of an overall balance. It was because of this particularity of timepieces that the movement of the alarm clock riding in the cheap suitcase in the fifth compartment of the second-to-last passenger car of the 12:32 local to Bar-le-Duc—freed of the weight of its minute hand—rotated slightly faster than it was supposed to go. By the end of its short trajectory it was nineteen seconds early, over and above the margin of error allowed by the artificer, in reaching the point where it touched the wire leading through the clock face to the bulk of the device.

When it did reach that spot, however, the concepts of advance or delay, of time itself, ceased to have a lot of meaning, at least in the immediate vicinity of the clock. In touching, the metal minute hand and the bared copper wire completed a circuit. Six volts of current flowed from the battery through the clock into the detonator. Inside the detonator the juice heated wire whose resistance was only one Ohm, and that heat was passed on to the surrounding solution of lead azide. Within ten-millionths of a second the lead azide reached a temperature of 5,000 degrees Centigrade and ignited. It busted out of the rubber plug at the buried end of the bronze pencil, and fired into the 1.7 kilograms of ammonium nitrate in the main charge.

The ammonium nitrate was built to be unstable. Subjected to shock its various molecules sought each other like long-separated lovers. The nitrates decomposed into each other to create nitrogen gas; the carbon and hydrogen elements melded with oxygen. The passion of their union created a heat and an expansion of gas far too great to be contained by the plastic envelope or even that portion of passenger carriage. Starting at the apex of the triangle, growing in power as they combined with the higher number of molecules lower down, the hot gases expanded in the direction of the triangle's base. Their maximum force was concentrated at an initial wavefront created by the massive compression of air. Here, at the very crest of the wave, energy maintained by the explosion exactly equalled the momentum conserved.

Because the triangle's base was directed along the slope of the luggage rack toward the forward bulkhead the main thrust of the blast was directed onto the bulkhead and, as soon as that collapsed, into the next compartment.

Frank was sitting with his back to the bulkhead when the charge detonated. He had in his mind two thoughts; first, that he, too, needed to piss; second—and this was a very general thought, more of a mind-color really, a thin layer of daydream that did not take or require definition—that Eva was still in the toilet and he would be pleased when she came back, both because it would mean he could use the toilet now and also because it was good to look at her. He already had decided, just as loosely, that after this trip was over he would not let her pass out of his life as casually as he had once, as they all had.

The enormous heat and shock caught him at shoulder level and snapped his spine like a carrot between the sixth and seventh cervical vertebrae. His brain, working at the speed of light, registered an instant of emergency and heat as his body was catapulted forward, but the great acceleration burst so many blood vessels that the areas of consciousness were terminally depressed within the fraction of a second before he slammed into Rohan directly opposite him.

Rohan understood "pressure" and a heat that had little to do with the not unpleasant and ongoing wash of visual impressions from the green-yellow country outside and the tiny undertone of recall, the high blue of Arctic—

Frank's body became part of Rohan's. The plates of his skull, driven by a shock front traveling at 1,200 miles per hour, shattered on impact with Rohan's collarbone. The malar and lachrymal bones as well as portions of the anterior frontal lobes were rammed deep into the Frenchman's upper chest cavity, pulverizing Rohan's ribcage and invading his right lung. Because the blast caught Frank high, the rest of his body curled as it moved. His abdomen telescoped and a mass of upper intestine, liver, shattered ribs and blood vessels was blown straight through the sternum into the center of Rohan's gut. The back of Frank's body, and the front of Rohan's, charred briefly in the heat of detonation.

The remains of the two men, along with the wood and formica splinters of the first bulkhead, an assortment of burned clothes, leather luggage, fragments of uncombusted ammonium nitrate, wine bottles, *forrás*-paprika chicken and Arab pastry, were blasted through the forward wall of their compartment as easily and casually as if they had been shoved by a drill punch the size of Detroit.

The force of the shock wave dissipated at a predictable rate as it traveled from the point of detonation but for the next ten feet you could not tell the difference. Due to its initial angle the wave blew Frank and Rohan and the accumulating wave of debris on a descending trajectory. As the wave traveled it ripped through the sides and floor of the railway carriage, bending or blowing the structure apart like something made of cooking foil. The two men collided with a horizontal steel member which cut off the lower half of Rohan's torso and took away Frank's left arm. Then the bodies were shot through the destroyed base of the car at a speed well over ninety miles per hour. They hit the gravel track bed, bounced, still together, into flight once more; rolled, disintegrating, down the embankment.

What was left of them was partial and hard to recognize. It came to rest in the weeds and wild dogbane that lay between the slope of the embankment and a field of corn six weeks shy of harvest.

The wave passed over the point at which the bodies of Frank and Rohan were ejected from the train. It was followed by a short period where blast pressure dropped steadily. Then came a front of negative pressure, a counterblast that caused a suction effect and made the wind of explosion flow in the opposite direction.

•••

The W.C. lay at the very front of the passenger car. Eva was sitting on the toilet with her jeans puddled around her shoes. In the background of her mind was a quick shimmer of the fear that had been with her every minute of the last two weeks. In the foreground stood a strong dislike for rough SNCF toilet paper. When the shock wave reached the W.C. Eva had more time to react than Rohan or Frank. Still she was conscious only of a big surprise and an automatic surge in her fight-or-flight centers as the panel behind her blew in and the monstrous concussion of the first wavefront smashed the frosted window, burst her eardrums, lifted her two feet over the toilet seat, and tore blouse and brassiere off her back.

Then, just as abruptly, the pressure dropped. The suction of negative atmospheres popped the W.C. door open and vacuumed away Eva's jeans and underwear and dropped her abruptly back on the toilet. Everything around her was an immeasurable noise very like the sound she heard when, as a human cannonball, she came surging out of the gunbarrel at the Cirque von Andau. The material world had been transformed into a chaos with no up or down to it. The train lurched, braked, lurched again. She fell off the seat and the car's unbalanced motion threw her back and forth between the toilet pedestal and what was left of the wall in front. Finally it crammed her between toilet and washbasin and a bent section of the compartment's sheet-metal floor.

The train screamed to itself. In an awkward, jerking, crabbed motion, it slowed, bucked, came to a halt; metal stressed beyond pain, wheel bearings buckled sideways.

Stopped.

Compressed air roared from broken lines. A woman started crying, the way an infant would, in short, breathy bursts.

Eva opened her eyes.

She was wedged on one thigh in a corner of the W.C.'s

floor. Above her she could see blue sky cut into curved grids by the remaining structure of the train's roof.

Where the passenger compartments had been lay only a fettuccine of black, contorted metal. In front of and under her, the stained granite stones of the track bed. Around, where the carriage once enclosed and protected, lay openness; trees, fields, a road.

She sat perfectly still. One ankle was bent the wrong way. Her back was ripped and punctured in a dozen places from the blast and accompanying shrapnel. Blood from punctured eardrums ran down her neck and breasts and arms. She felt very little. Except for her bracelets, she was naked.

Eva held up a hand, tentatively. It was scarlet with blood. For the first time in her life she felt no rise of disgust. Because there was no room for that amid the greater surprise. The only emotion she had room for, in her head, in the world, was this; an acceptance of an older truth, something it seemed to her she had forgotten or cast aside, only to have it brought home to her at last in this place:

Things happen without us.

She whispered the words to herself. Her lips scarcely moved and her crushed ears picked up nothing at all. But she heard the words nonetheless, loud in her brain, coming from a corner inside her that apparently could still function amid such huge contortions.

seventy-three

(. . .)

No birds sang.

Forty minutes after the explosion and still the curve of country in which the train had come to rest seemed to live in a protected instant from which normal sound and motion had been excluded.

Now and again a siren progressed in thirds up or down the scale as a rescue vehicle came or left. Someone shouted an order. A van with a television crew from a Reims station stopped at the police cordon by a level crossing.

A doctor arrived. A policeman walked him down the track and over to a patch of dogsbane lying on the edge of a corn-field perhaps ten meters from the rail line. Light-blue SAMU blankets had been draped over a couple of lumps that were hard to identify by shape alone. The blankets had gone deep dark ochre in patches where they touched the forms they veiled. The doctor lifted a blanket, took a brief look, and let it fall again.

Gendarmerie and track staff moved back and forth among the debris of the carriage. A patrolman from Eper-nay raised a wadded corner of metal paneling. He found a keychain holding several keys and what looked like a small rectangle of metal. He touched the metal to a steel frame. It stuck. Magnet, he thought, bizarre, and chucked the key ring in a box someone had set aside for personal effects. The box already contained odd bits and pieces; a silk scarf, a photo of the Riviera, a red-colored book of poetry in some unpronounceable foreign tongue. *Attila József*, the cover read. *Medvetanc.*

• • •

Eva Koszegfalvi d'Abruzzi lay covered with a blanket in the shade of a fire department emergency vehicle. A bag of Ringer's solution was suspended over her shoulder. She watched the random patterns made by the leaves of chestnut trees against the clouds and intervening blue. She listened to the astonished silence on all sides.

She was low priority, or so they had shouted, forcing words through her damaged hearing. Two men from her carriage were dead. The two available ambulances had been used to ferry a priest who had been in the same carriage, as well as an old woman from farther up the train, to the hospital in Reims. The priest was not expected to live. The woman, who had suffered a heart attack, apparently was in no great danger. No one else from her carriage had survived. Eva had a broken ankle, multiple lacerations, and ruptured eardrums. A young medical technician leaned a hip on the truck, keeping an eye on the Ringer's, listening to his portable radio.

They had shot her full of painkillers and there was something in the drip too but Eva knew this was not the cause of the great clarity expanding like a bubble in her mind.

What it came from was a new and fragile understanding of what she must do now.

In the fractured time since she was lifted onto this stretcher Eva had decided she must finish all the therapies prescribed by Doctor Makabeus. She would back them up with the conventional cures. She might even channel SEM in an attempt to find the corners of the brain that concealed the placebo effect, using the powers of her own brain to link up with the occult faculties of her cellular system.

Eva gritted her teeth, then gasped as even that small effort sent splinters of pain up her wounded back. Overhead a helicopter hovered in the southerly wind; "TF1," the letters on its belly read.

She would *not* kill herself. To hell with József and Szoltan and the whole romantic Magyar mania for self-destruction. A part of her that was more Hungarian than any such soggy melancholia refused to give in to the dominant trend. Death, she thought, had had its way too much and too often in these green and pregnant fields of France.

She could barely discern the clatter of the chopper overhead but she could "hear" *them* perfectly—they had been so alive, such a short, short time ago. Frank's crude laugh.

Rohan's way of mumbling, "Well," as he turned around a point.

An ambulance backed in close. SAMU men in blue jumpsuits buckled the stretcher straps and slotted her gently into the back. Eva's hands clenched, partly to fight the pain, mostly in resolution.

She would beat the darkness. That would be her mourning, for all of them. For Frank, Rohan, and Julián; for Serge and Tamas, Bobo and Hansi. Despite the small betrayals of herself and others. For all the people she had lost along the way to this specific piece of earth and time of day.

"*Vivre,*" Eva whispered to herself, though she could not hear her own words. "*Je vais vivre.*"

"*Mais bien sur que vous allez vivre,*" the SAMU man told her cheerfully.

They checked her pulse, her saline drip. One of them, kindly, used a tissue to wipe her cheeks. The doors closed and the ambulance lurched off the grass and down the road.

The news helicopter lifted higher. Following the directions of the cameraman it stalked the accelerating ambulance for awhile. Then the pilot banked left in a wide circle that would furnish them with an establishing shot of the country around; past Epernay; over the champagne warehouses; past the military cemeteries of Bligny, where soldiers from France and the German states were buried; past Blaizy, which held the graves of men from the American Expeditionary Force; into a promise of shadow from the east.

• • •

Under the chopper's path, a watcher sitting in a compact rental car on the other side of the police cordon noted the ambulance's departure.

It was finished. A small, chubby hand moved restlessly on

the wheel, then tightened on the ignition key. The rent-a-car's engine whined as it reversed off the shoulder. The car turned and accelerated down the Départementale toward the A-30 and Paris.

Branches stirred with the car's going. A nightingale retreated deeper into a copse of chestnuts. For a while now no siren had sounded and the bird felt the need to reassert its right to this stand of trees in which, after all, it lived and made its nest and fed its young.

The bird grasped the branch more firmly in its claws. It lifted its head, opened its beak, and drew breath.